A Holy Venom

A Holy Venom
Copyright 2024 by Kiarna Boyd
Cover illustration by Stasia Burrington
Cover design by Alicia Mikles
Edited by Josiah Eikelboom & Larry Clow
Proofread by Jason Knapfel
Interior Design by Holbrook Author Services

Published by Piscataqua Press
32 Daniel St., Portsmouth NH
03801

ISBN: 978-1-958669-26-6

https://www.patreon.com/Kiarna_Boyd

A Holy Venom

Kiarna Boyd

AUTHOR'S NOTE:

There are several non-binary gendered characters in this story for whom the pronouns they/them are utilized. These esteemed personages may identify as neither male nor female or they may identify as a combination. Misgender them at your peril.

CONTENT WARNING

PLEASE BE AWARE: This book contains graphic violence, gore, suicide ideation, and non-sexual child abuse (bullying).

For Autumnlily, who was the first to be kind.

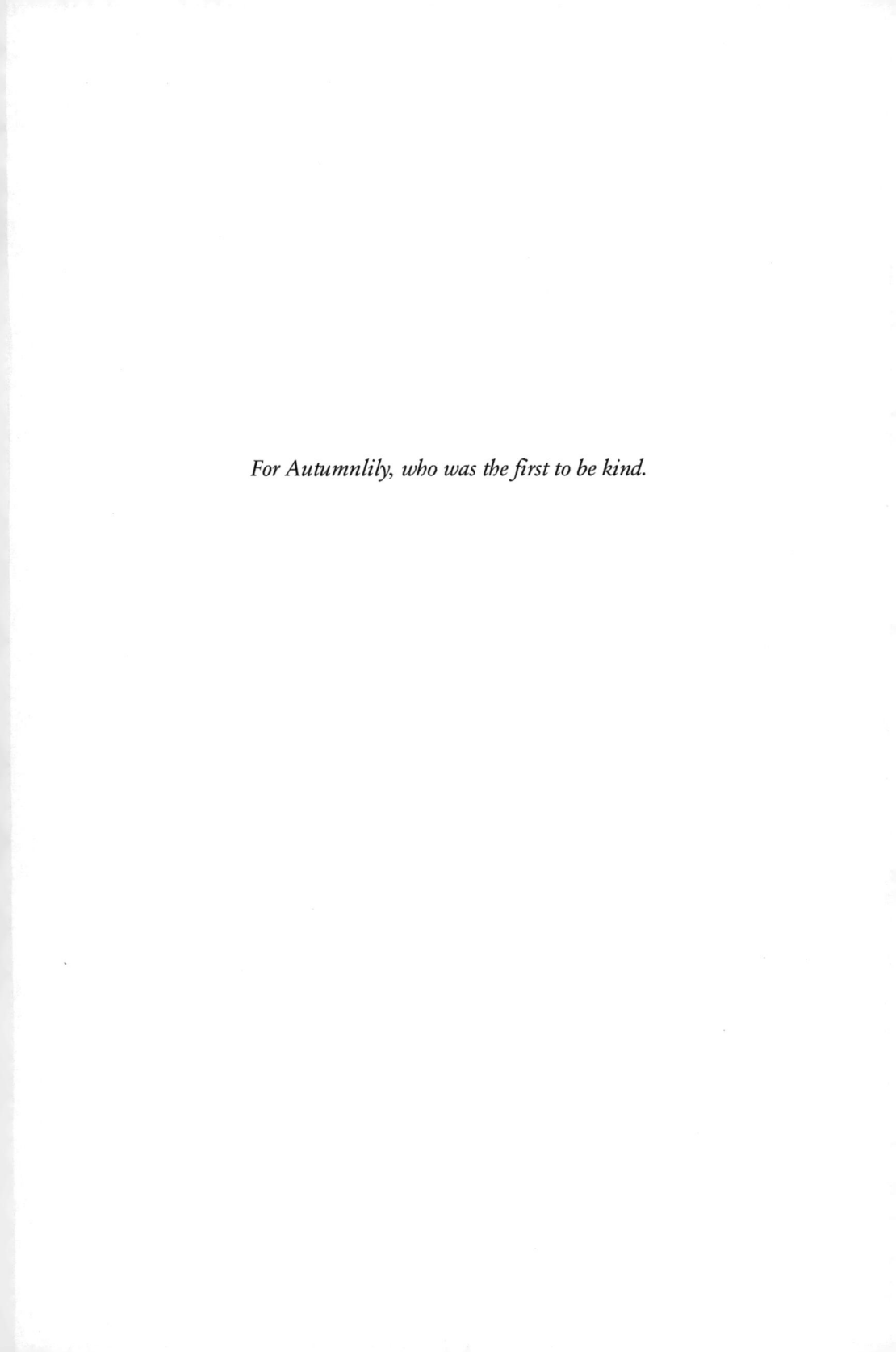

ONE

AT FIRST LIGHT, the cold mountain air filled with the excited caws of crows. The murder had discovered a banquet beneath the exposed granite of the high peaks. Whirling shadows swept in under the thick pine boughs and landed, wings sending dustings of fresh snow tumbling down to cover the bloodstains below.

Hungry beaks tore into ice-coated entrails looped and jumbled among the branches, the crows competing for the choicest scraps. Others waited opportunistically below, swooping to catch falling tidbits. The summit echoed with a jubilant cacophony.

Jostled free, a human arm landed with a thud. Before the powdery snow settled, the birds set upon the meat. Sharp beaks darted at ink-stained frozen fingertips as comrades squabbled. Pushed aside, a few crows danced off and pecked on another shredded chunk. Pine boughs bounced, showering glossy, iridescent feathers in white. Crystalline and scarlet, fragments of the decimated corpse scattered around them. The discovery of the liver and lungs set off a contest, theft and counter-theft.

Among the pines stood a glacial erratic boulder, free from snow cover. A ring of snow melt circled the hulking mass as it radiated an unnatural heat. A few young crows carried their breakfast to the stone and perched on the warm granite. From within the boulder came the crackling sound of movement. The birds stopped eating in unison and retreated to the protection of the trees to watch. A massive shadow coalesced out of the northern side of the boulder and the stone began to cool as its overnight guest pulled free. Startled, the crows raised an alarm, launching upwards. Snow and meat rained from the pines as the mountain peak filled with shrieking cries.

Kiarna Boyd

The older birds returned first, rattling their beaks in recognition as the form emerged into daylight. Two massive paws punched deep post holes in the snow as the shadow hardened, the towering shape becoming as solid as the boulder. Yawning, Aych stretched back, leaning against the stone. They glanced over their right shoulder, their frost-blue eye catching sight of the crows shaking more of the human intestines from the trees. Cocking their shaggy monstrous head, Aych focused their left eye, orange shading to liquid gold, on the worn hiking paths that wound through the trees. New scents wafted through. Plush fur and hard muscle condensed; Aych dropped to all fours. Billowing hot breath roiled through the frigid morning air. They shook their Big skin and inhaled the scents of the forest, their nostrils flaring. Hot, living humans and the odors of their mechanical and cosmetic indulgences drifted up from the southern trail. Saliva rushed over Aych's tongue.

New ranger's coming to see his first sunrise over the ridge? Aw, he's a sentimentalist out to make a happy memory on his first day. Their muzzle lifted into a grotesque parody of a smile, revealing a mouthful of pristine, sharp fangs. *Safe money is on him puking when he finds this mess.* They contemplated staying to watch the human become hysterical upon discovering the cathedral of carrion, but a second scent caught Aych's attention. Herbal and summery—the familiar perfume of the Caretaker lingered over the unbroken snow that concealed the northern trail down the mountain.

Yawning, Aych considered the two scents. As the sky overhead continued to brighten, they focused on the Caretaker's scent trail. With a loping quadruped stride, they barreled down the mountain through the pines, kicking up a snow squall in their wake.

A trio of deer scattered when Aych leaped over a granite ledge, the panicked ruminants sprinting desperately away from the elk-sized intruder. Blue jays shrieked in alarm.

Keep your pants on, I'm not hunting your kind. After leaping a frozen stream, Aych slowed their pace to push through the dense thicket of wind-stripped and bare brambles bordering the mountain's access road. Emerging, they squinted as the sun's first true rays reflected off the sparkling chrome and glass of a four-door behemoth of a truck parked in the layby. Half recreational transport and half luxury sedan, the machine menaced the quiet forest, as if ready to belch out a full regiment of deer hunters. Free of ice and snow, the vehicle looked out of place, like it had been driven directly from a dealership.

The Caretaker's scent hung on it, washing over Aych's tongue and mingling with the tang of metal, stale exhaust, road salt, and the distant traces of cold blood high on the mountain behind them. Remaining on all fours, they circled the truck, breathing a lungful of hot air over the driver's side window. Returning to the rear of the vehicle, they stood up on their back feet, reaching their full bipedal stance. A claw at the end of one elongated finger tapped against the metal roof. In response, the rear door unlocked and popped open. Aych stepped back and used their claws to hook the door and swing it fully open. The staged assortment of equipment in the back of the truck contained a mix of expected human camping supplies: backpack and tent, sleeping bag rolls for two, and food packets. A more discreet pile was set to one side, half-hidden under a tarp. This pile included clothing for one large human, three potable water jugs, and a toiletry bag. Noting the unfrozen state of the water in the otherwise frigid interior of the truck, Aych wrinkled their muzzle. *At least the Caretaker doesn't hang around to make small talk.* The fur along their spine grew warmer as the sun rose higher in the morning sky. Blowing a plume of hot breath, Aych stared at the pile of clothes. *Can't stay Big; need to fit in the fucking truck. No humans to see and the crows don't care. If anyone drives by, I'll call it a breakfast delivery.* They grinned, the sides of their muzzle curling up.

Anticipating the familiar agony, they let go of being Big and willed themselves to become Little. Pain blossomed, with the claws of magic tearing into their Big form, shredding it apart. Milky white ooze flowed out from their center as they pressed themselves inward, clenching tighter, forcing bones to contract, break, and reform. The pain traveled in serrated lines as fur sliced open and the white, viscous bone-white liquid laced over black pelt and muscle, coating it. The liquid solidified and grew tighter, pulling inward. The crushing awfulness of shrinking, being imprisoned made Aych snarl. The lines of magic seared and shrank, drawing tighter still, compressing flesh and folding it into itself. Nerves screamed as fangs contracted into a shrinking jaw. They reeled as their muzzle drove backward, slamming home into a shortened skull. They dropped and hit the side of the truck, leaving a dent in the door. The agonizing pain strangled and bent Aych from within, convulsions dragging them to the ground as every organ and muscle was reshaped to fit their Little human skeleton. Grunting, they stifled a scream as the changing magic struck in crippling shocks and boiled over, dazzling, tearing, and coiling inward.

Slowly opening their eyes, Aych watched a slim silhouette of a crow dart over the trees toward the rising sun. They pulled themselves up with a now human hand. Naked and smeared with blood and black ichor, they poured jugs of water over the new Little body and rinsed off the remains of the transmogrification. The newly sprouted mane of thick, shaggy black hair was free of slime. They cleaned the muck out from behind their ears, armpits and between their thighs. Aych could still feel their tail, nerves still registering the now vanished limb.

Pulling a hand mirror out of the toiletry bag, they inspected their new, smooth face. They confirmed eyebrows had regrown along with their mane, then frowned to create lines and furrows in the snow-white flesh. The human-shaped face was familiar, as it was always the same when they became Little: Wide-set eyes, still mismatched regardless of which solid form they wore, a broad nose and high cheekbones, completing the androgynous assortment of human features. The lips and eyebrows were full and mobile, the mouth prone to smiling too widely and splitting up the cheeks to reveal far too many teeth. For a very long time, this face had stared back from mirrors and still water, storefront windows and the eyes of terrified humans.

Toweling off with one hand, they lifted a pair of worn hiking boots left in a bag next to the set of hikers' clothing. *Ugh, made for narrow fucking human feet. Probably going to pinch across the toe box.* Wrinkling their nose, they dressed. They glared at the long boot socks, patterned with Solstice trees. Again they wondered how anyone could buy such ugly clothes in stomach-churning colors. *Humans can't see for shit, and I can't believe I have to wear this shit.*

Aych squeezed into the truck's cab, the Caretaker's summery woodland perfume lingering inside the vehicle. On the seat next to them, a thermos of tea and a hand-drawn map waited. The careful lines and notations were written in the Caretaker's elegant and sharp script, indicating the truck's location and route back to the city.

A Holy Venom

Retreat, hold, or advance? Ignoring the map, Aych considered the return trip south. *Can't leave him alone too long.* Downing a mouthful of tea, they dropped the map back on the seat and peered out of the windshield at the rosy clouds. *If I get stopped by a highway salt and it goes sideways ... I could eat a few salts without needing to sleep it off.*

Satisfied, they set the thermos cap in the cup holder and started up the truck.

Advance.

☾

Major Ota Hawthorne, retired, parked her truck in the first available spot on the third floor of the Twins Downtown Parking Garage. The garage felt cold and claustrophobic. She opened the truck's back door and stared at the empty cardboard box in the back of her vehicle. She was strangely tired. *Why was this hitting her so hard?* The death certificates had required the usual slog of dead-eyed paper shufflers and half-hearted condolences. It was still easier to think in terms of protocols and procedures than in terms of personal loss and grief. The apartment building manager, Iris Mae, had surprised her with a sincere offer of help and genuine concern for the deceased.

"As soon as you've got everything important packed up," she said, "let me know and I'll have the cleaning agency take everything else. No need to make it harder than it needs to be." The manager had patted her hand, the older woman's eyes still red from crying over her sweet, silly story about Baz helping her repaint the office in shades of dusty rose.

Hefting the box, Haw considered the manager's words: *harder than it needs to be.* How many deceased friends' things had she collected, how many apartment managers had she exchanged keys for a death certificate over the years? This was different though, wasn't it? Not a former squad member who had an accident or took ill or, worse yet, just up and gave in. Realizing she had been standing at the back of her truck with the empty box, Haw eased the door closed and headed for the elevator. The dull thud of her boots and the jangle of Baz's apartment keys bouncing in the bottom of the box echoed through the parking garage. Dark patches blotted the damp concrete. She walked out behind the parked cars and followed the faded yellow lines, avoiding the sheen of black ice on the unheated walkway.

Of course this bothered her. Her deceased brother's only child, her nibling, born before she was a parent herself. That first child of the new generation, that first tiny hand clasping her finger, emerging from the depths of all the blankets her sister-in-law had bundled to keep out the chill. The softness of Baz's cheek, softer than silk swathed in the cotton blankets that seemed much too rough for such a delicate thing. How she'd melted when those two dark eyes locked onto her face and that perfect, miniature hand squeezed tighter. Haw's chest ached. She felt the ghost of the infant's grip.

The keys rang against each other as she tilted the box to free up her right hand to press the elevator call button. Worry had consumed Haw when Baz confided they had a drug problem and were going to stay at a rehab in the mountains. She had been instantly confident in Baz's recovery. An unnoticed tear slipped down her cheek and dropped onto the box. She stepped into the elevator car. Pressing the box against the steel wall, Haw tapped the floor button. To distract herself, she recalled the chore list she'd written up that morning. *Easier to stay focused on the task at hand and get through it all,* she thought.

Collect a few innocuous things for the kids to remember their cousin by, maybe a sketchbook or a finished painting. Olive loved Baz's bright, cheery color palette and Haw knew how to take a hint from her spouse. *Check for any financial paperwork.*

Bag up anything potentially embarrassing and get it in the trash before the cleaners could gossip. Look for drugs. Empty the fridge.

Secure any valuables. Not likely there would be any, but remember to look.

Don't rush it.

The elevator doors slid back on the tenth floor. Haw froze and stared at dark welts embossed in the nap of the carpet. Her body tensed, ready to duck and roll. Her heart raced as she played in her head the best angle of approach to overcome her assailant. The elevator doors began to close, jolting Haw's mind free. She looked at the marks again. The marks were not boot prints signaling a hidden presence or signs of a struggle—only vacuum welts. Normal signs of everyday routine maintenance. *This is getting to me.*

A Holy Venom

She scanned the hallway. A cleaner's cart hugged the mirrored wall to the right of the t-branch hallway, while to her left a door opened and a couple jostled each other, trying to exit their apartment in a rush. Feeling a little guilty about her dirty boots on the plush carpet, Haw scraped the keys out of the box and kept her gaze forward as she walked, not meeting stares the exiting couple threw. Wide hallways. Clear lines of sight now that she'd passed the cart. A fumbling, loud and happy pair of youngsters oblivious to Haw's presence. Window at the end of the junction ahead of her. Situational awareness required she parse all the approaches and assess all unknown persons. Once she turned the key in the lock of number 239, she finally exhaled.

Haw blinked, trying to understand the scale and dimensions of the urban apartment. The open-concept apartment was taller than it was wide. *Like being in a matchbox turned on its side.* She surveyed the space for all potential exit and entry points. What she took to be a closet door sat at the end of the room, beyond the built-in floor-to-ceiling bookcase to her left. To her right, pencils lay scattered on the carpet as if dropped and forgotten in a rush. Deep pools of shadow crouched around the lumpy, coffee-stained couch that served as the only seating and sleeping furniture in Baz's home. Just beyond the couch was a small kitchen and bathroom. The few windows did little to illuminate the apartment. The lights in the high ceiling cast strange shapes around the sparse furniture. Coming out to the farm for Solstice dinner the year before, the twenty-eight-year-old had complained to Olive about not finding a new daybed that suited them as much as the relic from their art school days. They'd gone on about how the coffee stains on the couch fabric made it spotted, calling it their pet cat couch. A particular ache started in Haw's chest again and she forced herself to enter the vacant home avoiding stepping on the pencils. Baz was never coming back to flop on the couch or pick up their mess.

Baz's apartment was colder than the shared hallway. Haw set the cardboard box on the glass and steel table in the center of the room and looked up at the bookshelf crammed with objects. Each shelf was crammed with books and random ephemera arranged by hue and tone. The effect made it difficult to look at for long and Haw's eyes slipped off to the brighter tones arranged near the closet door.

Kiarna Boyd

The whole place reeked of expensive candles. Looking over the couch into the kitchen, Haw spotted two big glass candle holders. The kitchen was little more than an alcove. Two cabinets hung above the steel sink and two below with a meager counter to the right. A dishtowel covered in upturned glasses and mugs fought a cutting board and a hotplate for control of the minimal surface. Haw smiled at the steel coffee pot squatting on the burner, ready to take on any intruders to its domain.

The aromatic candles occupied a shelf wedged in below the cabinets and above the sink. *Tobacco and something else library-ish, not floral,* Haw decided. At the side of the alcove, the door to the bathroom was ajar. Haw used the toe of her boot to widen the gap and peered in. More candles lined the closet-sized room, filling the walls around the plastic shower surround and toilet. Haw glanced back at the kitchen sink wondering if the apartment's occupants and guests were expected to wash their hands in the same sink as the dishes. *Where the hell was the fridge for that matter?* Thankfully, the bathroom door opened out into the kitchen or there'd be no way to use the toilet. She muttered over the parsimony of whoever designed the so-called upscale living experience. She'd been deployed to the farthest parts of the world and been equipped with better shower facilities.

Baz must've loved the scent of these candles. Haw picked the glass holder from off the back of the toilet. Brushing her thumb over the designer label, she decided to take the candle home and carried it around the couch to place it in the box. No art supplies, no easel, no big tacked-up pieces of paper with pastels. Haw frowned; what had impressed her the most about her nibling's previous living spaces was entirely missing.

She examined the living room and reconsidered the door at the end of the tall bookshelf. She'd assumed it was a closet. Same off-white eggshell painted wood as the bathroom door with a matching brass doorknob, tucked between the room's single window and the bookshelf. Glancing out the window as she walked over, Haw noticed the railing of the fire escape was covered in thick stalactites of hazy ice, like a rippling, frozen fire. Her breath steamed against the glass. Something was making this part of the house much colder. "The hell?" she barked aloud, startled. She swung herself toward the door and clasped the doorknob. Feeling resistance, Haw pulled the door open, stopping the bottom with her boot before it hit the wall.

A Holy Venom

Air rushed by. She heard rustling and a thick, musty odor—almost sexual—spilled out of the room and overpowered the candles. Light from the living room cascaded through the doorway onto the hardwood floor. The room contained a second window facing the street. Neither the living room light nor the subdued amber cascade from the solitary window could illuminate the walls. Darkness pressed against the bands of light restricted to the floor as she ran her hand along the wall for the switch plate. Layers of papers heavy with paint and pinned to the wall confused her search. Water gurgled in pipes overhead and Haw froze in place, suddenly certain someone was in the room with her. Straining to see, she narrowed her eyes. *Was there someone in the far corner watching her?* The air, now still, did not carry the heat of another person nor the sound of breathing. Her instincts warned of danger, but she could not determine the source.

Wind gusted against the window glass. Diamonds of drifting snow sparkled and tapped. This room felt bigger and colder than the rest of the apartment. The sensation of being watched grew oppressive. Foundational imperatives drilled into her demanded Haw either secure the room or step back out. Paper ripped as she dragged her hand further along the wall. She winced at the sound and silently apologized to Baz. A bare patch of the wall met her fingers, and she flicked the light switch on.

The light flooded on in what must have originally been intended as the bedroom. The bare unshaded bulbs overhead did little to warm the dead artist's studio or push back the weighted darkness. Haw stared and gaped at the rich swirls of jet sweeping over the reams of paper tacked to the three interior walls, all the way up to the high, tin ceiling and the foam-encased water pipes. Interspersed over the raw white of the paper, black swooping spirals arched and crested bearing down on the far corner. There, diagonal from the door, a slender glass table stood. Layers of obsidian gloss rippled along the walls, all pointing to an object on the glass surface.

The room felt insane. She had cleaned up after hoarders, after alcoholics, and suicides. Former squad members off their meds stockpiling for imaginary disasters and invasions, friends entering early-stage dementia. Parents and elders left alone for too long living in their own detritus. None of those jumbled spaces bothered her the way this empty room did. She was familiar enough with Baz's artwork to know this whole room was an installation, but it was like nothing she'd ever imagined could exist in an art gallery, let alone someone's home. Gone were the rainbow and jewel tones of her nibling's gallery pieces or the whimsical pastels of the murals Baz had painted in the nursery at Haw's old house. *Was this all painted while Baz was on the Rot?*

Uncomfortable and chilled but drawn to what was clearly Baz's last work, Haw felt the room's intent press upon her. *Obsession, fear, and desire, of and for, whatever was on that table.* The feeling was inherent in the scale of it, the detail of it, the repetitive lines covering the walls. *Was the paint latex, or some kind of industrial sealant? What was that musky smell?* The paint was shiny in spots and matte in others. The rippling waves appeared to move and retreat as Haw took a few cautious steps toward the table. *What the hell is that thing?* She crept closer.

Ice crystals smattered against the window glass. She turned, breaking her gaze from the object. She blinked heavily and swallowed. Something suddenly weighed down her palm. She turned from the window and found herself standing next to the glass table, the stone sitting heavily in her hand. Her pulse raced. She could not recall crossing the scuffed wooden floor or picking up the stone. The object was rough, warm and round, fitting in her palm perfectly. *Why is it so warm when the room is freezing?* Haw turned the ball over in her hand. A grimacing face smiled up at her. Blunt and out of proportion, the grotesque imp's face changed in the light to something like a dog's head. As she looked, the two rough-shaped eyes appeared to blink and suddenly the stone was cold and heavy. Haw repressed a wave of panic and dropped it back on the table. On impact, the cement-like stone scratched the glass and rolled into the corner against the slick, nightmarish wall. Taking shallow, fast breaths, Haw looked at her hand. It stung as if burnt. Wiping her palm on her trouser leg, she stepped backwards until she was out in the living room.

☾

The cow bell on the music shop door jangled, the rustic rattling off tempo against the rock ballad of thievery playing over the sound system. In the rear of the narrow basement shop, Ky glanced at the security monitor and set aside the invoice he was reviewing. He clocked the shabby newcomer approaching the repurposed apple crates in the vinyl section as a nostalgia hunter. Reflexively, Ky tugged down the long sleeves of his shirt to conceal the mottled burn scars on his arms before getting up to assist the customer.

At the far back of the store, Yarrow, a lanky teenager with a poof of hair that created an unruly cloud around her bespectacled face, popped her head out of the break room. "I'll get this one," she chirped loudly.

Ky smiled at the resolve in her high-pitched voice. Wiping the cuff of her flannel over her eyeglasses, Yarrow went out around the memorabilia display counter and approached her target.

Picking up the invoice, Ky continued checking in the order. His awareness drifted to the expected patter between the customer and Yarrow, then back to the block of numbers on the recycled paper, and then to the shop speaker nested in the corner of the tiny stock room. He followed the current song's lilting, tragic notes and pushed his shirt sleeves back up to his elbows.

The music made him recall last night's omen-heavy dream. For a moment, his mind was full of images of the wintry forest and a menacing, hateful intent focused on him. There had been an important detail about crows. The rest he couldn't dredge up well enough to remember. Turbulent and harrowing, the dream was not his usual remix of nightmares about mud and sinkholes—dark, wet places to drown while pinned under crumpled support beams and cracked cement, dust and crumbled plaster blown into his eyes and lungs. All his major deployments during the Crisis had been to the jungles and deserts far to the south where snow was at best a postcard myth. The clarity of the dream troubled him. If he was honest, it had been a nightmare, waking him up and depositing him fully in the grip of insomnia, the portents leaving him apprehensive and in need of insight. It had been the kind of dream that would nag and haunt until he exhausted his efforts trying to understand. If he let the music work its magic, the answers would crack through, carried on the voices of the living and the dead. Scraping a hand over the nape of his neck, Ky scuffed at his short-cropped hair in annoyance. Like a ghost of a word escaping elucidation, the solution was somewhere in the music.

"... CWS?" Yarrow leaned over the counter full of rock band

memorabilia. "Hello? You in there?"

Ky shook his head and stared at the girl. "Sorry?"

She jabbed her thumb in the direction of the customer. "They're looking for some band called CWS. I haven't heard of them, can't find anything—"

"Caked With Spiders. In the dark synth section. I can—"

Yarrow flipped up her hand. "You do the inventory stuff, I'll do the custie stuff."

As Ky watched Yarrow bounce off, the next song on the mix began to play, another classic murder ballad. Listening to the lyrics, Ky leaned back and stared up at the tattered and water-stained concert posters stapled to the basement ceiling. The need to understand warred with his inclination to not compromise his work, as simple as it was. He justified playing the mix as multitasking and using the eclectic selection of music as an aspect of the store's personality. Knowing he was using it as a form of private divination added a subversive quality to listening—increasing the gap between the normal world and the strange, haunted reality encroaching upon him. The more he could widen his sense of that gap, the easier it would be to receive the weird information trying to come through. Intense emotions and a fully enlivened imagination, this is what the music could give him at the very least. At best, it would deliver a complete internal awareness of the threat, rather than the last-minute alarm of the physical countersignal. The playlist could answer his questions if he let it. He turned his attention back to the music: in the previous song, a suitor went bad, and turned into an obsessed stalker. The next song was about seductive and destructive, magical lovers. Albums selected by feel, songs chosen by setting the needle randomly onto the turntable. Half necromancy, half spirit-channeled, the resulting mix was divinatory. Ky listened, trying to fathom the message in the music. The warnings about murder were clear. The other songs formed a narrative about betrayal, desperate lovers, smuggling, stealing, and thieves. The outliers appeared to be about blindness and not seeing. Those confused the hell out of him, but his intuition and the spirits guiding the divination agreed: Heavy shit was coming.

He was accustomed to sleep deprivation, but this unease stirred up emotions he couldn't acknowledge. The feeling of dread refused to dissipate; the numbers on the invoice were hard to focus on. He could replace the mix

A Holy Venom

with the shop's showcase soundtrack and shake the troubling mood. No—there was still a piece evading his attention.

Yarrow returned to the counter with the grouty, rumpled customer in tow. Ky half-listened to her cheerfully ring them up and put their purchases in a bag. The familiar routine of the transaction added another layer to the ambient noise. By the cardboard stand up of a famous musician, the dehumidifier growled to itself as the cow bell noted the departure of a regular browser. He relied on the way sound stirred his unconscious and directly side-stepped his intellectual defenses as a tool for getting around his own assumptions and prejudices. This kind of divination offered an immediate kick, catching on his emotional reactions while bringing along a wealth of patchwork stories to sift through. Auditory cut-up magic incorporating the environmental noise and the fractious percussion of his own thoughts. The method worked more effectively for him than image-based divination. He needed to find the missing connection, to keep listening and to hear what he wasn't. The signal-to-noise ratio was off.

Yarrow turned to Ky. "I like your new playlist." The girl jerked her thumb at the speaker above the register. "It's like the soundtrack to a movie I'd want to see."

"You figure that way, do you?" If nothing else, he had to smile at her enthusiasm. Curious what she might be hearing, he decided to draw her out. "Any particular kind of movie?"

"Mmm ..." She scrunched her face up and pushed her oversized, cherry-red glasses up the bridge of her nose. "Definitely a horror movie, but not a straight slasher flick. Something supernatural. Atom-spheric."

"Atmospheric." Ky decided the dream images of being hunted by an unknown adversary were not relived memories from his tours. "A monster movie? Didn't know that was your type of kick, kid. Would've pegged you for the adventure flicks."

"Yeah, I don't like horror. But Fern likes scary shit, so..." Yarrow shrugged her shoulders up to her ears, as if to signal whatever her sweetheart liked was to be endured. "If it was, it wouldn't be one of those gloom boi monsters. All moody and brooding. Like *someone* I could mention." She gave Ky an exaggerated wide-eyed stare.

He chuckled. "You knocking me for not bouncing off the walls all the time, *like someone I could mention?*" He returned a mocking version of her own expression.

Yarrow shrugged and rolled her eyes. "You know what I mean. In the movies, there's always mopey monsters who hate themselves. All *'woe is me, I'm cursed to be this amazing thing…'*"

"Alright, you've got a point." Ky shook his head again. "It doesn't sound like that kind of movie." The girl's criticism of his moodiness touched a raw nerve. Yarrow might be less than half his age, but she was perceptive enough, especially if he wasn't concealing his shit properly. For a split second the sharp, sulfur flare of a struck match stung his nostrils and then vanished. The countersignal was clean and urgent, but this sensation was one of hidden shame.

"Oh, my mom wants you to come over for dinner this week." Yarrow held both her hands up to ward off her manager's reaction. "Don't worry, I told her you only flirt with the hot rock guys that come in. *Same attracted*, I told her."

The metallic ghost of the matchstick scent stuck in Ky's throat. "Way to make things awkward, kid. She likely wants to talk about selling, that's all." Inhaling, he tasted the papery stale air of the record store. Decades of incense used to fend off the clammy basement odors soaked up by the old, dried-up wood and cardboard, the crates of vinyl records and plastic cassettes were entirely devoid of the brimstone tang haunting his senses.

"Would you buy it?" Yarrow kicked her chunky boot against the base of the display case. "If you bought it from her, then when I get older, I could buy it back. You know, when you're all gentrified."

"Geriatric is the word you want. Sorry to disappoint you, but that kind of cash is beyond me. With what your mom pays me, I'm never making it."

"Yeah, you're just looking for an excuse not to buy because you're tired and don't want to carry boxes around." She rolled her eyes. "Not that I want to carry them now, but …"

"I could get cleaned up tomorrow night or the next and swing by. Ask your mom which is better for her." Taking the hint, he got up to move the heavier boxes of merch for the girl.

Yarrow put her hands up again and got into a fighting stance. "If you buy this place, that means you won't quit working here to open a combat school." The teenager bounced on her toes and gestured for Ky to come at her. "Show me more military stuff?"

"Never said I was going to do that either." He ducked under her arm and stepped to her side. Before she could turn, he flicked her on the back of the head. "Your mom could snag another buyer, easy. Already has a few lined up, the way I hear it."

Groaning, the girl dropped her arms. "Only other people that want to buy this place are those snobby art students. They won't let me work here and they would change everything and it would suck."

"Shit happens, kid." Ky shrugged and then nodded in the direction of the cardboard boxes by the back stairs. "Boxes don't unpack themselves either."

"Probably more moldy oldies. I'll make us coffee instead." Yarrow heaved herself away from the counter and stomped into the breakroom, the heavy soles of her fashionable boots adding to the ambient noise.

"Don't drink so much of that belly rot, it will—"

"I'm already taller than the rest of my class! It won't stunt my growth!" Yarrow yelled back.

The bass line in the current song surged, snapping Ky's attention back to the music and his surroundings. The familiar shuffle of hands searching through the salvaged apple crates resting on makeshift wooden tables, the water-damaged posters and album covers pinned to the walls rustling quietly in the recirculated air, the shredded remnants of flyers and notices on the message board by the front door that fluttered when the door opened, band stickers on every surface, and the ratty plastic tarps stuffed under the tables waiting in case the water pipes threatened to burst. All of it seemed at once eternal and suddenly so finite, a single moment of history already unraveling, like rats scurrying before rising water. As the moody song about sea witches calling their lovers to their deaths started, a sharp, burning sensation ran up along his spine and settled between the scarred gristle of his shoulder blades, throbbing. It was a lower level of psychic premonition, not the full-on assault of threat prediction he referred to as the countersignal. Ky snapped straight. *Pay attention,* he told himself. *Something is about to reveal itself.* Fission raised the hair along his arms and he listened closely. The information he needed was right here, if only he could hear it.

His body bent with his attention and he breathed the sound in willing the meaning to become clear.

Songs about dying and wanting to die he understood. The ones about murderous intent and jealous rivalry he had sympathy for, but the ones about loss of sight, blindness, chicanery, willful deception, and larceny made no sense at all to him. What wasn't he seeing or perceiving? Frustrated and annoyed with himself, disgusted with all of his categorized failings and shortcomings, Ky wanted to give up trying to guess what kind of a shit show was barreling into his life next.

He glanced at the security monitor again, half listening to Yarrow talking to herself as she made another pot of coffee. The guilty undercurrent he was trying to repress reacted to the plaintive vocals of the current song. He gripped the edge of the retail counter, willing himself to breathe as the psychic discomfort spiked along with the physical warning, a premonitory feeling, prickling his nerves on the scars along his shoulder blades. Every inch of his skin felt exposed. The sharp, cutting nerve pain flared in the scar tissue on his arms and chest. The feedback of strong emotional triggers of the music brought up the conflicted emotions he tried to push away. It was all jumbled inside him, the guilt and shame sitting like watchdogs at the threshold of deeper understanding.

The lyrics touched a nerve, accusations leveled against an unfaithful lover. Ky imagined himself as both the accused and the accuser, the one who forever fell into temptation and the one eternally asked for forgiveness. The secret about the dream and his uneasy sense of incoming danger were there, the answer his intuition promised if he would only face himself honestly. Exhaling and tightening his grip until his knuckles whitened, Ky thought of furnace-like heat and the comforting stink of gasoline. Like an alcoholic aching to grasp a forbidden bottle, he imagined pure grace enveloping him as he tossed a flaming match into a heap of trash piled along the wall of a derelict warehouse. The details filled themselves in, seducing him with remembered flickers of pleasure arising from the burning, writhing paper. The uneven, sparkling dance on the edge of the newsprint as it blackened to char and disintegrated. He leaned against the store counter as the song carried over into the single beat of silence before the next started. The omen showed itself, slowly forming along with the new song's intro. The

A Holy Venom

crooning, threatening voice of the singer intruded into Ky's vision as a second flame flared. This time a match sputtered in the shadows as an intruder lit a cigarette. The stranger's eyes met Ky's and judged him. An invasive presence knowing his sinister secret. Extinguished, the delicate, hopeful flames in the trash pile disappeared leaving only the bitter taste of ash.

Someone dangerous was coming for him.

TWO

THE BED SHIFTED and Haw turned over as her wife got up. Olive pulled on the checkered flannel bathrobe Haw had given her last Solstice and went around the carved foot of the bed to draw back the gingham curtains. Low-angled winter sunlight cut under the eaves of the house and streamed into the room. Dust motes danced over the handmade wooden furniture and settled on the wide pine floorboards.

"Five more minutes, hon, please." Haw buried her head back under the covers.

Olive cleaned her glasses using a corner of her pajama shirt. "Take ten. I'm going to feed the horde, and then you can get them to school." Casting a second look at Haw's bundled outline, she paused and smiled. "Actually, I can take them today. We finished early ahead of the deadline yesterday, so you can sleep all morning."

"You're a real doll." Haw peeped out from under the covers. "You don't mind?"

At the door, Olive flashed a smile over her shoulder. "Might cost you a pancake or three, but no added wife tax."

Sighing happily, Haw nestled back in under the covers. The door flew back from Olive's hand and a small girl trailing a large dog pillow darted past, multiple braids flying. She bounded up and onto the bed.

"Madda, Madda, you have to get up!" the child yelled, bouncing on Haw. "I waited all night to tell you about the ghost I saw! You can't stay in bed. MADDA!"

Burying herself further under the covers, Haw began to make snoring noises.

Berry scrunched her nose up. "MADDA!"

Olive hooked an arm under Berry's waist and carried the wriggling child out of the room. "You can tell her about it later. Now, did you wash your face, my girl?" She set the small child down outside the room.

Frowning, Berry nodded emphatically and tried to dodge back into the bedroom. "I haf—" She let out a crisp chirp as Olive snagged the back of her T-shirt. "But Maw, I waited all night and didn't wake anyone up and I did too see a ghost! In the house even!"

"You can tell the twins about it while we eat." Olive turned the small body around and gave her daughter a firm push on the backside down the wood-paneled hallway toward the dining room.

Fuming, Berry stomped and squeezed the pillow to her chest. The multicolored beads in her braids bounced angrily as she marched along the French doors. "Stupid twins won't believe me. They always make fun of me! They'll say ghosts and monsters don't exist." She shot her parent a sour look.

"Well, you can tell me all about it after you eat breakfast on the way to school, OK?"

"Nooo, 'cause then they'll be in the car too." Berry put her nose in the air and continued stomping into the dining room. Setting her dog pillow in one chair, she drew back another and sat down at the mahogany table. "I want waffles, not pancakes," she huffed.

Olive smoothed a hand over Berry's head and selected a ripe banana off the high board. "That's too bad, then. You'll have to find some kind soul – who isn't your Madda – to make them for you."

"Waffles!" Berry exhorted as she accepted the banana.

Emitting a small humph, Olive pushed open the heavy door into the pristine tiled kitchen.

"Morning, loser," two young voices taunted in unison.

Berry stuck her tongue out as her siblings entered. River stuck his tongue out in return while Ash snagged the dog pillow from the chair next to Berry.

"Hey! That's not yours!"

Ash pulled back their chair and sat on the dog pillow. "It is now, sprout. Go get the juice if you want it back."

Berry made a face and pushed her chair away abruptly. "I'm going to drink all the juice and you can have water." The girl marched into the kitchen, her forceful shove propelling the door to swing repeatedly behind her.

A Holy Venom

Flipping pancakes onto a waiting serving dish, Olive watched Berry stomp across the white tile. "You going to tell them about the ghost you saw last night?"

"No." Berry lifted the glass carafe off the shelf and hugged it to her chest. Her small hands cradled the container as she used her foot to push the steel refrigerator door closed.

"Why not?" Olive set down the spatula.

"Because they're mean and I hate them."

"Oooh, someone's in a mood, alright." Olive shook her head and picked up the platter of pancakes.

The noise of the children floated through the house. Haw was vaguely aware of the familiar clinking of cutlery and glass as young voices rose and fell like bird song. Warm and comforting, the familiarity of the crisp sheets and heavy blankets lulled her deeper into dreams.

She became aware of footsteps in the hallway outside the bedroom. The footfalls of a single set of boots, walking slowly on the historic farmhouse floors. Daylight receded from the windows as if the sky outside clouded over. Haw knew if she looked, the sun would be behind leaden clouds, darkness deeper than any summer rainstorm would bring. The footsteps stopped outside the bedroom door. The voices of her family disappeared and the house grew quiet. The house was afraid, Haw realized. Something was in the house, standing outside her bedroom door and the farmhouse was afraid of it. Haw started sweating through her pajama shirt.

She was suddenly in a mudbrick herder's hut in the South, the flimsy door made of nailed-together boards, shaking in the hot wind, gritty sand blowing through the cracks. The village was deserted and she knew she was alone hundreds of miles from the cosmopolitan southern capital. Gun in her hand, Haw tried to remember how much ammo was left, where the other squad members were, where Ky was, if he'd finished setting the charges, if the enemy was going to search this shack and find her. Fear and adrenaline charged down her spine, her muscles clenched and prepared for the door to open. Hot wind scoured the outside of the hut. There was no furniture to hide behind; everything had been burned. Haw backed up to the fireplace. Her boot heel ground into the wood charcoal, the stink of it lifting into the air and blending with a strange, musky odor. Not an animal smell; more like cologne. She watched the light seeping through the door, the sand whispering over the earthen floor. Was it on her? She inhaled the carnal scent, like sex and massage oil. The light dimmed. The door rattled as the dust storm howled outside.

Streams of sand snaked along the floor, strange patterns spelling something out. Ky would know what it said, what it meant. Her staff sergeant had an uncanny understanding of the strange, and what was happening here and now was the strangest. Wiping her forehead, Haw checked the safety on the pistol and willed her back to meld into the fireplace. Sand piled on the bare floor into flowing lines. The noise of the storm and the rattling door made it hard to concentrate, but there seemed to be a message forming. Haw wondered how higher-ups had gotten a message through but was grateful for the communication. Maybe it was from the resupply center. If only she could get the sand to stay still long enough to read it.

That scent was stronger, too, she realized. She could hear people fucking. The sheets twisting, soaking up the sweat and musk dripping from invisible bodies. Confused, Haw tried to watch the door while feeling the writhing, grinding weight of bodies fucking in the empty space. She felt embarrassed, as if she'd walked in unannounced and caught her squad members having a quick go of it in the showers. Desire built in her as the wind carried the low moans and cries. The hot air stroked over her hands and face, slipping under the layers of body armor and sweat-drenched cloth. Haw lowered the pistol. The wind outside dropped and the door stopped shaking. The gaps between the boards turned gray. Mud walls and the air in the room chilled as, unseen, the sun dropped below the horizon. All the wood was burned. Haw ached from the cold and the carnal urges in her bones. Without looking at the message, she walked over the words written in sand and pushed open the door to look up at the desert night sky. The cold sharpened as she felt the barrel of a gun press into the back of her skull. Hands flung her against the outside of the derelict building. Someone pressed their massive body against hers, pinning her to the exterior.

"Nice to meet you, Major Hawthorne." The scent of sex and cologne wrapped around her. A laughing growl filled her ear. "Let us see how long you can last." The teasing inhuman voice aroused Haw and shame burned

A Holy Venom

along her face and neck.

Haw kicked backwards, twisting into a joint lock, trying to face her assailant. A werewolf made out of stone with a terrible, grinning mouth full of sharp fangs pushed her down to the ground into the sand piled up against the wall. The grit burned on the back of her neck and scalp as she stared up into the monstrous thing's dark, hollow eyes. Its hands were vaguely human-shaped with long clawed fingers that caressed her face. Impossibly heavy, the thing crushed the breath out of Haw.

"Now, now, Major. If you make this difficult, they'll have to start their feast with your family. You wouldn't want them to do that, now would you?" The werewolf statue leaned closer, its rank breath stinking of corpses left out in the hot sun. "They are always so very hungry, you see. Centuries of hunger, all spent craving the sweet marrow inside your bones."

Unable to move, the weight of stone pressing into her, Haw cried out. The dark eye sockets suddenly glittered, one eye becoming a watery, sky-blue sapphire and the other a flame-orange citron, both reflecting her terrified face. *It sees me. It's looking at me. This is death, this is how I die.* Haw screamed as the stone fangs sank into the sides of her face, tearing down into the bone, crushing her skull.

Waking with a shout, Haw flailed and shot upright in bed. The dream faded rapidly and left a vulnerable sense of shame. Tangled in bedding and panting, Haw wiped a hand over her face and tried to recall what had been so upsetting. Fragments of nightmarish images, combat, and fear were all that remained. Soaked through, she grimaced and threw back the covers.

The farmhouse was quiet and empty, bright winter sunlight glossing the cherry wood wainscoting. Even in the full sunlight, Haw felt the unease she normally associated with nocturnal uncertainty. She pushed open the bathroom's oak door. Damp towels from the twins' morning shower lay rumpled on the racks by the tub. The faucet dripped and a banal glob of toothpaste lay half-smeared on the porcelain sink. Listening, Haw stripped off her pajama shirt and closed the door. Nothing was behind it except the antique sign admonishing users to flush the toilet. Haw's hand lingered on the oak and she looked deeply into the grain of the wood. *This was a tree once.* The thought struck her as foreign, utterly belonging to someone else.

Shaking her head, she turned to the toilet.

The unease stayed with her through the morning. She was only dimly aware of her actions as she showered, dressed, and made breakfast. She focused on the feel and sounds within her home and remained watchful as she washed the dishes and made coffee. The aroma of the brew brought her back to herself. There had been a perfume, a smell, sexy but upsetting. It almost came to her and then it was gone. Haw carried her mug to the back of the house to her office and tried to think about her architectural project work for the day.

The cardboard box on her desk waited. Heart sinking, she set the mug among the pens on the flat table next to the drafting board and looked out the leaded glass windows at the garden, snow mounded over the burlap-wrapped shrubs. Tempted to put the box in a closet and forget about it until spring, Haw undid the enmeshed flaps. Baz's candles and sketchbooks brought back the experience of the previous day. *Of course I had nightmares,* she thought. The folder with copies of Baz's death certificate tumbled onto the desk. Ignoring the mess, Haw dug out the rest of the items, thinking of whether she should give anything to the children now or wait until they were older. The back of her hand brushed up against something warm and rough in the bottom of the box. Tilting the cardboard, Haw scowled as the stone head rolled into the corner, making a dull ding as it struck a glass candle holder. *I meant to leave that damn thing behind.* Disgust came over her. Not wanting to touch it, Haw set the box on the floor and reclaimed her coffee. The sweet, honey tasting coffee beans Olive preferred were nothing like the strong, bitter grinds Haw drank back when she was active.

Flashes of the nightmare came back to her. The winter garden was replaced by a vision of the mud shack and Haw flushed. She looked at the phone on her desk and thought it might be worthwhile to call Ky. Maybe catch up and check in and see how he was doing. Find out how he was sleeping, if he *was* sleeping, considering his insomnia. Honorable discharge or not, she knew it was still hard for Ky to accept being packed off from the only career he had ever excelled at. Years had passed and her former staff sergeant still worked at a record store like a kid. Haw rubbed the back of her neck. She knew what she really wanted was to lay out what she could remember of the dream and have Ky calmly explain it away. Symbolic and primal, nothing more than grief. If there was anyone who would understand being unsettled by such things, who could be compassionate and laugh when it was needed, Ky was just the person. If she confided in Olive, well, what was there to say, really? She would listen and share her wife's grief, but Haw knew she'd leave out the darker parts of the dream. Thinking of that shameful feeling in the dream, being both the illicit voyeur and unwilling participant, brought a flush of heat right up to her earlobes, some flash of unwholesome desire.

☾

It was close to midnight when the twins' screams echoed through the house. Haw was up and out of bed before full awareness kicked in. Berry was huddled by the foot of the staircase, tightly clutching her dog pillow. As Haw raced up the stairs to the landing, Olive groggily came out of the downstairs bedroom.

"What happened, baby?" Olive asked as she wrapped her arms around the girl and watched Haw enter the upstairs bedrooms.

"The ghost came back." Berry wedged herself against her parent. "It was in their room this time."

River and Ash stumbled out of the bedroom with baseball bats in their hands. Ash dragged the sleeve of their pajamas over their face, wiping snot off their nose.

River put his hand on his twin's shoulder. "C'mon, Madda said to go protect Maw and Berry."

Haw emerged from the door to the twins' room and gripped the banister.

"Did you kick its ass, Madda?" Ash searched their parent's face.

"Couldn't find anything to kick." Haw glanced at Olive. Meeting her spouse's gaze, Haw put her hands on their older children's shoulders and guided them down the stairs. "You must've scared it off before I got there."

Ash squeezed the haft of the baseball bat. "I couldn't even move."

River grinned. "I screamed like Berry."

"*I* didn't scream last night when I saw it." Berry stood up, defiant.

"Let's go have a warm drink and then everyone back to bed." Olive swatted Berry in the direction of the kitchen.

"What about the werewolf?" The twins asked together.

"Werewolf? I thought you said it was a ghost?" Olive draped her arms over the older siblings' shoulders.

"I saw a ghost *last* night!" Berry shouted as she performed her stiff-backed march down the hall.

"We wouldn't be afraid of some old sheet-shaker like the loser is." River made a face at Berry's back.

"It was hairy and had fangs this long!" Ash held out their forearm.

"Yeah, and it had glowing eyes!" River turned back to look at his parent.

Haw absently nodded her head. "Well, there wasn't anything in there, so you must've gotten rid of it." Following behind, she was last into the kitchen. Catching sight of her daughter poking at something on the counter, Haw frowned at the stone head. "Did you take that out of my office?" The stone seemed to twitch, pivoting to face Haw. Its rough canine features seemed to leer at her.

Berry shook her head, the beads in her hair rattling. "It was here when I came in." She glanced back at her. "It's spooky, Madda. I don't like it."

"Where did it come from?" River nudged it further along the polished granite countertop with the end of his bat.

Ash squinted at it. "Looks like some ugly stupid doll head. Is it haunted?"

"Well, whatever it is, it doesn't belong on the counter." Olive shooed the children away and scooped up the head. "Is it cement?" She moved the children aside and dropped the head into Haw's outstretched hand.

"Maybe, I don't know what it is." Unbidden, the memory of Baz's unsettling studio came back to her. Haw frowned. The stone head felt cold and weirdly heavy. She wished she could throw it straight out the window over the kitchen sink.

Olive put her hand on Haw's shoulder and smiled. "Well, why don't you put it back in your office while I make us all—"

"Cocoa!" Berry shouted.

"Golden milk!" The twins countered.

Haw nodded. "Yeah, give me a minute." Only half aware of what she was doing, Haw went out of the kitchen to the front door. It was only when the icy air chased drifts of snow in over her bare feet that she realized she had opened it. Without a second thought, she chucked the stone head as far as she could into the dark winter night and shut the door firmly.

☾

Humans huddled near the entrance of the subway, warming themselves in the updrafts billowing out between the wrought iron gates. Ignoring the heavy scent of anxiety and discomfort the pedestrians radiated, Aych pressed through the crush of bodies out onto the busy city sidewalk. The grey winter sky stretched above the crowds, fat snowflakes obscuring the imposing skyline. Aych ignored the flakes; any that landed on their wool long coat and black hair melted rapidly in the preternatural heat of their body.

Foot traffic slowed on the corner of East Street and Tranquility Ave. as a titanic snowplow scraped through the intersection, pushing aside the mounting snowfall. The grating noise of the plow blade curved off to the right, down The Hill and away from the narrow streets of the Upper Quarters. Comparably diminutive plows bobbed and chortled over the cobblestone street, lifting their blades to prevent excavating the ancient granite. Neon splashed from the venues lining Tranquility, coating the compacted snow in bands of rainbow and shadow. A few taxis raced ahead of the plows, pulling up under the wide awnings to collect waiting fares.

Aych watched the humans mingle and divide, selecting from the many eateries on the Avenue. Cooks from the wide span of the Continent competed to draw in the largest crowds, each restaurant showcasing different regional cuisines. The opening and closing doors released gusts of steamy air, spicy and aromatic. The current fashion of wearing thick animal furs and imported perfume coated the tourists in an additional layer of exotic flavors. *Still only blood, bile, and bone under it all*, Aych thought. The dull ache of hunger contracted their throat, salivary glands throbbing just under their jaw. Walking quickly, they navigated away from the unpleasant stench of a nearby restaurant that specialized in charcoal grilling. The putrid reek of roast meat spoiled Aych's appetite.

To Aych, the city's veneer changed, but its underlying nature remained the same, as if it merely rotated seasonally through a fixed set of options, decade after decade, century after century. The Hunting Ground remained the same even as the humans inhabiting it busied themselves with putting up some buildings and tearing others down. Leaning over the street, the familiar ancient row houses shouldered together. Steep peaked roof turrets gullied with verdigris gutters steadily poured a deluge of snowmelt down into the sewers. Strained after endless years of holding heavy seasonal ice, the gutters pulled away from the brick and stone. Unmaintained, the copper bulged and birthed mammoth icicles that twisted into ice flows. Peaked porches protected the doorways on the ground floors and extended limited protection to pedestrians on the sidewalks. Along the Avenue, heavy curtains twitched in the windows of the second-floor residences, shedding flickers of golden light onto the tops of passing taxis. Further down the street, queues formed under heating lamps as off-work thrill-seekers waited impatiently to get into the bars and clubs. Aych recalled countless winters when barrels of coal and cauldrons of fire had offered pedestrians relief from the harsh wind of the Gales.

Laughter punctuated the conversations bubbling up from the sidewalks as the plows trundled around the next curve of timeworn homes reinvented as entertainment establishments and hotels—rooms available by the hour. Aych stepped out onto the cobblestones to bypass a shuffling party of uncertain tourists. Rounding a corner, the aromatic landscape changed again: the sweet stench of tobacco smoke, the pong of neglected hygiene, and the tang of myriad of cosmetic products. Clumped together and courting frostbite, under-dressed humans stood alongside the narrow facade of a former inn. The line undulated as those waiting shivered and avoided the massive icefalls jutting out from the gaping ends of looted gutter pipes. One human narrowed his eyes and spit on the sidewalk as Aych passed. Aych turned to the man and took in his scent. *Rotten organ meat. Liver and gallbladder are shit. Definitely a screamer.* Aych imagined the man trying to scream with his throat torn out. They locked a golden eye on the man and smiled, their lips pulling back impossibly far to reveal a glimpse of jagged tooth. The man instinctively took a step back, the brutal image set in his mind. *Have a nightmare on the house, fucker.*

Neon flickered on over the basement awning of a night club. The sign sent glimmers of ruby and cherry over the ice bulging from the drainpipes. A cheer went up and the queue surged under the awning and into the open doorway. Aych inhaled the warm air escaping the basement club. Snow piled up behind elaborate iron gates barring unused entrances between the restaurants and clubs. *No trace. If he didn't go last night, and he wasn't in line tonight, he might be at the Teahouse. As long as he's nearby.* Aych glanced across the street.

The Teahouse's door opened, a bell ringing as a large group of humans jostled to get inside. Multiple hands flung the door back; the Teahouse air escaped over the cobblestones. The scent of cedar panels and herbal infusions washed over their tongue and through their wide nose. Aych frowned. *Nothing recent. You better be somewhere warm and safe, psycho.*

Aych turned their head away from the Teahouse. Up ahead, The Velvet Door's incandescently bright vintage-style bulbs blazed in the marquee dominating the street. Heat billowed from the vents set among lights, creating a bubble of warmth outside the theatre. A taxi slid up to the curb, the rear passenger door aligned expertly with the red carpet. Liveried staff smoothly approached and helped a finely-dressed and haughty young couple out. Pointing at the glass display cases of antique posters, the delighted woman squeezed her companion's arm and squealed. The theatre staff gestured toward the entrance and ushered the couple through the embossed brass revolving door.

Muscular and bald with gold visible in his ears and nose, a brick of a man with a proprietary manner stood by the potted palms flanking the theatre entrance. As the doors swallowed the new marks, his gaze slipped over to Aych.

"Why you always dressed like you should be carrying a casket? This is a house of entertainment, not a grim salon." Vetch grimaced at Aych's sartorial choices. "Or are you out to scare the salts making like you're a dog? Get you a pair of those itty-bitty black mirrored sunglasses and you *might* pull it off."

"The dogs don't wear sunglasses. That's all horseshit." Careful not to stretch their mouth too widely, Aych cast an appraising eye over the Velvet's head of security. "You steal that coat from your mother?"

"This is Arctic wolf, I'll have you know." With an arch expression, Vetch opened the collar to reveal the coat's pink satin lining.

"One of your clients give you that for being so sweet?"

Vetch dropped his hand. "You *know* I don't work both sides of the curtain."

"But you're so pretty, especially when you're out here freezing your scalp." Aych leaned up against the sandstone facade of the theatre and took out a leather tobacco pouch. Creasing a cigarette paper, they sprinkled a mix of dried flowers and pungent herbs into the fold. "Bet you'd make good money preaching."

"If I did, I'd charge by the night, not by the hour." Vetch glanced over as another taxi pulled up. Tucking his gloved hands under his armpits, he looked back at Aych. "One of the have-nots came by end of last week looking for you."

"They say why?"

Vetch shrugged. "She didn't. Went back to The Cellar and haven't seen her since. Looked like one of the kid's friends. Had that trashy, everything-ripped leather look they all have."

Aych narrowed their eyes at the Teahouse across the street. "Anyone come around asking for me since?"

"Just her and only the one time. Why? You got a flock going over there?" Vetch nodded across the street.

"No way, no how." Aych shook their head. "If it's one of the kid's friends, she probably wanted to use me to scare off unwanted attention is all." They shrugged and nodded in the direction of the Teahouse. "Speaking of the kid, did he stop by while I was away?"

"Haven't seen him."

"You sure?"

Vetch stiffened. "I've known that one since he was standing on trashcans out back, still small enough to sneak in through the transom." He eyed Aych. "We all watch out for him. He's one of ours, no matter what anyone says. Got more enemies than you do, and unlike you, none of it's his own fault. If you're only going to talk horseshit and smoke, why don't you do me a favor and waste your night out in this damn cold while I go in and work the tables."

Striking a match off the sandstone, Aych cupped the flame to light the freshly rolled cigarette. "Wasn't it just the other night you were saying no one can spot a salt trying to sneak in like you can?" A spiral of bluish smoke uncurled from their lips. "Don't want to deprive you of your calling."

Vetch made a face, challenging Aych. "My *calling* would be to beat your ass at a table and show you how a shepherd makes a righteous living off their flock. Not stampeding them into rivers, as some think."

"Funny, I seem to recall taking five hundred or so off you last time we sat at the same table."

"I was lulling you. It's called giving you hope. But you just had to run off as soon as Lu snapped her pretty fingers." Turning halfway to look at the revolving brass door, Vetch narrowed his eyes. "What'd she need you to do? Water her high maintenance orchids? Carry one of her damn imported trees?" He tapped the tip of his alligator skin dress shoe against the ceramic pot of the tree next to him. "Not that I'd blame her, her overgrown twigs are a pain in the ass. She *should* make you carry all of them. Bet you wouldn't so much as break a sweat."

Aych let the smoke burn and curl searing through their lungs. Muscles relaxed along their spine and neck as the blend of poisonous herbs released their toxic bouquet. Their exhale sent a thick haze upwards engulfing part of the marquee. "Mudon decided to have an after-hours cocktail and favor us with his presence. Lu wanted me to keep her company and annoy him. See if he let anything slip."

Grimacing, Vetch looked back out at the street. "I don't know why Vee and Lu dally with that salt. Could be on the leash for all we know. Shouldn't trust—"

"They don't trust him. Only a fool trusts a salt. But the house needs a few bought and paid for friends in the Tank. You know that." Aych cocked an eyebrow. "Your eyesight must be fading. His *partner's* the one on the leash."

"Tosh? That one's too oblivious to be of use to anyone. Couldn't be more of a ram if you stuck horns on her." Vetch contemplated the cab pulling under the marquee. "Mudon can at least dress himself like an adult. I don't even know how the other one could be walking around in those sorry rags and not be embarrassed. She dresses worse than you do. Like once she made detective, they told her she could take off the uniform and she just walked around naked until a bagger took pity on her frozen ass and donated a ragged suit out of a trash can."

Aych laughed. The sound startled Vetch. "You should offer her lessons, take her shopping. Lift her pension while you're at it. Her spouse would thank you."

"Please, I'm not wasting my time on any salt, let alone one that's ..." Vetch made a pulling gesture. "If you're done smoking that vile shit of yours, stop hassling me and get yourself inside. There's a new anna on coat check. Tell me what you think of her and I'll buy you a drink."

Arching an eyebrow, Aych glanced toward the doors. "Not your flavor?"

"Hell no! She's full-on Stat. Got crazy all over her, like she just rolled out of there. I do not know why Violet hires drama. What they thinking? Like we need the extra work when it gets all messy and we have to talk everyone out of the chandeliers." Vetch cast a cool look back at Aych. "Speaking of, don't tell me you're just taking up my time out here until your favorite box of frogs gets done with work. You didn't tell him to come pick you up here, I hope?" He waved a hand in the direction of the Teahouse across the street. "Don't get me wrong. The kid's *gae-su*, but never once has he made dress code."

"There's a show down the block tonight, so he'd be going with the rest of the have-nots dancing in The Cellar." Aych stubbed out their cigarette. "If he comes to see me tonight, you could always lend him your coat. You could hide a whole ward full of Stats in that thing." Patting the fur, Aych winked at Vetch and pushed off the wall.

"I hear envy in you, Demon. You're just sad you don't own anything this fine."

"It's too small and the wrong color. Lu might take it off you if you're not careful." The corners of Aych's mouth twitched. As they headed into the theatre via the revolving spindle of brass, the temptation to flash a true smile, one that showed *all* their teeth, came and went.

Cascading light sparkled over the lobby as waves of heat whirled through the tinkling crystal chandeliers. The carved sandalwood screens of the Box Office, Front Bar, and Coat Check emitted a beguiling fragrance. Under the perfume of wood and the guests with their cosmetics and alcohol, an ancient trace of animal musk emanated from the circular, high-backed velvet couches. Humans shifted position on the diamond-tufted upholstery and released the ghost of centuries-old horsehair from the restored furniture.

A Holy Venom

Echoing percussively over the thrum of the heating system, live music drifted out from the gilded inner theatre. Low-pitched conversations and the continuous wind-chime bells of the chandeliers filled the expanse of the lobby, punctuated by occasional peals of laughter and the constant bustle of the Front Bar staff.

Aych removed the wool overcoat and draped it over their arm. Eyes half-lidded to shut out the atrocious sight of the velvet couches, they crossed the lobby. The couches put Aych in a foul mood. The noxious true color of the velvet always left a sugary, fetid taste of rancid fruit and leaf mold on their tongue.

Reaching the relative calm of the Coat Check, Aych assessed the new attendant. Barely a mouthful, the diminutive woman inhaled sharply as she returned their appraisal. The attendant's pupils dilated and the air shivered between them. Her pulse raced. Aych tasted the pheromones the human exuded over the tell-tale herbaceous stink of the Rot. *Ovulating. Genetic chemical imbalance. Probably off her meds and used Rot recently. Could have her now or later.* Maintaining eye contact, the woman leaned in, breathing deeply. *The sex would be urgent and rough. She'll be dead soon enough from her habit.* Aych considered the prospect of meat tasting like the poison the woman was becoming addicted to. *Price you pay for making deals with backwoods schemers.*

They gave the coat check attendant an enticing smile as they passed their coat over the polished marble. "That's quite a manicure. Must've been expensive."

The woman gazed sideways and laughed. "Worth it." She extended her sharp hot pink lacquered nails and grazed the back of Aych's hand. Bold and inviting, she maintained their shared gaze. "I've heard about you, you know." She set the hanger's chit on the counter with a click. "The Velvet's Demon Lover."

"That's too bad. I was hoping to make a good first impression." Aych tasted her scent again. Traces of other humans clung to her, leaving impressions of impatient, brief encounters. If she was a sex worker, she might have an arrangement with management to take frequent breaks in order to service clients. *Either that, or her addictions are making her unreliable and she needs the extra cash.*

"Good people don't make much of an impression on me." Carrying Aych's coat into the racks, the woman glanced back over her shoulder.

Aych slipped the numbered chit into their suit jacket pocket. "Then we'll get along just fine." Leaving a large bill on the counter, they turned away.

Applause for the last song echoed throughout the tiered amphitheater. Waitstaff glided among the islands of candlelit tables and followed migratory routes back to the pools of light illuminating the bar counters on either side of the venue. Beneath the now empty main stage, the spotlight spun over a quartet of musicians set up on the cantilevered bandstand floating over the elaborate parquet of the dance floor.

Aych descended the scalloped steps to the tier above the parquet. The quartet began playing a new song as Aych approached an alcove concealed behind jeweled curtains. Two humans in suits stood between the other tables and the alcove, pleasant smiles not reaching their eyes until they made eye contact with Aych. With a genuine smile, the woman on the left swept open the shimmering strands to let Aych through. They nodded to the security guard and stepped into the private seating area. Candlelight reflected off the golden back wall while orchids and lilies spilled from moss-lined urns on the long banquet table.

"*Tau-vik-lm!*" From the midst of the crowded table, an extravagant figure in an exquisite tailored suit cried out. Elegantly attired in satin and velvet, the elderly proprietor of the theatre waved Aych over. Violet's perfectly painted and powdered face wreathed into smile lines as they looked up at Aych. "You're back from your errand, I see."

"Only for a moment, *tau-lm*." Aych came around the curve of the golden wall to greet Violet. The elderly human's blossom-heavy cologne failed to conceal the bitter taint of their venerable *ve-vik* habit. Aych could smell the old-world drug clinging to the organs within the human, sweetening the meat, even enhancing the flavor—unlike the newer more fashionable drug the coat check attendant was taking. "I brought Lu a gift."

Established members of the household seated around their elder nodded or inclined their heads to Aych while the humans new to the high table stared or nervously averted their eyes.

"*Tau-vik-lm, tu tau-ve-lm.* Our demon and our goddess, such close friends." Violet's face wreathed into soft wrinkles as they addressed their guests. They turned their dazzling performer's smile back to Aych. "You have time yet to make your offering to our goddess. She'll be in her dressing room. She goes on in a half hour, but be sure not to delay her. We cannot be kept waiting for our evening star to rise." Violet gave a little flourish as they waved in the direction of the stage. "Thank you, *Tau-vik-lm*, for averting evil from our house."

"Thank you for the honor of allowing me in as a guest, *tau-lm*." Aych winked at the consummate shepherd.

As usual, the whispered questions from the night's flock started up as soon as Aych turned away. Titillated, the guests were eager to hear about the so-called demon. Eyeing their chosen targets, the household was more than happy to fabricate stories while refilling glasses and stroking thighs under the draped table linens.

There were additional guards stationed between the bar flanking the left side of the theatre and the hallway leading backstage. They each reflexively stepped to the sides of the shadowed passageway as Aych approached. The younger guard stared challengingly at Aych. Shooting a warning glance at his junior, the other guard inclined his head.

Aych dropped a hand on the senior man's shoulder. "The new anna at Coat Check is going to give the house trouble, Vine."

"Holy Mother. First Vetch and now you." Sighing, the man shrugged. "I told Vee that. What she do, offer to preach right there in the box?"

"Not to me, but she's on the Rot and …" Aych made a low gesture as if throwing something away. "Soon enough she'll either not show up for her shift or catch hell for preaching on the wrong corner. The salts are one thing, but you do not want the talent feeling disrespected in their own house."

Further down the passageway, Aych paused to watch oversized silhouettes on the bricks. Backstage, humans ran and walked in all directions, the frenetic energy of their approaching performances carrying them throughout the warren of passages. Burdened by equipment or tasks, stagehands hurried along while the house performers bickered and rehearsed together. Up on the catwalks, ropes creaked and swayed, fine lines of ancient dust drifting down. Centuries of human scents imbued the bricks and floorboards with a living presence. The velvet stage curtains carried more than a little trace of blood, both animal and human.

Aych hungered, and the discomfort quickened their progress to the dressing rooms. The urge to smoke and repress the hunger warred with the perverse pleasure of delaying gratification until the kill.

Stretching on the wooden crates stacked up against the inner wall, the waiting dancers threw long-lidded looks at Aych. The humans smelled delicious and Aych swallowed back a fresh wave of saliva. *You can wait a few more hours to eat, fiend.*

They knocked on the door. A barely audible voice inside bade them to enter. Crushed up against mirrors tacked to the brick walls, racks of sparkling costumes and expensive arrangements of hothouse grown flowers crowded the star's dressing room. The floral offerings from her admirers pushed out the last of the human scents from Lu's domain. The dressing room was an intoxicating tropical paradise.

Seated before her reflection, Lu applied a lurid shade of lipstick. Silken skin clung to the sharp outline of her clavicles and the lithe, powerful muscles along her neck and shoulders. "There. That should do the trick." She met Aych's eyes in the mirror and smiled. "What do you think? Am I perfectly gorgeous?"

"No matter how lovely you choose to look for them, when your scales catch the moonlight, I think you're a thousand times more gorgeous."

Lu laughed and the notes of it rang like falling water. "I forget you can *see* me." She looked at her reflection for a moment. "It's so odd living as if I am only this. Tell me, what do you see? What am I in your eyes?"

"I see reptilian, immense coils. Silver-dusted jet scales shimmering and filling this entire room, iridescent. A jeweled serpent's head with fangs the length of a grown man's arm towering over my head. Your forked tongue tasting the air. You've got diamonds for eyes. You look magnificent." Aych smiled and let the corners of their mouth open wider. *Rain on hot stone, verdant jungle, and lake-born thunderclouds.* Tasting an always present and impending lightning strike, Aych nodded to Lu. "How they must've screamed when they witnessed your true glory."

"Flatterer. You look famished." Capping the lipstick, Lu turned in her chair. "Have you not eaten?"

"Not enough." Reaching into the In Between, the inexplicable bridge

A Holy Venom

between the Hunting Grounds and the Silent Woods, Aych retrieved a lacquered box from thin air. "After I did the divination with the candidate's guts, I had a couple of hikers in a tent for a snack. Like candy bars out of a vending machine." They took a step closer and handed the glossy box over. "Thought you might enjoy a souvenir. They were addicted to the Rot, so it might have gone off."

The wigs on the dressing table fluttered as a breeze swept out from under the costume racks. Lu opened the container revealing a fresh human heart lying on a handful of snow.

"It's darling!" Lu pressed her hand over her sternum. "Where did you find one of this quality?"

"The lure's previous selection. You would've liked their artwork, though I drove them completely batshit." Aych's smile widened into a grotesque wolfish grin. "They made some kind of modern art shrine around the lure. Still, they seemed like your preferred kind of human: Pure, but approaching corruption." Aych looked around at the stacked flowers. "Once it was clear the candidate was only a link to the next one, I killed them. I didn't want the meat going bad before I could get that tidbit for you."

Lu scooped the heart up and admired it. Taking a dainty bite, she closed her eyes in pleasure. "Suffering a gruesome death does heighten the flavor. Before you used them for divination, you scared the poor thing quite badly, didn't you? What was the augury?"

"We're getting closer. Some more warnings, like last time. Too many players on the field." Aych shrugged. "Promises of finding the right candidate soon."

"Pure-hearted sweetness." Sighing, Lu replaced the rest of the human heart back in the box. "You are missing out. Sure you don't want any?"

"It'll only make me hungrier." Aych avoided looking at the reflection of their Little form in the dressing room mirrors. With its wide set features and smooth, new skin, the face hanging there triggered ghostly fragments of a half-forgotten dream, something from years long turned to dust, yet still troubling. One of the downsides to Lu's company was the constant presence of mirrors.

"Speaking of, you said that was the last one the lure found?" Lu scrunched up her perfect human features. "They couldn't have lasted even one minute."

"Not even ten seconds. I suspect the lure used them as a connection for the next one it wants me to interview. It seems to be operating by linking humans who know each other. Pain in the ass way to go about finding what we need. It's already showed me the next candidate. Ex-military. On the raggedy side, but might last a few minutes. I'm letting it nip her heels and see if she's worth my time." Tipping a hand, Aych indicated the box. "If the lure keeps wasting my time on fools—"

"You'll find the right one soon. Don't worry so much about it." Setting the box on the dresser next to trays of cosmetics, Lu stood up and stretched. Aych looked over her human body, unmarked without a blemish or scar, the terrible wounds on her back hidden from sight. "The Rot is addicting more humans every week. Not that I mind the taste as much as you do—"

"That was the plan, wasn't it?" Aych growled.

Lu arched a delicate eyebrow. "Sales have been increasing. *Ve-vik* is no longer in fashion for being too tepid and too expensive, comparatively. Though the overdoses are happening more quickly than I'd like."

"Good riddance. Fuckers."

"Mind that mouth of yours, please." Lu rolled her eyes. "You're missing the point of all of this. If it carries too many off at once, they'll stop buying because of fear. Our associates don't want that—they want live users. Not that I believe for an instant their new potion can make humans change, mind you."

"They're all going to die from overdoses anyway." Aych flexed their toes inside their dress shoes, trying to stretch the leather. No matter how often the Caretaker replaced Aych's wardrobe, the shoes and boots always pinched. "It's not our concern though, is it? Just doing a trade to get what we want."

Slipping a sheer robe off the rack, Lu nodded in the direction of the door. "Vine's coming..."

Aych cracked the door, catching Vine just as he was about to knock. "What can I do for you?"

Startled, Vine dropped his hand. "Vetch says there's a have-not asking for you out front."

"Thanks, I'll be right out." Closing the door, Aych glanced back at the empty spot in front of the dressing table. "I should go."

"Maybe eat while you're out." Lu called out from behind her rack of wardrobe selections. Hanger hooks clattered on the rod as she pushed the gowns roughly. "Not too many, though. Can't have you napping. Or eating whole apartment blocks and kicking off rumors of roaming gangs of murderers. Again."

They smiled. "When will you be done tonight?"

"First will be at ten, second closer to one." Lu peered around the rack. "Why? Are you worried about the *gae-su?*"

"Yeah. I should go check on him. I don't like leaving him alone for this long, especially if he hasn't come by to see you." Aych kept their fingers draped on the brass doorknob.

"The time between attacks is decreasing. If you need me, come get me. I worry about him too, you know."

"Thanks." Stepping out into the hallway, Aych looked back at Lu. "I know you'll knock 'em out like you always do, but try not to shock all the seats into cardiac arrest at once."

Lu put her hands on her hips and winked. "Where would be the fun in that? I prefer to slowly destabilize their sense of reality until they end up at the Statler, fantasizing about me and only me."

☾

Out front of the theatre, Vetch eyed Aych as they emerged from the revolving door. "Should have grabbed your coat. Told 'em to wait across the way for you. They stunk."

"Thanks," Aych nodded. "And you're correct, the anna at coat check is an empty seat waiting to happen."

The wind blowing through the city carried the scent of the Twins. Icy gusts cut through the wool suit and settled against Aych's skin. Their gaze swept the far side of the street, searching the golden glow of the Teahouse's kitchen windows.

Taxis slowed as Aych navigated the slick cobblestones. To the right of the timber-framed building, a hunched figure stepped out onto the sidewalk.

"You said to come tell you if..." The scrubby human shrank away from Aych. "I came right away like you said. I did what you told me, checked up on him every few days like you asked."

Annoyance flared, waking the spike of their hunger. The man was diseased and filthy, unappealing outside and inside. "Where's Ruin, Dan?" Aych took another step closer, driving the human backwards.

"He's not nowhere! That's what I came to tell you. Like you asked. Not at The Cellar, not here, not at any of those places." Dan's arm flippered up against the side of the Teahouse. "I checked the Stat, too, just so you wouldn't be bothered." The man's voice dropped to a whine. "I asked around, too, like you told me. No one's seen 'im for days."

Aych repressed the urge to smack the man's head clean off his shoulders. "You're certain? Take a minute and think for me, Dandelion. You're not lying or pretending you checked everywhere?"

"I wouldn't, I wouldn't lie to you, Aych. Not to you. I checked all them places and asked the people you told me to. Even asked his boyfriend." Dan's arm flippered again. "Shine said he hasn't seen Ruin either, he's been looking everywhere too. He knows we're friends, that I'm worried, like you! You can go ask him if you don't believe me. You believe me, though, don't you? You believe me, right?"

"Yeah, I believe you." Aych searched the night sky. The snow clouds were gone, replaced with distant stars scintillating in the vast and frigid vault of the Heavens. *Where the fuck are you? You better not be doing what I think you're doing...*

THREE

THE AFTERNOON SUNBEAM ARRIVED, syrupy and golden. Infiltrating the narrow gap in the stained hotel drapes, the wedge of light shone across scuffed and filthy walls. The sunbeam traveled steadily along the gloss of nicotine coating the wallpaper to the unoccupied chair in the dingy room, eventually inching far enough to illuminate the exposed stuffing sticking out of the fake leather. A tuft of cotton caught the light, flaring like fairy treasure. Motes spiraled and fluttered, sailing out of the light as the masked man occupying the other chair moved to turn a page in the paperback he was reading, rolling another page into the meat of his left fist.

A boy crouched in the corner opposite, watching the anticipated wedge of sunlight appear. He pulled his knees closer to his torso and waited. His body itched all over and his hair felt greasy. Allowed to only wash his hands and face on bathroom breaks, he could see the weeks of dirt clinging to his bare feet. His toenails were too long and there were gross crescents of dirt and blood under his fingernails. As he lifted his toes off the rug, the stained sleeves of his shirt rubbed over the fresh scabs along his forearms. The friction of fabric against the burns made the boy bite the inside of his cheek, raising a new welt. He watched the sunlight, remembering what its appearance in the room meant. He needed to distract himself and to keep from scratching. If he gave in, he would keep scratching until he bled and then the man would roar and slap him with the paperback until the boy's ears rang. Looking for a distraction, he glanced into the cardboard box of toys next to him. Neglected now but showing signs of wear, the wooden alphabet blocks inside the box sat alongside chunky animals clumsily carved from roughly sanded wood. Toys meant to entertain a younger child. His hands remembered the feel of the smooth woodgrain and each shape. Dog, cat, snake, something like a bird or a bat and something like a bear or a wolf. *A is for asshole, b is for baby, c is for club, d is for dead, e is for escape, f is for fuck this, g is for guts, and h is for…* The boy's fingers flexed as he remembered the useless weight of each dinky lettered block.

He focused his gaze on the pock-marked rug. His eyes played tricks. Imaginary bugs crawled through the fibers like slow moving armies of elephants. The sunlight swept along the scarred carpet revealing burnt wool threads, cigarette ash, and crumbs from endless bags of crisps. There was a single full-sized bed between the boy and the hotel room door, the slim space underneath the cheap bed frame crammed with boxes of junk food and more paperbacks.

The sunbeam caught the foil on the homemade cardboard mask taped to the kidnapper's eyeglasses and the light flared. Behind the cheap disguise, the man the boy called Foil-head hissed and leaned forward out of the sunbeam's range, focusing again on the pages of the worn book.

In his corner, the boy watched this silently, trying to stay invisible and review his plan. His heart began to race as the light inched behind Foil-head, crawled along the doorframe, and then skipped back into the bathroom with its small glass window overlooking the fire escape. The moment the light reflected in the mirror, the boy's heart kicked up and he dropped his head. *Any minute now.*

There was a sharp rap on the door and then a second later it eased open. A parade of adults slunk and swaggered in, suddenly filling up the small room with chatter. The bed heaved and the springs gasped as some of the newcomers sank into it. Four leather shoes and boots on the carpet, then two sets of high heels, one with a stray, unnoticed gingko leaf wrapped around one of the stiletto spikes. Perfume, cologne and tobacco smoke wafted out thickly, encircling the boy.

The pointed toe of a high heeled shoe prodded the boy's right shin. "This is what a hundred pounds of gold looks like in easily moveable form." The voice was feminine and cruel, heavily accented. "Sad little rich boy. His desperate parents will pay us any day now. Papers said they were liquidating their entire fortune to meet our demands."

Like the inside of a goldfish bowl, the cramped hotel room filled up with cigarette smoke until the boy felt it burning his eyes and mouth. Laughter rippled through the smoke. Plumes wended along the curtain and sought escape through the borders of the concealed glass.

"Is he sick or something?" a voice with a local accent asked. The question was punctuated by a rough kick to the boy's thigh.

"Nah, he's just learned our librarian friend over there doesn't like to be disturbed." The smoke churned with their rasps of laughter.

Fingers wrapped through the boy's long hair, dragging his head up. He blinked, eyes watering as he stared up at six crappy tinfoil masks looking down at him.

"Shame he's so skinny. Would've been a pretty one. You feeding him enough?" One of the adults in a suit and rain-damp trench coat turned to glance over at the man in the chair.

The man the boy thought of as Pie-tin stared at Foil-head, expecting an answer. The side of Pie-tin's face was visible, a line of clean-shaven skin not covered by his mask. The foil stayed in place tied with elastic over the man's battered cauliflower ears.

Foil-head answered in a squeaky-thin voice. "Eats enough to shit and stink the whole place up." He shrugged and went back to his reading.

"He deserves it." A woman hissed and kicked the boy with her boot. The woman with the heavy boot wore a taped-on piece of foil like a bag of snacks. Her mouth formed a snarl of anticipation. "His whole family deserves to die. I didn't come here to worry about this piece of shit's diet. You said –"

"Oh yes, you wanted to do the honors today, didn't you?" Cutting Bag-face off, Pie-tin shook the boy's head. "Roll your sleeve up, you. Time to pretend you're getting your medication."

The room filled with malicious laughter.

"Don't think we feel sorry for you, you awful piece of trash. Your family is trash. Diseased –"

"But lucky for you, they're the wealthiest!"

Like a rerun on television, the joke came with a laugh track and the audience wriggled, pleased with the punchline.

Another masked face leaned down from the circle of adults pressing in on the boy. "Just pretend you're up at the Stat where you belong, about to get a shot. Every day, they'll come in the ward and then they'll—"

"If he lives that long!" Bag-face growled.

"Oh, we won't kill you." Pie-tin prodded the boy again. "But maybe we'll experiment on you –"

"Like the dogs do!"

The laughter was nervous this time, the joke falling shy of the intended mark.

A different woman slapped her gloved hand at the boy's face. "Hurry it up, we haven't got all day. He told you to roll your sleeve up. Do as you're told."

Bag-face turned her back and pushed her makeshift mask away from her face. She lit a cigarette. The plume of tobacco smoke curled over her shoulder as more hands grabbed at the boy's limp arms, shoving up the stained shirt sleeve on his left. Circular scabs and a few weeping wounds dotted the boy's skin. One burn mark for every day he had spent in the confines of the room, enduring the group's daily visit to torment him.

"Maybe we could cut out one of his eyes instead. They'd still pay to get the rest back."

"Or a finger."

"A toe!"

"Hold his hand out so we can burn him again. That was great fun!"

The suggestions on how to torture their captive kept coming as Bag-face inspected the ember at the end of her cigarette then pasted her mask back over her face.

"Hold him," she hissed. "I want to watch him cry while I do it."

From far away, in whatever sanctuary of spirit the boy's mind sheltered, a slender, fragile thing broke. It was, he thought, not like a vase falling off a shelf to shatter, fragments flying. Instead, it felt heavy, like a worn lock wrenched off a horse paddock gate, the stall door bursting open, the creature inside escaping. Except this feeling in him wasn't beautiful like a horse. It was ugly and heavy, yet still leaping and quick. He felt made of nightmares. The force crashed and hurled itself through the hole in his spirit, now broken open and spiraling wider.

"Fuck you!" he screamed. The words came on their own, rushing up his throat as he slammed his forehead into the face of the woman holding the cigarette in front of him.

The kidnappers staggered back as their normally docile prisoner went wild, thrashing and fighting.

"I hate you! Die! Die!" the boy yelled, balled up his fist, and punched Bag-face. Careening around the hotel room punching and kicking, he raced toward his objective.

Foil-head rose from his seat too late to stop the boy's trajectory into the bathroom. As he passed the man, the boy flung an elbow into Foil-head's stomach, knocking the adult off balance. He slammed shut the bathroom door, its rudimentary lock clicking into place.

"Stop him! He'll ruin everything, you assholes!" Pie-tin man shouted as the others clambered over the bed and each other. "Kick the door down!"

"Fuck you! I *will* ruin it!" Grabbing the top of the toilet tank, the boy hurled the slab of porcelain against the grungy bathroom's window. It shattered just as he hoped. Barefoot and bare handed, he hauled himself over the shards of porcelain and through the jagged glass that sliced into his legs and arms. Furious pent-up hatred pounded in his head and propelled him head-long out the upper story window onto the rickety fire escape. Behind him, the bathroom door exploded open. Masked faces appeared at the broken window, yelling. Under the boy's bare feet, the rusted grate of the fire escape deck whined and shimmied from his weight, slight as it was. The cold metal burned his feet as he paced the tiny square of grating.

A woman yelled to the rest. "Who is the smallest? You! You go out there and get him! Before the salts spot him!"

The boy looked out over the city. The wind blew shredded leaves and gusted rainwater off the railing. Truck horns and emergency sirens blared. The boy ignored the noise and stared down the twenty stories to the traffic-jammed streets below. Blood soaked through his clothes and he started shivering. The sirens wailed and grew closer, the scanning beacons of spotlights chasing over the sandstone exterior of the hotel, dazzling his eyes. A patrol car stopped and two uniformed officers piled out. One yelled into the radio clipped to her collar while the other flagged down a second patrol car and pointed up at the boy on the fire escape.

"If you come back in now, we won't hurt you," a different adult's voice wheedled from the bathroom window.

Newly freed, the ferocious thing in the boy refused to let him turn around. Before him, over the pocket-sized safety of the fire escape, the city sprawled, the burning horizon opposite the rising dark. He oriented himself using the location of the Twins and the Basilica and at last knew how to get back to where he belonged.

"If you try and get me, I'll jump. You know I'll do it! I will!" His child's voice cracked around the defiant proclamation.

The anger in his heart was growing, spreading wider and wider. The crack rippling inside his head was getting louder. Unable to restrain it, the boy screamed to let it out. Distant and echoing, it might have come from the box of toys left in the hotel room, it was so strange to him. Below, the patrol car's searchlight swiveled and fixed on his location as long, screeching howls of pain rose out of his throat.

☽

Waking with a gasp, Ruin fumbled for a lighter in the front pocket of his jeans. Afraid and feeling alone, he instinctively longed for Aych. The subway train wheels clattered and sung over the tracks. On either end of the car, the sliding doors gasped and sighed. Faint music played from a nearby passenger's headphones and the tin-thin notes swam through the train. The accordion junction between two cars flexed as the subway tunnel flashed light-dark-light through the windows. One second, he saw the subway tunnel; the next, somewhere else. Ruin caught a glimpse of a bleak forest, cursed and angry, skeletal, bare trees. Snow drifted between the trunks as moving shadows hunted him. Somewhere in the dark, a small bell jingled. He closed his eyes against the invading scenery.

"You got out," he whispered as he ran his thumb over the lighter's spark wheel. "You aren't in that hotel anymore." He resisted the urge to touch the knife in his jacket pocket. He glanced at the subway map above the door opposite. Three more stops and he would arrive at the Greenway. Ten minutes after that and he would be halfway to the practice space. Half an hour later, the music would drown out the rest of the world, taking his nightmares with it.

The train slowed and stuttered as it pulled into a stop. Station announcements crackled through the blown-out speakers as the car doors gusted open. Bodies moved in currents, some in, some out, bringing new sounds and strangers' voices. The scent of roses and sandalwood wafted through the humid, hot air. A woman in a fitted long coat and high boots took the empty seat across from Ruin. She fished around in her designer purse and sighed noisily, unable to find whatever she had been searching for.

The sickness inside Ruin woke up. Voices whispered to him and corrupt impulses stirred. His diggers called it a 'traducer's chorus,' songs of violent abuse and grotesque compulsions looping in his mind. Ruin thought of it as a chorus of imps, malicious and hate-filled.

He looked up at the woman. She was flawless, featureless, like a storefront display mannequin. Not a human—an artifact. Witnessing himself dehumanize a potential victim ignited a litany of useless coping mechanisms harvested from years of therapy. But none of the diggers' suggestions controlled the urges, though he tried them all, like a washed-up singer trotting out a tired set list.

Taking the lighter out of his pocket, he cupped his other hand over it and bowed his head. Fear of fire, fear of pain, both could keep the imps quiet. The rubber band wrapped around his wrist might work for a minute or two. The thought of the lighter cooking his flesh brought back the nightmare. Shrinking back into his seat, Ruin ground his teeth and put the lighter away. He dreaded what was coming, what always came after the urges started up. Across from him, the woman opened a cosmetic case and checked her reflection.

Ruin bit the inside of his cheek until he tasted blood. Around him, the subway rumbled and clattered through the deep tunnels of earth. Hidden from the sky, the sun, and the moon, he wished to be anything else. He wanted to die. Only, if he died, there would be no music, no more hope, no more dreams, no more time with the people he loved. The shit-bags in the hotel room would win. They would be right.

Searing pain ringed his skull. He dropped forward over his knees. The imps showed him what they wanted him to do. They made pictures for him: blood-splattered walls, a magazine photoshoot of a murdered stranger's apartment, a tilted doorway leading into his victim's skewed bathroom, filled with broken toiletries and crumpled towels, and a knife, his knife, rattling into a dry porcelain sink, leaving a wet, glossy trail beneath a mirror slathered in blood. Flashes of an eviscerated body in the tub, her sliced and severed skin. The woman's wide, lifeless eyes staring blankly into his, a torso splayed open revealing glistening bone and viscera. The stink—no, a perfume of blood and sweat stinging his nostrils. Waves of nausea rose up. *Run*, he mentally screamed to the woman seated across from him. *When the doors open, run for your life.*

A throaty laugh jolted him. He looked up. A woman, seemingly made of glass, sat next to him, her translucent shoulder touching his. *Pretty darling, it's OK to want to kill her, to hurt them all, pretty darling of mine.* Synchronized to the click-clack of the train rushing over the rails, the realness of the woman flickered. Younger than Ruin yet somehow older, her vintage clothes and jewelry shifted from two-dimensional detail to three-dimensional opacity. She was the photo image of his aunt cut out of a family scrapbook and pasted into the world. Then suddenly, she was rounded and curved, a mirror reflecting the warped spaces inside the train car. Back and forth, the ghost flickered in time with the train going over the tracks. *Clack-clack-clack-clack.* Ruin snagged the rubber band on his wrist and snapped it over and over until a welt appeared.

You'll need something stronger than that to keep me away. The imp chorus in his head cheered as the ghost laughed again and stood up. Her form materialized fully as she moved to sit in the same seat as the woman across the aisle, the two forms phasing in and out. *Here,* the ghost said, gently turning her glass chin and tracing the shimmering neckline. *This is where you cut, and all the water will jet out and you can drink her down.*

Ruin shuddered. He wanted rid of the ghost of his aunt and wished Aych— Time stuttered like the train, slowing and accelerating unevenly, glimpses of the skeletal trees of the Silent Woods and the underground tunnel of the Hunting Grounds alternating through the windows. The screech of brakes and squeal of metal on metal stopped Ruin from hearing or seeing anything.

Then his perception lurched into motion, throwing him from one moment to the next. He was off the train and staring at a water fountain. He didn't remember getting here. *So thirsty.* He pounded the palm of his hand on the broken water fountain, willing it to work. Breathing in the fetid subway air, his throat felt raw and parched. *Can't even manage to whisper let alone sing.* An imp laughed. Ruin rolled to the side of the fountain and slid down the tiled wall, shuddering. He sank into the rat-shit covered newspapers and crushed paper cups. The station lights hovered above, hyper-real and crisp burning whiteness. The laughter started again, creaking and sawing through Ruin's throat. As he sat, a steady tide of commuters pushed through the stiles, off to work, or home, or wherever. Bored station attendants scanned the crowds, pretending to watch for fare shirkers, their eyes sweeping over him. He was just another stat, invisible. Water dripped down the steps beyond the exit spindles. Ruin shivered and tried to ignore the terrible thirst gnawing at him. The world stank of piss and garbage, but a hidden chain of perfume enticed him away from the platform. His body pushed to stand, trying to latch onto the smell.

To the left, along the train platform, a faint sound drew his attention. *Tap, tap, tap.* The sound grew louder as he hung against the wall. He closed his eyes, his heart pounding. *Tap, tap, tap.* High-heeled boots, reckless fashion to navigate in the ice and snow. *Tap, tap, tap,* louder against the yellow warning lines. The sound cut through him, piercing his skull. *Tap. Tap. Tap.* He knew what he would see when he opened his eyes: two legs branching up and hip bones and the sweet warmth between them and cold water running in veins like hidden wellsprings deep in the woods.

Strands of brunette hair, long and glossy and bound in a single long bundle, appeared in his line of sight. Around him, the Hunting Grounds sharpened into focus. High heels tap-tapped to his right and stopped in front of him. The woman was impatient. She kept checking her wristwatch, flicking her hair back and forth over her winter coat. Hips tilted, denim clinging to skin fading into fur-lined boots. Ruin's fingertips ached to dig into the woman's pelvis. *Catch her neck in your teeth while you're at it,* a doubled voice slurred in his ear. An electric rush of excitement raced through Ruin's body. The thought of biting reminded him of—

He glanced up and the top of the station gave way to a starless sky. An ancient, unchanging sickle moon flickered between the high branches. Apricot and copper, it cast no light on the barren forest below. Neither the station workers nor the commuters could see the Silent Woods creeping in. The length of brunette hair twitched impatiently as the woman looked at her watch again and sighed.

Train brakes tightened on the rails. The ear-splitting noise set fire to the roof of Ruin's skull and he squeezed his eyes closed. Sparks danced behind his eyelids as the car pulled into the station. Speakers sputtered updates about delays, setting off a wave of groans from the waiting passengers. An additional jumble of noise echoed over the canned door closure warnings. Ruin felt the woman moving away and opened his eyes. As she started away from the delayed train, his back unpeeled from the wall. She was going up to the street.

Passing through the turnstile, Ruin watched the S&P officer leaning against the service booth. The man was laughing, sharing a joke with the subway employee behind the shatterproof glass. The checkered bands on the officer's rain vest chattered at Ruin, the squares shifting and pulling into demonic faces, mocking him. The officer glanced over and met Ruin's gaze. Ruin dropped his head and shoved his hands back into his leather jacket. The choking heat of the station pushed him up the wet stairs. Thick white noise muffled the people flowing up around him, making them distant even as they jostled into him. The scent of his prey mingled with the dirty-salt tang of car exhaust and overflowing garbage cans.

The silhouettes of the other commuters blurred into a river of shifting trash and islands of conversation. Headlights and streetlights added to the cacophony muddling his senses. The warm cloud tumbled out onto the sidewalk and deposited him on Macer Ave. Head down, he let his boots find the path. He broke into a jog, suddenly panicked at the idea of losing her scent.

Then, Ruin was clutching the bricks of an unfamiliar building, the streets of the city suddenly foreign. The tidal surge of the changing landscape made him afraid. He could feel the brick through callouses on his fingers and willed the solidity to hold him in place, to keep him in one world. The imps howled and lashed out, hating him for losing sight of her. Water dripped off the fire escape above, conjuring images of the woman reclining in some nearby apartment. He could feel her perfect body glimmering. If he focused, if the imps would shut the fuck up, he would be able to find her. Then—

Gasping in horror, Ruin smashed his head against the bricks. Anything to make it stop, he would do anything to make it stop. All he wanted was

A Holy Venom

the music. All he lived for. "Liars. You're all fucking liars!" he screamed and swung his head again. The brick shredded skin off his cheek. "I won't do it. I won't be like her!"

Ruin closed his eyes against the voices and the hallucinations. His fingers found their way along the padded lining of his jacket to the zippered pocket inside. He took out one of the slim paper tubes stored there and tore it open with his teeth. The powder burned on his chapped lips and caught at the top of his throat. Ruin repressed a cough long enough to swallow the mouthful dry, the medicine scraping down his throat like glass shards. Tears leaked from his closed eyelids.

He felt the weight of the knife in his back pocket. Through the layers of denim, he felt it burning. "Help me, please." Dragging in a breath, he glanced out into the street as a bus went by. If he timed it right, he could— Pushing off the wall, he bolted into the street. Car horns blared and walls of light crashed around him. The air burned in his lungs as he ran blindly through the street. With each breath, he anticipated the bone-crunching impact. He teetered on the edge of the choice. He wanted the music, he wanted to hear it again just once more. "If you don't do it now, they will make you kill someone. Again," he whispered.

He prayed he was running west toward the Twins. Even a fuck-up could manage to fall into the freezing rivers and end it. He would rather die than become her.

He had nothing and no one left to ask for help. There was no one left to pray to. The Holy Mother hated him. The voices were Her punishment for his sins and the sins of his family. The imps clamored for his blood. They wanted him to turn his arm over and set the tip of the blade between the tendons, draw it down to the crook of his arm. They showed him how to open his skin and let them move in and out. Not for the first time, they showed him how to kill himself.

He missed his friends. He wished he could see Squash and Shine and tell them how much everything they'd done for him meant. He wished he wasn't a waste of everyone's effort.

"Aych," Ruin whispered as he stared at the sickle moon through dead tree branches. He missed Aych the most and wanted, if only for a minute, to bury himself in their arms until the voices stopped. His whole chest ached with longing until he stumbled.

The stairs under his boots wavered. He floundered in snow between the barren tree trunks and then tumbled down the tiled stairwell back into the station. The lights in the station dimmed, fading under a layer of inexplicable darkness. Fear seized him. An icy wind sluiced from the train tunnel. Staggering, he turned and saw his aunt's ghost standing alone on the platform. Gone were her designer clothes and arrogant demeanor. She looked afraid, harried, shivering in hospital pajamas. She wrapped her arms over her chest and stared back at him frantically. Frost zigzagged along the wall tiles and ice built up on the platform under her bare feet. The tiles began to crack and fall away as gnarled tree roots cracked through. Long, serpentine trunks spawned forth, each tree unfurling clawed branches that lifted and tore through the station ceiling.

His aunt's apparition screamed at him, *"It's coming to kill you! Run!"*

The lights in the train tunnel went out as the wind howled. Panicked, Ruin sprinted for the stairs. Behind him, his aunt screamed in agony, her cries echoing off the station walls. Pain exploded in Ruin's lungs. The compulsion to escape faded as his legs gave way. He stumbled, caught himself on the railing, and glanced backward. The station vanished. Snow gusted around vitrified trunks, the tangled, angry branches merging with the starless sky.

"Fuck." Ruin's warm breath dissipated as the endless night of the Silent Woods bore down on him.

Despair dragged at his bones. He lost his grip and skidded down the slope into a snow pile and lay there. Death would be coming now ... if not something worse.

FOUR

PASSENGERS EDDIED AND POOLED on the stairs leading into the subway station. The fusty air blasting from the ductwork hanging overhead billowed coats and scarves as boots trampled food wrappers and churned the strewn debris into unidentifiable clutter. The faces of those passing by formed a swirling cascade of the curious and the concerned. Other commuters rushed by the onlookers, uninterested in the spectacle.

"Hey, can you hear me?" Officer Pike called as he knelt next to Ruin's crumpled body. "Did you hit your head?" The transit officer turned his head to call into the radio clipped to his collar.

A massive, pale hand fell on his shoulder, covering the radio before he had a chance to speak. "My friend has been having an adventurous night, officer," Aych enunciated each word in a clear, low drawl. "Too much to drink."

"Hold it," the transit officer demanded. He stood up as Aych started to move toward Ruin. "Or it could be he's on a kick and you're looking after one of your customers."

Aych ignored him and moved to Ruin's side. "You've got a sharp eye, officer." Aych propped Ruin into a sitting position. "Could be this kid's on the Rot. Maybe his rich parents are worried about their poor darling causing a scandal and hired me to bring him home."

"Yeah, well, you're not doing a very good job playing babysitter," Pike crossed his arms.

"Lucky for them, you were here when it mattered." Offering a handshake, Aych flashed a tight-lipped smile.

With a frown, Pike took Aych's offered hand. Palming the concealed money Aych passed him, Pike huffed. "You'll get 'im out of here and seen to."

"Of course, officer."

Pike waved the remaining onlookers away. "Alright, move along. Kid had too much to drink, he'll be fine."

Aych hooked Ruin's arms over their own and stood up with the human over their back. Aych inhaled Ruin's fear and desperation as the young man's head rested on their shoulder.

At the curb, a taxi driver got out of the first car in line and came around to open the door for the pair. "Hitting the limit a little early tonight?" she teased Aych.

"Thankfully," they replied dryly as they arranged the unconscious human in the back seat.

"Where you headed?" The woman angled her rearview mirror and met Aych's glimmering eyes. She inhaled sharply.

"Ten twenty Tranquility, in the New Quarter. Across from the Velvet."

"From this side of things, that's going to take some time," the cabbie replied, shaking off her passenger's strange appearance.

"We're in no rush."

The taxi jostled forward as it pulled away from the station exit. Ruin slumped against Aych, the human's head coming to rest on Aych's left arm. Irritated, Aych shifted, putting their arm over the top of the back seat. Ruin's body slid to rest against his protector's chest. Aych softly brushed back sweaty, tangled strands of dark hair from Ruin's face as he slept.

"Fuck. You smell like shit, you know that?" Ruin's leather stank of coppery sweat and his skin emanated a strange metallic odor that reminded Aych of burnt electrical insulation and rubber. With their free hand, Aych fished the pouch of herbs out of their suit jacket and leaned forward toward the driver. "You mind if I crack a window and smoke?"

The driver lowered Aych's window. "Go ahead." She cranked the heat up to compensate for the sudden cold.

With quick practiced movements, Aych assembled and rolled a cigarette one-handed. Putting the finished roll in their mouth, they fished out a brand-new lighter, lit it, and inhaled deeply. The lungful of potent fumigants edged into Aych's blood and dulled the edges of their irritation. *That last candidate was a waste of my time. I should've been back sooner before*

A Holy Venom

that fucking degenerate, shit-bag malison tried—

Plumes of thick, pungent smoke slipped out of the gap in the window. Taking another lungful, Aych relaxed. *His new meds aren't worth shit.* Along their ribs, Ruin's slight body rose and fell in a counter rhythm. *He's safe, and I've bought us some time until Lu can fix him up. That's all that matters.* The familiar scent of Ruin's skin and hair lay under the sewer stench of the subway and countless hours pressed into a tin can with hundreds of other humans, each coated in cosmetics and their own gland-driven excretions. Aych glanced down. *You smell like a grocery aisle in hell, psycho.*

Under all the others was something darker, a hidden scent: an icy-cold void and eldritch magic. *Snow that never melts nor can ever quench your thirst; lifeless, thorny tree bark; ancient bitter shale and granite that longs to slice your skin and sup on your blood. Betwixt and between.* With their thumb, Aych gently tucked Ruin's hair back behind his ear. *You were scared to be In Between, hunting and being hunted in the Silent Woods. Alone and yet never alone.* Soft under the grime and grit of sweat, Aych touched Ruin's cheek and the fragile bones beneath. *Dehydrated, half-starved, over-medicated, scrawny, the meat would taste . . .* Aych caught the thought and took one last, long drag from their cigarette. When they let it go, the ember flew out the gap, a cherry-red speck disappearing into the night. *I leave you alone for a few days and you end up worse than if I dropped you in the House myself.*

Putting up the car window, Aych watched the Hunting Grounds shift and fade in streaks of jarring white light and blocks of shadow. Ice-coated buildings loomed up around frail-looking humans scurrying along the sidewalks, every one of them afraid of their own city. The window gap snapped shut dulling the wet, slopping sound of tires plowing through slush and the never-ending clamor of car horns and sirens.

Rainbow neon marked the taxi's entry into the New Quarter. The artificial light rippled in vibrant waves over the vehicle as the driver weaved through the warren of constricted streets and clumps of pedestrians. Like a beacon, the lights of the Velvet's marquee blazed up over the tops of the nearby buildings. Traffic slowed as limos and taxis queued in front of the nighttime oasis.

"There's a driveway just up on the left. Right after the hydrant." Aych passed a large bill over the driver's seatback.

"Thanks! You OK to get your friend in on your own, yeah? You need any change?"

"Keep it, we're all set."

The taxi dipped back into the street, ignoring the crowds in front of the Teahouse trying to flag it.

"How far up you want me to go?" The driver eased down on the brakes.

"Enough so I can open the door. This is fine. You can back out as soon as we're clear." Aych waited for the car to come to a full stop in the courtyard. They got out and carefully eased Ruin from the back seat, cradling the sleeping man in their arms.

The driver inched back into the street. Aych adjusted their hold on Ruin and carried him over the snowbank. Post-holing through the deep drifts, they reached the carriage house and hit the outdoor switch for the first of the two bays. The garage door on the right churned upwards as the lights and heating system kicked on inside.

That *stingy, nagging fuck could've just left the heat running.* Aych growled in annoyance.

Packed with tools, machinery, and motorcycles in various states of disassembly, the garage stank of gasoline and motor oil. Wrinkling their nose, Aych carried Ruin to the center of the least cluttered bay and set him gently into a folding chair. Aych took off their suit jacket and began going through Ruin's pockets. They found a knife and crumpled packets of medication. Pushing the paper packets back into the leather jacket, Aych dropped the knife into their trouser pocket. They slipped a wad of cash into the inside pocket of Ruin's jacket and zipped the leather up to keep him warm. Aych studied Ruin's face and frowned. "I need to get Lu over here, but if I leave you alone, that fucking thing will reattach."

They stalked to the open bay and stared out across the snow to the back of the Teahouse. "I can feel you looking for him, shit-bag." With a snarl, Aych hit the switch to shut the garage door and returned to the center of the bay. They studied the engine pulleys suspended from the support beams and poked among the piles of equipment. Aych found a utility power cord and began tying it in knots. They glanced back at Ruin and then up at the pulley system. *This will have to do.* Hooking one of the knotted loops over the hook on the pulley, Aych wrapped the remainder of the thick cord around Ruin's

A Holy Venom

chest several times and knotted it. They picked up Ruin, hugging him against their chest with one hand. With the other, they hauled on the pulley chain. Still unconscious, Ruin's body hung limply in the air as Aych checked the ties and chains for stability. Satisfied, they raised Ruin up until his boot heels were a foot off the garage's cement floor and tied off the pully chain. Eying the human's prone form dangling like a fly in a web, Aych frowned. *Fucking thing has been at him for days this time. Shit.*

On the other side of the garage, Aych located a large, shallow pan full of motor oil and carried it through the ranks of stripped motorcycle frames. *I shouldn't have left him for so long.* They placed the container of viscous sludge under Ruin and nudged it in place with the toe of their dress shoe.

The garage work lights cast odd, iridescent shadows on the slick surface of the pan. Bending under Ruin, Aych let the reflection of their face fall on the oil then slipped a finger into the filthy muck. Releasing the bone-white flesh off their fingertip, Aych let the skin dissolve into the fluid, sorcery sloughing with it, enchanting the liquid in the pan. They sensed the ragged, torn edges of the malison nosing around the garage in search of Ruin. *I've got more in my bag of tricks than you can imagine, you low-rent piece of shit.*

Aych stood. Their finger quickly reassembled itself as the ripples on the surface of the oil stilled, reflecting the bottom of Ruin's boots. Aych slipped on their suit jacket and studied Ruin's face. *Sleep and sleep some more, if you know what's good for you.*

The door engine cranked on again and a squinting, gray-haired human ducked under the trundling panels. "What the fuck are you playing at?" the man demanded, glaring at Aych. "Saw the lights on and—" The human stopped as he spied Ruin's limp form dangling from the pully. "What the fuck is wrong with you dangling him over … what the fuck *is* that?"

"Took you long enough," Aych snatched a rag off the lounge chair and wiped the remaining muck off their hands. Taking the knife out of their pocket, they wiped Ruin's fingerprints off it and dropped it back into their trouser pocket. "Protection until I bring Lu back. If you touch it, Mat," Aych snarled, "I'll gut you for lottery numbers."

The head apothecary of the Teahouse was saturated in the aromas of herbs. *And that other stink. Cut grass and fresh turned earth, clean-picked bones, and cedar forests.* Like a spray of musk and piss on a territory marker, a

Presence lingered on the man. Aych couldn't decide which they hated more, the man or the stink of Other that clung to him. Mat reached out his hand. Aych thundered a warning, "*I said don't touch anything!*"

"I was only going to check his pulse." the herbalist snapped, cringing.

"Too fucking bad, you'll have to take my word that he's fine."

"You can't hang someone up like a side of beef. Especially when they're hurt. Can't be good—"

"Shut the fuck up. I said it's to protect him." Aych glared at Mat. "Even a half-assed practitioner like yourself can tell what it is."

"He could be injured and you're trussing him up like meat." Mat shook his hand at Ruin's sleeping body. "It's not right."

"You think I'd fucking hurt him?" Aych growled low in the back of their throat and took a step closer. "Do you?"

"No, of course not." Mat shook his head and held his hands up in defense. "I didn't mean it that way. I'm only worried, like you."

Aych threw the rag onto the workbench. "Then stay here and keep watch while I get Lu. Don't break the circle under him. Don't move the pan. And don't fucking touch him."

Mat muttered and lowered himself into the battered folding chair. "Well go on, then. Get her."

"I'd be halfway there if you weren't nagging at me," Aych muttered on the way out of the garage. "Fucking useless."

☾

Outside the Velvet, Aych nodded curtly to the woman standing by the revolving doors. The security guard nodded back and resumed watching the new arrivals walking the carpet. Lu sailed through the bustling lobby, diamond clips sparkling in her finger-wave coif. She glided through the chaos like a sovereign surveying her court, dispensing and receiving roguish compliments and offering shaded innuendo while Vetch discreetly followed.

As Aych approached, Vetch draped a voluminous white mink coat over Lu's bare shoulders.

"I must be off now." Lu handed her cocktail glass off to one of her admirers. "Do enjoy the rest of your evening."

"Will you be back tonight?" an overly eager woman asked, pressing her hand into Lu's fur coat.

Vetch caught the woman's fingers delicately and lifted them to his lips. "Have you forgotten your promise to me? If I remember correctly, *le-lm*, last time we chatted, you said you wanted to see the gaming tables?"

Walking toward the exit, Lu waved and smiled at her disappointed fans. "Where's the *gae-su* now? How bad is it?" she murmured as Aych fell in next to her.

"Close to a full possession. I've got him across the street, in the garage."

"Oh, that will be chilly this time of year. I suppose he can't go into the Teahouse quite yet or you would have brought him here." Taking out a pair of gloves, Lu pouted. "If it is that bad, you were right to keep him outside. It is going to be chilly, isn't it?"

Throwing an apologetic look down at Lu, Aych increased the ambient heat radiating off their body. "It should only take us a few minutes to get inside. I'll keep you warm."

"Ah, that would be lovely." Lu stepped into the compartment of the revolving door.

Admirers swarmed Lu. Aych pulled up to their full height and Lu slipped under their left arm. Aych glared at the humans surrounding them until even the drunk ones backed off.

She smiled up into Aych's face. "Security *and* my very own heating lamp. No wonder I keep you around."

"I thought it was to get rid of your leftovers. The crunchy bits you don't like to eat."

"That too. But this is a nice side benefit," she snuggled closer, adding to the flirtatious illusion. "How badly is it affecting him?"

Aych guided her along the red carpet. "Full of useless medication and completely unhinged. Either his new meds are fucked up or he's taken something that's not playing well with others. Doesn't smell like *ve-vik* or Rot. Some other synthetic medicine that smells like he's sweating plastic and talc. I managed to take a bite out of the shit-bag this time, but the connection is getting stronger." Aych paused and caught Lu's eye. "There's more. Ruin was falling Betwixt when I found him."

She gave an elegant shrug in response. "He was instinctively looking for you, perhaps? That's usually why he goes there, isn't it? Despair and desire combined open many doors."

Lu squeaked in surprise as Aych scooped her up into their arms and started across the street. "I hope you do get a chance to demolish that thing. Filthy *pikma*." She draped her arms around Aych and rested her head against their neck. "Its entire existence is offensive. I sincerely hope you tear them apart."

"Me too," Aych smiled maliciously. "One of the few things I can honestly say I want to shred into tiny, tiny pieces without eating."

"The tiniest pieces." Lu tapped a finger against Aych's jaw. "You haven't eaten, have you?"

"No, I had to find Ruin. He was already following someone." Aych strode up the icy driveway leaving wet footprints in the gravel. "He had a knife."

"To make an offering of cut hair again, or to—"

"Does it matter?" Aych stepped over the crest of the snowbank and followed the trail into the garage. "If he'd been stopped by the salts with the knife, it would've been all over. The salts would've dumped him up at the Stat no questions asked." Once through the door, Aych glared at Mat, still in the chair. "You didn't touch him or anything else?"

"No, I told you I wouldn't." Mat stood up slowly and gave Lu a relieved, welcoming smile.

Carrying her between the toolboxes and dusty machines, Aych brought Lu to the center of the garage bay.

"You can put me down now." Lu slipped gracefully out of Aych's arms and tugged the glove off her right hand. She furrowed her brow and leaned into Ruin, setting one finger on his chest. "Your nose is right about his meds. There's definitely a poison in his bloodstream. It's not from a plant source, and it's not any of the synthetic street delights I'm familiar with." Lu leaned away and slipped her glove back on. "He's safe to enter a dwelling now. You successfully broke the connection. The *pikma* won't follow him in until they recover from your attack. I've restored my influence over him for now, but..." She eyed the tray of motor oil below the unconscious human. "Oh, what an excellent idea. I will have to remember that trick! Though, I would

A Holy Venom

prefer a cleaner medium."

Mat sighed. "Thank you for coming over so quickly."

Lu threw the herbalist a dazzling smile. "I want to repay you for your generous help, so whatever I can do for your family is my pleasure." She glanced up at Aych. "Settle him inside. I can walk back on my own."

"Are you sure? It's below freezing."

"It won't kill me. I can walk myself back like a grown woman. Besides, you can't leave him hanging like that forever." Lu tipped her fingers at Ruin. "You know, I only hate the cold. It doesn't hurt me. We brumate, not hibernate. And I quite like being carried and treated as a dainty, precious thing, if you must know."

Mat reached out to take hold of Ruin. "I can get him inside while you take Lu back to the Velvet."

"You'll drop him and break your damn hip in the process. We need you to finish your fucking job," Aych prodded Mat in the chest. "Go draw a hot bath, if you want to make yourself useful."

Confused, Mat glanced between them. "For Lu?"

"No, you fucking pervert. *For Ruin.*" Aych waved Lu back and moved the oil pan.

"Well, you didn't say that, did you? How was I supposed to know?" Flustered, Mat started out of the garage. With one hand on the seat of a motorcycle, the man paused. "There's a whole goat in the walk-in fridge in the kitchen. In a cooler right inside the walk-in."

With their arm around Ruin's waist. Aych stared back. "You trying to kill me now?"

"No! You seem hungry is all." Mat stormed out of the garage muttering. "Fucking asshole."

Lu called out, "Mat, your nephew will need to go on a saline drip once you get him to bed. He's terribly dehydrated."

"I already planned on it." The apothecary shot another look at Aych. "I was listening."

"Thank you!" Lu turned back and pointed at Aych. "Come on now, Mat isn't going to poison you. I don't think even I could manage to take you out if I bit you myself. And you'd taste terrible."

"He could decide to try out your special request on me." Aych lowered

Ruin over their shoulder and unhooked him from the pulley. "Just because you trust him and the Awy doesn't mean I do."

Lu sighed and began picking her way out among the clutter. "After you get the *gae-su* settled, eat the goat Mat thoughtfully provided for you. If you don't, you're going to overeat when you hunt and then sleep too long. Didn't you say the lure found another candidate?"

"It did. It's warming her up for me." Aych repositioned Ruin and followed Lu out of the garage. They smacked the garage switch and the door clattered down the rails behind them. "Can you make it back in those heels or do you want to wait in the kitchen for me to carry you back?"

"Please," Lu gingerly stepped through the snowbank, her long mink coat leaving ripples in the snow. When she lifted it, her spiked heels left diamond imprints instead. "I have lived in this frigid hell of a city long enough to manage to get my own self home in higher heels than these. I just like letting you do me the favor of toasting my perfect backside."

Aych smirked. "Don't freeze and turn into a snake-scicle on the way home. That'll be difficult to explain to the locals."

"I'll have you know my lake back home is fed by cold springs." Lu turned her nose up and started picking her way over the gravel drive. "Shouldn't you be getting your precious jewel inside already?"

Aych glanced into Ruin's face. "How long until it starts up again? Until the shit-bag malison latches onto him again?"

"A few days is all my influence can manage for now. Five, maybe less. You best be back as soon as you can. And I have told you not to refer to it by that term around him, it's too telling. If you must call it something, say *pikma* or something similar." Lu stopped. "You do know it would be so much easier if only you would relent. You're not the same. If only you'd reconsider, we wouldn't have to—"

"We are sticking to the plan." Aych hugged Ruin tighter. "Three days is more than enough for an interview."

☾

The stone head stared malevolently at Haw. A ring of water around the thing pooled and seeped into the antique wood of the desk. Not even ten minutes ago, Haw had thrown the head out into the cold, watching silently as the stone plummeted out of the sky and cracked through the ice of the farm pond behind the house. She swatted the wretched object off her desk.

No matter where she left it, or threw it, it returned. Even now as it rolled on the floor, the carved features appeared to mock her efforts. No human hand had returned it, she knew that much. Haw's stomach churned. *Was it a psych-ops attack? Was a former adversary after her and her family?* None of the state powers she could think of would target a retired veteran out of misplaced vengeance. Haw had adhered meticulously to the rules of war. No crimes against civilians, always treated POWs as fellow human beings. She could not think of any motive for this uncanny hostility. She clenched her jaw. There was a sledgehammer in the barn and if nothing else, she would knock that thing's creepy face right off.

"Everything OK in here?" Olive rapped a knuckle on Haw's office door and glanced in.

Haw tried to fix a calm expression on her face before turning around. "Yes. Everything is fine."

"Don't you try that on me," Olive pushed the door back and raised an eyebrow. "When's the last time you were even able to sleep for more than an hour?"

Haw sagged against the desk. "I just don't know what the hell is happening."

Olive came over. "Could be a psychological operation. You piss off any old enemies? Any contacts you want to tell me about?"

"I was …" Haw caught sight of Olive's teasing look and guffawed. "I wish it were. Then I'd know what to do."

"What *would* you do? Call S&P? Call your squad? Buy more guns?"

Sighing, Haw shook her head. "There's nothing I can show anyone, nothing I can even tackle. Hell, if I tried to shoot it, I'd be afraid of hitting the kids or you. I'm not even sure it's really happening. We haven't actually seen anything."

"The kids have. I believe them that something's going on in the house." Olive glanced at the stone head leering at them from the corner of the room. "What's that?"

"Nothing. Just a rock I picked up outside." She quickly got off the edge of the desk and snatched the head off the floor.

"Oh? Can I see it?"

"Never mind that thing. It's dirty," Haw quickly dropped it into the waste basket. "What did Dr. Plate suggest?" She knew she was deliberately deflecting Olive's attention. *Why don't I tell her? Why don't I want Olive to touch it?*

"She said we should put the nursery monitors back in the kids' bedrooms. See if they record anything. If they don't, we should have the kids listen so they know nothing is in the room with them."

"And if they *do* record someone in there?"

"Then we call S&P and have them do something about it. You don't think there's someone actually coming into the house, do you?" Olive suddenly looked worried.

Haw tried to shake off the maddening desire to tear the farmhouse apart looking for hidden passages. "The kids aren't lying, but beyond that, I don't know." Glancing at the wastebasket, she considered if something more disturbing was happening.

Olive squeezed Haw's arm. "I'll dig the baby monitors out of storage and set them up. We'll all feel better once we prove there's nothing going on except scary stories and overactive imaginations."

Coming back around the desk, Haw kissed Olive's cheek. "I'm sorry I'm not more help."

"You might have a virus. Night sweats can indicate a range of medical issues."

Haw laughed. "Once a medic, always a medic."

"I have to go pick up the kids. Why don't you take a nap until dinner?"

"I need to finish up the final designs for the townhouse project. But that sounds like a plan for after."

Olive paused and glanced back at Haw. "If it is something, I don't know, supernatural, maybe we should ask Ky about it."

"Ky? I don't know if I should bother him over …" Haw blinked as she considered her former staff sergeant. *At least he would understand about the nightmares.*

"We haven't had him visit in forever anyway. Why don't you call him

A Holy Venom

and see if he could come out for a few days? You know the twins would love to see him. Berry's hardly ever spent any time with him." Olive smiled reassuringly. "Besides, I miss him too."

"I hate to ask him to come all this way and take time off from work if they're only making up stories." *You know they're not. You know something is really happening. Why are you lying? Why don't you want to call Ky?*

"If that's all it is, then we'd still get to see him. If it's something spooky, at least he'll take it seriously. He's the only person I can think of that's interested in this stuff who wouldn't scare the kids."

Haw could almost hear Ky's voice, reassuring and calm as always, telling them everything would be alright. "What the hell. I owe him a call anyway."

Olive smiled. "Give him my love and tell him there's plenty of pancakes."

☾

Ruin's eyes fluttered open. Discomfort nagged at him. He was on his back, lying in a soft, welcoming bed. Above him were familiar swirls of pale color. He followed them as they shifted from misty clouds to a diving seagull wing. He was in the garret of the Teahouse. The inner point of his elbow joints ached inexplicably. His face felt paper dry and crisp, his lips chapped from exposure. How long had it been this time? He wondered if he ran his fingers over his chin and cheeks if there would be patchy spots of stubble. It took days for the sparse, blunt-tipped hairs to regrow and if there were any... He followed the whirls and patterns of the faded ceiling mural, as he'd done so many times as a child. Childhood memories tumbled, most happy, with a few painful ones trailing behind. The evening neon light seeped through gossamer curtains. Feeling the pinch of tape when he moved, Ruin looked down at the IV in the back of his left hand. With practiced movements, he pulled the needle and tubing out of his vein and swung his legs to the side of the bed. The sheets tangled around his feet as he stared at the empty saline bag hanging from the IV stand next to the four-poster bed. A tray of raspberry thumbprint cookies and a carafe of grapefruit juice sat on the nightstand.

Groaning, Ruin picked up a medicine packet that someone, probably his uncle, had left pointedly resting in an empty water glass. He tapped the paper tube to settle its contents then tore off the end and poured the white powder into the glass. Then he lifted the carafe and poured the juice over it. The bittersweet citrus barely concealed the metallic tang of the antipsychotic. Ruin gulped it down quickly and grimaced. He crammed a cookie into his mouth to kill the aftertaste.

"Fuck!" Suddenly remembering his promise to Squash and Shine, Ruin tore off his pajamas and searched the tiny, circular bedroom for his clothes. He located a stack of laundered clothes half under the bed. In the garret's closet-sized bathroom, he quickly shaved and brushed his teeth, checking his reflection to make sure he looked halfway decent before grabbing his leather off the hook on the bedroom door.

Jogging down the tight turn of stairs, his stomach growled. The cookie had only made his hunger worse. When was the last time he had eaten? He contemplated raiding the Teahouse kitchen for breakfast but knew his uncle would want to talk to him. He needed to get across town to the practice space as quickly as possible. Shoving his hand into the inside pocket of his leather to check for the practice space keys, his fingers closed on a wad of cash. He smiled, relieved; he could afford to take a cab.

His smile faded as he realized what the money meant. Aych had found him after all. Had he pissed himself? Had he been covered in his own blood... or someone else's? Fragments of memory slid and tumbled like snapshots without sound or context. He possibly followed long-haired, beautiful people and likely thought about hurting them. Shame heated the back of his neck and made him stumble as he pushed through the oak door to the stairwell off the second floor. On the other side, an elegant staircase appeared, spiraling down the cerulean walls of the circular tower. He tried to focus on getting out of the Teahouse without running into anyone. He needed to hail a cab, not get a thousand and one questions from his uncle about where he had been. Not that he could answer, anyway. In his head he saw a pair of mismatched eyes and a familiar husky voice, tinged with disappointment, admonishing him. Shame heated his neck again. He hated the idea of disappointing Aych. He pushed open the door at the base of the stairs and stepped through the cedar panel behind the Teahouse register.

Half hiding behind the fronds of the fern on the counter, Ruin checked in the direction of the guest rooms and then down the hall toward the front of the restaurant. Half expecting Mat to catch him, Ruin rounded his shoulders and bolted for the exit.

Once out on the busy sidewalk, he avoided looking across the street to the Velvet. Praying he could catch a ride before anyone spotted him, Ruin rushed to a cab dropping off passengers at the end of the red carpet.

Hanging onto the door while the startled couple quickly made their way to the Teahouse, he dodged around and slid into the back seat. "You free?"

"Am now." The cabbie replied, barely glancing up. "Where to?"

"1300 Canal off of Still."

"That's up by the Distillery?"

"Yeah, it's the Cannery." Falling back against the patched seat as the vehicle pulled away from the curb, Ruin tried to remember what exactly he'd done. Guilt and shame kept surging up, though he couldn't pin down any of the fragmented images in his head. He glanced at his hands and saw his nails had been scrubbed clean. Had they been caked with just dirt or had there been something worse, something far uglier under them? Scraping his calluses, he felt the sickening surety whatever he had done, it had been unforgivable. He spent the rest of the cab ride practicing what to say to his bandmates.

When the cab arrived, he pressed the fare into the driver's hand before the car had even stopped. Bounding out, he rushed up the granite steps to the looming entranceway of the former industrial building. He pushed aside the metal door and stepped into the dank and humid foyer. Checking the rest of his jacket pockets for the practice space key, he pulled his hands out empty. He swore under his breath. Event flyers and studio rental notices covering the wall around the intercom flapped in the rush of air as the heating vent kicked on. Tapping the number into the pad, he sagged against the wall.

The intercom speaker crackled. "Yeah? Who is it?"

Ruin closed his eyes in relief at the woman's familiar, high-pitched voice. "It's me, Squash, who the fuck else would it be? I lost my key."

There was a long pause. "Ruin? You're downstairs?"

Sighing, he pushed off the wall. "Look, I know you're pissed—"

"Stay right there, OK?" Squash's voice faded out slightly as Ruin listened.

"Just don't fucking move. Shine's coming down for you. Just wait, OK?"

"Can you buzz me in already? I need to take a piss."

"I can't, it's broken, that's why Shine is—"

Ruin groaned. "I'll take a piss around back by the dumpsters and be right back."

The intercom crackled as the woman shouted. "No! Just wait, OK? He'll be there in a second!"

Before he could respond, Ruin glanced over as the inner door flew open.

Panting from his sprint, a frantic young man in a moth-eaten sweater grabbed Ruin by the arms. "Where the fuck have you been?" His worried brown eyes searched Ruin's as he shook him. "Are you hurt? Did you get locked—"

"No, nothing happened like that." He could feel Shine's panic in the way the other man gripped his arms. Ruin gave him an apologetic look. "I know I said I wouldn't miss practice, but shit happened."

"I was fucking worried. That was a week ago. Where the hell have you been?" Shine shook him again. "What happened to you?" He enclosed Ruin in a tight, silent embrace and then pushed him away. Holding his returned boyfriend at arm's length, Shine glared. "Were you with Aych?"

Ruin shook his head. "No! You know it's not like that—"

"Were you up the Hill then?" Shine's expression softened as he studied Ruin's face. "Did you get—"

"Don't fuck with me." Ruin shoved him away. Nightmarish images darted through his mind. "You know I don't like jokes about—"

"I wasn't making a joke. It's been over a fucking week. You were supposed to meet us on the seventh. It's the fourteenth." Shine's expression shifted from relief to fear.

"The fourteenth?" Ruin sagged against the wall. "You're fucking with me; I just saw you at Janky's."

"I'm not fucking with you. That was last week." Shine pushed the inner door open with his boot. "Get upstairs. Squash has been worried sick about you. We've been looking all over the fucking city for you. She even went to ask Aych to find you." Pain showed in Shine's eyes when he repeated Aych's name again. "By the look of you, I'd say that's who finally found your sorry ass, isn't it? When shit gets bad enough, that's who pulls you out of the gutter

A Holy Venom

every fucking time. I don't know why you even—"

A wave of nausea hit Ruin. He sank to the floor and covered his eyes. A week. An entire week lost this time. He dreaded what he might remember. A half sob caught him off guard and he crammed the side of his hand into his mouth and bit down. He was going to have to check the mausoleum. If there were trophies, he wasn't sure what he would do.

FIVE

AFTER GOING OVER the bank accounts and reviewing her open project list, Haw gave in to the heaviness of her body and retreated to the bedroom. She laid down on top of the bedspread. A twenty-minute nap would do. Haw stared at the ceiling. *I should call Ky*, she thought. *What would I say? Hey, I'm having trauma nightmares that are weirdly arousing and my kids think there's a werewolf or a ghost, or a ghost werewolf, in the house? Could you drive five hours to Delmont to visit us and check under the beds?* Groaning, she flopped onto her side. When she finally fell asleep her dreams were claustrophobic; an endless crawl through sewer pipes, her arms dragging her body forward, inch by grueling inch.

The house was quiet and cold when she got up. Still exhausted, Haw went into the kitchen and found Olive washing the dinner dishes. "How long have I been asleep?"

"You were out cold when I checked in at dinner. Thought I should let you rest. Should I have blasted a foghorn under your ear?"

"No, though I *am* hungry."

"I made you up a plate of wings and veg in the fridge."

Haw picked the last bits of sleep from her eyes as she shuffled over to the steel refrigerator. As she clattered through the shelves, Olive turned up the volume on the baby monitor by the sink.

"Should be right—"

"Yeah, I'm looking for the mustard. Your wings deserve the hot stuff."

Olive laughed. "It's in the door, *where it's supposed to be*."

"Must've been the kids moving things around because I just found it on the shelf." Haw leaned on the counter across from her spouse. Peeling off the plate wrap, she nodded at the baby monitor. "Anything interesting so far?"

"The twins were gossiping about their classmates, but they've gone to sleep. Berry was out just like her old Madda." Olive set a baking tray under the faucet and filled it with hot soapy water. "Did you call Ky before you passed out like a bear entering hibernation?"

Haw swallowed a mouthful of chicken. "No, I'll give him a call tomorrow."

Olive shot her a strong look. "If you don't, I will."

"Was that Berry?" Haw leaned to turn up the volume on the monitor.

Olive shut off the water and listened. Their daughter's voice floated out of the speaker. A second voice, lower and gruff, replied.

Her adrenaline surging, Haw raced out of the kitchen and flew up the stairs to Berry's door at the top. Haw wrenched on Berry's bedroom door but it wouldn't budge. Frantic, she put her ear to the door. She heard muffled voices. Taking a step back, Haw aimed a well-placed kick next to the doorknob to force the latch. Unyielding, the oak door gave no indication of the impact. She stared at it, surprised. Desperate, she thought of the sledgehammer in the barn and if she dared leave to go get it. "Berry! Can you hear me?"

Inside the room, Berry sat upright in her bed unaware of her parent calling to her from the landing. "I thought you were a ghost, but you look real now," the girl stared at the monster taking up half her bedroom. It had tall pointy ears that moved when it listened to her speak, a long wolf-like muzzle, and huge tail that almost swept the floor as the monster stood in front of her. It was covered in thick, shaggy black fur. When it opened its mouth, there were long, sharp teeth and a black tongue behind them. Its strange eyes stared at her—one blue and one gold. Both looked like dog eyes, only much, much bigger. Berry squeezed her dog toy tighter. "Why are you in my bedroom? Are you going to eat me?"

Aych smiled, showing all their fangs. "No. I don't eat children, only adults."

"*You're sure you're not going to eat me?*" Berry tilted her head and narrowed her eyes at the monster.

"I told you, I don't eat children. But I'm deciding if I want to eat your parents." Settling on their haunches, Aych thoughtfully scratched the black

A Holy Venom

fur along their jaw with their claws. "I could tell you a story first before I decide. Unless you don't want to hear a story. Then I could go eat your parents now."

"Tell me the story!" Berry blurted, tightening her grip on her toy.

Aych flashed the child an amused smile. They took a breath and began.

✸

Once, a very, very long time ago, there was a little girl who had a hard life.

The adults she lived with made her do endless chores and hit her when she didn't do as they liked. They hit her when she was slow, or when they were mad, or sometimes just because she was there. She was tough, though, and brave. One morning before the Sun was done with their long journey through the hours of night, the girl escaped and went alone into the woods. The woods weren't like the ones you have here. No, these were ancient and scary Woods. The trees hated humans and the animals in the Woods feared hunters.

The kind, good parents told their children to stay out of the Woods at all costs. But the girl had no good parent to give her advice or worry about her, so she went deeper and deeper into the forest. She heard a dog yip in pain. And though she was tired and hungry, she ran off to help without a thought. But instead of a dog, she found a huge wolf, as dark as chimney soot and its eyes like flaming gold, caught in a hunter's trap. The iron teeth of the trap bit through the wolf's paw and the girl knew it must be in terrible pain.

Now, she was afraid of the wolf, and it's important you know she wasn't cruel or stupid. She knew the animal was likely to eat her, but she also knew how it felt to be trapped and in pain. Knowing this, she said to it, "If you promise not to harm me, now or ever, I will free you."

The wolf watched her with his big, gold eyes and said, "If you release me, I promise not to harm you, now or ever."

With that, the girl got a thick, long branch and wedged it into the trap. She said to the wolf, "This is going to hurt. I'm sorry to cause you more pain."

"Worry not, child. Do your worst," said the wolf.

The girl pushed with all her might and the jaws of the trap squeaked apart. The wolf eased his broken and bloody paw out and began licking it.

"Well, I'll be going now," the girl said, backing away from the wolf.

"You didn't ask for a reward. Don't you want one?" he asked.

"No thank you. I know what it's like to hurt and have no one help."

The wolf thought a moment and pointed his snout at the path. "If you keep going, you'll come to a House made of obsidian standing alone in the Woods. There's a chimney that spills smoke out every hour of every day and every night. The smoke from it smells of fresh bread, or of roasting meat, or of sweets and spices. Would you hear my advice about this House in the Silent Woods?"

The girl thought for a moment. "Yes, I would hear your advice."

"Don't go that way. Go back to the place you came from and tell the people who hurt you that you found the House and that it is filled with treasure. Tell them to bring carts and horses and take all the treasure from the House. But heed me: don't go with them, as no human ever leaves that House alive."

The little girl looked sadly at the wolf. "They won't believe me, and if they did, they'd make me carry a sack of treasure on my back. They work me to the bone all day and half the night."

The wolf thought for a moment and said, "Wait here." With that, he limped off in the direction of the House.

Well, the little girl waited and waited, wondering if she had been a fool to trust the wolf. Every time she thought about leaving, she looked at the bloody trap and decided to wait a little longer. Soon, the wolf came back. His paw was healed and he carried in his mouth a goblet made of gold.

He set the golden goblet at her feet. "Take this back to the people who hurt you as proof that the House is full of treasure. When they force you to come back this way tomorrow, I shall run out of the woods and snatch you up. Don't be afraid; I will not forget my promise. But you must scream and scream as if you are caught in an iron trap while I carry you away."

Neither stupid nor trusting, she considered his plan carefully. "I will take your advice," said the little girl. "But why are you helping me?"

"I too know what it is to be in pain and wish someone would help. You did not ask for a reward, so instead you shall have my help." The wolf licked the little girl. He did this not to taste her, but to comfort her. Without another word, he trotted into the woods and disappeared.

Being a brave and smart child, the girl did as the wolf instructed and took the goblet back to the people who made her do endless chores and hit her for no reason at all. The adults rolled the gold in their hands and held it up to the sunlight to

A Holy Venom

see the jewels sparkle. After fighting amongst themselves, they decided they would go to the House in the woods at dawn and steal everything they could.

They told the little girl, "If you're lying, we shall hang you up by one foot over the fire until all your hair burns off. Then we will hang you by your other foot in the pond until you drown."

"I'm not lying," the little girl answered firmly. "The House is full of treasure. It smells of fresh bread and roasting meat and sometimes of sweets and spices." She knew the wolf had told her the truth. In fact, quite often, should you wish to lay a trap, the truth is better than any lie.

"You better not be lying," said the cruel adults.

"You'd better bring all the horses and bags and crates," the little girl replied.

In the morning just as the Sun finished their journey through the long hours of the night and touched the trees with gold, the mean and foolish humans loaded up the horses with bags and crates. Just as she predicted, they made the little girl carry a sack.

Into the deep, dark woods they went with the little girl leading the way along the path. Darker and darker, quieter and quieter the woods became until they were in the very heart of the Silent Woods, where no human should ever venture.

"How much farther?" asked the adults.

"Oh just a bit more," said the girl. "Soon you will smell the delicious smells coming from the chimney."

She took one more step, and the wolf sprang out of the woods and snatched her up. "Help! Help!" cried the girl as if she had been caught in an iron trap.

The adults only grumbled that the girl was dead and could no longer carry gold or do chores. They did not think to help her or go after the wolf for even one minute. Instead, they bickered over who should carry the child's load of treasure and kept following the path until they smelled the delicious smells.

The wolf carried the little girl back to the humans' house she had come from and set her down gently. "This is your house now, and you may live here without fear."

"But what if they come back?" the little girl asked.

"No human ever leaves the House in the Silent Woods alive." the wolf replied.

"What of the horses? Will they be killed too?"

"They might or they might not. If they live, I shall bring them back to you."

The little girl reached out and hugged the wolf. It was the very first time she had ever hugged someone and the very first time the wolf had ever been hugged.

"Thank you for saving me," she said. "Thank you for being my friend."

"Thank you for saving me. And thank you for being my friend." he replied. "Now if anyone comes and asks where the adults are, you need only tell them about the House in the Woods and the treasure they left to collect."

The little girl looked at her empty house. "Will you stay with me? I'm afraid to be alone."

"I will come and visit and teach you many things," the wolf answered. "Eventually you will meet kind humans who will not ask too many questions. They will live here if you ask them to."

"I'm afraid of humans," the girl replied. "Won't you stay with me instead?"

"No, but I will visit. You will see. There are others like you." With that he licked her again, not to taste her but only to comfort her, and went back into the woods.

☾

Finishing the story, Aych stopped speaking and listened to the adults frantically trying to gain entry to the child's bedroom. Snapping their jaws, Aych released the enchantment on Berry's bedroom. The door tore off the hinges, flying back to bang against the bedroom wall. Out on the landing, Olive and the twins screamed in surprise.

With practiced movement, Haw rushed in, dropped into a defensive stance, and assessed the room. Her eyes locked on the creature in the corner. Out of the impossible darkness, its blazing, terrible eyes stared back. Haw froze and her body numbed. It was a thing of nightmares and yet it was there, in front of her. The form burst into ghostly shadow and smoke, the wisps caressing her skin sensually even as the tendrils of shadow curled back into the vines and flowers of the room's wallpaper. The scent from her dreams hung in the air. Her mind reeled. Sweat stung her bulging, stricken eyes. It smiled at her then, impossibly wide, teeth glimmering in the darkness. Her whole perception cracked and shifted, sliding sideways like the deck of a ship on a stormy, tumultuous sea. Only the presence of her child kept her from screaming. Flashes of dark shapes loomed like afterimages burned into Haw's mind. Echoes of strange and familiar voices chattered, yelling her name.

Her daughter was screaming, Haw realized. The twins were yelling out on the landing and Olive was asking questions. Numb, Haw sank to her knees. The impossibility of it invaded her consciousness. Real and yet unreal, flesh and smoke and death and desire. It felt primal, ancient, dangerous. *It was a monster, here, in this room. I saw it and I heard it. Not psychops, not a hallucination, not a dream. It was real. It was here.*

"Madda!" Berry shook her mother's shoulder. "You've got to get out of here before it comes back to eat you!"

Olive scooped Berry up and shushed her. "It's OK, baby, it's OK." She glanced at Haw. "Was there someone in the room?"

Haw felt herself turning to reply, moving slowly like she was underwater. *Olive didn't see it? No, she didn't, or else she would be*—A delayed kick of adrenaline hit her, speeding up time and action. Haw jumped to her feet and herded everyone out of the room. "You've got to take the children out of here. Go to Bush Farm next door. Call S&P from there and don't come back until they've sent a car out. Do you hear me, Olive?" Haw pushed a protesting River away from the twin's bedroom door. "You're all going. *Now.* Put your coats and boots on. Don't worry about socks." Gently as she could, she forced everyone down the stairs and along the hall toward the front door. Things needed to be seen to and steps taken to secure the family.

"Ota!" Olive pushed back. "What has gotten into you? What's going on? I will not be shoved out the door like this! Tell me what you saw!"

"Later." Haw threw her spouse a pleading look and glanced at their children's terrified faces. "Right now, I need you to get them out of here. I need all of you out of here."

"I'm scared, Madda." Berry clung to her legs. "It said it was going to eat you both."

"I know honey, I know you're scared. But I'm going to get rid of it then you won't have to be afraid." She kissed her daughter's head. "I need you and your siblings to go wait next door so I know you're safe." Looking at Olive, she held her spouse's gaze. "You need to take them and go. There's no time to argue about any of it."

"I'll call S&P …"

"From the Bushs' house. Right now, you need to not be here." Haw began taking the children's coats out of the closet and pressing them into their hands. She lifted a heavy duffel bag full of emergency supplies off a hook and slung it over her shoulder. "I'll carry the holiday kit bag to the car for you. Keep it in the back." She shot her spouse a look and handed Olive her winter coat.

"The holiday kit? I don't understand, if you just want us to go to the Bushs', why do we need it? I don't understand what is happening." Olive accepted her coat and started pulling it on. "If you think we need to take precautions and go, OK, but shouldn't you come with us? Why are you staying?"

Because it wants me to be alone. The thought chilled Haw to the bone. "So someone's here when S&P comes and it can't be you or the kids. OK?" *I'm lying again. Why am I lying? Because I don't want them to get hurt and if they stay...*

Olive helped Berry with her snow boots as the twins surged forward to hug their mother.

"Kick its ass, Madda." Their voices were muffled as they pressed against her chest.

"You take care of your sister and each other, OK?" She tussled their hair and took a step back. "Don't break into the supplies unless you have to, OK?"

River and Ash nodded and started getting their jackets on.

Silently, the family went out into the dark. Haw walked behind, hustling her family toward the car. She moved deliberately, watching the barn and the long winter shadows for anything that might lunge out at her loved ones. Slashes of white and black afterimages, tendrils of smoke, and bestial claws flashed across her vision, confusing her. She shook her head. *Focus.*

Olive started the car up and Haw set the supply bag between the twins' feet then buckled Berry in. Backing away, she watched the headlights sweep around the driveway. The farmhouse felt quiet and sad, but not empty. The urgency of getting her family out gave way to the familiar bone-deep sensation of imminent combat.

A wave of vertigo hit Haw and she leaned against the doorway, steadying herself. Nightmare images of somewhere else dragged at her. Splices of a haunted forest at night, children's frightened faces, and some awful half-remembered terror clawed at her. She could feel it; it was coming for her, for her family. *To devour them all.*

Haw stalked back to her bedroom to get dressed and to load up. The garments shoved to the side, Haw stared ahead unblinking into the closet as her hand flicked a dial in the vault door in the back of her bedroom closet with quick, automatic movements. The numbers of the combination lock clicked into place and she wrenched the lever. The thunk of the door unlocking grounded her in the present moment. She swung the door open. Her gear waited inside just as she had left it. Armored vests and rifles hung on the side of the vault, ready. Knives, small arms, and other tools sat on the shelves. *Whatever the fuck you are, I'm going to put a few new holes in your hide.*

The familiar heft of the reinforced vest felt reassuring. Haw tapped each of the body armor plates from habit. The pistol on her left hip was canted in its looped holster for easy access. She slipped it out and popped the magazine in. She slipped a serrated combat blade into the sheath along her back, the tension grip holding it in place with a drop pull over her right flank. The feel of it sliding into place eased her mind. The vest hip pouch under her left hand was already full of shotgun shells but Haw clipped another pouch on then picked up the shotgun and cracked it to drop two rounds into the double chambers. Loaded up, she eyed a locked iron box on the shelf of the vault. Uneasy, she dialed the second combination and pulled out the field explosives. More than a flashbang, she contemplated the metal casings of the one-twos and then clipped a pair onto the front of her vest. *I'm not taking any chances.*

Her hands sought out the rhythm of the equipment check. Buckles, ammo pouches, extra magazines, holster angle, and finally the easy feel of the hilt of the blade above her kidney. She pulled on her gloves and repeated the check. Satisfied, Haw chambered a round in her pistol and set the safety.

The stink of decaying flesh and woodsmoke stung her nostrils as a shadow slunk across the inside of the closet. She slammed the vault shut and shook her head. *What the fuck is wrong with me? This is insane, I should have gone with my family. What if it goes after the kids? I can't fight this thing alone. Why am I acting like someone's pulling my strings?* Her hands followed the familiar routine drilled into her muscle memory as she checked and rechecked, preparing for war.

Kiarna Boyd

☾

Moonlight glittered on the frozen pond. Aych watched from the knoll of pine trees above the house as the human went through her preparations. The woman was repeatedly checking her guns and examining a selection of knives and other equipment. Seeing Aych in their Big form had unleashed a terrible enchantment. Any adult who witnessed them Big was infected with a spiraling paranoia and the compulsive need to confront the monster. Inside the house, the nightmares the lure had planted had borne devastating fruit. Aych could feel the human's thoughts unraveling, leaking nightmares and fear into her waking life.

Aych grinned. The former soldier's trained threat response was easy to manipulate. The baneful enchantment blossomed as Haw's last pieces of self-control fell to Aych's summons. *That's it, lose your grip a little more so I can reel you in. Then we'll get this party started. You don't need a good reason to die. Just come and play with me, human.* Aych reached out a clawed hand and pulled the invisible thread that tied the lure to its maker. *Come.*

The full moon inched along the dome of the winter sky. Cloudless, the stars scintillated without any moisture to dim their distant light. A wedge of electric light thrown across the backyard and the fresh scent of human activity indicated the woman was coming outside, loaded with a portable arsenal of body armor and weaponry. Aych chuckled. *Steel, rage, and gunpowder against claws, fangs, and magic.* The scents of the human's tools interested Aych less than the woman's unique mix of resolve, confidence, and madness. *She's experienced similar mayhem before. Went out to battle unknown enemies and she's remembering she lived through it. That she won.* Aych smiled again, the long sides of their muzzle stretching back. Their black tongue slid across eager fangs. *Let's see if you can make it to five minutes against my kind, Major.*

The itch of being surveilled and the lack of cover between the farm and the trees grated on Haw. The moonlight was a serious disadvantage, and she knew she should have leveraged the house or the barn rather than going outside, but there was an irresistible pull, like a chain hauling her forward, dragging her up toward the pines.

A Holy Venom

The wind was blowing from the north, pushing at her back and driving fresh powder over the settled hard-packed snow. *First-timer's mistakes and this many mistakes will get you killed.* Yet, against all better judgment and training, here she was sweeping up the hill, bold as brass. *Might as well be bugling on my way up.* Grimacing, Haw tried to keep her attention on the line of trees up ahead. *It's up there waiting for me and it's not going to attack until I get up there.* The sudden knowledge hit her. It was orchestrating an ambush and she was walking into it like a damn animal to the slaughter. Still keeping her shotgun ready to fire at the sign of movement, she slogged through the packed snow, her boots breaking through. *This is beyond stupid; I should turn around and use the damn house or the barn. Wait for daylight and S&P. Call Ky, he would have ideas.*

The thoughts piled up as Haw watched herself trudge up the hill. Turning her back would be impossible, she would have to retrace her steps backward and keep her gaze forward out into the darkness. The snowy fields felt silent but not safe. *Where was it? Where and why did such a thing come from?* Sweat and her steaming breath kept Haw company as she leaned forward against the weight of her gear. All the indicators of an escalating threat had been present, but so weird and ridiculous that it had been easier to ignore them. The visions shuddered through her, glimpses of her nightmare, whispers from impossible voices, the weird stench and sultry incense of Baz's apartment. Sensory memories flooded her as the wind set the silhouettes of the pines creaking and swaying. *Why had it picked her family?* Haw thought of Baz ripped apart on the mountain. It was no random accident; Haw's nibling had not woken a bear out of hibernation or been attacked by some other normal animal. It wasn't a stalker. It was this *thing*. Even a human serial killer would have been easier to accept. Haw grimaced, realizing with her long list of combat kills she would at least have a sense of common humanity with that kind of scum. But this *thing* had been in her child's room, had been stalking her children. The paranoia and adrenaline aligned, feeding Haw's resolve. *You picked the wrong family to fuck with, beast. I'm going to put you down!*

The wind moaned through the pines and a halo appeared around the moon. Aych marked the lunar disc's position as the lure's chosen candidate entered the circle of trees. Stepping into the light, Aych growled low and steadily. *Here I am human, now what are you going to do about it?*

Hearing the growl, Haw swung the shotgun up and fired. She threw herself to the left, attempting to catch sight of the enemy. Her body acted on its own, rolling, dodging, running, firing, moving in a zig-zag pattern to avoid return fire. Snipers were not always in high perches but could be low in the brush or behind a mound of snow. The anticipated counterfire never erupted out of the tree line. Throwing herself against a tree trunk, she waited, wondering if she had been able to hit the monster. Where was it? It had growled, communicating violent intent. Without counterfire or movement, she was uncertain of the creature's current position. *It's still out there! Keep firing at the last location. Lay down a pattern east to west and flush it out. Make it move, show itself to you.* Haw yanked a one-two off her gear belt and pulled the pin. With a fluid movement, she lobbed it across the opening between the trees and braced for the resulting explosion.

Aych lazily snatched the grenade out of the air. The air ripped as their hand disappeared and dropped the explosive harmlessly into the In Between. *You've got to risk a bit more if you want to play with me, lady.* Aych eyed the pine boughs obscuring the moon. *Bullets and bombs aren't enough. Come out and dance.*

An itch of uncertainty plagued Haw. There was no explosion. No flash of light. Only the wind sweeping over the snow and the creak of branches. Had the device been faulty? Did the enemy have a means of disarming it? Every muscle, every nerve in her wanted to run screaming into the clearing firing until her magazines emptied and ... *what then? Dumb ass, that's a sure way to end up in a body bag.* Her frenzy cooling, Haw assessed the situation with steely calm. She knew better than to risk a direct frontal attack on an unknown enemy. *Wait. It will move and then you'll have a target. Only then when it takes the risk do you feed it a hot bellyful of surprise.*

Aych clicked their claws and snapped their jaws in impatience. A cautious hunter was of no use to them. This retiree was likely to spend the whole of the night wasting their time hiding behind a tree trunk taking potshots from a safe distance. The kind of hunter Aych needed would put themselves forward, wriggling on the hook deliciously up close and personal and then and only then, playing hard to get. This one wasn't even willing to put on the five-minute floorshow Aych required. Disgusted, they studied the

A Holy Venom

mottled impact craters on the surface of the moon. The House in the Silent Woods had existed before that skull-white and lonely sphere had been new and smooth like a river pebble, freshly cleaved from the body of its parent and flung far away from its diurnal twin. *Retreat, hold, or advance?*

Advance.

Hunched against a huge pine, Haw heard the sound first, like fabric tearing slowly; then came the heat of a massive body next to her. The steam of its hot breath billowed out like smoke in the winter air, obscuring her vision. A clawed hand seized her wrists, binding them together in a punishing grip. The shotgun fell into the snow. Bone snapped and flesh tore and Haw screamed. The monster, haughty and cruel, stared into Haw's eyes.

Not even five minutes. Disappointment boiled into rage. Aych carried the human out into the moonlight, blood trailing from the human's wounds, marring the white furrow of fresh snow. Aych raised the woman up into the air.

Haw stared down at the frenzied creature's face. *Not an ambush. It was a duel. I lost.* The monster held her up as if she was impaled on a pitchfork, nothing more than a bale of hay to be tossed aside. *It's angry and disappointed in me.* Haw laughed, choking on the blood welling in her throat. Releasing her mutilated wrists, the creature sank its claws into her shoulder. The impaling hand ripped free, disemboweling her. Blood splattered over fur and snow and Haw could not help being surprised at the manner of her death. So much for dying a wizened crone in bed surrounded by grandkids. A pang of regret and a sense of sadness came and went. Then there was nothing.

Aych tossed the woman's body aside. Under the light of the exiled moon, they studied the ex-soldier's steaming entrails for auguries. The liver and gallbladder had tumbled out a little further from the intestines and the kidneys were half in shadow. *Secret agendas.* Aych narrowed their eyes and read the positions of the other organs in relation to the cardinal points and then turned their attention to the condition of the victim's liver. Glossy with health, it shone wetly under the moonlight. *Success is promised, an indentured servant arrives, destruction is salvation. A great victory.* Mollified, Aych threw Haw's entrails and organ meat up into the pine boughs for the crows to find in the morning. An offering in exchange for all they had given and all Aych had taken. Licking their claws clean, they turned toward the rest of Haw's corpse. *Well, at least there's a late-night snack.*

SIX

AN S&P OFFICER CAME down off the Bushs' wide farm porch to intercept a gray sedan pulling into the driveway. She waited as the car pulled to a stop then moved to the driver side door and gestured for the driver to roll down their window. She assessed the middle-aged driver's stubble-lined face and rumpled band T-shirt. Visible under his short sleeves, burn scars pitted and stretched over the muscles of his upper arms and continued up to his neck. The officer noted the stack of empty coffee cups and food bags in the passenger seat. A leather jacket and a threadbare military surplus duffel bag took up the back seat. "Can I see your identification please, sir?"

Handing his license out, Ky glanced back at the porch where Olive was stepping out into the frigid morning air. A cloud of suffering and grief emanated from her. "Is this necessary, officer? The family asked me to come."

Relentless throughout his five-hour drive, the prescient knowledge of Haw's death had warred with Ky's hope for her to be found alive. As soon as he had turned off the highway exit toward the village, he had known she was gone. As always, the rock-solid sense of knowing the worst was true before anyone else made him feel like shit. It did however allow him to prepare for the emotional turbulence he was about to step into.

Under the pristine snow shrouding the slumbering fields, the loss of Haw and her gruesome death whispered to him. The farmland she loved was mourning, the trauma imprint staining the fields of snow with the brutality of her murder.

The officer's expression was uneasy. "Sorry for the extra trouble, but you understand there's a safety concern while the search is ongoing. You can park over there, by the barn."

"Thanks." Ky accepted his license back then nosed the car over to the barn next to three empty S&P cruisers.

Olive was walking over from the house as Ky got out, pulling his leather on to keep off the chill. Haw's wife looked exhausted and angry. "Thank you for coming so quickly. I know it must've been a long drive for you."

"You know I'd drive anywhere any time for you two. Did they find anything?" Extending his hands, Ky instinctively braced against the tide of emotions curling off of her.

"They told me to expect the worst." Olive took Ky's hands in her own. "The medical examiner said she couldn't have survived that much blood loss. They found…" her voice trailed off. "I haven't told the children yet. In case…"

Ky held Olive and waited as the anger, pain, and denial washed over them. "Have they secured the farm? Have you been able to go back yet?"

"No, they said we had to wait until it's been searched and all the evidence collected." Olive turned back. "I'm sorry to keep you out in the cold, but there's things I need to say and I don't want the children to hear. I should've brought a thermos of coffee out with me, I'm sorry I'm just not thinking right…"

"Not needful, I've been drinking coffee all night." Ky smiled ruefully. "When I stopped to get gas, I filled everything up."

"Let's walk a bit to stay warm." Olive glanced at the house, the children's faces visible in the kitchen window. "I wanted Haw to call you, tell you what was happening. Things were off for a few days. Haunted, you know? Nothing was right in the house. The children were having nightmares, Haw wasn't sleeping, and then…" Her voice drifted off as her eyes glazed over with sadness.

"S&P find anything, or is it too early for them to update you yet?"

"After I called last night, they sent officers over to our place. All the lights were on, the doors were open and Haw's boot tracks went up out the back way. They found a … crime scene in the pines. Said it looked like a wild animal attacked her, maybe a bear." Angry, Olive squeezed her arms around herself. "They just dismissed the children's accounts out of hand. Said there was no sign of forced entry. They asked if Haw was taking anything, if she'd been high." She stopped and swallowed. "I told them we

A Holy Venom

heard it, on the monitors, we heard it talking to our baby girl! Ota wasn't high, she was furious!" Olive locked eyes with Ky as she stared at him desperate and dismayed. "Who the hell was in our house? Who the hell hurt my wife?"

Her anguish hit Ky in the solar plexus like a well-aimed kick. "I don't know, but Haw wouldn't have taken any risks unless she thought she had to."

"She did it to protect us. That thing was in our house! The detectives said it was an animal out in the woods, said it must've carried her off and they're still searching, but no, they haven't located—" Tears welled up in Olive's eyes. "It wasn't a bear, she wasn't high. The children, the kids kept telling us it was a monster and I thought they were making it up. Holy Mother, she was still in good shape. She wasn't some pushover, and now they're telling me something wounded her and possibly ate her. Ate her! That's just not the world we're in. People don't get eaten, do they?" Olive threw Ky another desperate look. "Monsters aren't real, right?"

"Whatever it was," he pulled her in for a long hug. "Haw went out to protect all of you and punch that thing's clock for threatening the kids."

"You believe me? What the children said, what Berry said she saw? My wife wasn't a paranoid drug user!"

"I believe you." Ky gazed out across the silent fields to the snow-crusted fence poles where the Bushs' property abutted with Haw and Olive's farm. The rupture of violence hung like a discordant, grating sound, inaudible to most. A ribbon of injustice and grief flowed in from beyond the line of pine trees on the far edge of the pasture. He turned back to Olive and squeezed her hand. "And Haw was formidable. She has always been a solid, state-issued, piece of kick-ass."

Olive gave a half laugh and smiled sadly up at Ky before letting him go. "I don't know if we should go back to our farm, even once S&P says we can. I'm thinking it might be better to take the twins and Berry to my parents up in Bladshaw for a few days. I called them this morning and they suggested it. It's just, I'm not sure about leaving before they find her. What if she's not dead? What if she's hurt, out there, freezing?" Olive started to cry, her sorrow long held back, demanding release. "What if she's ..."

Ky wrapped his arms around her again and felt her anguish surge and crest. "Let's go in. You can call to see if we can go over. Just the two of us. Then you'll know what you need to do."

"It is cold out here, isn't it." Olive wiped the tears away. "Did I thank you for driving all the way out here? I'm sorry, I just can't remember if I did. Delmont must be a six-hour drive from Thursby? You must be exhausted. Here I am having you standing out here—"

"It's no trouble. I'd be plenty hurt if you hadn't called me straight off. You know that." He brushed his hand over her cheek wiping a stray tear.

"Yes, that's true, I do. And I'll feel better if we go over, if you're with me when I first go in there." Olive wiped her hands on her hips. "We'll go into the Bushs' and you can talk to the children while I call S&P and let them know we're going to come over."

"I think that's for the best." Ky kept his arm around Olive's shoulders as they walked back to the house.

River and Ash scrambled out of the door, flying down to rush at Ky.

Olive frowned and admonished them. "Don't crush the man, give him some space."

"Ky, did you come to kick its ass?" River grabbed his hand.

Ash grabbed onto Ky's arm. "Did our madda kill it? Are *you* going to kill it?"

"What did I just say?" Their mother scolded. "You go on with you, I swear. Give him a chance to get inside, I raised you better than this." Olive looked over to where Berry waited, clinging to the pillar along the edge of the porch steps. "Girl, where's your jacket? If you're going to be out here—"

Berry's small voice rang out. "Did the monster eat our Madda?"

The twins glared at her. "No way, loser," they shouted in unison.

Olive pushed them up the steps. "Berry, do you remember Ky? He is a friend of mine and your Madda's. You were only a—"

The girl looked down at Ky. "No." She turned and ran into the house, slamming the door behind her.

"Sorry, Ky, she's a baby." River tugged him up the stairs. "Are you going to stay with us?"

"Ky can stay in our room." Ash glanced at their parent. "He's going to stay and wait for Madda, isn't he? Aren't you?"

A Holy Venom

"I've got to make a few calls, you two show Ky where the bathroom is and then take him to meet the Bushs." Olive opened the door. "They have coffee and food for everyone in the search parties laid out in the kitchen."

An ancient hound dog sauntered up as Ky came into the house. The dog nosed his hand then lazily returned to flop in his dog bed by the farmhouse stairs. From between the railings, Berry watched the remains of her family file in.

Ky untangled himself from the twins. "Can you get me a cup of coffee? No milk or sugar, please."

"I'll get it!" River yelled first. With his twin on his heels, the boy raced into the kitchen.

Berry watched as Ky unzipped his jacket and sat on the lower steps to stroke the hound.

"That's Lemon." She wrapped her arms through the railings. "His feet smell like crackers. My name is Berenith, but nobody calls me that except at school."

Ky nodded his appreciation of the introductions. He stroked the animal's head until the old dog toppled sideways, showing his speckled belly. The dog was calm and Ky did not sense anything out of the ordinary in the neighbors' house. A couple of former disincarnate residents slipped up and down the hallway upstairs, roused by the currents of anxiety running through the farm fields. Invested protectors circling on the lookout for more trouble. Given the circumstances, the grief, anxiety, and the children's high-strung fear that was to be expected.

"My Madda's dead." Berry watched Ky. "No one will say it, but I know she got gobbled up."

Ky leaned back on the step and watched the girl. "You think she got gobbled up?"

"The monster told me a story and before that, they said if I didn't want to hear the story, they were going to eat my parents. But they did anyway. Well, just my Madda. Even though I listened." She kicked at the railing leaving scuff marks. "It was a liar."

Considering his words, Ky watched the girl for a moment. "Did it say why it was going to eat her?"

Berry shook her head sending her braids bouncing. She resumed watching Ky pet Lemon's belly. "Is it my fault? Did it eat her because of me?"

"No, sweetheart." Looking into her eyes, Ky shook his head. "It was the monster who made that decision, not you."

The twins reappeared and Ash proudly carried the mug over to Ky. "I got it for you!"

"But I poured it!" River squatted on the floor next to Lemon's dog bed and stuck his tongue out at his sister on the stairs.

Sipping his coffee, Ky watched the three children. A miasma of sooty residue stained Berry's outline. Out of the corner of his eye, Ky caught only a vapor of it trailing off the twins. Sinister and prickly, the contamination was confined to the children. None of it adhered to the dog or to Olive.

The dog and children looked up as Olive walked in from the living room.

"We can go when you're done with your coffee."

"Are you going to find Madda?" Ash searched their parent's face. "Can we go too?"

"You need to stay here for now. We're only going ..." Olive's voice trailed off.

"To answer questions," Ky added. He handed the mug back to Ash. "Keep this handy for me."

Listless, Berry watched Ky stand up. The stain flickered and curled over her reacting to his movements. Behind them, Olive opened the door and Lemon heaved himself out of the dog bed.

"I'll take him out to pee." River jumped up as his parent let the farm dog shamble out the door.

Olive spoke soothingly to Berry. "We'll be right back. Don't you worry."

☾

Olive was unsettled on the car ride over, broadcasting her anger and heartache in spiky jagged bursts. Ky considered the children. The girl especially needed to be purified, the twins would assuredly benefit from the same, and it was likely their house was going to require work. He considered if sea salt would be enough. He needed more information to ascertain the methods required to keep the family safe.

A Holy Venom

As they drove closer to the family's farm, Ky consciously shut off the loop of songs he kept running in his mind, an endless background wall of noise circling inside his head. Without the constant playback, the blare of other signals in his proximity swelled, a psychic inrush of radio station chatter broadcasting a mix of strong emotions and occult disturbances. Picking out the signals he wanted, Ky listened intently.

Olive glanced over. "Are you still managing the record store in Thursby?"

Ky nodded and focused on her. "Pay is shit, but it gets me first choice on whatever comes in."

Olive flicked on the turn signal and braked to turn into her driveway. S&P vehicles lined the side leading up to the house. Two marked vans occupied the parking spots alongside the house forcing Olive to park in the snowplow turn near the barn. "We won't be here long." She glanced at Ky. "Right?"

"Only as long as you need." Ky caught the murmur of unsettled spirits moving inside and around the ancient barn. In a centuries-long cycle, death was laid in the foundations of the former dairy farm, yet the ghosts and guardians of the place were highly agitated. Whatever happened overnight had the ethereal inhabitants of Haw's farm riled up and on the defensive. *What makes the dead afraid?*

He stepped out of the car and into the pulsing contamination imbuing the house. The noxious waves screamed at him—wished him death and agony. Curling his hands, he rubbed his thumbs over the sides of his index fingers. *Fuck right off. I will fuck you up.* Under the supernatural imprint of invasion, Haw's death pooled in the soil. Focusing on the trail of roiling hatred, he listened in and tried to track the source. There had been a quick battle; he sensed the echoes of it coming from behind the house. Haw's shouts and the growling engine of her doom merged into a single bombastic mix of gunfire, agony, and despair.

Even with the horror of the night before laid bare, there was relief in discovering Haw's death had been quick. His friend had been spared prolonged anguish—something he had experienced and did not wish upon anyone.

Feral and skittish, the tendrils of shadow and noise dodged and shifted as an S&P detective came out to greet Olive. The heavy-set woman displayed a lack of residue, her presence scrubbed clean by long adherence to attending high mass. Ky studied the upper windows of the farmhouse and the roofline. If the killer was here, he needed to find it and get rid of it. If it wasn't, he needed to purify and protect the house so Haw's family could return and grieve properly in comfort. Tasting the residual hatred of Haw's murderer, like graveyard dirt and bloody meat, Ky pushed back against the dregs of unclean magic. A house blessing would burn the miasma back and salt water would seal the boundaries afresh. For the rest, he would need to do more divination.

"This is the family friend I mentioned, Ky Drew." Olive gestured to him.

"Mr. Drew." The detective offered Ky her hand. "I'm Detective Tray."

Ignoring the unwanted information in her touch, Ky shook her hand. He jerked his chin at the medical examiner's van. "Have they found anything?"

Tray watched Olive out of the corner of her eye. "There's nothing additional to add at this time. I'm sorry to say." She directed them toward the house. "I can answer your questions inside. No reason to keep you out in the cold."

The tendrils slinked up alongside Ky, following him up the front steps. Once he crossed the threshold, the shadows shrunk and contracted further into the house. "May I look around, Detective? The kids are nervous there might be someone here and I'd like to reassure them."

"Yes, of course. The team's finished with the inside. I'd like to ask Olive a few more questions." She looked at the widow. "Unless you would prefer to check the premises?"

"No, go on ahead, Ky. We'll be in the kitchen. I want to pack up some food for the children so they don't eat the Bushs out of house and home."

The wood-paneled hall and upstairs landing held impressions of daily life. There was a rush of fear and anger, ghostly shouts echoing from the stairs and upper floor. Ky caught the replay of Haw's agitation and anxiety. Traces of an influence lingered under Haw's emotional patterns and Ky tried to sense the intent hidden in the malicious residue. He kept his hands in his jacket pockets and followed the chatter into Haw's office. The furniture and books gave off the solid reassuring quality of their deceased owner. Ky exhaled. There was an ache in the way the light fell through the window and a loneliness in the venerable wooden beams over the desk. The house mourned with Ky, grieving for the one that would never return.

From behind the desk, he caught a flicker of movement. Sinister, it scuttled out of his line of sight. Condensed darkness leaving ripples of mischief, a thing of hatred, corruption. Madness trailed in its wake.

Cautiously, Ky took his hands out of his pockets and approached the desk. Nothing moved. The sting of the countersignal on his back prompted Ky to assess the open office doorway and the leaded glass windows. All the other dissonance he attributed to replay and leftover taint ... but this signal meant there was a live, present threat.

Keeping his awareness on the periphery as well as the area around the desk, he slid the waste basket aside with his boot. Nerve pain tapped along the skin of his right shoulder and he tensed, anticipating an attack.

The pain he thought of as a countersignal first began warning him after a mission far to the south went sideways. An explosive charge timed out early, leaving him buried under shattered concrete. He lay there for days under the heavy weight, waiting to die. For a while, he thought the sensation tingling in his skin and flaming the length of his spine was some kind of sciatic nerve damage, pinched and flickering on and off like shitty house wiring. Then a pattern emerged. The pain always flared when an enemy patrol scouted the decimated building or the predators came out in the cold desert night. Over time, even after he was rescued, he started to notice the pain flared with certain kinds of threats, primarily imminent violence or magical attacks. Like an animal picking up the cues of trouble discernable only to itself, the physical sensation of the countersignal would raise an alarm and leave Ky guessing at the cause. Here in Haw's quiet office, the signal escalated from an itch to full searing pain.

A stone head rolled along the level floor to the corner under the windows. Squatting, Ky studied it. Shadow movement writhed over the grotesque face as it smiled hideously at him. The haunted object was aware and watching him, pleased. Its unhinged glee pissed off Ky. *This is war magic.* Keeping an eye on it, Ky reached into the waste basket and took out a piece of paper. Folding it in half, he used it to pick up the head.

"Go fuck yourself, you tiny piece of shit. I'm going to smash you into a thousand grains of sand." Ky wrapped more discarded paper around the stone, careful not to touch it. He grabbed a few more sheets out of the waste basket and clumped them to conceal the ghoulish object. Whoever had killed Haw, Ky was now certain their methods were supernatural, targeted, and openly malicious.

☾

Adjusting their necktie in the motel room's bathroom mirror, Aych paused. Water from the faucet dripped into the cracked porcelain sink as they stared into the mismatched eyes reflected back at them. *That was fast.* Aych resumed straightening the square knot tied in the silk. The information the lure sent was scant; this new candidate was canny enough not to have touched it directly, and it was on the move. *Contained and being transported and moving in this direction.* That was unexpected and intriguing. *Retreat, hold, or advance?*

    The motel was in the village closest to the last failure's demise. It was entirely reasonable the new human the lure was now attached to was driving close to here on their way elsewhere. Aych checked their wristwatch, thinking of travel times back to the city versus the opportunity to scout the new candidate immediately.

    Advance.

☾

The winter sun was low on the western horizon as Ky stopped at a gas station in a small village off the main roads. Wrapped in a garbage bag and tied with kitchen twine, the thing he had taken from Haw's office sat on the back seat. He kept an eye on the bundle through the rear window, while he filled the car's tank. The quality of the spirit inhabiting the stone head bothered him. Not quite human and not quite animal, it exuded a low, chittering noise, as if it was constantly snickering or whispering. The magic oozing out of it felt at once enticing and repulsive. The influence was disturbingly seductive. As he considered the soundtrack it provoked, the debauched thrill of anonymous trysts in grimy bathrooms with dangerous rejects came to mind.

A Holy Venom

Visceral gambling with sanity and safety for a darker desire.

Ky popped the trunk open and took out a spare gas can. Unhooking the nozzle from the car, he unscrewed the plastic top and filled the container. Whatever was seated in the head was intelligent and Ky had every reason to suspect it had played a significant part in Haw's death. Either it killed her or it marked her. Either way, it was a locus and had to be seen to.

The street was quiet, with only a few cars pulling into the grocery store across the way. Next to the parking lot, a newly constructed brick building contained the town's relocated post office and a tax accountant's office. Ky scanned the street. To the west, a leaning church spire rising above the tree line caught his eye. He focused on the crooked needle of the structure and immediately caught a tinge of neglect and decay.

Hooking the gas nozzle back into place, he checked the street. He sensed someone's gaze resting on him, then the sensation abruptly receded as quickly as it had started. He waited a moment to be certain he was not being watched and got back into his car. Behind him on the seat, the thing in the bag trilled and gibbered incoherent noise in Ky's head. Whatever it was, the piece of malevolent shit was extremely pleased with itself.

On the drive to the church, the homes grew sparser and less well-tended until there were only trees and tall brambles lining the poorly plowed farm road. Alone next to a modest-sized cemetery, the dilapidated church hunched in a lavender-tinted moat of dusk surrounded by snow. Paint peeled from the wooden boards and there were no tracks in the snowbank leading up to the padlocked doors. Musty and miserable, the sobbing murmurs of sexual abuse and alcoholism coated the former place of worship.

Ky drove further down the road. He pulled over into an access lane cutting through the forest under the powerlines. Grabbing the wrapped head off the back seat, he went around to the trunk. Purification of the stone head was his most important task as it was war magic and linked to the contamination surrounding Haw's children and home. Ky held the garbage bag uneasily. Destroying the thing would be throwing away his chance to get more information on whatever killed Haw. The bag was strangely warm in the cold air and Ky realized he had been standing with the trunk open, staring at the gas can.

Kiarna Boyd

☾

Aych drove past a line of rundown houses and then pulled over onto the shoulder careful not to get hung up on the snowbank. The lure was moving again. Slower and coming back in this direction. The human was carrying it but still not touching it directly. In the distance, Aych could see a broken-down church through the trees. The lure was there. Curious, they rolled a cigarette and watched the abandoned church. *He's trying to get rid of it on consecrated ground. Good luck with that.* The lure stopped moving and there was a strong sense of amusement from it. *What the fuck is he doing in there? If you think the Old Lady will help you, you're in for a sad surprise.* The head channeled back the sensation of heat and the tang of smoke. Inhaling the cigarette smoke and catching the scent of gasoline on the wind, Aych laughed and slapped their palm on the steering wheel. They watched as smoke began rising from the former church. They backed the car up and turned it. *Wait until I tell Lu.* Delighted, Aych's cheeks split revealing their true smile.

☾

After checking no one was around to observe him coming out of the woods, Ky got back into his car. He started up the vehicle and drove off as the first strings of smoke snaked over the trees. The head was in the basement wedged into the broken cement. Ghosts of misery had crowded around while he had set up the three-four. The impressions and memories oozing out of the filth made him weep as he rigged the accelerant. The place was a raw wound of wretchedness so strong even the thick-headed locals refused to enter it. Unlike other abandoned churches he had purified in the past, this one was free of graffiti or any sign of teenagers breaking in to party. The secret history of the worst abuses of power and authority made themselves all too clear in the echoing cries locked in the aged lumber and drystone masonry. Fire would free the spirits trapped. The breath quickened in Ky's throat and the excitement ran along his body under his clothes. One spark from the three-four had started it, then nursed it slowly, giving him time to

A Holy Venom

get far enough away before releasing the flames to be nourished and unravel, spooling out their righteous, sanctified beauty. The gold and amber light curled and blazed, growing larger, the crisp symphony of oxygen transforming into heat and shining light. In the process, the wood and stone took the heat into themselves and released the buried pain upwards. His eyes flickered to the rearview mirror. The spirits ascending in the charcoal reels of smoke, the knowledge of the expansion of the flames, consuming and swelling expanded the choked pain around his heart. The fire burned. As it did, Ky felt useful. This was his purpose. This was right, no matter what morality the world imposed on him. Things like the stone head and cursed places like that abattoir of slaughtered trust needed to burn. The desert had taught him it was holy, this ancient and sacred rite of devouring flame. Now, with the obscene head gone, he could focus on purifying Haw's family and their home.

☾

The susurrus of hushed voices mingled with the clink and clatter of glassware, filling the lower rooms of the farmhouse with a constant hum. Outside, politely distanced from the somber exchanges of the civilians, boisterous clusters of retired and active military personnel traded favorite memories of their dead comrade, their stories punctuated by laughter. Ky made his way upstairs, feeling the exhaustion of the last few days catching up to him.

At the top of the landing, he cracked open the repaired door to Berry's bedroom. He had asked Berry if it would be alright for him to come back to check the room for her. Now with the house full of family and friends and most everyone from the local village filling their mouths with potluck and their ears with other people's private business, Ky was almost grateful for the chance to check the forlorn bedroom. *Almost*, because the floral wallpaper in the corner across from the door still carried a trace of what he could only label as spatial insanity. There, in the tight corner above the pink cabbage rose, he could sense the impossible warped tangle of dislocated space. No matter what he tried with salt and herbs, blessed water, or whispered song, Ky could not purify it or close the invisible gap. He knew better than to trust his inclination to light a bowl of isopropyl alcohol and ignite the blue flame. True to their purpose, the flames would bring their promised purity. Then his hand would tremble and slip, letting the flame leap out of the bowl, splashing the fuel and enabling the living released Presence to burrow through the wallpaper until it reached the seasoned, venerable oak behind it.

Sitting on the girl's bed and picking up her scruffy dog doll, he tried to put the vision of the vapor curls of blue-tipped fire out of his mind. He stared at the spot between the small chest of drawers and the stencil of the robot on the toybox lid. Berry had told him about the killer and its nocturnal visit before it had lured her mother out to slaughter. The countersignal was quiet, yet the hairs on the back of Ky's neck prickled as he sensed the uneven quality of the air hanging near the wall. Without thinking, he was up and moving with his free hand outstretched, half expecting his fingertips to pass through the dusty paper and its frosting pink flower.

"Should've known I'd find you up here." Behind him, a man's accented voice called from the doorway. "Find any ghosts?"

Dropping his hand, Ky turned and shrugged. "Not the ones you'd be interested in, Lieutenant."

"It's *Detective* now. I'm out too." Mudon eyed the dog doll in Ky's other hand. "You hunting for Haw's ghost? Or praying for her soul?"

"You interrogating everyone including the family, or just me?" Ky swallowed back harsher words and used returning the doll to its place on the bed as an excuse to avoid looking at Mudon. He had known there was a chance the former intelligence officer would show up to Haw's funeral to pay his respects, but he had hoped the spirits would have warned him. Ky felt Mudon's eyes watching him, reminding him of a house cat watching wild birds through a window. *Waiting for his chance.*

"Don't be like that, *pen*," Mudon shut the door as he stepped into the girl's bedroom.

Ky shot him a warning look. "Let's get one thing clear. You are not, and will never be, my *dapen*," he snapped. Ky hoped to forestall any of the other man's attempts at claiming an imaginary, retroactively-invented bond.

The detective put up both his hands. "I get it. This business with Haw dying like this, out in the sticks, has you worked up. Still, those aren't

A Holy Venom

reasons to cut up so rough. She was my friend too, if you recall."

Ky narrowed his eyes and nodded at the door. "You mind opening the door? I'm uncomfortable without a clear line of retreat. Certified combat trauma survivor, remember? You should, you're the one who got me discharged."

"Now, don't be like that." Mudon shot him a sour look and eased the door open a crack. "Let's not get off on the wrong foot. I wanted to check in with you. Haw was an important friend to both of us."

"Sure, and you're thinking about asking a pretty farm girl you meet downstairs at the funeral buffet to marry you. What you want is to ask questions. That's what you always want." Ky focused on the wallpaper. "You want to ask me if the rumors are true, if there's something supernatural here." He shook off the former intel man's scrutiny like brushing off a horsefly before it could bite. If he wasn't careful, Mudon would cause him worse pain and aggravation.

The S&P detective shook his head and moved near the dresser. "No reason to ask." He glanced over and held Ky's gaze. "I've seen this plenty of times. Nothing supernatural about it. Oh, there's some that want it to read that way. They use a lot of hackneyed temple stage tricks to dress it like there's a mystery here, but no. Just drug dealers being scum." Mudon's tone hardened. "I'll tell you straight. It's a criminal organization pushing illegal street narcotics. They've got a new product and it's sweet and fast and deadly. They're branching out into rural areas and these backwoods towns." He made a dismissive nod at the door. "My bet's on Haw falling afoul of them one way or the other. Maybe the sticks at the local Tank think it's the Shepherd himself that came for her. I don't know and I don't care. Maybe Haw went looking for her own answers and picked up the wrong regard while she went about it. Or she decided to work for the dealers." He watched Ky's indignation flare. "Maybe, they offered her enough to pay for her litter's college fund."

"That's horseshit!" Ky was in Mudon's face now. "Haw wouldn't have—"

"No? Her nibling was dealing the Rot up in the Capital. Olive tell you that? No? They got killed off the same way a few weeks back. Hacked to pieces and strewn over a mountain top to scare the locals. That's what this organization does when the relationship with the local drop breaks down, apparently. They send out their enforcer and this sick fuck makes it look like an animal attack. The sticks in the Tank let it ride as a cautionary tale for the rest of the seats. If I put money down on the identity of this particular sick fuck, I could retire in two weeks. Trust me, I know this asshole's work."

Mudon tilted his head and moved closer to Ky. In a lowered voice, he continued. "You're on edge, *pen*. Don't tell me your imagination has been getting to you. You look a little tired. Maybe you're sleep-deprived. Insomnia and that replacement for shut-eye you do with your album collection. Too tired to think straight." His gaze swept over Ky's face. "Or maybe you've been staying up late, making your homemade insurance policies?"

Realizing the game, Ky backed off. "If you're insinuating …" Fear flared and cooled almost at once as Ky considered this was what the dreams had been warning him about: Mudon's eyes catching him in the dark.

"We're not in some rundown trainyard or rebel outpost," Mudon stated, holding Ky's gaze. "Tell me, *staff sergeant*, if I asked the local Tank to check your car for traces of accelerant, what would they find?"

"Not a damn thing," Ky growled and then shrugged forcing himself to calm down. Mudon was shaking him hard just for old times' sake. "Shove off, *lieutenant*, before I slug you. That's the only warning you'll get out of me before I snap it. If, after I adjust your attitude, you wanted to charge me for assault, I can press charges for psychological bullying. We both know the civilian courts don't take kindly to former officers leveraging psych intel on combat survivors."

"I got you honorably discharged and you would still bite me for it after all these years," Mudon smiled bitterly. "Fine then, play it that way." His expression became stern. "So long as it doesn't involve murder, I'll overlook your … hobbies. Not your fault you're unstable, considering the services rendered. You know I went easy on you. Could've brought you up on charges, but what can I say? I sympathize with you."

"Go fuck yourself." Ky moved passed him toward the door.

"I know who killed her." Mudon grabbed him by the arm. "If you want to get revenge on the people who left Haw's family without so much as a body to bury, I could use your help to get evidence."

Ky swatted Mudon's hand away. "Sounded like you knew all about them a second ago. Now you need help? And why should I after you throw the past in my face? Or were you thinking it would make me feel all warm and friendly to relive our shared time in the interrogation cells?"

Mudon was silent a long moment and then gave a quick nod. "It's complicated. Doing things the right way, legally, means gathering evidence. It's slow going and the other side is not slow. They're fast and getting faster. Your talents with people would be useful." His shrewd eyes searched Ky's face. "Maybe I'd like to get you out of that shithole you're living in, offer you a way out. I could do you a favor, maybe even get you on full-time."

"As a fucking informant? As your cat's paw?" Ky raked the other man with his eyes, thinking again about locked rooms. All those hours spent shouting his innocence. All those hours of Mudon fucking with his head. "If you want to do me a favor, there's a woodchipper in the garage you could crawl into. Preferably while it's running."

Mudon chuckled. "Listen to you, getting all brutish when you're mad. Just like I remember. Next, you'll be suggesting I drop some change in the jukebox and you'll tell me which numbers to press. You miss dancing with me?" The detective raised an eyebrow. "Because if you want me to keep asking uncomfortable questions, I will."

Ky became still. "I'll say it more clearly, then. Fuck you and fuck your favor. If you know who did this, do your job and arrest them."

"Funny how we're always having chats like this in unusually cramped rooms, isn't it, *pen*?" Mudon looked around. "Maybe you want to keep living in that shithole and playing hide and seek with the stick forensic teams until your heart's wish comes true and you get a bigger, nicer room rent-free at the Statler. Can't have you do that to yourself. After all, I went to so much trouble to keep you out of there last time. Staked my reputation on you being a solid, law-abiding citizen."

Resisting the urge to punch him, Ky turned his back and swung open the door before stepping out onto the landing.

Behind him, Mudon came out and leaned on the door jamb watching as Ky went down the stairs. "I'll be keeping an eye on you, *pen*."

SEVEN

AYCH TOOK THE BACK WAY down the alley and arrived at the Velvet before it opened. They glanced up at the backside of the theatre and cast a disparaging eye over the thick ice weighing down the alleyway dumpsters next to the loading dock. This was the Velvet's hidden face: dark and leering and dangerous, a stark contrast to the facade of neon glamor the wide-eyed seats swooned over. Noting that at least the stage entranceway stairs were clear and sprinkled with grit, Aych rapped a knuckle on the pitted stage door. The porthole window shot open and a pair of human eyes inspected Aych's. The window closed with a snap. Bolts scraped against the metal frame.

"Evening, Rue," Aych nodded to the guard as the door opened.

"Evening." The stocky man set his back against the metal fire door. "Violet wants to see you when you have a minute. Says to come by their office after you see Lu."

"Sounds important," Aych took out their tobacco pouch and glanced up at the stagehands prepping the rigging in the catwalks. The staff called back and forth while traipsing along the grated metal walkways. "Anything happen while I was out?"

Rue brought the rolled magazine in his hand up to hip level and made a cutting gesture. "A couple of salts came around trying to make like they were tourists. Tried to sit in on a game."

"Who let them in?"

"No one. Our fella turned 'em away at the front door. Told 'em they weren't up to the dress code."

Aych smiled and sealed the cigarette paper. "They never learn."

"Dumb shits," Rue grinned.

"I'll tell Vee you told me to stop in." Sliding the cigarette behind their ear, Aych headed for the grated metal stairs.

Rue settled onto his stool and went back to the magazine. Overhead, Aych navigated the first level of scaffolding to the backside of the main house. The stagehands and lighting techs stopped their tasks and moved aside to let them go by.

Aych knocked on the inner fire door and waited. The door cracked open and a woman peered over the chain, closed it, and then fully opened the door.

"Fire marshal won't like that chain," Aych gestured as they stepped through.

The security guard put her back against the gold-flecked wallpaper. "Neither it nor I will be here when they come by." She eyed Aych warily. Meeting their gaze, her eyes went wide and her body tensed.

"This is the first time we've met, isn't it?" *She's sensitive and afraid of what she's picking up off me.* Aych leaned into the delicious aroma of fear. Their proximity heightened the woman's terror, making her scent almost irresistible. Eyes half-lidded, Aych stopped a few inches away from the woman and reached out to rest their hand on the wall next to her head. "Am I that ugly? Or maybe ..." Aych leaned in closer.

"Don't ..." The guard's voice waivered and her eyes started to water. She stiffened with panic.

"Don't what?" Aych let their gaze flicker down the length of the guard's body and then back up to her eyes.

"Hey, babycakes," Lu called out from the doorway of her extravagant suite. "There will be no workplace harassment tonight, thank you." A silk dressing robe hung off Lu's shoulders, the luxurious cloth clinging to her curves.

"Tch. Hypocrite." Aych dropped their hand and moved away from the guard. "You do it all the time."

"When I do it, it's called flirting. Get your pasty, fish-belly white behind over here and leave Tansy alone."

Tansy slipped down the wall. The vaseful of flowers on the table by the fire door trembled as the guard kept herself from falling to the floor.

"You pay them no mind," Lu called out in a soothing voice. "They're all bark and no bite."

Aych snickered as Lu swatted their backside in passing. She closed the door and raised a disapproving eyebrow.

"What have I told you about leaving the household alone? Do you want to make more enemies?"

"She knows what I am," Aych said. "Might have a good guess about you, too."

Lu crossed her arms. "What's that girl going to know about anything? That you're a creepy shepherd that makes her uncomfortable? That I'm the best stage magician, anna, *and shepherd* in this entire city? You're only looking for an excuse. You give them too much credit. They won't let themselves even imagine what we are."

Aych picked up a cut crystal lighter off the marble mantel. "Maybe I just think it's funny when you get mad enough to call me *babycakes*. It's the closest you get to swearing at me." Taking the cigarette out from behind their ear, they lit it as Lu glared. "You want me to apologize? Take a class on sexual harassment?" Their eyes followed Lu as she draped herself on the couch in front of the fireplace.

"Don't mess with the house. We have a hard enough time hiring decent people without you going around driving them over the edge. Half the city is on the Rot and the other half are pure fools. As for making me angry, don't think it's cute. I could char your flea-bitten pelt to a cinder."

"I will behave myself. Promise."

"I know you will. Or else." Smoothing her hand over the plush fabric, Lu patted the couch back. "Tell me your news."

Aych unbuttoned their suit jacket and sat next to her. "You were right. The lure found another candidate right away. Might be what we are hoping for."

"Go on," she said, a pleased smile curving her lips into a bow.

"Mid-forties, excellent condition, probably trains every week. Ex-military, either a practitioner or close enough to recognize the lure. Either way, a magician. Twitchy, like he's half here, half somewhere else."

"It found a *real* magician, not a stage magician? Not some illusionist pulling rabbits out of his behind?" Putting her feet across Aych's lap, Lu adjusted her dressing gown. "And? There must be more. You're grinning like a snake that caught *all* the birds."

"Psychic." Aych let the smoke curl out of their mouth in rings. "At least an empath, maybe more. And that's not even the best part."

Lu clicked her tongue. "That'll just cause you trouble. If he knows what you are, he'll be more difficult to manage. Here you were not ten seconds ago threatening to eat that poor woman—"

"I thought you said they won't let themselves admit we're real." Resting their arm over her legs, Aych settled back into the couch.

"The ones we hire here. You think I'd let Violet hire a legit psychic? Please."

Aych grinned. "Fair enough."

Lu poked them in the shoulder. "What else? You're not going to tell me they're a trained monster hunter from some long-forgotten pedigreed family sworn from birth to destroy your kind?"

"Like those even exist anymore." Mirth twinkled in Aych's eyes. "Better."

"Better than a trained hunter?" Lu gave them a surprised look. "Well, out with it then."

"They tried to get rid of the lure by burning it."

Lu's expression went sour. "That's nothing. A high school kid might try that just from watching movies."

"What high school kid sets a church on fire to get it done?"

Her eyes went wide. "Don't tell me …"

Aych smirked. "Arsonist. Practiced at it. We found ourselves a crazy-ass firebug, one who's easy as hell to push over the edge. He's ready for the bright lights and big time."

"He sounds *dangerous*. We don't need a wild firebrand setting the wrong things ablaze." Lu leaned forward. Her gown opened, revealing the soft, elegant curves of her human form. "What did you learn about his magic?"

"Couldn't get close enough to catch a whiff and he hasn't touched the lure yet. Watched him from a distance and he knew I was at it. Didn't want to risk tipping him off."

"Well, look at you talking strategy for once. You do have a brain in that pointy skull." She poked Aych again. "Ex-military. An arsonist and psychic. Magician. He can fight?"

A Holy Venom

"Don't know until I give him a run-through. Moves like it. I'll know more after he touches the lure."

"And if he doesn't? What if he's smart or experienced enough to not touch it?"

"If needed, I'll go there and shove it down his throat."

"Where's he now?"

"Sticking around for the last candidate's funeral. They were friends. He's pissed off and knows it's not over."

"Oh, that will make it easier for you."

"If he's the right one, if he can go five minutes with me, we can—"

"If he is, we can get to it as soon as the herbalist is done." Lu watched as Aych leaned forward to stub the cigarette out in a crystal ashtray. "If he's not, then the next one will be. Don't get your hopes up. Not yet."

Aych squeezed her hand and smiled. "I want this one to be the right one. I want to get this fucking done and I want you to be whole. We're running out of time—"

"Please. What you want is an excuse to cause trouble," she said, poking Aych again. "That and for me to return the favor and purify your favorite human. That's the only thing you care about. To free him before it's too late."

Avoiding her eyes, Aych nodded in the direction of the door. "Speaking of humans, Violet wants to see me. You know anything about it?"

"I imagine it's about that fool across town." Her tone turned harsh and Lu slipped her legs free. "There have been more overdoses with the Rot over at The Jewel. That *pik-un* running the house is either cutting it with something or selling too much to other fools. Too many empty seats. Even if you and I are fine with humans seeing themselves out, Vee will stop distributing it if they think it is too dangerous. They do not share our … motivations."

"Well then, I should probably go repay Vee's hospitality and look into the matter, shouldn't I?"

"Yes, yes you should. Make an *honest* living from your brutal arts." She pointed a long, white lacquered fingernail at Aych. "Don't overdo it and sleep in. You need to check on our would-be hunter. I want to know everything about him."

"We don't even know if he can last two minutes …"

"I said *would-be*, didn't I? And that's exactly why I don't want you sleeping on this." She looked at them from the corner of her eyes. "I feel it in my bones; this is the one we want." She held her hand out palm facing Aych. "Don't whine at me if he turns coward after five seconds because of your lack of finesse. But if he makes it a full five minutes, then you can say that I told you he was the one. Remember, we want him obsessed enough to come after you. For that, he needs to be up and moving, not locked up and raving. Though, if they commit him to the Statler, we would be able to retrieve him when—"

"You're a piece of work, you know that?" Aych buttoned their jacket. "Calling me out on hassling humans when you're worse than I am. Disparaging my looks and my lack of grace."

"I get consent before I work them over. Make them want it. You have zero interest in subtlety and rely on that raw, charismatic excuse for charm of yours to rope in the weak ones. When that doesn't work, you just roll them straight over into their base fears. Doesn't take talent to stampede the herd when you are," Lu waved her fingers at Aych. "Whatever you are."

"Are you saying I lack class?"

"I'm saying you are *lazy* and don't put any effort into being seductive." She threw an arch look. "Not that any human in their right mind would find you attractive. Giant block of a thing with too many teeth in that rock you call a head."

"There you go again disparaging me. You trying to hurt my feelings?"

"You don't have feelings. You have appetites. Though you could at least use what you have rather than being a bully. You can have integrity about it. Put on a better show before you kill them."

"That's how we go about things differently, you and I. You gain their confidence until you have every morsel at your feet believing they have a chance with you for real. But," Aych winked, "You don't keep me around here to make them feel at ease, now, do you?"

Lu smiled wickedly. "No, I do not."

☾

Vetch opened the office door and gave Aych an appraising look. "Still look like you work at a funeral home, but the cut's an improvement." Behind him, a cage full of brightly plumed songbirds fell silent in the windowless office.

Aych averted their gaze from the head of security's carefully selected ensemble. The human's choice of fabrics clashed violently, threatening to give Aych a migraine. "Thank you." *And you look like a street carnival threw up on itself.* Aych smiled and nodded to the elderly human seated at the desk. "*Tau-lm.* I trust your health is good and your house is happy. Rue said you wanted to see me."

The Velvet's proprietor smoothed the glittering, embroidered silk scarf tied around their neck. "Ah, *tau-vik-lm*, my dear, come and sit so we can talk about that." Violet glanced around Aych to look pointedly at Vetch.

In response, Vetch raised and dropped his fingers, giving the stagehand signal for all clear. "No whistles in the house, *tau-lm*."

"Thank you, dear one." Violet relaxed and let their chair hinge back. "I'm afraid I need to ask you for a favor, Aych."

Aych avoided the bird cage and took the seat closest to the desk. The birds huddled together and eyed them nervously. "Always my pleasure, Vee."

"This … this I think will be over at The Jewel, one of the flower houses we own, Eldridge has overstepped … or, should I say, overstayed his welcome."

Vetch sat next to Aych, tilted his head, and spoke pointedly. "Too many kids and too many annas who have gone home early to the Holy Mother were seen at The Jewel right before they left. Too many untimely departures in general. The numbers are bad. The attention on The Jewel is high at the Tank and you know what that means. They'll be over here next."

Aych turned to look at him. "I heard you had to tell a pair of salts to shove off. Were they on the leash or sniffing around on their own?"

"If they weren't on the leash, the next set will be. Like I said, the numbers are bad. I'd take care of it myself …"

Aych grinned. "But you know how much I love doing Vee a favor."

"One like this, yeah. It's your specialty. Adds to your legend," Vetch rolled his eyes.

Aych turned back to Violet. "Just Eldridge, or you want his whole house?"

"We think the house is likely OK. Legae is from Grava and she knows how things should be done. She risked much coming to have a word with Vetch and she did the right thing. Eldridge is putting all of us at risk." Violet's expression sagged into a parody of disappointment, while the elder's eyes remained full of sharp-edged anger.

Vetch nodded. "Legae respects Violet, she understands hospitality, what it means to have a house. Treats the annas well, doesn't push too hard, doesn't take too much. But Eldridge, he doesn't respect the traditions, our ways of hospitality. He's pushing things. Says he's trying new things, new ways ..."

Sighing, Violet put their clasped hands on the desk. "When he came to me and asked if he could open a house, I thought, times change. Even if he wasn't raised in a *gra-doon*, I shouldn't be prejudiced. When it was only *vevik*, he never over-sold. No one died from these overdoses. I welcome everyone, I *want* to welcome everyone. I told him he could sell the Rot for us but ..."

"He's selling too much and to the wrong people. I gotcha, Vee." Aych looked from the elder to the younger and back. "Do you have the script lined up, or do you want me to improvise?"

Violet took a black metal card out of their breast pocket and set it on the desk. "Fifty thousand. The story is you got it off a closed game here and now you want to spend it."

"No one will be surprised if you show up asking for an assortment. Hell, Eldridge will be drooling over the chance to talk to you privately." Vetch indicated the credit marker. "He'll offer you the best and then ..."

"Thinking that I'm all tired out and amiable, he'll invite himself in for a chat." Aych slid the marker off the desk. "You think he's that much of a fool? Everyone in this town knows I work for Violet."

Violet tapped their fingers on the empty space where the card had been. "Oh, well. We know it, don't we?" Their usual flamboyance submerged under a sudden steely tone of anger. "Fucking around with the chance of bringing the dogs down on all of us. Only the worst kind of arrogant fool would risk that."

Noting the change in Violet's manner, Aych closed their blue eye.

"You're really worried they'll show up over some bodies full of Rot? Not write it off as just some kids going home early?"

Violet looked pointedly at Vetch.

He shook his head. "Those fanatics don't want anyone going home early. They don't even allow themselves to send anyone over. They get off on scrambling brains instead. They'll send the salts to net as many of us as they can then work the weakest over in the Tank, or worse, in their kennel. Whoever they take will end up talking until their brains run out their mouths. And then, when the dogs are done, they'll dump their scraps in the Stat, useless as a boiled vegetable. We can't risk it. The salts we can use, we use. But the ones on the leash?" Vetch shook his head. *"Dogs don't make deals."*

Aych shrugged. "You want it done so as not to get their attention, but clear enough that all the other houses know."

Violet shared another look with Vetch and sat back, dramatically raising their hands to the ceiling, signaling their satisfaction. "Our house is blessed by this one's directness."

"And the fifty comes back from The Jewel to you, Vee." Aych slipped the card into their pocket. "All this is costing is the real fifty The Jewel should be making off the flock rather than playing with me."

Nodding, Violet made a small flourish with their hand. "Cheap enough to fix the problem and plug the hole in the boat. Hopefully, in time."

"And if it isn't in time? If the Perlustrate already has enough to come here, then what?" Aych watched as both humans winced.

"The *dogs*," Violet emphasized the euphemism, "are not going to come here as long as our star, our *tau-ve-lm*, has the Mother Church's favor. Her glory keeps the High Priestess enraptured and we enjoy the benefits. Meanwhile, we keep our salts sweet and they find other places to exercise their curiosity. It's the smaller houses under our protection the salts will shake, to make a show for the dogs and the flock. To look, as those in the Tank would say, *effective*."

Vetch tilted his head in the direction of the street. "If they do for some reason want to knock us around and make a show of it, The Velvet's got more than a fair share of tricks in her bricks. I'll get Violet and Lu out if I need to. You worry about your end of things."

"Ah, yes, the advantages of fabricating our schemes out of a venerable magic house." With another flourish, Violet gestured at the framed posters of former stage illusion acts decorating the office walls. "Now they see us, now they don't."

"Then what? You'll relocate to Grava and take an early retirement?" Aych smirked. "Doesn't sound half bad."

"Unless you hate losing—and we hate losing." Vetch shrugged. "Our house, our city. Fuck the dogs. Excuse me, *tau-lm*."

"No need to apologize, dear one. Indeed, *fuck the dogs*." Violet locked eyes with Aych. "If they ever dare take my house and you're in this city, promise me you'll punish them, *tau-vik-lm*. Make them bleed. All of them."

Aych nodded. "I didn't mean to ruffle you and you don't have to ask. You know it would be my pleasure. Only reason I haven't already is Lu says it would spoil her fun up the Hill. You've been good to me all these years. This fifty included." They tapped the pocket holding the marker.

Puzzled, Vetch watched their exchange. "You might be asking too much, Vee. Shouldn't Aych try to get out too? No matter how good a shepherd they are, what's one person going to do against the whole Chapterhouse?"

"You are too modern, *pen-lm*." Violet sighed. "I love you like my own child, but if you're asking that question with this one sitting right here in front of your own eyes, I can't retire and leave things in your hands. Not yet. When you understand, then I can leave The Velvet and the other houses in your hands. Look, child, and see what sits before you." They unfurled their arms in a sweeping motion at Aych.

Aych got up and shot Vetch a wry smile. "When you figure it out, try not to piss yourself. You'll never get the stink out of those trousers."

☾

The stairwell reeked of cat piss. Ky hefted his duffel bag and spun his keys on his thumb as he climbed the tenement stairs to his apartment. It was late and he tried to be quiet as he scaled the steps to the top level of the brick building, but no matter how careful he was, the empty hallways and stairwells sent echoes of his footfalls rattling and banging like the air-filled water pipes. Discarded food wrappers glinted in the corners of the stairs and slush from other residents' boots slowly melted on the rubber safety treads. Reaching the top, he pushed open the metal door and crossed the wide floorboards. The loneliness, depression, and anger of the other tenants seeped out from the low-income units. Legacy imprints from the factory production days, anguish from accidents and deaths in the machines, ghosts of the alcoholics reliving their drawn-out suicides in slow motion, all of it existed in stasis, archeological suffering under modern angst and despair. To make the place bearable when he first moved in, he had lit the blue flame of isopropyl alcohol to burn out the patches of sexual assault and intergenerational misery. How he had fought to keep his hand steady and how he had wept with effort, extinguishing the divine fire when the rite was done. Now all that was left flitting through the halls were shades of dead children unwilling to leave the familiarity of their brief lives.

Unlocking his apartment door, Ky halted. A foreboding pressure hung in the air. He prodded the door open with his boot. He readied to swing the duffel if needed. "Hello?" He scanned the apartment.

He snapped the lights on. The cramped living room was as he had left it. Bolted together milk crates filled with horizontal stacks of vinyl, the stereo console untouched, music magazines scattered on the coffee table. Coffee filter in the trash and traces of incense in the air—no scent of other people. The kitchenette along the side of the living room was untouched, save for the mug in the sink he remembered putting there before he left for work.

At the far end of the room, the blinds covering the original arched window rustled in the updraft from the radiator. Ky set his bag on the stacked twin mattresses set up as a couch. Trying to locate the point of disruption, he approached the bedroom door. The hinges sighed as he pushed it open with his fingertips and waited. No change in the air, yet the sense of otherness seemed stronger, more immediate. The countersignal stirred, sparking a faint staccato of nerve signals flickering over the skin on his back.

Flipping on the light, Ky glanced around the shoebox of a bedroom. The scent of incense was stronger. The sheets were thrown back and rumpled as expected. Books neatly filled the milk crates holding up the mattress. One book lay on the apple crate employed as a nightstand, next to it the desk lamp and bladed fan sat on the wool rug. A pot of grass sat on the window ledge and snow was stacked against the glass outside on the fire escape. By the foot of the bed, a thin radiator hissed and chortled, trying to chase out the bone-deep chill.

He checked behind the tapestry cordoning off the end of the bedroom. Between the shelves of clothes, the altar cabinet remained closed. The ash of the morning offering of incense remained in the bowl of sand in front of the wooden cabinet. Perplexed, Ky unhooked the latch and swung the altar doors apart. The countersignal stung and scalded in warning.

Inside the cabinet seated among the framed photos of deceased friends, sat a rough, hand-carved wooden statue of a jackal. After the wild desert animals found him half alive under the rubble, he developed a sentimental liking for their sharp faces and inquisitive eyes. Careful footed and clever, the sight of the jackal nosing through the debris brought relief to his despair. It had not occurred to him to use the last of his ammo to kill it. At the time, he was too obsessed with needing to save the remaining rounds for himself. Trapped as he was, the scavenger could have made an easy meal out of his seared body or gone for his face. Instead, the jackal had watched him for a moment with a curious look before loping off. It ran into the desert dusk, its tail whisking through shattered cement blocks. That momentary glimpse of the sand and black fur kept Ky alive, gave him a reason not to use his pistol and keep waiting for rescue. When it came, the medic told him the trackers had followed the paw prints through the broken remains of the compound.

Instead of the usual comfort the memory brought, Ky felt a sick twist in his gut as the countersignal flared, hot then cold. The stone head from Haw's house lolled at the bottom of the altar cabinet. Untouched by the fire at the corrupt church, it lay at an angle, resting against the jackal statue. The head's deformed canine features insolently smirked up at Ky.

Infuriated, he reached out to seize the profane thing and then stopped himself. The compulsion to grab the head and fling it across the room made his fingers itch. Catching in the periphery of his eyes, an unanchored shadow moved. The shadow slunk behind him along the bedroom wall. The tapestry billowed and the leering stone taunted him. War magic and

A Holy Venom

ambushes, traps and manipulation, all of the warnings from the playlist returned and he swore under his breath. It had not been about Mudon after all. The profane magic was setting off the countersignal and the resulting electric shock warnings made the nerves in his hand ache.

"I don't know how you got in here, but you're not pulling a fast one on me, fucker." Ky grabbed a T-shirt from a nearby shelf and doubled it up. Using the cotton as a mitt, he extracted the head from his altar. Carrying it at arm's length, he went out to the kitchenette, opened the freezer, and shoved the wrapped ball of hatred under the frost bulge in the far back. Slapping the door shut, he considered the thing's appearance. Paranoid, he thought of Mudon's target, the sleazy criminal organization selling street drugs. Had they broken in and placed it as a warning? Yet the spirit seated in the stone was the same or close enough to the one he had dealt with at the church. The thing was no stage prop. The slow roast torch party hadn't managed to lock it down, nor had it sent the enemy spirit packing. Thoughts of the uncanny, wavering wallpaper in Berry's bedroom and the sense of a hole in reality supplanted scenes of dealers selling kicks on street corners. Paranoia in full bloom, Ky glanced over at his record collection. He began the slow process of creating a new divination playlist.

Long after the new mix was done and the countersignal finally quiesced, Ky lay on the stacked mattresses he used as a couch. He listened. Water-stained squares of drop ceiling covered the underside of the mill floors. The irregularly shaped splotches of dried leaks played tricks with his eyes, while the cheap material muffled the sounds of his upstairs neighbors brawling. He focused on the music and closed his eyes, ready for another night of insomniac contemplation. The sound of his neighbors' argument grew distant and trailed off as Ky slipped into unexpected slumber. Then the dream seeped in. It began quietly, then started rolling like an arthouse film and Ky felt like he was coming in halfway through the plot.

☽

"You aren't listening to me!" Baz yelled. "It stole my dreams! *Invaded my dreams!* Don't you understand?" They dug their ink-stained nails into the rough wool of the chair. A dusting of snow blew against the rectory windows. "It hates me! If it doesn't kill me, *it will take my eyes!*"

Panic rose in the artist's throat. They looked frantically at the drug rehabilitation advisor, an attentive woman sitting across from them with her hands folded placidly in her lap. How could she be so calm, so unaffected? Couldn't she feel it, the creeping doom suffusing the air, infiltrating the parish house library? It oozed through the walls and shelves of leather-bound tomes, viscous impending terror dripping into the room. Baz felt nauseated, cold sweat beaded their skin. "I'm telling you, it will find a way to harm me, to make me suffer."

The nausea brought with it a clanging headache. They swallowed nervously, keeping watch for the peripheral glimmer of migraine halos. If the fractal shimmering started up again, there would be no choice but to retreat into a darkened bedroom and burrow head to knee under the weight of blankets. Sleep would stroke cool fingers over the crisp sheets and slip under Baz's eyelids, bringing relief. But at what cost? Each time they dreamt, the nightmares came and took away that much more of their waking life.

Surges of light splashed through the transparent mica set in the iron door of the wood stove. Dappled waves leaped and waivered over the half-moon cinder rug protecting the thick woven carpet emblazoned with traditional folk motifs. Baz stared at each texture, the smoothness and gloss, the crinkle and jumble of dust, and the slick, knotted silk. An antique porcelain bucket hand stenciled with flowers lay tucked into the cavern of the original brick-lined fireplace. Groans, clicks, and sighs of the combusting logs filled the silence as the wood shifted, crumbling and falling into glowing embers and ash.

Mother Irin tapped the end of her pen on the notepad balanced on her knee. "Basil, I want to draw your attention to your use of the word 'it'. Neuter, for an object. Not inclusive, not—"

"*It's not human! Why won't you believe me that it's real?*" Baz writhed with arousal and shame, remembering the last dream, the last nightmare. The encounter left the scent of sex lingering on the sheets, the erotic aftermath of horrible, hidden desires. It had to be real! Baz swallowed as their body flushed at the memory of their bestial tryst.

Irin sighed loudly, breaking Baz's reverie. "As a matter of faith, I have

A Holy Venom

difficulty accepting the Holy Mother would allow any of her children to be so ... *haunted*." The skin around her eyes crinkled with concern. "I tend to agree with your therapist that this is a matter of the Imaginal. He suggested it is your guilt. Past experiences of your fans stalking you and your general habit of overwork, combined with the recent loss of your partner, have created this fantasy. Your addiction—"

"It's not a fantasy. It's a *thing*. it gets you in your dreams first—it killed him! When C.S. told me," Baz choked, saying the dead man's name. "I didn't believe him. Not at first, but then I started to see it. To smell it." Baz flinched at the memory of that scent. Not even a fortune's worth of candles could obliterate that inimitable, carnal fragrance. "I know you don't believe me, but it's true. It's a monster. Doesn't the Church have any way to get rid of such things?" Baz dug their fingers deeper into the chair's arms. The threads cut into their skin.

Through the window at the opposite end of the library, the sun began to fade and withdraw the unyielding glare of the winter's day. Outside, beyond the skeletal apple trees, the cemetery between the rectory and the hunched church would disappear, the mounds of snow covering the granite gravestones becoming shapeless until the line of the wilderness blurred and consumed more as night took hold. The grounds of the rehabilitation center would disappear into the darkness—as if, Baz thought, a brush dipped in watercolor gray had passed over the house.

"The Church does perform exorcisms when there is confirmed supernatural activity. However, what you're describing is not an account of the restless dead or the relic of a traumatic event imprinted on a place."

Watching Baz over the tortoiseshell rim of her glasses, Mother Irin waited, then spoke slowly and purposefully. "Your partner died of an overdose; no one killed him. We've gone over the official report together. There was nothing found to indicate another party was involved, supernatural or otherwise." The counselor softened her tone. "No one can make you color-blind, Basil. As a painter, your unique vision, your years of developing your technique, your imagination, these are the most precious tools you have. I need you to understand what's happening: your fears and misplaced guilt are manifesting through your dreams. Your greatest talents are giving rise to these torments.

Kiarna Boyd

"You feel guilty about your partner's death, and that makes you vulnerable. As a result, you've created a self-perpetuating punishment—the loss of your creative abilities. But I need you to hear what Dr. Birch and I have told you, Basil. No one is after you. You're safe here. C.S. died because he self-administered the wrong dose of a street narcotic, not because a creature from your dreams killed him. S&P is checking on the whereabouts of your problem fans, and so far, there is no sign of an active stalker. No one knows you are here except my most trusted staff and your therapist in Newton. I know you're afraid, but you need to stop confusing the past with the present. You need to be kind to yourself. No one is trying to hurt you. The Holy Mother would not allow the kind of horror you're describing to exist. I need you to consider that this may be a result of withdrawal. This drug is new enough that the doctors aren't certain of its long-term effects."

As the light outside the window dimmed, the mantel and paneled walls of the library became murky. Oval shadows pooled out from beneath the drip trays under the potted plants. Elongated triangles drooped from the corners of the framed landscapes hung between the bookshelves. Baz slumped back into the overstuffed chair.

"It's not the Rot. The monster is real. Why won't anyone believe me?" Baz shuddered. "C.S. knew how much he could take. We both knew. I didn't use as much as he did, but he was always careful. It was intentional, not a mistake! It drove him to do it. It's real, and it hates *us*, don't you see?" They stared at the elongating shadows, watching as the point of one triangle rotated like a midnight inversion of a sundial, tracking the loss of daylight. "My dreams ... all my best ideas come from my dreams. I used to see so vividly, shades and hues, gemstone and washes so subtle. Like waterfalls of layered rainbows. Always there, in the palace of my imagination and ..." They stopped, blinking. When they resumed, Baz's voice was dull and monotone. "Now, there's nothing. Even if it doesn't kill me, my life is over. C.S. is gone. Next, my talent, and then, finally, my sight. I'll end up in the Stat scribbling on the walls. I can't live like that. I won't."

"But you described it so vibrantly," Mother Irin murmured. "Detailing how it appeared to you, it doesn't sound like your dreams are limited to black and white." Irin flipped pages and tapped her pen. Paper rustled as she searched. "'Skin like the Twins' frozen ice, long hair like the entrance of an alley you're afraid to pass, and lips smeared with blood.'" Her eyes sought Baz's.

Baz whimpered through their clenched teeth. Half-formed, a figure turned in their mind's eye, cruel and uncaring, full of fury; all wide strokes of charcoal and hatred on bare plaster walls, wet lips smeared and dripping. The bone structure both heavy and delicate, impossibly perfect skin stretched around a mouth too sensual and too wide to be human. Luminous, bewitching eyes over lips wet with human blood, the shimmer of sharp teeth barely concealed. Unclean, alluring, enraged—it was with them now, in the rectory. Baz's memory shifted—altering, cracking, peeling—the layers curling and burning, revealing bleached bones piled like primer and sealer in the metal cans ready to be applied and never again taken out.

That life was over, Baz was sure of it. They stared at the stained skin around their fingernails and the charcoal wedged under the cuticles like so many speckles on a robin's egg. There would be no more murals, no more whimsical, light-hearted beauty ... not from these hands. In their mind they saw the thing in the nightmare raise a strong, perfect hand. The hand grew claws, frosted talons of glass shining under the glare of streetlights. Memories of the city poured in. The steep-roofed houses of the tourist quarter beneath the summer's vast peerless canopy of sky, chipped, flaking, and cracking into the abysmal, constant darkness of winter. Newspapers and discarded syringes, their tell-tale orange caps frozen in dingy snowbanks, churned under the sidewalk plows along with the rest of the avenue's filth. Memories of lines of powder on the varnished coffee table, like a dusting of spilled eyeshadow or some strange imported seasoning arranged in rows on the cramped counter next to the sink.

"I want you to understand you don't have to punish yourself for what happened to C.S. It's not your fault, Basil. There's an epidemic ..." The lulling cadence of Mother Irin's voice shattered Baz's nightmarish reverie.

Baz turned their attention to the advisor, their eyes dull. "It was in the Twins, C.S. said. He found it mud larking." Releasing their grip on the chair, Baz stared up at the firelight dancing across the tin ceiling. The library rocked as if it was sinking so very quietly to the bottom of the sea. "But that was a lie. C.S. never was much for getting his hands dirty." Emotion fluttered in Baz's chest like a restless bird and then stilled. "Maybe he did, maybe he fell in, but I can't imagine him climbing down there with the sharp rocks and the ice and the tires the truckers dump in there. They still make you get shots at the hospital if you fall in. He hated anything medical..." Baz wearily turned their head to look at Irin. The room steadied as the priestess returned Baz's gaze. "It all started when he brought that rock home. I told him it wasn't as special as he thought. It looked cast, not carved, not like a museum piece. But he insisted it was his ancient treasure. Probably picked it up at a gallery sale. Some sculptor he was flirting with." The artist curled forward, cupping their clammy hands against their ears. "Holy Mother, why did it have to kill him?" Sobs wracked the artist's body. The migraine blossomed, cracking like thunder, and the halos fractured the world into hazy, jagged slivers.

Irin reached to comfort Baz. "It wasn't your fault, Basil." Her tone kind and sad, Irin ran her hands over the artist's shoulders. "The Holy Mother would not want you to suffer so. The Saint's words will give you comfort. Will you pray with me now?"

As Baz's voice joined Irin's in prayer, the firelight flared. The light leaped across the carpet to stretch up toward the tin ceiling and trace the rivulets of designs imprinted there. The gilt titles of books caught the flickering glow. Behind the armchairs, the bookshelves appeared to stretch and writhe. Outside, the wind picked up. The soughing whispers murmuring and creaking through the pines as the night winds began to howl in earnest.

☾

Ky woke with a shout and fought back the uncanny sensation of being someone else. The speakers in his living room hummed. The playlist had ended long ago.

EIGHT

ANIMATED NEON BLOSSOMS opened and closed on the sign above the pleasure house, casting the sidewalk below in bursts of garish pink. Stepping out of the limo, Aych finished their cigarette and surveyed the twelve-story hotel. Golden light spilled from the window casings, strings of bauble lights concealing the tacky tropical-themed rooms behind the original windows. A steady stream of couples and trios entered The Jewel's arched entrance while a trickle of solitary humans used the more discreet side door.

Shutting the passenger door behind Aych, the driver shared an amused look with them. "Call me when you want to run back to the Velvet." The woman glanced at The Jewel. "I know it's traditional to wish you satisfaction and happiness, but I think I'd better wish you health and safety. You keeping up with your shots?"

"Don't worry, Daisey, I'll take a shower before I get back in the car."

"The car I can clean. Just don't bring anything back to the Velvet ... and I don't mean their towels, if you catch my drift."

Shaking their head, Aych flipped up a hand and started for the gaudy entrance. A bright-eyed attendant rushed to open the door. Inside, the mirrored lounge was full of scantily-clad sex workers chatting up potential clients. Attendants with trays of cocktails plied the guests while dark-suited security staff watched from the periphery. Over the chatter and clink of glassware, the sound system thumped out an endless mix of high-energy dance music. The annas and their clients negotiated through shouting and lewd gestures before finalizing arrangements.

Aych inhaled the mix of flesh, cosmetics, and chemical highs with disgust. *Be better off eating out of a trash can.* They waited.

After a few moments, a tall, graceful woman in a sheath dress and glittering gems approached, her regal stride closing the distance between them. Two of the suited staff members trailed in her wake, though Aych got the impression they were more ceremonial than protective. The guards stared at Aych from a few paces behind the woman.

"Welcome. I'm Legae." The woman's surgically modified voice cut through the background noise. "We are honored to have you visit The Jewel." She made an elegant gesture toward the back of the lounge. "Arrangements have been made for only vegetarian dishes to be served to you and your entourage, per your request. Our best and most delightful flowers are waiting for you in the VIP area."

Aych kept their smile to human standards and offered Legae their arm. "I'm all yours." The scent of artificial hormones rose from the woman's skin like an exotic hothouse perfume. The traces of Legae's feminizing surgical procedures were so subtle that Aych was barely able to spot the fine scars under her makeup.

Legae pressed her body against Aych. "As you've requested an ensemble, I'm sad to say I'm not joining tonight's festivities. I only preach solo. You understand." She smiled apologetically and the lights of the lounge reflected off the sparkling gems in her ears and at her throat. Her warm regard swept over Aych; her practiced expression of desire was skillful enough to seem genuine. "I'd be flattered to be included in any future one-on-one requests."

Aych gazed into Legae's eyes. Under the synthetic aroma, the woman smelled deliciously healthy and clean. Strict vegetarian and a non-drinker, most likely a means to preserve her youthful looks, given her profession. The familiar pang of hunger roused first and started to sharpen as Aych's salivatory glands ached. The roots of their teeth throbbed as the need to rip into human meat cramped their stomach. "Oh, I've no doubt I'll want to see you again. Alone." Legae's flesh would be succulent and tender. *Fall right off the bone.*

"I'm certain it would be my pleasure." The anna dipped her head, the pulse in her neck slow and steady as they walked through the crowd.

Security unhooked the flimsy chain to let their group pass into the onyx vault of the VIP lounge. Under swirling lights, dancers paraded on and off individual stages while clients in the round private booths watched their undulating bodies. Legae directed Aych to a large seating area next to the

A Holy Venom

main stage and nodded to her escort. The two staff members waited for them to be seated and then bowed before departing.

Legae leaned into Aych. "I hope you will make him suffer," she whispered sensually, her light tone belying the anger flickering in her eyes. "He's *vik* and endangering us all." She laughed and shook her head, as if flirting.

Aych raised the human's hand to their lips and locked eyes with her. "It will be worse than anything you can imagine." The dull ache in their chest made this gentle gesture an act of great self-control.

She sighed and smiled. "In that case, I will definitely owe you a favor."

Kissing her knuckles, Aych felt their throat tighten in response to her proximity and warmth. They let their teeth graze her skin ever so slightly. The temptation to taste was crowding the back of their tongue. "Let's hope so." Aych slipped the black marker out of their suit jacket and held it out between two fingers.

Legae accepted the card and looked up as a string of decadently attired humans appeared at their table. "And now, here are your companions for the evening. Our very best. I hope you will find their company pleasing."

Keeping her hand in theirs, Aych languidly glanced over at the people posing for review and approval. The sickly-sweet scent of Rot rolled off the youthful flesh, along with an onslaught of competing colognes and perfumes. Mixed into it was the warming perfume of excitement and desire. One of the young women in particular gave off a lush flavor of exquisite fear and arousal.

Aych waved her over. "What's your name?" The violet blue of the young woman's eyes reminded them of small flowers that appear first under the spring snow in the Hunting Grounds. The human slid into the booth, her heartbeat so rapid as to shiver the air. *An armful of purity in a place like this.*

"Em. My name is Em." The sex worker lowered her long lashes. "It's an honor to meet you—we've all heard so much about you. You honor our house tonight with your visit."

The smell of her skin was punctuated with fear and pheromones. Aych could feel her trembling, as if at any moment she might faint. *Pure, but not psychic. But what then to be so afraid of and aroused by me?* Aych whispered into her ear. "Do you want me to fuck you with the rest, or save you for later tonight when we can be alone?"

Her eyes widened. She put her small, delicate hand under the table and stroked Aych's thigh. "Alone, if I could have my wish …"

Ah. This is how she greets her death when she sees it. Aych leaned back toward Legae. "I'd like to reserve Em for later. As a reward. When I can take my time and not put on a show."

Legae dipped her head and smiled approvingly at the younger woman. "I'm delighted one of ours made a good impression. I shall arrange that. What of the others?"

Aych appraised the annas and leaned back. "All of them look quite satisfying."

"I assure you, they will be." Legae stroked Aych's arm and gestured for Em to follow her. "We will see you later, then?"

"Not too much later." Aych stroked Em's thigh as she stood up. They turned their attention to the other beautiful humans awaiting introductions.

Waiters brought dishes of cooked and raw vegetables, along with numerous bottles of sparkling wine and strong spirits. Laughing, the sex workers gracefully surrounded Aych and began the work of an orchestrated group seduction.

After a suitable amount of time drinking and feeding the humans, Aych gestured to one of the nearby attendants. "If you can direct us to a suite, I think it's about time the next round of the evening began."

"Of course." They inclined their head and waved in the direction of the elevators. "We have everything set up for you."

"Can we stop by the vending machines so everyone can select their favorite toys?" Aych draped their arms around two of the more curvaceous annas.

"And preferred lube!" One of the men giggled. "Allergies, you know!"

"Right." Aych pretended to be mildly drunk and slurred their speech accordingly. "Lube, condoms, gloves, toys. What am I forgetting?"

"More booze!" one of the women roared.

The attendant smiled as the group stumbled and groped on the way into the elevator. "I believe you'll find all of those items in the suite, *Tu-lm.*"

"No cameras?" Aych leaned over them as many hands hauled them back into the elevator.

A Holy Venom

"Your privacy is assured." The attendant waited until Aych was otherwise engaged and then stepped in and selected the button for the twelfth floor.

"How many of us are there?" Aych mimed a headcount. "Six of you plus one of me. Good. It will be a new personal best to fuck all of you properly." They eyed the attendant. "I'm not sure about this one. They look a little too boring."

A jeering cheer went up from the entourage. "All of us at once?"

"Even if you are a demon, you can't please all six of us, honey. You best pick your favorites."

Aych pulled the man out of the group and into their arms. The kiss was long and lush as the elevator echoed with whoops and whistles.

With a ravenous look in their eyes, Aych released the half-swooning human. "Tonight, I'm going to make you all believers."

☾

Aych was in the shower when the humans were roused and herded out of the bedroom. They heard the complaints, groans, and sleepy protests over the water jets and through the dark marble lining the bathroom. Relishing the hot water, Aych let it sluice over their head and back as the sex workers angrily filed out of the room. Washing off the stink of humans, they smelled at last their own familiar scent and smiled. *Soon, blood and warm meat.*

Aych leisurely combed out their long mane. The sex had been entertaining, but now hunger was making sharp demands. The irritating restraint of being Little made the need to feed worse, especially with tantalizing human flesh so close. Self-restraint was necessary for the job. *But not for much longer.*

In the main room, the satin covers had been thrown over the island of a bed and the trolleys of alcohol and room service leftovers whisked away. Seated under the painting of an erotic tryst was a man just entering the prime of his life. He was overconfident and eyed Aych like a shepherd sizing up a ram. Through the sweaty, post-coital cloud, Aych could pick out the bakery-case frosting scent of a diabetic incorrectly medicated. Aych stepped out of the bathroom and tied their bathrobe sash into place.

"I suppose I could flatter you by suggesting you star in a movie, but then, that wouldn't be utilizing your real talents." Eldridge watched Aych pad barefoot across the carpet.

Yawning, Aych shrugged and settled in the wingback chair adjusting the robe. "If you want to make money off me, I'll listen so long as my cut's the biggest." *Tell me your tale, human, and I'll tell you one of mine.*

"This is about money, isn't it? You like having it to throw around. Not just this fifty, but ten times that. Tell me, what if I offered to double—no triple—whatever Violet is paying you?"

He is even more of a fool than Vee thinks. Aych whistled appreciatively and retrieved their tobacco pouch. "That much? For a couple of movies? Don't get me wrong, I like your household just fine, but that seems excessive for a few hours of handling flesh."

"Not for movies. Not for … this," Eldridge sneered at the bed. "Everyone knows Violet has you do the messy jobs that Vetch won't dirty his hands with. Why?"

"I like messy." Aych let the first drag of the pungent herbal smoke roll off their tongue. The lick of the poison dulled the hunger enough to toy with the man before absolute need kicked in. "I ask for those jobs." The hazy blue vapor filled the space between them. *Because I like playing with my food.*

Wrinkling his nose, Eldridge leaned back. "You could be doing much more, with your skill at the tables, your reputation—"

"What do you know about my reputation? What do you know about me, or anything for that matter?" Aych raised the eyebrow over their frost blue eye.

"I know you like violence and sex and winning."

Aych watched the human lose his cool. "This isn't going the way you expected it to. You know you haven't set the hook correctly, but you don't know why or how. Am I right?"

"I want us to be friends, to be family. I want you to join my house." Eldridge gestured at the hotel room door. "I had my people give us privacy so we could come to an understanding. Alone. To show I trust you, that you can trust me. Whatever you want, just ask and I'll make it happen. Like I said, I want us to be friends."

"You don't want to be my friend." Aych inspected the glowing end of the cigarette's ember and then glanced over. *And your bodyguards are long gone—called away by a woman who hates your guts—ensuring there's no one outside that door to hear you scream for help.* "You don't know anything about me. You're here because people are scared of me and you want them to be scared of you."

"You're right. People are scared of you. But I'm not." Eldridge sniffed. "I wasn't born in Grava, I didn't come from one of the inbred, old imperial families there. I was born here in this city, a foreigner from outside of any household—like you. Violet thinks I'm just one of the flock putting on airs, but I'm—"

"It's good you're proud of being from here," Aych cut Eldridge off. "Of being an outsider." They tapped the cigarette on a forgotten plate left on the side table.

Surprised and unsettled, Eldridge dropped his hands to his knees and peered at Aych. "Aren't you? It makes us different. The southerners use us, but don't want us in charge …"

Ignoring the man's attempt to bond over geographic and temporal misconceptions, Aych smiled. "There's a story about this city. About before the city even existed, when it was still a village in the mountains. The High Priestess told it to a friend of mine, and she told it to me. It's about the Shepherd. Want to hear it?"

The man scoffed. "Saint Anna and the Shepherd, of course I know it. Every child here has heard that story. Tourists hear it when they tour the Basilica and see the sacred fountain."

"This one is even older, and most people haven't heard it. Not the southerners, not the locals. The only record of it might be in the Church archives, written in the Saint's own hand. It's that ancient. You're proud of being from here, but you've never heard this story. Shall I tell it to you?" Aych watched the human. "Would you like to hear how the Shepherd came to be?"

Eldridge gave a short laugh. "You want to tell me a story, now? Here?" He lifted his hands and stretched his arms along the back of the couch. "Shouldn't we be discussing a deal? What you want, what I want, how we will take the city for our own?"

"Haven't you ever wondered about where the name of our shared vocation comes from? Why people call us shepherds?"

Irritated, Eldridge exhaled. *"Annas have to preach and shepherds have to punish.* Again, every child—"

"You know the idiom, but not what it means." Aych shook their head. "If you don't know the story it came from, how can you or anyone else understand what it means to be a shepherd? You want me to believe you can run this city?" Aych took a long drag off their cigarette. "You're an ignorant, ambitious child playing a game you don't even understand."

"Fine, tell me your damn story." The human rolled his eyes at the ceiling. "You want me to understand what it means to be a shepherd, the stale code of leading the flock."

"I do want you to understand. I want you to listen like your life depends on it. Will you do that? Can you listen like that?" Aych ground the cigarette out on the plate and glanced over.

"I'll listen and then we'll make a deal?"

"You'll listen without interrupting, and yes, then we can make a deal."

"Go ahead, then." Eldridge waved his hand. "Tell me your bedtime story."

✱

Long ago, before the city existed, the mountain was here.

People were here too, living below the mountain in the foothills, in a village. The name of the village is long gone, its ancient stones long shifted from the shoulders of the mountain to the houses and paddock walls that were moved again to build the Holy Mother's first church here. But this story is older than that, older than the Church, older than the story of the Saint and her passion and her promise, or even why she gave both to the Shepherd. This is the story of how the Shepherd came to be and why all right-minded people are afraid of the mountain and this city. Why people remember to fear black dogs that come in the night but don't remember why ... or who those dogs serve.

Just like now, the winter then was harsh. The villagers worked together to survive the long, hard, cold months and struggled in the short summer to fatten their flocks. Crops were difficult to grow on the slopes and tricky to keep from failing. But the soil was rich from manure and the thaws kept the grass green. The

A Holy Venom

mountain pastures were fertile and so too the sheep, fat and healthy. The Twin Rivers wended through the trees and joined at the foot of the mountain then, and those same rivers still remember the lost village now.

It was the tradition to keep all the livestock in common in the summer months up in the high pastures and bring them down to the village near the water in the autumn and through the winter, until the spring lambing. For the high mountain was treacherous, full of wild beasts and ill winds that brought sickness. Lambing season was always dangerous, and so tending to the ewes and keeping them close for human aid was an important task.

After the lambs were born, the children of the village old enough for the chore herded the sheep up the mountain to the spring pastures. Laughing and free, they went with the village dogs up the sides of the mountain, sharing the work and cheerful company. The youngest ones staying below were sent halfway up once a week to leave bread and cheese, or whatever the adults could spare. This was the way of things for countless generations. In the autumn, when the winds grew chill and the winter Gales closed in, the grown and wild children would return with the sheep and the dogs, parading through the village into the arms of their families and envious younger siblings. So it was, and so the village always thought it would be.

Now, one year an inexplicable illness came on the heels of winter after the Gales, taking with it the very old and the very young. So many died that there was no laughter and no song when the flocks went up the mountain. Heavy was the earth with mounds of stones over the dead and heavy were the tasks left to the living. Families worried for their children on the mountain; would they be safe? Would the sickness come again? So great was the loss of the young that the adults had to bring the bread and cheese and often had no time to undertake the chores of the village while caring for those high up on the mountain. Hard-pressed, and without the guidance of the lost elders, the parents longed to see the faces of their surviving children, and so they made excuse after excuse to call them back. Family by family, they justified this son or that daughter or that child back from the summer pastures needed for the work of the village.

This went on until only one boy remained on the mountain with the dogs. All of his family had been taken by the sickness and there were none to miss his face or worry over him or call him back. So, he stayed on the mountain, without the other children, through the long summer nights, warmed by the fire he built with his own hands and the company of the dogs. No one thought to bring him bread or cheese, no one thought of his loneliness, no one thought of him at all except that he was there and capable, for surely the dogs did most of the work.

The boy tried to understand. He missed his family and the company of the other children. He missed the herding songs, which never sounded the same when sung by only one voice. He tried to understand, and he tried to focus on keeping the dogs fed and the sheep safe. But the mountain was a treacherous place for a lone human. Strange winds blew through the crags, and weird howls rose from the caves. The ravens and the crows tried to keep the boy company and warn him of the dangers that come in the night, but he worried they were after the sheep and paid their urgent caws no mind. The dogs worried too and kept close by the boy. They knew their duty to the flock and to the village and this one child left alone on the high slopes of the mountain.

Spring went and the summer drew to an end. The days grew shorter, and the boy was relieved to be soon going back to the village. He knew his childhood home would be empty and sad, but in his naivety, he thought perhaps another family might welcome him. Might he not have earned praise for his bravery? He caught wild hares to feed the dogs and foraged edible plants for himself; he feasted on the sweet summer berries that grew on the high slopes and drank from the freezing cold streams. He found joy in the dogs' playful games and relief in the work of tending to the sheep's silly plights and minor ailments. He tried to love and he tried to understand. Most of all he tried to live.

Now, had the eldest of the villagers still been alive, they would have warned against any human being left alone on the mountain for too long. For they knew there were worse things than those beasts that killed and ate sheep in the high places—evil things lurking, plotting, waiting, in the dark places and caverns burrowing deep under the mountain. The elders would have berated their grown children who dared to call themselves adults and threatened to drag their tired bones out of bed and up the steep paths to fetch the boy and bring him back to the village. Such was the wisdom and kindness lost after the long winter of sickness.

Indeed, those dark and evil things watched the boy and his dogs more than they watched the sheep. They watched his struggles to understand and grew delighted when he stumbled. The worst of them, the great, bitter wind that caused sickness and hated all the humans who dared traverse the mountain or the foothills below or any part of the earth, watched the boy most closely. And so it was in the

A Holy Venom

late nights of summer that the ill wind blew out of the caverns and circled the boy's hut. She listened to his dreams and blew into his ears, giving him night terrors until he knew naught but trembling and fear.

Waking in the night, huddled with the dogs, the boy would think of checking for danger—of checking for wolves. Wolves, the lean hunters of the mountain, left the flocks alone in the warm months, preferring the red-tailed deer in the forests below. In the winter they might come near to the village, smelling the easily hunted penned-up sheep, but in the summer, they were only stories told to scare the youngest children new to the mountain.

The ill wind listened to the boy's fears and learned and shaped herself into a great, shadowy, nightmare thing of a wolf with glowing red eyes. At night, she howled and tore up the sheep, leaving the carcasses to scare the boy. She injured a dog so that the boy was forced to end his beloved friend's suffering, a decision that tormented the boy. Every night the monstrous wolf circled the boy's hut and howled. Every day the boy found grief and loss in the pastures, bloody and maimed.

One night, the boy, sleep-deprived and half-mad with anger and sadness, burst out of the hut. He carried a torch and his knife. He shouted, "Come then, kill me! But know I will kill you!"

The giant wolf came then and she circled in the shadows where the torchlight never reached. Her red eyes glowed and her rough, raw voice growled. "Why are you on my mountain, boy? Why are you here with your dogs and your sheep? Are you not afraid I will kill you and eat you?"

Afraid and angry, the boy replied, "No! I'm here to protect my village's flock, so we might have food in the winter."

The wolf laughed her rough laugh and her great eyes glowed ruby and scarlet. "Your village? They have forgotten you. You think they will welcome you back? I will slaughter your sheep, and your dogs, and you, and they will forget you ever lived. They will only mourn the sheep and the dogs."

The words of the she-wolf stung the boy. "They will not, they will come for me and they will kill you."

"Oh child, they could not even remember to bring you bread and cheese. They do not care if you live or die. They only care if their own children live, not you. Not you. They have forgotten you."

"You lie." Even as he spoke, the boy feared the she-wolf was right, that the villagers had forgotten him.

"Come then, see with your own eyes. I will carry you on my back and you shall see."

"You will eat me up."

"I will eat you up anyway, but first let us see which one of us is right."

And so the boy dropped his torch, and leaving his dogs to guard the flock, he got on the back of the giant she-wolf, who was really the ill wind of the mountain. And like the wind, she carried him down and down the slopes of the dark mountain to the village.

They looked into the windows of each and every house and in each the boy saw it was true. The children and their parents had forgotten him. In beds asleep safely, or laughing around the hearths, the villagers carried on happily without a moment of grief or worry for their sheep or the boy or even the loyal dogs high up on the mountain.

The sadness in the boy swelled and his anger grew and grew as they went from house to house. The she-wolf felt him getting heavier and heavier on her back and licked her lips, for she knew despair would make his meat that much sweeter. When they had looked in the windows of the last house, empty and cold and full of dust, for it was the boy's own, it was no longer a boy she carried but an angry young man.

Up and up, she carried him back to the sheep and his dogs. His anger swelled as he thought of villagers laughing and singing lullabies to their children. He thought of the young people he had witnessed kissing and thought of the lips that would never brush butterfly soft against his.

"Now we know who was lying and who was telling the truth." The she-wolf set him down amongst his dogs and laughed. "Now, I shall eat you up."

"No," said the angry young man. "You will not."

The she-wolf laughed. "How can you stop me? Neither your knife, nor your fire, nor your dogs can harm me."

"No, they cannot," the man said. "But my anger is greater than you and I can devour you in one bite. You killed my sheep and my dogs, and so I will punish you the same way. I will pierce your flesh with my teeth."

"Try it," said the wolf, still laughing. Who had ever heard of such a thing as a man eating a wolf, let alone eating an evil spirit?

But the young man had grown from a boy on that mountain. He had eaten the wild hares and the wild plants and drunk deeply from the wild streams. He

A Holy Venom

was as much of the mountain as the ill wind. And so knowing magic in his own wordless way, he opened his mouth as wide as he could. "My anger is greater than your ill will and I shall have both."

And so, he inhaled, and inhaled and inhaled with all his might, drawing in the wind in her wolf shape, until he had indeed eaten her all up. But she was a thing of magic, and the man had her inside of him and the two mingled. His anger and her hatred, his flesh and her spirit, until there was only one that was both and neither.

They howled and howled and howled until the villagers below heard the terrible noise and the dogs lay on their bellies and the sheep huddled in fear.

Down and down, they went, as one—something between a wolf and boy, a man and an ill wind. Not either, but all. They went down the mountain and brought their terrible punishment upon the village. That night the houses were full of blood and terror, and none escaped the anger and hatred that came down upon them.

In the morning, the one who was no longer alone fed their dogs strange meat and drove the sheep into the caverns of the mountain. And so they lived, going in and out of the mountain, growing blacker and blacker until the dogs were as black as coal and the sheep blacker than night. Eventually, the ill wind was indeed consumed, devoured by the one who had been only a lonely boy. He punished any who stepped foot on the mountain until the day the Saint came to beg for the healing water of the sacred spring hidden within the mountain.

But that is a story for another time.

☾

Eldridge yawned. "So, the Shepherd was driven mad by the mountain. Not a very good story. I can see why no one tells it."

Aych walked over to the couch and put their face above Eldridge's. "You are not one of the dogs, but only a villager living below the mountain, and you have forgotten this fact." They grabbed the man by the throat and pulled him up off the couch.

Gasping for air, Eldridge clawed at Aych's hand. Watching the human thrash, Aych drew their arm back and threw the man In Between. Eldridge vanished from the suite and Aych stepped through after him, the rip in reality sealing behind them.

Eldridge lay stunned against the trunk of an ancient, craggy tree. Gusts of cold air billowed between the trunks and carried the coppery scent of blood through the Silent Woods. Barefoot in the hotel bathrobe, Aych walked through the snow and prodded the man with their toes until Eldridge's eyelids flickered.

The waning sickle moon hung above the ancient forest, unchanging and unmoving, the amber shape shedding no light. The crystalline snow spat and swept between the cursed trees drifting over the human's legs.

"I've got a date with a beautiful woman who wants to die and it would be rude to keep her waiting." Aych bent and slapped Eldridge on both cheeks. "Let's get this over with."

Moaning, the human opened his eyes and flinched from the shock of pain in his wounded head.

"Not quite ripe, but I've just the thing." With a puckish smile, Aych undid the sash of their bathrobe and let the garment fall into the snow.

Disoriented, Eldridge glanced around. "What? Where …" Desperation tinged his words. "Help me …"

"I should think not." Letting go of being Little, Aych stretched themselves. The white skin ripped and tore as the blackish-gray smoke within hardened and lengthened. Their mouth distending and jutted, the fangs erupting from elongated jaws. Aych's eyes burned sapphire and molten gold as they glared at the man.

Eldridge could only stare at the horror coalescing before him. The cracking sounds of bones breaking, the half groans of pleasure and pain, the monster dripping obsidian ichor and oozing bloody fluid terrified him. Whatever instinct to run he might have possessed vaporized as the mismatched gaze of the monster nailed him against the tree.

Relief and pleasure followed the anguish, the perfect release of pressure from the confines of being Little. As the rolling transformation hardened and rippled fur across muscle and new skin formed between, Aych slowed the release of their change. Slower and slower until every claw, every inch of hide and fang was in place. The desire to expand lingered, the temptation to grow and become Bigger sizzled from their tail to their ear tips. *Let go, let go, let go and devour everything. Don't stop! Advance, advance, ADVANCE!*

A Holy Venom

The human gibbered, the man's mind splintered by the magic of the reveal. Aych stroked his hair, their claws now wet with fresh blood. Around them the trees whispered, the scent of human suffering flying on the frozen wind—calling.

"Not quite enough misery to satisfy everyone," Aych's unmodified voice rumbled from their chest. "An easy death would disappoint Legae, if not Violet." They raked their claws over Eldridge's face, the tips rupturing the supple orbs of the human's eyes, blood and viscous fluid cascading down his chest.

The man's screams echoed as the aroma of fresh available meat dripped from his wounds. Blinded and sobbing, the human curled up into a ball, exposing his back. Aych inhaled the delicious scents and howled a long, drawn-out summons. From deep in the forest another howl erupted, angry and challenging. The ground began to quake and the snow sifted in ripples as some Other approached at a tremendous speed.

"There, now. That's all arranged." Aych bent and slipped a bloody claw tip through the loop of the discarded bathrobe. "You'll be torn apart soon enough and I won't get yelled at for overeating." *There's tastier meat waiting for me back in the Hunting Grounds.* Aych casually slung the robe over their shoulder, smiled a true smile, and vanished.

NINE

Ky knew he was dreaming. He watched sunlight stream through eerily familiar windows, the dust motes drifting lazily in the air, and tried to remember the house. He looked around the living room. The jade plant and prickly cactus in the window, potted violets, and succulents arranged on the wire plant stand, the crocheted, pastel-colored blanket across the couch, the avocado-hued shag rug, the antique sideboard along the wall, a colorful bowl of fruit meticulously arranged in its center. It was strange but familiar to him, half-remembered, a fabricated dream space combining childhood memories of neighbors' homes and other houses he had passed through.

He looked at the brass clock face hanging above the sideboard. The second hand moved in an orderly fashion as he marked the position of the minute and hour hands. He glanced at the brass and nickel faceplate of the antique radio and noted the tuning marker was set in the high eighties, then looked back. The clock face remained the same as it had been, only the minute hand progressed to a further position. Surprised by the dream's linear consistency, he reached out and laid his fingertips on the mahogany sideboard. The wood was warmer in the sun, cooler out of it. He dragged a finger through the dust around the base of the fruit bowl, leaving a clean trail on the wooden surface. Ky picked up a banana from the top of the arranged fruit. The fruit was soft and smooth, entirely real to his touch, and gave off a sugary, rotten aroma that mingled with the cigarette smell emanating from the nicotine-stained walls. He glanced at the photos lining the room. They were of faces and places he recognized, but a composite of misplaced memories. He scanned the room again, trying to note any presence or purpose in his surroundings, but it was disturbingly quiet.

Resting a hand on his chest, Ky found his heartbeat. His pajama bottoms were the ones he remembered putting on in the waking world and his body looked as he expected it, scarred and aged. Bemused, he walked down the hall leading out of the living room. He passed the bathroom—tiled in robin's egg blue—and the den—full of old sports trophies and dusty bookshelves—and the details crept into his memory. A single-family home, all one level, bric-a-brac of emerald glass sherbet cups in the hutch standing next to the swing door into the kitchen, and at the end of the hall, the bedrooms. More photos, sun-faded, of faces he half-remembered but could not place. A house staged and created as if it were entirely real. Never would anyone replace a light bulb, or shit, or masturbate, or go to bed drunk here. Only his absolute sense that this was a construct kept him from believing he was awake. A house, yes, but never a home.

He opened the door to the first bedroom and found four child-sized beds, each perfectly made, with the sheet top folded over the edge of a worn, fuzzy wool blanket. The pillowcases were vintage, washed countless times, the floral linens matching the sheets. A colorful rag rug lay between the beds. He caught sight of the bookcase. The books were all fairytales. He opened a book and the words were well-ordered and legible, the usual dream jumble missing. Ky bent and took another one off the shelf. Opening it, he could read the words. The pictures of the familiar childhood tale remained unchanged as he turned a page and then flipped it back to check it again. If he was in a dream, he would expect the text and the illustrations to be unstable. *The clever kitten carried off the butter dish...*

A large shadow glided by the open bedroom door.

"Hello?" Ky called, dropping the book. He rushed to the hall. "Hello?"

In the living room, a stranger stood with his back to Ky, looking out of the large picture window into the yard. "Hello yourself, gorgeous," the figure replied, not turning. Ky frowned. The voice was masculine and familiar.

"Is this your house?" Ky asked as the man's shadow cut a cool line across the ray of sunlight.

The stranger turned. Ky took an instinctive step backward as he beheld his own scarred face looking back at him. His double smiled. He wore an expensive suit, tie, and dress shirt, all in the same inky black hue. "No and yes." The double's voice was Ky's own—as it sounded in his skull—his

A Holy Venom

internal voice, not the timbre of his recorded voice. "I have no house in this wild wood to call my own."

"We're not in a forest." Ky glanced at the yard outside.

"That's only an illusion. Look out the front door and you'll see."

Ky went back in the hall. His double appeared in the bedroom doorway and smiled as Ky passed, the corners of his mouth grotesquely stretching to his ears. Sunlight streamed through the three diagonal window panels of the front door. Ky set his hand on the brass knob and turned it. The metal was cold enough to burn. He glanced over his shoulder. The man had moved and now leaned casually against the open doorway of the den.

"Open it," the stranger indicated with a languid hand.

The brass knob was freezing. An icy wind blew in around the sides of the door as Ky slowly opened it. Before him, the night sky was a black bowl, and an amber sickle moon hung over a cursed forest of bare and angry trees. The ancient, unchanging crescent was an uncanny shade of rust but cast no trails of light on the shadowed forest below.

Ky frantically shoved the door closed. "Where is this place?"

"The Silent Woods. You remember that much, don't you? The House in the Woods that lies In Between."

"In Between." The words curdled in Ky's mouth. "The House in the Wood." Dread crept up his spine and the sunlight coming through the windows dimmed. "The House of Sorrow in the Silent Woods..."

"That's right. You remember. You've been here before." The double turned his head in the direction of the far end of the house. He looked back at Ky, pity in his eyes. "If you escaped, why the fuck would you ever risk coming back?"

The question made Ky sick to his stomach. "To make sure it was true. That I wasn't still trapped here, only imagining I was free." The sudden uncontrollable fear made Ky shake. His feet were glued to the rug, the itchy strands worming between his toes. He stared at the kitchen door and awful memories loomed in his mind. He could feel the sweat on his skin despite the wintry air. His stomach clenched and his heart pounded. *The kitchen...* he remembered the horrors inside it.

"Your bones ground for flour to bake bread. Your blood to wet the dough, your meat for the pot, and..."

"Your heart for dessert." Ky remembered the story of the clever kitten he had found in the bedroom. The kitten had escaped ... but *he* was still here and the kitchen was still here. "All to feed the Owner." Even as he spoke, Ky knew he had fucked up by completing the phrase out loud.

The house darkened and grew frigid, all the heat drained at once. Shadows slipped and coiled from the pictures on the walls. Ky now understood the precisely detailed furnishings were the bait in a trap now slamming closed.

"Oh dear." The double set his hand on his chin, feigning concern. "I suspect you've done it now. You're so fucked. She'll catch you, you know. Even if you cut her head off, it will roll right back on, as loyal as a dog. Then it will all start over again, won't it? Nothing in here will harm her and you've brought nothing to trade. She'll eat you, marrow and all. Poor boy."

The House began to change. The colors and textures dripping off into the corners and crevices as the walls stretched up into the elongating roof beams.

"Shit." Ky spun around and grabbed the doorknob.

The door opened and he tumbled out into the snow. Overhead, enormous wings rushed through the trees, blotting out the moon. The House was heaving and rising, drawing boulders from under the snow. The stones rippled from beneath the ground and floated up to join the towering walls as the structure grew. The House's transformation became deafening.

"You have two minutes on the clock." Leaning in the doorway, his black suit drinking in the light from the interior, the other tapped his wristwatch and shouted over the din. "Do you think you can manage it? Before the Owner catches you? If not, you'll end up in the Pot."

Ky tried to find a direction to run. The ground reverberated. At the edge of the darkness of the Woods, the trees shook, sending clouds of snow drifting to the ground. Howling, growling, and yowling filled the air. He remembered the enormous shadow against the moon and knew other monsters were loose in the Silent Woods.

"How do I get out of here?" The terror of unseen enemies and the awful knowledge of being eaten alive for all of eternity pressed in on him. Panic seized his heart. The scars on his torso seared and burned, the flesh cooking all over again. He smelled the scent of roasting meat wafting from the

A Holy Venom

chimney, the marrow in the bones roasting in the stove. Dead children being cooked after suffering unimaginable horrors. All of it came flooding back to him. The years and hours mingling into an endless cycle of repeating nightmares.

The double bent down and brought his face next to Ky's. "You got out before. Or maybe you didn't? Maybe your whole life since then was a dream and you've always been here. Perhaps you never left. Can you recall how you got out, child? Did you ever truly leave?"

The pain vanished. Surprised, Ky looked down and found he was a boy again. A stranger with a different face leaned over him, their skin as white as the snow and their eyes glowing, one amber like the moon the other witch-fire blue.

"I remember you. Help me," Ky heard himself say in a child's voice. His tiny hand reached for the stranger. "Before they come, before they take me back. Please. I don't want to die in there. Don't let them eat me." He trembled.

The stranger knelt and wiped away his tears. "I will help you only this once and never again. Because you asked, I will help you. But you will owe me. Remember that."

Ky felt his heart ache. Glancing down, he saw blood welling up, staining his pajama top. The warm wetness ran along his stomach and dripped onto the snow. The stranger wrapped their arms around him and whispered into his hair. Ky could not understand what they were saying. He only heard the soothing lilt of their voice and the cadence of the words. But he *felt* the message: *It would all be alright, it would all end and he would wake up and would be safe.*

Ky woke with a gasp. The ache in his chest lingered as he glanced at the radiator at the foot of the bed. Steam hissed and the metal pipes rattled.

The dream faded in the dark of the bedroom. Trying to keep ahold of it, he got up and headed into the living room. He ran his fingers over the stacks of albums in the milk crates. Whenever an album shuddered under his fingertip, he pried it out of the stack and went on to find the next. The countersignal brushed up through his fingertips until he had removed an armful of records. Placing them on top of the speaker next to the stereo, he opened a case of cassette tapes waiting for the countersignal to prompt additional selections. When it failed to do so, he flipped on the living room lights and went into the kitchen to make coffee.

☾

Alone in the Magnolia suite, Em paced from the bedside table to the door and back. She ran her hands over the satin slip anxiously. When the knock came, it was soft, almost inaudible.

"Who is it?" She leaned against the door and looked out the peephole.

"Room service." Aych's voice carried through the wood, amused and low.

"Come in. I wasn't sure if you'd be coming by tonight." Unhooking the safety latch, Em stepped back.

Sizing up the smaller hotel suite and the nervous human inside it, Aych inclined their head. "Legae suggested I might have a nightcap with you." They glanced at her satin nightgown. "Maybe I'll tuck you in and then see myself out."

"No, stay. Unless you're tired." She poured two drinks and offered one to Aych, her trained hands steady despite the anxiety wafting off her. "I know you had business to take care of, and there was the party earlier. You don't have to visit with me if you don't want."

"I wanted to see you." Aych gazed at her face. The human's aroma of fear, arousal, and excitement knotted every muscle in their throat and chest. Impatience and hunger flared simultaneously. Throwing back the drink, the alcohol burned, numbed their throat and dissipated too soon. The ache remained and they moved closer sliding a hand along the woman's thigh and hip, touching the hem of her satin nightie. "And you wanted to see me, didn't you?"

"I did." Em lowered her lashes and then stared up with the same desperate look she had earlier. "I want to ask you for a favor, but I'm afraid you'll say no."

"Try me." Aych pressed closer. Setting the empty glass on the bar, they ran their thumb along her jaw. "Might be I'm interested in it too, whatever your proposition entails."

"Unlikely." Turning her head away, the woman slid her fingers into

A Holy Venom

Aych's. "You'll think I'm sick, maybe. Disgusting. Maybe tell Legae I'm no good."

Aroused, Aych bent and kissed her collarbone. "I doubt there's anything you want that would surprise me. Try me." She tasted of soap and flowers, clean with a rare sweetness that lingered on the tongue. *Lu would surely want to taste this one.*

Em turned away abruptly. "They say you kill people. That you'll do it for money or for favors. Is it true?" She took a drink.

Aych gently turned Em back to face them and let their teeth graze her shoulder, pressing slightly on the bone beneath. Moving their lips against the fluttering pulse in her neck, they murmured. "Yes." Blood moved under Aych's skin along all the compressed nerves imposed by their Little form. Aroused and starving from multiple transformations, they struggled to maintain the knife edge of control.

"Anyone? Anyone at all?"

"Yes." They licked the sweet skin along her throat and whispered in her ear. "Is there someone that hurt you?" Drawing her face closer, Aych gazed into her eyes. "Someone you want murdered?"

"Yes." Em stared back. Her voice trembled and the scent of fear blossomed. "I want you to kill me."

As I thought. "Why would a healthy, beautiful young person like yourself want that?" Aych released her and reached for the decanter. Pouring another drink, they moved aside and watched the anna from the corner of their eye. "I'd understand if you wanted to get away from here. Try another city, another life. But just outright die?" They set the crystal topper back into place and raised the full glass to their lips. "I don't understand."

"Haven't you ever wanted to end it? To be done with the never-ending sameness?" Em wrung her hands and resumed pacing.

"It's never the same for me. And no, I haven't." *Play it out, make yourself wait, let her sell you on it.*

"You think I'm crazy, that I should check myself into the Statler and let them make me want to live, don't you?" The woman stopped with her back to Aych and spoke over her shoulder. "You think I have every reason to want to live, but I don't."

Aych closed the distance between them and dropped their mouth to her bare shoulder. "Explain it to me so I can understand," they murmured against her skin. They tormented themselves with the need to rend and tear and let their desire for the human ripen that much more.

"I've always hated being alive." Sighing, Em relaxed back into Aych's arms. "Some days, some nights, weren't bad. I've had fun, moments of real happiness. But the feeling comes back. I feel trapped. It doesn't matter where I go. I'm not running from pain, or from effort, but existence itself. I want to be free." She looked up, her eyes desperate.

"Trapped by what, exactly?" Aych lifted Em's arm and brought her fingers to their lips. "By your job, your family, other people's expectations?" Each gentle kiss was an act of willpower, each time they released the human an act of self-restraint.

"No, none of that." The woman rested her head against Aych. "This body, this skin, waking up every day."

"It's the middle of winter. When spring comes, there will be flowers and birdsong. Won't you miss all that?" *Bones cracking and marrow spilling hot and sweet...*

With a sad smile, Em looked up into Aych's eyes. "No."

"Why haven't you killed yourself then? Why ask me?"

"Oh, I suppose I'm a coward. I don't want to do a bad job and end up stuck here but unable to get out." She gave a little laugh. "I'd rather hire an expert to make sure ..." Twisting in Aych's arms, Em clutched them. "Oh please, won't you help me? I've got to get out of here, out of this life. Haven't you ever felt so low you wanted to die? It's like that, only it never ends and it's never going to end until I stop breathing ..."

"I have bad days, but I don't want to chuck it all in and shuffle myself off."

She pushed herself away and sat heavily on the bed. "No, I don't suppose you wouldn't. I imagine you cheer yourself up and go right on with living." Her eyes flashed with pain and something akin to anger.

Aych set their glass on the nightstand. "I enjoy killing too much. Eating, fucking, fighting, they're up there, too. Gambling, hunting, and making humans suffer never gets old." Sitting next to her on the bed, Aych pulled her closer and kissed the top of her head. "When I feel shitty, I borrow the joy of the crows and the wisdom of the ravens and promise to pay them back. Go talk to my friends. I know it's hard to believe I have any, but I do. One like you, pure and hurt by the World, and one like me, twisted with rage, and prone to hurting others as a result. If, after doing all that, I still feel low, I'll go a little crazy, indulge a little too much. Then sleep it off for a few days and pull myself together."

"You can't understand, then. What it's like to always be thinking of death, of wanting to be dead, the constant desire to just not be anything at all. To be free of being."

"Oh, I understand that fine. A friend once explained it to me. Suicide ideation, he called it. His diggers told him it was always a cry for help, but under that, it's often a misunderstanding of the desire to escape pain in the present by thinking death is a way out." Aych smiled. "I told him about a delusion called the Gambler's Fallacy, when a player on a losing streak thinks at any moment their big win is fated to happen because they can't keep on losing. It's a similar delusion, the Suicide's Fallacy, thinking your pain will only end in death, that release is the next hand you're due. You don't know what's on the other side of your death any more than you know what next week will be like, or next year, for that matter. All you know is your singular desire for the pain to end. You could be exchanging the hand you've got for a worse one, or maybe only a different hand in a new game. It's the same risk you take by waking up each day. You can leave the table but you can't stop the game."

Aych lowered Em to the bed. "And I understand you might fantasize about it, about me killing you right now. How thinking of that might be exciting, turning you on, making you wet ..." They slipped their hand between her thighs. "You might spend nights dreaming of someone killing you. But it's a fantasy. People have all kinds. Perfectly sane people get excited thinking about being ravished or even raped. But they're in control, playing it out in the safety of their imagination." Aych let their weight press against the human. "If I was to snap your neck right now, it would be all over. Quick, clean, painless. You'd get that next hand dealt to you on the other side of your death."

Em's breathing quickened and she gripped Aych's shirt. "You'd do that for me? You'd break my neck and kill me?"

Aych gently ran their fingers over the thin fabric covering her. "Now,

I'm just sweet-talking you a little, telling you what it might be like. You're excited by the fantasy and you're enjoying thinking about it while I'm touching you. If you were dead, you wouldn't feel any of this, couldn't be excited by this. It would be a one-time-only ride."

"That's what I want. Oh, please." Em tossed her head against the pillow. "Do what you want with me and when you're done, snap my neck like that. That's what I want."

"That's a fantasy. Nothing wrong with wanting the game of it. But if you want me to kill you, not play at it, you'll have to give me something in return. I don't get off on painlessly killing humans. You're asking me for something special, something I don't do. You're asking me to give you a gift and I want to know what you'll give me in return."

"Money…" Em groaned as Aych stroked her. "I can get you money…"

"I've got enough and I can get more. What do you have that no one else can give me?"

Tears filled the woman's eyes. "Anything, I'll give you anything. Just promise you'll do it. Promise you'll kill me."

"And if I tell you that once you're dead I'm going to eat you, going to tear you apart and leave this room a bloody mess, would you still want me to keep going?"

"Oh, yes, I would." Rolling her hips, Em pressed into Aych's hand. "What can I give you, what do you want?"

"If I did you my preferred way, you'd die in terror, screaming, and in the worst pain you've ever experienced." Aych murmured and kissed Em's collarbone again. "I'm not going to lie. I hate your kind. I hate humans more than you can ever understand or imagine. What you're asking is for me to be generous." Lowering their head, they licked the woman's erect nipple.

Groaning, Em squeezed her thighs together and arched her back. "But you said—the crows, you get joy from them. Won't you take mine too? Please?"

"They're better at it than you are." Aych smiled sadly. "You're ripe now, wet and wanting, but that's not joy. That's not the exuberance of life flooding out in celebration. You've got need and want to spare, but I've rooms full of those treasures."

Em clutched their arm and pulled them down into a kiss. Tears leaked

A Holy Venom

from her eyes. "If you do this for me, if you'll kill me, I'll love you for it." Her eyes shone as she tightened her grip. "Please."

A rare gift indeed. Aych brought the woman over the crest of orgasm. They felt her muscles contract and spasm as she bucked under their body. "Alright then. I'll fuck you and when you've had enough, tell me. I'll kill you, painlessly. In return, you'll love me for it. When you're dead, I'm going to eat you, except for one piece that I'll gift to a dear friend, the one who is, like you, pure and hates being in this world. Do you agree?"

"Yes."

"No safe word, no backing out. No changing your mind. If you do, I can't promise you a painless death. I'll be angry and it will hurt. You'll suffer and be afraid." They kissed the woman gently on the lips. "Last chance to change your mind and say it was all just a fantasy. All pretend."

"I want it to be real. I want you to do it. Please."

"All right. We have a deal." Aych smiled then. It was a true smile, showing all their teeth, and they rolled the rare enchantment of seduction out of their skin until Em swooned in intoxicated pleasure.

☾

Opening her bedroom door, Lu stared up into Aych's face and then stepped back, waving them inside. "Your audacity is a thing of legend. I just fell asleep. You best either be in trouble or have excellent news."

Aych waited until Lu had slid back into bed to hand her the lacquered food container. "Sweet, but not as sweet as you prefer." They went over to the window and watched the plows clearing the recent snowfall.

"Dessert could've waited." Lu opened the box and smiled at the human heart nestled among ice cubes. "For this, I might forgive you." She set the box on her bedside table and brought her knees up under the silk sheets. "You're quiet. Don't tell me you're sleepy after only eating that mouthful."

"She asked me to kill her. She offered to love me." Aych leaned against the window casing and stared at the ancient buildings higher up the slope of the city. *Dawn will catch rose in the high spires and the sky will be on fire. Two fewer humans beneath it all, by my hands. So many more to kill.*

"Did she? Odd."

"She loved the pretend human who murdered her. I could see that much. Gratitude and affection for the one who set her free. But she didn't love *me*, didn't see *me*." They looked ruefully at Lu. "You must get that kind of one-sided adoration all the time."

"Oh, yes. They love being in love." Lu linked her arms around her knees and rested her chin between them. "The grand drug, their greatest high. They will crack themselves open and spill it all out, every drop. They want the grand illusion, not the awful truth. You know that."

"I do." They lowered their gaze to the Teahouse across the street. "But it eases my disappointment hearing you say it."

"*Lu tau su vun vik,*" Lu recited. She pressed her cheek against her knee. "Only one of them is strange enough on his own to ever love you, even knowing what you are. But if you go to him and let him do just that, he'll never be free, not even when he dies. You will possess him for all of his future incarnations. That's what you're afraid of, the only thing you're afraid of. Trapping the one you love."

"You don't have to mention that part. I know I can't fuck around with his particular affliction." Aych growled. "I hate the shit-bag that's fucking with him too much to slot myself in as a replacement. I'm an unapologetic asshole, but I'm not that much of a jerk."

"Yes, you are. That's why you bring me gifts at five in the morning and use foul language in my bedroom. All so you can stare out my bedroom window and wonder if he's sleeping across the street." She grabbed the pillow next to her and threw it at Aych. "If I wasn't around to tell you you're being maudlin, you'd have crawled into his bed by now. Don't tell me you are a paragon of restraint. You'd eat him whole if you could spit him back out in one piece. Repeatedly."

"First you give me shit because I won't, then you give me shit if I want to." Throwing the pillow back at her, Aych stepped away from the window. "As much as you claim to hate humans, you still protect them."

"I'm only testing your resolve before we start this job. You are uncertain when it comes to the *gae-su*. If you don't want to possess him, we have to move quickly before the *pikma* fully claims him." She stuffed the pillow behind her back. "Don't you have more important things to be doing?"

"Than bothering you? Nah, that's my number one priority in life."

A Holy Venom

Dragging a hand through their hair, Aych shot another glance at the window. "I'm taking the eight o'clock to the anthill our new candidate lives in. He's in a craphole called Thursby."

Lu relaxed back against the pillows and watched Aych pace at the foot of her bed. "Do you think he'll do?"

"He's got my interest, but after the last one, I'm not holding my breath."

"If he passes, we can get started as soon as Mat is done with both batches."

"If he passes, I'll leave him with a hook in his head. We can reel him in when we want." Aych shrugged and stopped pacing. They touched a bioluminescent orchid blossom growing along the ornate mirror of Lu's dressing table. The deep amethyst flower dimmed and then brightened when they moved their finger away. "What's holding up the herbalist, why hasn't he finished?"

"Mat's got one vial ready, but the deal was for two, remember? It took forty cases of Constalia and more than six months to make the one, but he did it. He's the only human in two thousand years the flower has given her secrets to. You should keep that in mind the next time you feel like eating him."

Aych touched their fingertip to another orchid causing the flower to dim. "Did you test it?"

"Are you volunteering?" Lu raised an eyebrow. "That tincture would knock down one with even your robust constitution."

"Maybe. Maybe not," Aych shrugged. "All I ate as a wee thing were nasty, bitter herbs. I grew up in a venomous garden, remember?"

"Plants and fungi are poisonous. Animals and insects are venomous. And you survived your ordeal only to graduate to eating trash like a possum and bones like a dog. Peacocks consume poisonous berries and in turn grow exquisite, unrivaled feathers, their brilliant glory. You, however ..."

Aych smiled. "You know just how exquisite I am when I'm at my Biggest."

"You mean when you're eating entire neighborhoods?" Lu sniffed. "No one is going to be admiring your splendor when you're massacring everyone in sight. They're too busy running away trying to preserve their sad, slow behinds."

"Speaking of, I think we ought to have a plan for making a surprise visit to the Perlustrate on our way out."

"Why? For Violet? Or because you hate them for being your only local competitors in terror?"

"Bit of both. You're going to take out the High Priestess, so why shouldn't I do my part to improve the city? The Awy think the Church is ready to collapse, so let's give it a harder shove."

"You just want an excuse to eat hundreds of humans at once," Lu laughed. "Why you look forward to it I'll never understand. It's not like you even bother to savor your meals." Lu rolled her eyes and flopped back. "I am too tired for your nonsense. Go dump it somewhere else, you absolute snow cloud."

"Remember this before you fall back asleep," Aych tapped the box containing the heart. "The ice will melt. It's too good to waste."

"And you get yourself back here." Lu put her hand on Aych. "I'm not sure how much longer I can keep the *pikma* off the *gae-su* if you're not here to chase it off."

"If I crawled into bed with him, I could rip her to shreds every night."

"Tsk. Don't justify your evil fantasies to me. If you did possess him, you'd never know if he truly loved you."

"You're cruel when you're overtired. Get some sleep."

"And whose fault is it that I'm still awake!" Lu buried her head under the pillow. "Don't overestimate the hunter and hurt him too badly. We need him in one piece."

☾

The lines of a magical ward flared and broke as Aych tapped their fingers on Ky's apartment door. The dead bolt unlocked and the door swung open of its own accord. Stepping in, they closed their eyes and inhaled. The apartment smelled of coffee, stale food in the trash can under the sink, and a human male with his adrenals on overdrive. The residue of the lure coated the walls and furniture with a sooty, charcoal stain. *Lives alone, no frequent guests. That's a pity. No leverage gained by tormenting a roommate or lover.*

The refrigerator started shaking—something in the freezer was banging around. Aych snapped their fingers. The freezer door flew open and the stone head launched out and into their palm. They smiled fondly as the enchanted object trilled and purred. "Yes, I am pleased with you." They pocketed the head and examined the kitchenette and living room.

Human magic flared again in lines over the arched window and Aych caught another trace of it from the bedroom. Curious, they pushed the door open. There was a third ward, also recently refreshed, over the bedroom window. *No guns or weapons, his only knives are in the kitchen drawer. What does he use to fight with?* The head trilled and Aych pulled back the tapestry, exposing the altar cabinet. The faint stink of a Presence caused their upper lip to twitch. *More than a church, less than the Teahouse.*

Gingerly, they opened the cabinet and bent down to examine the jackal statue. The ghost of a Presence was seated there, faint and sleeping like a territory marker long exposed to the elements and never refreshed. *Desert sand, turquoise waters flowing in an ancient river, all belonging to another World. Another kind of place where the sky is the rose of first light and sunset, eternally.* Aych breathed through a rush of resentment and spite. They wanted to break the statue. Instead, they took the lure out. Bouncing it in their hand, they eyed the statue and then the head. Mischief glinted in their eyes as they swapped the head into the altar and pocketed the wooden icon.

Walking over to the bed, they unbuttoned their long overcoat and suit jacket. The dent of the human's head marked the pillow and Aych settled onto their back, mirroring the regular occupant's repose, their longer legs stretching off the mattress until their shoes rested against the radiator. *This one has skill with magic and common sense.*

Aych breathed in the stink and sweat of the human. *This one has killed many other humans. Shock, sadness, but not completely unhinged. Not ripe; altogether still too sane. That's easy enough to fix.*

With Ky's scent firmly in mind, they got up and went back out to the living room. *Retreat, hold, or advance?* Buttoning their suit jacket, Aych went to the freezer and wedged the jackal statue behind a bag of peas. It was petty and childish, but delightful.

Advance.

☾

Kiarna Boyd

Aych followed Ky's scent through the parking lot, along a packed trail of snow around the back of the building, and eventually to the iron gates of the local convent. There, Aych inhaled again. *Withered flesh, failing organs, and rancid regrets.* They pushed open the gate and surveyed the cloister's marble walls.

Ice covered the statues of the veiled Holy Mother and her Saint. Elderly priestesses in their scarlet garb, visible through the convent windows, hobbled back and forth, performing their tiresome, pointless duties. Aych sneered at the statue of the Holy Mother. *They pray to an absentee landlady and her equally absent janitor.* Aych walked around to the back of the convent house and inspected the snow-covered garden. *This will do.*

The convent sat on a graded hill above a granite ledge. Below, the frozen river cut through the mill town, a milky, white road no one dared traverse. The town's industrial wealth and religious enthusiasm had long faded and only the old buildings remained as monuments to ambition and faith. Aych eyed the low position of the winter sun on the western horizon. The candidate's scent was stronger in the direction of the river.

Advance.

☾

The clang of cow bell interrupted the song as Ky sorted new inventory in the back room. He listened to Yarrow welcome a customer. As Ky turned back to the inventory, the countersignal suddenly flared white-hot. Startled, he dropped the packing slip and rushed out of the back room to check on the girl.

Bouncing on her toes by the entrance, Yarrow was humming along with a new song on Ky's latest playlist.

"Everything OK out here?" Through the entrance glass, Ky caught sight of a tall figure leaving, their trouser legs and polished shoes climbing up the shop steps back to street level.

Yarrow turned halfway. "Yeah, just a tourist asking for directions. Rich folk from the Capital." Beaming, she tapped the corner of her cherry-red eyeglasses and cocked her head. "They said my glasses are *fashionable.*"

A Holy Venom

"Yeah? Good for you." Ky rubbed his back. "As long as they didn't lift anything. Rich people steal more than poor people in stores like this." He rubbed the ache along his shoulder blade and headed back to the supply room. "Fuck." He picked up the dropped paperwork off the floor.

The next song crackled through the speaker mounted on the wall. Ky tried to remember if the static in the mix was in the original bootleg from his pal at Hot & Heavy or if the speaker was crapping out. Then the male singer's voice roared through the music and Ky smiled. The countersignal continued burning along his spine. He tried to remember the name of the band on the original cassette tape as the song's chorus repeated. *In the dark, alone, you know I'm the one you want, the one you need.*

"This is just swell, might as well chuck it all and live in a cave." He rubbed the spot again and tried to finish correlating the packing slip with the contents of the order. "What the hell was that?" Unsettled, he listened to the music and tried to decipher the warning hidden in the pain.

☾

Outside, Aych rolled a smoke. *Protective of the girl and afraid of what he's picking up. Psychic, but not trained. That's good enough to start with.* Lighting the herbal mixture, they glanced up Main Street at the meager assortment of stores and restaurants the rural town had to offer. They strolled further along the sidewalk searching for a tea shop. The streetlights buzzed and flickered on, casting a shadow off Aych's shoulders. The condensing darkness pooled off their body and trailed down, covering the stairs to Last Chance Records in blackness.

TEN

ON HIS WAY HOME, Ky turned his attention to how the stone head wound up on his altar. Certain it was the same object he'd tried to burn, he recalled Mudon's warnings. Ky stopped. One of the criminals involved in the drug-running scheme could have left the stone as a warning. If so, they might even now be watching Ky or waiting in ambush. He eyed the pools of streetlight and the patches of wet asphalt with mistrust. Dirty slush and deep puddles of ice water lurked at the edge of the sidewalk between the snowbanks. The heavy, damp chill bit, slicing through wool to drag on tired joints. It would be a long, dreary walk, even without stopping to check for surveillance agents or clumsy locals hired to keep tabs on him.

Haw had been prepared and that hadn't been enough to stop whoever, or *whatever*, had killed her. A restless uncertainty gnawed at him. It would be simpler if Mudon was right and it was all sly tricks in service of a reckless and unsavory trade. Ky focused instead on the practical vectors of attack on his route. The small-town salts would be sitting around warming themselves inside the Tank down by the frozen river. The peaked slated roof of the armory was visible over the cement block and brick modern buildings on Main Street. The drunks and the rougher crowd would be on the Eastside, near the bars and boarded-up rowhouses. The salts might drive by, but they'd never bother to get out of their warm cruisers to inspect a shabby property, even if it was on fire.

The thought curled Ky's lips. Even if Mudon had put a notice out on him, thanks to the weather, the likelihood of anyone paying him a visit tonight was low. He considered if the floor show at his place could have been a bored detective from the Tank setting up a scripted set of stage tricks. Nothing had been stolen or tossed and there was no way a salt would miss the opportunity to trash a brown bag's apartment. The covert precision of it worried him more than the intrusion. His bias toward the thing's magical agency was, in some sense, one of comfort. Ky snorted at his habit of trusting magical thinking over material reality.

Reaching his apartment building, the stairwell stank of the usual spilled beer, piss, and regret. There was something else, a lingering carnal perfume. The seductive unfamiliar odor, a mix of hothouse flowers and incense, prompted memories of funeral masses for dead friends and lovers. A snippet of the bootleg song from his last playlist repeated, the singer's voice looping in Ky's mind. *In the dark, alone, you know I'm the one you want, the one you need.* The Ruined Saints—Ky finally remembered the name of the gutter band from the Capital. The song was off the live venue cassette the manager of Hot & Heavy had mailed him. Frowning, Ky considered the strange perfume in the stairwell again and recalled a former instructor, blinded in her generation's forgotten war – *"Smell is one of the most primal senses. It will carry the truth to you if you let it."*

The countersignal sizzled when he reached his floor. His apartment door stood ajar, the magical wards broken. Ky became drilled in, hyper-focused on everything around him. He inhaled sharply. The air carried the same strange fragrance as the stairwell. He went into an automatic state of assessment and response. Easing his bag to the hallway floor, he kicked open the door and waited for a reaction. Warmer air drafted out of his apartment. All was quiet and still as he slipped around the doorframe.

Nothing but the slight moan of wind interrupted the stillness of the apartment as snow blew into the living room. The bedroom window was wide open, letting in the cold and scattering of snow. Slamming the window shut and locking it, Ky quickly checked the three rooms and the closet for any sign of the enemy. Nothing. The countersignal flared still, scalding his nerves until it felt like a burning handprint on his back. The front door squealed when he closed and locked it. Returning to his bedroom, Ky yanked the tapestry back and opened the altar. Tied to a torn page of a magazine, Yarrow's cherry-red glasses tumbled out. "CONVENT GARDEN. NOW," was scrawled in fresh blood over the page. The stone head rocked side to side, leering.

"Fuck!" Flying into the kitchen, he lifted the phone receiver. The coiled

A Holy Venom

cord was severed and hung uselessly off the square yellow box. He slammed the receiver into the cradle and seethed. His only thoughts had been to cover himself, not protect Yarrow, not to consider anyone else might be in danger. He went into the bathroom and hauled out a milk crate of cleaning supplies and carried it into the living room. Cursing himself and his shortsightedness, Ky debated going to the Tank to leverage Mudon. But the thought of Yarrow, alone and afraid, made the decision for him.

He retrieved a recycling bin full of clean glass bottles from under the kitchen sink. Pulling on a pair of rubber gloves, Ky grabbed two chemical bottles and began to work. With practiced movements, he put inflatable balloons in each bottle and then filled each balloon with the first household chemical. After tying off the rubber end, he gently pushed the stems in and filled the rest of the bottle with the second fluid.

There was a clattering sound and Ky caught sight of Yarrow's red eyeglasses lying on the floor of his bedroom where they'd fallen out of the cabinet. Answers to the questions posed by the divinatory songs started falling into place. All the filtered omens and auguries slotted into the soundtrack in his head. This time, someone had been in his apartment and left the note. Whoever they were, they had Yarrow. Shame and regret washed over him. If only he had considered Mudon's warning more seriously, she might not be in danger. Years of training prompted him to push away the invasive thoughts and to focus on the task at hand. The mental beat thumped in time to the fragments of his dreams and Ky ground his teeth working faster to assemble the one-two's.

☾

Hidden among the iced-over trees bordering the garden behind the convent, Aych watched the lights in the priestesses' rooms switch off one by one. Leisurely scratching, they dislodged the last of the pale ooze from their luxurious coat of new fur. Soon, only one light was on in the convent. From their vantage point halfway up a giant oak, Aych glanced through a blood smeared window on the top floor. Impeccable and without a single bloodstain, Aych's suit and outer coat hung on the closet door inside. *There's a 5 AM train back to the city. That should do nicely.* Sticking their tongue out between elongated front incisors, Aych caught a descending snowflake. It tasted of car exhaust.

The wind brought with it Ky's scent. *Anger, alertness. No guns, but he brought the knives from the kitchen ... and he has something nasty in that bag he's carrying.* Aych sniffing. *Reeks of chemicals.* The human was anticipating violence, but he wasn't irrational. Their eyes narrowed. *Interesting. He's pissed off but sane. The lure hasn't unhinged him.*

Ky entered the garden from the right. In one hand he held a canvas bag. Moving slowly as if he were feeling his way, the man followed the shoveled pathway into the garden. He made no attempt to hide. Aych snorted in surprise. Unlike the last candidate, this one knew such tactics were useless.

He's wearing a blindfold! Easy enough to take it off him ... But he is clever enough to have thought of it. Or one of his protective spirits tipped him off. They watched as Ky set his equipment bag on the path and took out his gear. *This might actually be fun.*

"I'm here," Ky shouted. "Let the girl go." He held a glass bottle in one hand and the straps of the canvas bag with the other.

Aych was amused. *Smart in some ways, stupid in others. His divination didn't tip him off it was a bluff. Blindfolded, but confident he can hit me. What a joke.* Aych dropped out of the tree. *Maybe the next one the lure finds will be less of a fool.*

Eyes closed under the blindfold, Ky exhaled and inhaled. The inhuman vortex of corruption and hate had left its perch above the garden and was now moving toward him. *So much for Mudon's theory about thugs.* Not knowing exactly who might be listening, Ky prayed to the gods of righteous death and battle. *Let me avenge Haw.* The one-two in his hand was one of ten and he had the knives tucked into his belt. All he needed to do was respond to the countersignal. He could hear the distant noise of traffic and the hiss of the snowfall. No screams or struggling, no sense of Yarrow out in the garden. He felt a flush of shame, realizing he'd been suckered by his adversary's ruse. Shaking it off, he knew he wouldn't have done anything different. He had ten chances to hurt whatever he was facing, two knives as a last resort, and whatever protection he was to be granted against an unknown adversary capable of exceptional harm. *It killed and ate Haw.*

He gripped the glass bottle in his hand and waited. The cold ate into his boots and snaked down the collar of his jacket, chilling his throat. The red scribble of rage out in the dark zig zagged in his mind's eye, the thing's turbulent frenzy reconfirming it wasn't human.

Aych loped toward the man. *Let's get this over with. I can catch the last train tonight and not have to wait for the morning one.* They launched to the right side of the human and hooked a claw under his blindfold, slicing it off. Aych chuckled, letting their breath steam along the human's face and neck. *It's no fun unless you die screaming in terror.*

Ky kept his eyes closed and pivoted to sling his arm around. *Wait until you get a face full of this, you evil and arrogant fucker.* He released the bottle and grabbed another. The creature nimbly dodged the first. Grotesque, bestial laughter and rough breathing filled the garden as the bottle harmlessly plopped in the snow, unbroken.

Flinging themselves across the snow, Aych slashed Ky's back. *Open your eyes and see me, you dumb shit.* Claws raked through the man's padded jacket and drops of blood danced in the air. A second pass scored the backs of his legs.

Ignoring the pain, Ky screwed his eyelids shut. The familiar kick of adrenaline heightened his awareness. In his mind's eye, the outline of the creature sharpened. The long ears and distinctive lupine head shape were unmistakable, the bipedal, burly form and long fingers tipped with vicious claws. *It* wants *me to see it.* The message in his divination confirmed, Ky took aim again.

This one is used to throwing his toys without a clear line of sight. Aych considered tossing the bag of chemical bombs into the trees. Lunging, Aych rushed from the edge of the trees. *He's vulnerable, a tube of muscle and shit foolish enough to believe he can fight me head-on. Just like the stupid shits that show up at the House looking for treasure.* A familiar anger stirred in Aych. They remembered all the clanking adventurers in armor, striding up armed with clever plans to steal what they thought would be easy to take. Their resentment of humans, of *adults*, soured the saliva in their mouth. *Enough wasting time on trash.* Aych spit. *Advance.*

The warning launched up Ky's spine. Heat swept along his nerves into the palm of his hand as he released the second bottle.

Mid-leap, Aych caught the scent of an unfamiliar animal. A Presence erupted into the garden, spilling out through the human and blazing across the snow. Olfactory and energetic, the Presence encircled Ky. A rose quartz sky at dusk and dawn; jade-cool water in basalt-lined ponds. The Other tasted of ancient dust and dry lands. The territory of the garden was now in dispute, invaded by another who claimed the man. Aych roared in response, as the bottle, unnoticed, smashed on their side. As it shattered, the flying shards cut the balloon releasing the second chemical. The mixture ignited and liquid flames seared Aych's fur and skin. They screamed in rage. *Fucker!*

The divine aura shivered in the night, shielding the human as Aych howled. They willed insanity and terror into the man. The Presence deflected the unclean enchantment as if it were a gentle wind. Wrath ignited in Aych's bones, churning and searing through their skin. Erupting with hatred and fury, they barely noticed as their skin bubbled and split, ichor seeping from the wound made by the homemade incendiary device. *This one you want to save? Of all the times and all the humans, this one you come for? You choose him? Fuck you! I will eat him, then you, and shit you both out!* Outrage crested over into madness as Aych howled and cursed. With each breath, their bones cracked and split, bursting with lust for revenge and mayhem. *I will murder all of you, wherever you hide, and then feast on your unfeeling, uncaring flesh until there is nothing left! I will destroy all of you!* Eons of torment coursed through the obsidian ichor and boiling blood as Aych's skin tore. *I will become Bigger—BIGGER!—and destroy you all.*

Ky buckled under the crushing waves of insanity and fury, unaware of the conflict around him. He fell to his knees. The third bottle slipped from his fingers onto the icy path and rolled into the snow below the bushes. As the ravening monstrosity contorted and expanded, his sense of where exactly the monster was diminished. The erupting rage filled the garden, spinning upward to the sky and out beyond the borders of the convent property. He could hear screaming from inside the building. Woken by the terrible howling, the priestesses stared from their windows, watching the unfathomable battle in the garden. Behind him, Ky felt the women's minds and hearts shattering as they succumbed to the creature's noxious contamination. No human could witness the creature's presence without breaking. He screwed his eyes closed and bowed his head. The howling and gnashing grew closer. The heavy thudding of terrible footsteps neared. The weight of the creature's rage forced Ky's body closer to the frozen ground as if a mountain lay on top of his back.

Exhausted and helpless, he kept his eyes closed and raised his head, straining against the invisible weight. The strange scent he had encountered in his hallway washed over Ky. With it, a sudden impulse entered him, triggering the same song to loop in his head, music selected and curated by the dead and the living. Ky shouted at the storm-shaped fury, reciting the lyrics running through his head. "In the dark, alone, you know I'm the one you want, the one you need!"

As the man spoke, the foreign Presence consolidated, covering the human's huddled body with its canine-shaped aura. Aych snarled. The lingering incense of ancient resins mingled with the perfume of rain on dust. Not submitting, the Other noticeably quiesced, drawing inward. Not fully retreating, but backing off. The mollifying posture communicated: only this one human was claimed, no further territory was disputed.

Aych halted. Saliva dripped from their fangs and their eyes blazed, twin orbs matched in ferocity. The claws of their right hand hovered in the air above the man's head. Through a haze of inconsolable pain, Aych considered the offer of truce and the human's words. Not a plea, not an incantation, not a prayer, but a song. A song Aych had heard countless times—Ruin's song, one his band played at every show. *You know I'm the one you want, the one you need!*

Aych thought of Ruin trapped, possessed by the shit-bag wraith, forever twisted out of his mind, unprotected and abandoned, the plaything of the diseased spirit. How could this human know *that* song? Aych shook their head, trying to dispel Ruin's voice. The shouted lyrics were the psychic's way of stalling for time. Recalling at last Lu's admonishments, Aych knew they must not become Bigger. They snarled in frustration and snapped their jaws in Ky's ear. In this moment, the man's trickery was a good sign. He had lasted the duration of the interview. This human was a hunter and he could be used.

Hold.

Inside the convent, a priestess shrieked and smashed out her bedroom window with her bare hands. She screamed pleading prayers to the Holy Mother. Aych's head flew up in response to her frenzied ranting. *There is no one here to protect you. Your God does not care, and I will have my fill.*

Ky gasped as the creature leapt from the garden, smashing into the broken window frame and disappearing into the convent. With the oppressive psychic weight finally off his body, he collapsed into the snow. Behind him, the shrieking intensified. He tumbled into nightmares of remembered battlefields. Horrific memories of slaughter and human torment replayed in time with the screams echoing from the convent. Blackened bodies shriveled in clouds of smoke or fell from high windows. Children crawled bleeding from shattered buildings. Face down in the snow, Ky sobbed as oblivion closed in.

☾

Awake, panic seized Ky. His left arm was pulled taut. His thoughts caught up with his body. There were bandages taped to his back and gauze wrapped around his upper legs. His heartbeat raced. The aching pain in his muscles prompted him to sit up in the hospital bed. The clattering sound of metal on metal brought him to full consciousness. Confused by the restriction on his arm, he tugged again.

"Easy there," Mudon murmured. The detective was close to the bed. "You'll hurt yourself, cranking on it like that."

Suddenly awake, Ky found the detective looking at him from behind an opened newspaper. "Where the fuck am I?" His wrist was handcuffed to the hospital bed railing.

Mudon watched him. "I said take it easy. If you keep thrashing around like that, the nurse will put you under again. You almost tore your IV out before."

Ky glared at Mudon. "Are you going to tell me what the fuck is going on or am I going to have to—"

"You're under arrest. For trespassing ... and potentially worse." Sighing, Mudon folded up his paper and tossed it on top of the encased radiator under the room's solitary window. "In fact, if it wasn't for me putting in a word for you, you'd be in the secure medical ward under full restraint instead of wearing that flimsy piece of jewelry. I know you can get out of it, but do me a favor and keep it on while I convince the local salts you're well-behaved."

"Trespassing?" Memories of the fight in the convent flooded back and Ky experienced another wave of panic. "I can't stick around while you play *da-pen*, pal. That *thing* could come back at any time."

Mudon watched him for a moment. "I don't know what you think you saw out there, but the local emergency crew found you at the scene of a massacre at the local retirement convent." He nodded his head at the hospital bed. "Lucky for you the white coats took one look at those slices on your backside and put you on the side of the martyred saints. If they hadn't, you'd be in some serious trouble, my friend."

"You're not my friend, you traitorous piece of—"

"You know what your problem is? You don't think these things through." Mudon leaned forward. He tapped the side of his jaw near his ear and raised an eyebrow then looked pointedly at Ky. "The forensic team found your bag of tricks. Asked me why a record store manager would be carrying around homemade explosives. I had to tell them you've got a vigilante streak. A do-gooder veteran without the sense to mind their own business. And after what happened to your military friend and her nibling, you've been tracking the Rot dealers on your own."

Ky glanced over his shoulder and spotted the surveillance device nestled in among the cables of medical equipment. He glowered at Mudon. "You told the Tank I was out for revenge?"

"I thought I'd talked you out of it at the funeral, but, good citizen that you are, when you found out the local dealers had gone to ground in the convent, you worried about the safety of the sisters. If you'd shared what you knew with the Tank, maybe they could've saved some lives. You never think these things through. Could be if you'd gone in and argued your case, some of those annas might still be among us." Mudon shook his head. "I've explained to the locals that I need you for an undercover role. We finally got a shot at network distributing this new shit and I need your talents to gather intel. The Tank here isn't happy about letting you go, but they agreed it might be better for everyone if you leave town for a while." Mudon spread his hands wide and then picked up his newspaper and tucked it under his arm. "Now that you're awake, I'll put in the transfer request and we can be on our way."

Ky tugged on the handcuff. "Any reason I need to keep wearing this?"

Mudon took out the key to the cuffs. "The white coats will need to clear you, then you can get dressed." He paused and pocketed the key again. "I'd better wait until then. You'll get ideas."

"Fuck you. I'm not an errand boy that you can drag around whenever you want."

Mudon put his mouth next to Ky's ear and whispered, "You stay here and the local Tank's going to look at those one-two's you left in the sisters' garden. Won't take them too long to piece together who's behind the unsolved torch parties in this part of the country." He looked into Ky's eyes and spoke in a normal tone. "I think you know the best way to avoid further tragedy is to be a team player and do what you're told. You want to take the fuckers down, but you know this solo approach is wrong."

Slumping back against the pillows, Ky fumed. Mudon might be a double-dealing salt, but he wasn't wrong.

"I'll tell the nurse you're feeling livelier." The detective looked him over. "If we're lucky, we can catch the ten o'clock sleeper and have you ready to start infiltrating the distributors' main location by tomorrow night."

Ky glanced over in surprise. "I can't up and fucking leave. I have a job and rent to pay. I manage a store. People depend on me."

Mudon shrugged. "I'll make sure you don't get put out on the street. This is important work; the community will appreciate your service."

Ky glared.

The detective grinned. "Don't go anywhere, I'll be right back."

Ky's panic grew. Time alone with him in a train car was too much like being interrogated. Contemplating the mess he was being dragged into, Ky wished the thing in the garden had killed him.

☾

Aych was greeted by the expansive bliss of an unclouded firmament stretching over the snow-shrouded earth. The midday noise of traffic and winter birdsong slowly anchored them back in the waking world. A lingering sensation of relaxed comfort suffused every nerve, every bone, every inch of their skin. In the absence of hunger, intense pleasure remained.

A Holy Venom

Shit. Once again Little, Aych sat up on the roof parapet. *How many bags of bones did I eat?*

A garment bag hung off a lighting fixture by the metal door leading back into the marble building. Beneath it, Aych found a matching toiletry bag. Naked and groaning, they scrubbed at their face with the heels of their palms. Considering the blood-soaked state Aych had left the convent in before taking their nap, the Caretaker had no doubt removed any trace of their presence before the salts showed up. As Aych rubbed their face, the accumulated dirt of sleeping outside on the convent roof came off on their hands.

Yawning, they tapped the roof access door to unlock it and carried the bags inside the unused attic. Compared to the chill of the parapet, the attic was warm and scented with the fustiness of the ancient rafters. Opening the next door into the top-floor residences, the recycled air carried the taint of cleaning solutions and bleach. The coppery tang of blood and shit—the stench of disemboweled humans—was long gone. Further inside, the floors below were devoid of the habitual sounds of human activity. From the attic to the brick arches in the basement, the convent stood vacant, save for an atmosphere of dread. Even the ghosts were gone. *How long have I been asleep?* Shaking their head, Aych exhaled sharply. *Lu is going to be mad as hell. Ruin better be close to the Velvet.*

After locating showers in an abandoned dormitory wing, Aych washed the grime off and wrapped a towel around their waist. *Check on the hunter, then catch the next train.* They wiped the condensation off the mirror over one of the sinks and adjusted the new skin around their eyes and mouth. Satisfied with the reflected face, they unzipped the garment bag. The Caretaker's distinctive perfume wafted out. *If I don't hurry, Ruin might be getting into trouble about now.*

Adjusting their necktie, they checked and discovered the lure was still untouched. It was where they had left it, radiating hatred throughout the human's home. The hunter had left the area and the lure was unable to locate him. The stone head was unhappy and actively searching.

With a growl, Aych tore the sink off the wall. *If he's getting away, if someone has interfered, if I have to start this entire fucking process over again ...* Jets of water sprayed over the bathroom floor as they fumed and smashed the porcelain against the tiled wall.

☾

The first-class cabin attendant rapped on the door. "We will be arriving within ten minutes, honored guests."

Ky sat on the edge of his bunk and watched the frozen landscape pass by the train window. Viewed from the height of the trestle, the snowy plateau stretched to the base of the looming mountain range, growing larger and more imposing as they approached. The crowned spikes of the mountain summits reminded Ky of fangs. Ice sheeting the vertical crags caught and reflected the rising sun, golden and glowing. The reverberation of the train intensified as the track entered a mountain pass, leaving the plains behind. Now the window showed only the dark bones of the earth locked under bands of ghostly green ice.

Mudon broke Ky's reverie by dropping a folder on the bunk next to him. Cabin lights illuminated the lurid crime scene photos that slipped out. "In case you have any doubts we're after the same assholes." The detective watched as Ky flipped through the photos of bloody hotel rooms and taped-off crime scenes.

"I told you, it's not human." Ky dropped the images back into the manila folder. "I fought with it, in the garden." He thrust the folder back at Mudon. "It's a werewolf."

"Fought blindfolded and with your eyes closed." Mudon shook his head as he took it. "I'll tell you again, you fell for temple tricks. In Grava, the gambling houses have been murdering people and making it look like accidents for at least a thousand years. You going to start telling me Mlolm is real, capsizing boats and drowning people? Or are you buying into the legend there's some local cryptid in the heart of the capital, gutting shepherds in the Heights and eating them whole?" The detective's expression was pitying. "Get you a VIP room at the Statler with that noise. 'Werewolf' is what our forebearers called serial killers—especially those with sick sexual kicks—back before the steam engine was invented. They couldn't imagine a human fucked up enough to do this kind of shit and reasoned it had to be a supernatural form of evil. Haw's not coming back to life with a bad case of

A Holy Venom

magical rabies."

"I don't give a rat's ass if you believe me or not." Exhausted, Ky pinched the bridge of his nose. "We've been over this all night. Whatever outfit is running your new drug, they didn't kill Haw."

Mudon opened his mouth. "Haw—"

"She wouldn't have had anything to do with that shit!" Ky snapped. "She wouldn't have put people's lives at risk, no matter what horseshit conspiracy you come up with!"

"You're not listening to me. I've told you, there's good reason to think Haw found evidence in her nibling's apartment, something linking the kid back to these people." Mudon slapped the folder. "She went the same superstitious route you're taking thinking this diversion, this psych-ops shit, and she died for her mistake. She should've called in the Tank. If she didn't trust the locals, she had enough contacts she could've called."

"If you're so sure it's all smoke and mirrors, why do you want me in on this? You've got plenty of local hands that can go in there and whistle for you." Ky stared at the detective, wondering, not for the first time, what the man's consistent harassment indicated. When they had both been in the service, Mudon had dogged his steps, waiting, Ky thought, for him to fuck up. Yet when it came down to the final disposition, the lieutenant had covered for him, vouched for Ky's innocence, and requested an honorable discharge on his behalf. The man had partially been responsible for sending Ky on his final mission, so maybe it was guilt. Or maybe Mudon had some vestige of conscious. Whatever it was, Ky didn't trust it enough to keep his neck off the line.

Mudon glanced at Ky. "It's not that I haven't tried. For months now I've worked my angles and tried getting more evidence, more intel on these fucks. I need your skills, your abilities, the way you know things about people—"

"Just swell, you want me to listen in. How many times do I have to tell you? I'm not a fucking radio receiver."

"No, you're not." Mudon leaned against the edge of the cabin bunk. "I don't exactly know what the fuck you are, but I trust your hunches. If anyone can walk in there and get me what I need without dying for it, it's you. You're my wildcard."

"Your card?" Anger swelled in Ky's chest. "You have the fucking nerve to knuckle me into this bad business of yours, and now you want to sugar me? After everything that happened?" He glowered at Mudon. "Let's get this straight. You sent me into that building, and when it all came down on my head, you fucking left me under the rubble to die. In the dark. Alone." Anguish tightened his throat. "Didn't even bother to try and dig me out, to see if I was alive. Left me in that fucking hole like it was my tomb. Then you came after me, saying I was a firebug, that I was at fault."

"I'm sorry. Is that what you need me to say?" Mudon returned his gaze evenly. "The report from the scouts came in that you were dead, that the blast was triggered early and you didn't make it out. I had to worry about the living. I followed my orders. We were under attack and it would've been against procedure to send in search and rescue. Anyway, you lived through it, didn't you?"

There was no way to explain the feeling; the agony of abandonment, heavier than the concrete; the pure hell of waiting to suffocate, thinking each breath would be your last. Disgusted, Ky turned to look out the window and caught sight of the city spiraling up the terraced heights of the mountain. Flashes of gold and lapis blue flickered above the granite warehouses crowding the river.

"Look, I get it. You hate me. That's understandable, I worked you over as hard as I could. If there'd been another high ranking officer in the area, they should've interrogated you. But if they had ..." Mudon dropped his gaze and then looked back at Ky. "That was years ago. You lived, you were rescued, and now I need you to help me catch these assholes before they kill more people. They know you are onto them, and you will be next."

Ky scoffed. "You're so worried about me, but you threaten to whistle to the local Tank and dangle me over their torch cases? That's a hell of a way to show you care."

The muffled noise of the other passengers filtered through the cabin walls as they readied to disembark. In a moment, the view of the waterways fell away, the intensified rumble of the wheels on the tracks faded as the train entered the open stockyards. Industrial warehouses and factories built of mountain stone loomed over the raised trestle. Graffiti and vandalism marred the back side of the Capital city.

A Holy Venom

The train diverted onto another iron trestle and the waters of the Twin Rivers churned below. Slabs of ice rode the waves as the current twisted and slammed around the bridge supports. Striking the metal, the slabs broke apart, dropping chunks and fine white powder back into the froth around the footings. The momentum of the train slowed, the clatter of the wheels growing quieter while the noises of the other passengers grew louder. The train slowed again and the wrought iron station gates passed over the cabin window.

Inside the Northern Imperial Railway Station, hundreds of people milled about the marble platforms beneath the glass and iron-buttressed domes. Gusts of steam billowed out from under the locomotive newly arrived at Track 10. Shouts echoed under the leaded glass arches of the station as porters responded to the mournful, final blast of the train whistle. Battered yellow ramps were unfolded and locked into place. A fleet of luggage carts surrounded the sleek train carriages. Pigeons tumbled off the roof struts while a flock of starlings wheeled out of the potted trees. Crows dived and snatched food scraps, their raucous calls echoing through the station interior.

Mudon dropped Ky's bag onto the cabin floor and hefted his own over his shoulder. "You'll be staying at the flophouse not too far from the place I told you about. Your contact will make sure you get hired on and tell you about where you're rooming. Here's the address. Go around back to the stage door." Mudon held out a business card for the theatre. "My number's on the back. If you get into trouble, call me."

Ky glanced back. "And if I say no and walk off this train with no intention of doing your shit work?"

Mudon shook his head. "Then I make the call to the Tank. You'll get picked up on suspicion of arson. Doesn't matter where you skip out to, we'll find you."

Ky snapped the card out of Mudon's hand. Hefting the straps of his duffel bag, he picked it up off the floor of the cabin. The sing-song cries of the porters cut in over the other sounds filtering through the cabin walls.

"I'll check in with you when I can. When you get any leads, you call me straight off." Mudon reached out and put his hand on Ky's arm. "Don't trust anyone, no matter how friendly, no matter what story they give you. Don't get yourself killed like Haw did. Remember, it's all an illusion. None of it is real. Thousands of years of playing to the seats. There's nothing supernatural after you, werewolves don't exist."

Ky looked at Mudon with disgust. "Now you just sound like one of those tired hoary shepherds you spent all night warning me about." Ky slid open the door.

Out in the passageway, the other passengers shifted to make space. As the train carriage door opened, humid, torpid air roiled into the compartments, bringing with it the saline scent of the steam engine. Tropical birds zig-zagged over the jostling foot traffic, flitting from one potted tree to the next, the winged escapees adding to the din of the station. Ignoring Mudon as he slipped into the crowd, Ky followed the other passengers across the station platform.

The indoor concourse erupted into view. A motley assortment of shops sprawled out behind crates of imported fruit and giftware. Restaurants and bars crammed the niches under the vaulted arches while buskers and dancers entertained behind cordoned-off patches marked by their placard licenses. Warm sunlight filtered through the trees and dense, hanging foliage. It was a chaotic swirl of activity, the reinforced glass and iron cupolas above amplifying the heat and noise.

Ky shouldered his way through the commotion towards the transportation hub. Sharp-eyed children dashed through the crowd and Ky navigated away from their inquisitive hands. The young pickpockets and beggars assessed his worn leather jacket and faded black denim and turned their attention to the better-dressed tourists. Ky emerged through the outer doors and took his place in the taxi queue. Mammoth plows turned onto the street, forcing the other vehicles to the sides of the road. Accustomed to the interruption, local commuters stepped under covered granite porches allowing the nimble sidewalk plows to pass. A few kind locals hauled a couple of confused tourists out of the path of the machines. The line moved quickly. Ky's turn came and a taxi swiftly pulled up to the curb in front of him.

"Where you headed to?" The taxi driver extended his hand for Ky's luggage.

"The Velvet Door on Tranquility."

A Holy Venom

"I know it." The driver threw Ky a friendly smile and tilted his head at the waiting car. "Get yourself in and out of this cold."

"Thanks." Ky got in as the driver slammed the trunk and slid behind the wheel.

"Come to see a show?" Adjusting his mirror, the driver watched Ky settle into the backseat. "Maybe visiting friends?"

"Work."

The driver swung the car into an opening in traffic. "Oh, you got a job at the theatre?"

"Something like that." Ky considered throwing away the card in his pocket.

"You should be sure to see a show while you're there."

"If I stick around, I might." Between the tops of the rowhouses and financial buildings, Ky caught glimpses of the Heights, the wealthy district of the ancient city higher up the mountain, close to the Basilica, and home to the clergy. The funicular cable lines broke the ranks of the orderly street grid. Gradually as they drove upward along the twisting streets, the sandstone facades began to appear. At first soot-stained and neglected, the restored sandstone brightened as they drove into the wealthier neighborhoods. The cable-pulled carriages glided overhead with tourists and locals alike peering down at the streets below.

"Best stage shows in the whole city. On the whole continent! They've got real talent there. Not just the best dancers, but the acts! It's expensive or I'd go every month. You don't gamble do you?"

"Not usually."

"That's good. Stay away from their tables. Just go for the acts. Real talent, like nothing you've ever seen. You wouldn't believe me if I told you half of what I've seen there over the years." He laughed.

"The dancers are good?" Ky tried to get his mind on something else.

"Oh yeah, they do the best razzle dazzle! That's what they call it when they shimmy down to the tassels. Lots of places have that, but the Velvet is the best! I suppose some people would recommend it for the soft trade." He glanced in the mirror at Ky. "If you're interested in that sort of thing, it's the best too. But expensive. Not that I step out like that anymore. A poor man like myself keeps it at home if you know what I mean." He chuckled. "If you have the money, I tell people, get a seat in the theatre itself, right up front if you can, so you can see there's no wires or any of that funny stuff."

"Wires?"

"Yeah, like they use in other places. For the ruses, you know, the illusions."

"It's a magic show? Stage magic?" Recalling Mudon's warnings, Ky frowned. "I thought it was a pleasure house?"

"Yeah, didn't anyone tell you? Oh!" The man laughed. "I thought you knew, seeing as you said you'll be working there. Sorry, I always think everyone knows these things. It's the best magic house in the city. They get their headliners from Grava: legendary illusionists, trained families going back generations, that sort of thing. 'Glamorous and divine,' they call it. Real temple magic!"

☾

Ky knocked on the metal fire door next to the loading dock and waited. When the peephole slid back, he leaned forward. "I'm here about the—"

Ky stepped back as bolts scraped open and the heavy door swung out.

"Get yourself in and stay quiet." Rue looked him over. "No word about how you heard about this beyond *Somebody told me to ask,*' got it?"

Ky nodded and watched as Rue heaved the door back and slid home the bolts. The enormous theatre rustled and bubbled with gallivanting spirits, yet the countersignal along his back stayed quiet. Ghostly forms and opaque shadows billowed through the multistory curtains, prolonging the cold draft Ky had brought with him through the stage door.

"Not that anyone is likely to ask you about it." Rue beckoned him to follow along the brick wall between the heavy curtains and thick coils of rope snugged to iron wall anchors. "We get strays coming through enough that the only questions you're likely to get are about what can you do and can you hold your own at a table." The man stopped and looked at him. "Well, can you?"

Ky shrugged. "I know how to keep my hand to myself."

"Good answer," Rue winked and then kept walking through the backstage labyrinth of equipment stacks, props, and stacked crates. "Lined up a bed at Prickle May's. That's out the front and three streets down, you'll see the sign for rooms to let. Cheap broom closet, but I put a deposit on it so you won't have to worry about bugs. Might be knives in the floorboards there, so I wouldn't go digging around if I was you."

Picking up the subtext, Ky nodded. "How much I owe you for the deposit?"

"We'll settle up after you get hired on. Big man will want to ask you those questions I mentioned and see if he likes you well enough to be more than a push broom." Stopping outside a flimsy wooden door barely hanging on the hinges, he looked Ky over again and stared at the bag in his hand. "Any chance you brought a suit with you?"

Ky shook his head.

"Lucky for you, we keep a few racks in costume for have-nots. Should be able to find one in your size." Rue pushed the door open and waved Ky through. "If he likes you well enough."

Ducking his head, Ky dodged a bare light bulb and tramped down the rickety steps.

"There's a cot and fixings for coffee." Rue called from the top of the stairs. "Probably some crackers and cookies, maybe something in a tin, though I wouldn't eat it. Books in the little room on the back of the toilet. Sleep or read until he comes to get you."

Glancing around the windowless basement hole, Ky called up the stairs. "How long do I have to wait down here?"

"Six, seven hours at most." Rue started to close the door.

Grimacing, Ky took a step back toward the stairs. "I could come back later."

"It's part of the interview." Rue shut the door and locked it.

"For fuck's sake," Ky sighed.

☾

Hours later, Ky heard the locked door open. A well-groomed man in his late thirties stepped jauntily down the basement stairs. He exuded the confidence of a trained fighter, and Rue followed close behind. Jewelry glinting at his throat and from his ears and nose, the man stepped under the light of the bare bulb hanging from the ceiling and smiled broadly at Ky.

"Welcome to The Velvet Door," Vetch eyed Ky's jeans and T-shirt. His smile relaxed into the appearance of genuine pleasure. "You're interested in working for us? What exactly did you have in mind?"

Returning the man's open and easy smile with one of his own, Ky replied, "Anything you need except kitchen work— I can't cook." He stood up and offered his hand. "I'm Ky."

"Vetch." Heavy gold rings adorned the ring fingers of both of his hands. He smiled and waved at the stairs. "Let's go upstairs and I'll give you the tour." He clapped a hand on Ky's shoulder. "Tell me a little about yourself. Used to carrying church iron long distances, I take it?"

"They kicked me out. Nicely of course, with all the fancy paper only they care about, but no extra cash." Ky switched his jacket to his other arm and dropped the strap of his duffel across that shoulder, keeping the arm closest to his escort free. "I could use a job."

"Shameful." Vetch pursed his lips and shook his head. "Lot of our folks carried iron back in the Crisis. Here you'll get only respect for the time you put in. From all of us."

"I appreciate it, but I'm not looking for special treatment, just …" Ky glanced over his shoulder at Vetch as he stepped over the threshold back on the stage level.

"Honest work." Vetch nodded at Rue.

Rue winked at Ky and wound his way through a set of curtains as a team of stagehands came through with a sizable painted backdrop. In their wake, the dappled star motif on the freshly painted wood released a trail of rogue sequins over the scuffed floorboards.

"Need to be fast on your feet this end of the house." Vetch steered Ky out of the way of the stage techs. "We'll swing by wardrobe then I can take you out front, once you're looking respectable." Keeping his hand on Ky's elbow, Vetch got them both through the cramped passageways between the layers of screens and curtains and over to the inner brick section of the backstage area. "You can leave your things here too. No one will fuss with your belongings." Eyeing Ky's build, the head of security waved a pair of shrunken seamstresses over from their perches atop tall chairs. "Ladies, come take pity on this new employee of ours. I need him looking his best

A Holy Venom

for the front of the house." Vetch rolled his eyes as the elders groaned and adjusted their towering wigs and the layers of flimsy gauze that floated like glittery clouds around their bodies. "Sorry to interrupt your break."

"The sequin tuxedo!" One of the diminutive creatures announced.

"That moth-eaten thing? Hah!" Her companion fired back.

"Ladies, ladies, just make him look decent. He's not walking the boards, he's just a watchdog for the lobby." Vetch winked at Ky. "Any three piece on the rack is fine. Here, try this one." He pulled a garment bag off the steel rack and tossed it to Ky. "Those boots are fine for now."

"Why'd you interrupt our tea for nothing?" The seamstresses shot Vetch withering looks as they climbed back up on their chairs. "You bothered us for no good reason."

"If I hadn't called you down, you would've reported me to the guild." Drawing his hands back, Vetch dipped his head as they sneered.

After he was dressed, Ky tucked his duffel under the rack of suits and followed Vetch. The two men walked under the catwalks and down a curving corridor lined with shipping crates upon which numerous performers appeared to be napping. A few stared at the two men and a child in a cat onesie stuck out her tongue as her eyes met Ky's.

"Back of the house and front of the house have a friendly rivalry," Vetch explained. "The only people you need to impress are the proprietor of this fine historic theatre, Mixter Twalum, also known as Vee or Violet, and our star performer, Lutauvelm." Vetch stopped Ky and undid his tie. "Most call her Lu. They're both easy to spot. Vee's the dapper elder, usually with me or being trailed by more security than you can imagine for someone not a high priestess. And Lu's …" Vetch inhaled sharply and shook his head. "Lu's the most beautiful person any of us have ever been blessed to behold." He held Ky's gaze for a second while maneuvering the borrowed silk necktie. "If you're at a table and by some miracle, there's two captivating, devastatingly gorgeous creatures there with you, she's the one who also looks like she'd laugh herself sick watching you get stabbed in the stomach. Try not to swear when you're around her. She prefers we stick to clean language." Finishing with the tie, Vetch lightly patted Ky's face. "Then there's the foul-mouthed iceberg with dyed black hair that follows Lu around. That's Aych, and they dress like a color-blind undertaker who happened to shepherd their way to a tidy fortune. Deadly at cards and dice, they will absolutely empty your wallet. Avoid sitting at any game they're in. I can tell you that from experience. And," Vetch leaned in. "The only other thing you need to remember is no one likes a thief. Don't steal from the house, don't bring dishonor to the house, don't pick fights inside the house. If you can remember *that*, you'll be fine. Any questions before I introduce you to the rest of the family?" Vetch gestured at the door separating the theatre from the lobby.

"One," Ky gave him a lopsided smile. "What exactly is my job?"

Clapping him on the shoulder, Vetch pulled him toward the door to the front of the house. "We'll figure that out as we go. Could be standing around keeping an eye on things, or fetching and carrying for the talent, or maybe escorting a guest out to be revived by the refreshing night air. Could be you get to wheel around all of Lu's tropical plants while she decides where they go today. Tomorrow she might have you move them back again."

Laughing, Ky shook his head. "Whatever you say."

"Oh, one more thing. You'll want to keep these on you." Vetch took a square tin container out of his breast pocket and held it out to Ky. Then he pulled his hand back slightly and frowned. "You're not allergic to honey, are you?"

Eying the tin, Ky shook his head. "Not that I know of, why?"

Vetch nodded and slipped the slim box into Ky's suit pocket. "These are charcoal pills, in case anyone steps on a guest's drink. Or yours. Been known to happen, sadly." The head of security stared into Ky's face. "If you feel woozy or start hallucinating, pop a pair and swallow 'em straight off. If a guest seems like they've been drugged, ask 'em the question about the honey allergy and then feed them a pair if it's safe. If they don't know or don't answer, just hold off until I can make the call. Apothecary across the way makes them for us special. A bespoke mix of wood charcoal and honey. A few folks are allergic to bee products and can have a bad reaction. Well, less than if they hadn't taken them at all, mind you. Draws any poison out. You can also use it if you get cut with a laced blade."

"Sounds like a lot of risk for carting plants around."

Vetch laughed and clapped Ky on the shoulder. "Happens when there's a house full of the fattest sheep in town, all swanning about the place in search of ways to shed their hard-earned cash while you watch their wallets for them."

"Might be easier if we lightened the load for them."

"That's what I like to hear." Vetch swung open the fire door. "Welcome to the best house in the city. I'm sure we'll find something you're good at." He clapped Ky on the back propelling him out into the front of the Velvet.

The security detail at the bar greeted Vetch and sized up Ky as the pair entered the lobby. Besides the main entrance, there was a fire door set between one end of the bar and the passage to the nearby restrooms. The venue staff lounging at the nearest end of the bar congregated next to a gilded cage of an elevator. The atmosphere of curiosity increased, filled in with low-pitched comments from the security guards as they noted Ky trailing behind their boss.

Two other staff members wheeled tropical trees out and set the pots on either side of the revolving brass door while a third was inspecting the red carpet leading to the curb. Cleaners polished the carved sandalwood of the Box Office and Coat Check and brushed lint off the magenta couches. The lobby of the theatre was infused with a surging, electric quality, vibrant and absolutely threatening. Ky realized he might as well be walking into a thunderstorm.

ELEVEN

DUST MOTES DRIFTED through the beams of afternoon sunlight that cut between the small studio bedroom's blinds. Shine sat up naked on the edge of a mattress laid on the floor nested among the clothing-strewn boxes and furniture harvested from sidewalk leftovers. Ruin's boyfriend and bandmate reached for his jeans.

Ruin watched him dress. "I'm sorry."

Shine paused and glanced back. "It's your new medication, isn't it?"

Rolling over onto his side, Ruin covered his eyes. "Yeah, I think so." The sunlight crept up his foot. Ribbons of self-inflicted scar tissue wound up his arms and across his chest. Spiraling patterns of tattoo ink crisscrossed the scars, forming intricate patterns.

Shine scooped a shirt off the floor and shook it out. "I have to go in for my shift."

Ruin sat up. "You want me to—"

"No need." Shine grabbed a pair of boots. "You should take a shower and go see Dr. Tansy like you promised. Get yourself sorted out. While you're at it, remember to pick up more grapefruit juice to take with your meds. The last carton went bad while you were gone. Had to throw it out."

"OK." Ruin wrapped his arms around his knees. As clouds moved across the sun, the sunbeams softened and vanished, dimming the tiny apartment.

"Practice is at seven. Don't lose your key, I can't afford to keep replacing it." Shine got up and walked out of the studio, without ever meeting his lover's eyes.

Ruin resisted the urge to yell. He pressed his face against his legs. The tears came quietly as one of his hands balled into a fist. His hand, his fist, wanted to go into the wall. It wanted to smash into the plaster, over and over again. One good punch; maybe it might take a few more. "Sorry." Feeling his guts twist, Ruin looked at the glass next to the bed. It would be so easy to squeeze it until it broke. All he had to do was give in and all that bright, sharp pain would rush up his arm and burn the agony out of his heart. It would feel so good ... but then they would know. Shine and Squash would know what he was, who he was. They would have no choice but to throw him out of the band. He would end up at the Statler, drooling and raving like everyone said he would.

He knew what he wanted, what he needed. No one would be at the practice space now. If he could play his bass and sing, maybe he could release enough pain without having to cut it out. Then he could go find Aych, to explain ...

Wiping his face, Ruin stared at the scars and cigarette burn marks on his hands and arms; maybe he was too damaged. Maybe he belonged at the Stat.

☾

The session with Dr. Tansy and Ruin's few errands ate up the day and he barely made it to practice on time. Tangled cables, running from the drum kit to the mixing board, snaked across the stained, burn-pocked patchwork of rugs covering the worn wooden floors of the factory practice space. The centuries-old window frames rattled as a train rumbled along the raised bridge outside the Cannery. Setting his mic back, Ruin pushed a cord closer to the cobbled-together stomp box with the toe of his boot. His heel caught on the rug releasing the malodorous ghosts of stale beer and spilled ashtrays. Gently settling the body of his bass against the brick wall, he hooked the strap over the repurposed coat rack bolted above, then looked expectantly over at Shine.

On the other side of the rehearsal space, Shine wiped his sleeve over his head. "Better."

"What?" Leaning over her drum kit, Squash pulled one of her earplugs out.

Shine set his guitar against an amp and reached over to ruffle the lemon-colored fluff on the drummer's head. "I said, it's better."

The two musicians shared a look and glanced over to Ruin. The band's

A Holy Venom

singer squatted with his back against the cold bricks, staring unblinkingly at the ceiling.

Aware of their scrutiny, Ruin got up and moved through the stacks of equipment to the couch at the back of the cluttered room. His body was still buzzing from the last song. He looked over the room. Squash and Shine were talking quietly with their heads together. Behind them, the stolen hotel flag covering the open window billowed up from the glass. Dutifully, Ruin got up to close the window. He started to ask about it being left open as he reached behind the flag and stopped. The window was shut and locked. As he checked it again, he caught sight of a woman standing staring on the train trestle across from him three stories up.

"Ruin!" Shine shook his shoulder. "Are you asleep on your feet or what?"

"Sorry, I was …" Ruin turned around.

"I've been trying to get your attention for five fucking minutes. What are you looking at?" The guitarist brushed back the makeshift curtain and glanced out at the trestle.

"Nothing. What's up?" Heading back over to the couch, Ruin rubbed his fingers together. He felt a lingering prickling sensation in his extremities.

Shine's eyes followed him. "You take your meds today?"

"Yeah, why?" Meeting his boyfriend's gaze, Ruin dug his thumbnail into the callous on his right index finger. He knew why Shine was asking and he hated himself for not concealing his lapses.

Shine cocked his head and watched him for a minute. "You with us?"

"Yeah, thinking through the last song." Ruin gave him a lopsided smile. "I fucked up a few times."

Squash came over to flop on the cushions then pulled at Ruin with her legs. Dragging him backward into her lap, she put her arm around his neck and squeezed him. "It's alright, that's why we practice." The drummer smiled up at Shine. "Right?"

"Don't think sweet-talking me is going to change my opinion on that stupid high-hat shit you keep throwing in at the end of every fucking song," Shine crossed his arms.

Squash jumped to her feet and yelled back. Ruin lost track of what was being said as the itch in his fingers demanded his attention. Scraping at the tough skin, he got a whiff of perfume. The artificial, flowery scent reminded him of someone, like a memory from childhood.

"Well, what do you think?" Squash flicked him in the head. "Is this dog's ass right or do you like the way I've been finishing on *Worms & Cries*?"

Shine groaned. "If it was just on that one fucking song it would be fine, I told you. It's not like I don't want it ever, but not *every* fucking song."

Out of the corner of his eye, Ruin saw the flag moving again. The synthetic silk rippled as if a breeze was coming through the window. "Is there a draft in here?"

"What?" Confused, Squash looked at Ruin.

One beat behind, Shine repeated the question. "What?"

Ruin glanced from his bandmates back to the window. "Sorry, I thought maybe there was a draft coming in."

"If you're cold, put your jacket back on." Shine went over to his amp and lifted his guitar off the stand. "We can't afford to add another heater."

Squash wandered in the direction of the sink. "It's going to get brutal up here next month. This shitty building will freeze solid. They never crank the heat up enough to compensate for the Gales." She took a bottle of water off the stack and turned to look at them. "Hey, if we're getting money for the gig, can we put it toward buying a van? I heard Flashbang is splitting up. I bet I could get Dinky to sell me hers for cheap."

"We should use it for studio time. We need a decent demo more than a van. Only thing we got going around right now is that set we did at The Cellar last year." Shine clicked one of his stomp boxes with his boot.

"Fuck a demo. We've got enough people asking, we should put out a proper album. Everyone says *Deathless* should be a single." The drummer looked over at the couch. "What do you think?"

"We should make our first record. We've got enough songs now," Ruin glanced up at Shine. "I've got a good name for it."

The guitarist strummed his instrument and listened to the sound through his amp. "Yeah? How would we pay for it though?"

"I'll do a few extra late shifts at the Teahouse. Thought we should start fighting over the name of it first." Getting up off the couch, Ruin walked by Shine. "*The Wrong Dogs*."

Shine curled his lip. "Sounds more like a band name than—"

"I like it." Squash walked between them and put her water bottle on the upturned crate by her drums. "If you can get us the cash for studio time, I could ask Rel if she'd record us."

Ruin gave her a wide smile. "It would be great if she would."

Shine glanced up from his board. "If we're going to make an album, we need more killer songs. Headliner material. No more opening shit."

"Headliner," Squash wrinkled her nose.

They both looked at Ruin expectantly.

With a solemn expression, he nodded. "Headliner." He opened his mouth to tell them about a new song idea when the door to the practice space creaked, opening. He stared into the dark sliver of the gap as the door slowly swung open with a low moan; the entire room compressed, squeezing his body until he was on the verge of suffocating.

A woman in a hospital gown stepped into the practice space. The air filled with the scent of freshly turned earth, pinesap, and wood smoke. Chills raked up Ruin's spine as she looked at him, her eyes locking onto his. He opened his mouth to shout, but his voice shriveled, the words dying on his tongue.

As he stared, pinned in place with fear, her wide, staring eyes liquefied, dripping down her face. The vacant sockets never left Ruin as her skin shimmered and shifted to the bright translucence of a polished mirror. Two perfect mirrored orbs swelled from her skull, filling the bony sockets. Long artificial lashes rimmed each silver eye, taking on the visage of a metallic doll. Ruin stood shaking, unable to look away, as the thing reflected back to him all of his past atrocities.

Icy panic sluiced over him. Nightmarish faces bubbled up under her transparent skin. Disembodied hands banged inside the unyielding curves of her face and neck, as if underwater, and lumps pushed against the fabric of her hospital gown.

She stepped closer. The flailing limbs within her vanished into darkness. Inky smoke coiled from her mouth and nostrils, spinning out of her, crossing the room to enfold him. He opened his mouth to scream a warning to his friends but the phantasm collapsed into a cloud of vapor and gushed into him, freezing his blood.

Staggering back against the battered couch cushions, Ruin flailed. He gagged and clutched at his throat. Tears streamed from his eyes as he choked and lurched off the couch and stumbled for the door. Behind him he could hear his friends' voices diminishing in the distance as the practice space faded around him, dwindling to utter darkness. Pressing against him, burned, scarred trees burst from the factory walls, their sinister branches clawing and scraping through his hair. He had to hide, he had to make himself small and quiet, he had to shrink until there was nothing left to catch. He ran down the rotting, leaf-strewn stairs, desperate to reach a safe place, hunting for the secret place only he knew. Outside, streetlights flickered a blood-red pall as wind and snow moaned. The streets were empty except for dark craggy trees bursting through cracked pavement and faint, distant howls. Above him, the sliver of a moon hung ominously in the sky. Ruin ran. He ran down the street and through the trees. He ran past hollow-eyed corpses and down the stairs of the nearest subway station, down into its recesses, praying for safety.

Slime dripped from the walls. Thick and syrupy, the infected pus of the City oozed from the tiles of the station. Ahead, the subway car pulsated—a glistening serpent, its slick scales waiting to swallow him. Keeping his chin down as he boarded the car, Ruin tried not to see the things swimming in the slime. Shadowy figures melted through the walls and serpentine shapes wriggled under the floor mats. The stench of rotting bodies hung in the air like dead fish. He squeezed his eyes shut. The belly of the serpent contracted as it moved, pushing all of the dead half-digested things into him. Hot, torpid air skimmed along his back and the monsters near him fought over the choicest morsels among the corpses. Claws ripped through tender skin, spilling glistening, wetness onto the floor. Without his knife and without his lighter, he was helpless, one more tiny creature to be devoured and digested, one more useless ghost trapped in intestinal tunnels hundreds of miles underground. The imp chorus started up again. Wheedling and howling, the voices sang in unison until he covered his ears and wept.

"Shut the fuck up!" Ruin screamed.

The other passengers of the westbound train moved away from him. An older man tucked his newspaper under his arm and glared. Two girls dressed for an evening out whispered and stole glances at his shuddering body.

"Make it stop," Ruin sobbed. He wrapped his arms around his leather and prayed. "Help me, please, help me." His body ached and burned as the

A Holy Venom

hated memories replayed. The kidnappers' voices began to replay, telling him their plans. He felt the twisting scars running up his skin and bent forward, wishing the pain would finally kill him.

☾

Ruin sat on a bench between the vending machines and pretended he was dead. He had made it to this station, disgorged from the charnel house train. The walking, decomposing corpses tottered past. With his sweatshirt hood up and his leather zipped closed, he concentrated on being still, hoping the flayed bags of meat would walk by without noticing the thudding in his chest or the sweat dripping from his face. The softly pulsing electricity of the machines on either side of him offered a kind of protection. He promised to write a praise song to thank them when he was free, when it was safe to sing again.

He counted under his breath. A captive snake train squealed into the pit. Maggoty skeletons shuffled into its rotting coils while others stumbled off. He counted and waited. When the time was right, he would stand up and spring from his hiding spot. It had to be when the imps were quiet and the platform was clear. He had to make a run for it. Up the stairs, turn right and run until the snow was waist high. Then find the iron gate. Climb over it and keep running until he could see the safe place. He had to get inside it before they found him, before the snow started falling again, before it got too cold. He had to run for it. He had to get to the safe place. And once there, he had to wait.

☾

A few of the kitchen staff glanced over the stainless steel prep tables as Aych came through the backdoor of the Teahouse. Striding through the steam-filled workspace, they passed the walk-in fridge and went through the archway into the apothecary. There, the humans concocting herbal mixtures at the high wooden benches looked up as Mat rushed by the shelves of glass and ceramic teaware to grab Aych by the arm.

"Where have you been? You have to find Ruin, now!" Mat yelled at

Aych. "You need to bring him back immediately!"

Growling, Aych slammed the herbalist against the steel door of the walk-in. "What—"

"He's been drugged, stepped on!" Mat's features contorted and he glanced around the kitchen. Mat looked at Aych with a mix of anger and desperation. "I don't know who did it. Doesn't matter right now. Find him and bring him back here before it's—"

"What the fuck are you going on about?" Showing their teeth, Aych stared into the human's eyes. "If he's not here, how do you know he's been poisoned?"

Mat continued to try and drag Aych out the back door. "I sent his meds in to be analyzed. The instructions weren't right. I thought it was a typo, but the whole thing—"

"Why the fuck did you have his meds analyzed?"

"Listen!" raising his voice, Mat grabbed Aych by their lapels. "Go fucking find him and then I'll explain. I know you can find him! I've told Lu everything in case you went to see her first." Mat's face twisted and his eyes welled up. "Kill me, I don't care. But we need to get the drug out of his body—"

"Calm the fuck down." Aych pried the human's hand off their coat. "I heard you. I'll bring him back." *You better not be dead or possessed and you better not be over there ...* They opened the back door and a billow of hot air from the kitchen rushed out twisting over the snow.

Mat nodded weakly and collapsed against the doorway. "I'll have everything ready upstairs. Get him here as soon as you can."

"You called his apartment? Checked with his bandmates?"

"He's not with them. Squash called me," Mat shook his head. "He ran out screaming while they were practicing earlier tonight. Scared the hell out of them both."

Aych exhaled and stared up at the heavy clouds hovering over the city. Throwing up a hand, they let go of the door. "I'll bring him back."

☾

A Holy Venom

A silver sky loomed above streetlamps, the cumulative nocturnal light of the City reflecting off heavy storm clouds. The unnatural glare filtered through the stained glass windows of the mausoleum and cast pumpkin-tinted shadows. There was a rhythm, an incomplete song, tapping against the glass and inside Ruin's skull. He sat in the pool of half-light surrounded by the raised stone tombs inside the crypt, humming and rocking himself. Above him, the Saint and her sacred spring stood silhouetted in the lead lines of the glass. Opposite, in his own stained glass window, the Shepherd reached out to Ruin and offered a cup brimming with spring water. Humming another section of the song, Ruin imagined the taste of the sweet, clear water, diamonds of rain and snow melting on his tongue. He bit the inside of his cheek. Tears leaked out of his eyes as the song tried to move through the cotton packed in his throat. He had stumbled through the thick, ice-crusted layer of snow in the necropolis and used his family's secret way into the locked crypt to wait.

The ancient stones could keep him safe. Safe from everything but *her*. They could do nothing to prevent his aunt from finding him; her skeleton was laid in the casket entombed behind him. Long white bones in a dimming taffeta dress, her luxurious hair tangled in the dust of countless flowers, the diamonds around her collarbone, and others from her rotted ears lost under her grinning skull, fallen away like forgotten stars. She had made him bring her offerings once, ponytails and twin tails cut from his middle school classmates' heads. Stolen trophies laid out on her casket to bribe her back to sleep. After that, he could no longer let himself date anyone his aunt might find too beautiful, out of fear she would demand their lives as tribute. The less interest she had in his lovers or his friends, the safer they were. Everyone was safer if he was locked up in here, or, if he had no other choice, in the Statler.

It's lost you know. The fountain they say is hers is a sham, his dead aunt's mocking voice echoed in his head. *The real spring dried up thousands of years ago. Pretty story though, for orphans and fools. One sip and you'd be cured. But not of me. Never of me. You can pray and pray and neither the Saint nor the Shepherd will free you. The Holy Mother hates you.*

"I know," Ruin kept rocking, boot heels to tailbone and back again. The song in his head was looping, glitching, and spiked. It was like the white noise of air conditioners and broken heating vents, singing lullabies of dying galaxies and the sorrowful lives drowned in the Twin Rivers, suicides escaping their misspent, beautiful lives, like suns diving into an infinite cosmic abyss. All the shit and piss streaming away in the fast-moving current until it disappeared into the vast ocean far away from the city and the mountains.

You belong to me, child. The ghost ran her hand through Ruin's hair. *Before you were born, you belonged to me. Your mother was stupid, your father was stupid, and the rest of them ... well, you know what I did to the rest of them.*

"They caught you and they locked you up. You died in the Statler," Ruin shivered; the mausoleum, already frigid, was growing colder. The sweatshirt under his leather was damp with sweat and the thin black denim he wore was no match for the chill from the paving stones. He thought about crawling back into the rumpled sleeping bag by the sepulcher.

And then you were born and took my place there, didn't you? In my perfect, stylish suite of rooms with my lovely things, while my idiot cousin screamed and screamed all night one suite over. He kept you up, didn't he? Your real uncle. Screaming and crying every day and all night until even you *wanted to kill him.*

"He was in pain. He was apologizing," Ruin hid his face against the top of his bent knees. "He wanted to die." His uncle's body was lying in dust and stillness in his casket, all his sobbing silenced and sealed away. Ruin envied the quietly departed dead.

How did it feel to kill him?

"I didn't kill him!"

His aunt's ghostly laughter echoed off the granite. *You can lie to the diggers and the salts and even to yourself. But I know what you did. You killed him. Barely grown, you murdered your own family. Whispered through the heating vent and told him your mother was dead. That the bad people came and killed her. That strangers broke into the house and set it on fire. Because of what he did, his only sister was murdered.*

"Because of what you did! They all died because of you!" Ruin screamed until the sound echoed off the stone and into his bones. "You wrecked his life, just like mine!"

The lock in the bronze doors clanged open. The frigid night air swirled in, gusting against Ruin's back. Before he could look over his shoulder, he

A Holy Venom

felt the winter night peeling away as warm relief poured over him like hot water. The comforting musk of Aych's sudden embrace made Ruin's eyes roll back in his head. He began to sob uncontrollably. "I waited for you until you came, I waited—"

"I'm here." Aych arranged their limbs around Ruin's and brought their head alongside his. They held the human as Ruin's long, uneven cries wracked his body. *Be warm, be still, be safe.*

"I'm so fucked up, I fucked up, everyone—"

"It's not your fault," Aych began to ease Ruin to his feet. "Your uncle's waiting to give you an antidote. I'm going to bring you back."

"It's never been like this." Ruin stared up into Aych's eyes. "I'm seeing things, hallucinating my ass off. Not just hearing them. Everything's fucked. Everyone's afraid of me. I can't stop her. She wants me to kill all of them. The spring dried up and there's no cure anymore." He pointed feebly at the Shepherd in the stained glass. "I have to kill like he does, but everyone is afraid of me and I can't get close enough."

"You know I'll never be afraid of you." Throwing a glance at the images of the Shepherd and the Saint, Aych slowly turned Ruin and walked him closer to the exit. "We need to get you home."

Breathing in Aych as they left the mausoleum, Ruin fell into a swoon. His body began to sink toward the frozen ground below the granite steps. The billows of his breath churned in the air and strange faces peered back at him. "You say that, but when I'm alone, there are so many people in my bed. But never you."

Holding Ruin upright and tapping the bronze doors of the crypt shut, Aych sighed. "I'm sorry. I don't want to leave you alone, but I also want you to be free."

"I found you once, in the Woods. Like in the stories. You were there, but not like this. You were Big. I saw you. You were so beautiful." Through the long void, waves of sleepiness tugged at Ruin. The warmth and comfort lulled him. A sudden sense of urgency made his eyelids flutter as his body went rigid against the sinking pull and the cotton in his mouth dissolved to honey. Did Aych know? Had he ever said it out loud? The words rang and glittered in Ruin's chest. "I need to tell you," he tried to focus on Aych's face. "You need to know."

"I do," they replied, their voice softer, more tender. "I already do. Go to sleep. I'll be with you when you wake."

☾

"Get him out of his leather." Mat gestured impatiently while Aych stripped the jacket off and laid Ruin on his bed. Once Aych stepped back, the herbalist took his place and shined a light in Ruin's eyes.

"Keep him asleep," Mat asked, glancing at Aych. "I know you can do that."

Clicking their tongue in annoyance, Aych looked back at Ruin's face. "What else your bumpkin friends tell you about me?"

"Enough. Look, I don't want to fight with you. I know you have a problem with me, but I don't have one with you." Mat lifted the sleeping man's arm and pushed the tattered sleeve of Ruin's sweatshirt above the crook of his elbow. Taking a length of rubber tubing out of his pocket, Mat tied it around Ruin's upper arm and checked the resulting raised veins. He swabbed one with an alcohol wipe.

Aych tightened their jaw. "You going to explain what's wrong with him or do I need to see Lu for a conversation with an actual adult?"

Mat took a syringe out of his work smock and uncapped it. With practiced movements, the herbalist pressed on Ruin's arm with one hand and slid the tip of the syringe into the vein with the other.

"Now, we wait and let him sleep."

Aych took out their tobacco pouch. "I'm running low."

"I'll refill it for you, there's a new shipment just in. You'll need to be careful. Don't smoke it indoors around people … humans. The new batch of nervine came right off the upper moor on Blue Mountain last season. The primary compounds are more potent."

Sifting the crumbly mixture into the crease of the rolling paper, Aych glanced at the line of cars pulling up to the Velvet. They looked back at Ruin. "Is he going to be alright?"

"Should be," Mat ran his hand over his brow, suddenly looking much older and exhausted.

"How did they find him?" Aych cracked the window and an icy draft

A Holy Venom

blew in over the lip of the sill. Aych pushed the panel closed and tucked the cigarette back behind their ear.

"It was his prescription. They must've found him through his pharmacy records." Mat scowled. "He's been on a new antipsychotic just over a month." The herbalist steepled his hands together, resting his forehead against his fingertips. "The Aya called to tell me it's like the toxin the Perlustrate uses on their prisoners. A psychogenic drug. In a large dose, the drug intentionally causes brain damage. Except, in this case, some fuck waited until the new med was prescribed to Ruin specifically. Then they changed the instructions on his prescription packets. The way he took the dose changed it from the antipsychotic he was originally prescribed to the drug the dogs use, N-piperyl-2,4 methoxyphenyl propyl 1-methylhexyl amine. The lab report listed it as n-PMPMA."

Aych growled. "How the fuck can he be targeted by changing the fucking instructions on a med packet?"

Mat shook his head. "When you brought him back last time, he had the new meds in his jacket. Regular pharmacy packets, each one with a label printed out with his full name and dose instructions. That's nothing new, the pharmacies print those labels when they fill the script and hand-apply them to the packets for each patient. But the instructions listed on all the doses Ruin had on him stated 'take only with grapefruit juice,' which is fucked, pharmacologically." Mat stood up and nervously scrubbed at his ribs through the smock. "There's an enzyme in grapefruit that interferes with all kinds of chemical reactions. It's less common with herbal decoctions and tonics, but it happens enough that we get drilled on it as apprentices. When I read the instructions, I called up the pharmacy and double-checked it wasn't a typo. I thought maybe it was supposed to be *'don't* take with grapefruit juice.' And that's what it said on all the other prescription records for the drug! But on Ruin's record, the instructions clearly said *'take with.'* His pharmacist was as confused as I was."

Mat shook his head again. "I didn't want to risk saying anything in case he skipped his meds. Normally grapefruit would only render a med ineffective, it wouldn't weaponize it! Instead of going with my gut and flushing all the packets, I left them alone. I didn't want to scare him; I didn't want him to stop taking his meds. To find out if I was being paranoid, I sent a packet by fast boat to the Aya. It took a while to run the cryptotoxicology. The Aya only called me back with the lab report this afternoon." The herbalist's expression hardened. "Her divination also indicated it is a bespoke drug, engineered to target a specific patient—Ruin." He held Aych's gaze pointedly. "All an asshole would have to do is make it look like a random typo on Ruin's dose instructions. After a few days mixing the compound with grapefruit juice, he would have a full-blown psychotic break with psychogenic hallucinations and uncontrollable paranoia. That's what they wanted."

Aych growled. *Someone at the Stat is going to whistle. I'll start ripping apart the kitchen staff and work my way up.* "You checked this out? At the Stat?"

"He's my family, of course I went up!" Mat held his hands out defensively. "I know it was against Lu's instructions, I know it was risky, but I took the back stairs during third shift and checked the in-house pharmacy's records."

"Any fuckshow with access can just look up his info? It's that easy?" Growling again, Aych crushed a fresh wave of anger. *Hold. There will be time later after Ruin is safe.*

"That easy to find and read patient records, yes. But it's much harder to change them." Flinching away from Aych's expression, Mat glanced at the cigarette behind Aych's ear. "The Statler's records don't list a known address under his full name, but there's at least a dozen people who could've changed the instructions. They only had to wait for his doctor to prescribe it, which they would, even if they're innocent. Because it's a hereditary condition, even if he was being tracked under a false name, there'd be a trail, a matching pattern in the medical record. If you know how the diggers work, it's only a matter of waiting."

"Fuck!" Snarling, Aych smashed the side of their fist against the window jamb, leaving a dent in the wooden frame. "He's going to have to leave with Lu, go to Grava, get the fuck away from these shit-bags before they find him again." Opening their hand, Aych stared into the dazzling lights of the Velvet's marquee until spots burned across their vision. After a moment, they glared at the herbalist. "The Aya tell you what to use as an antidote? That's what you gave him? With the syringe?"

"Technically, it's an antivenin." Mat's expression closed up as Aych's

A Holy Venom

eyes narrowed.

"Antivenin? That's why it smelled …" Aych reached out and grabbed Mat by the throat. They shoved the human against the closed bedroom door. "Don't you fucking tell me you used Lu's venom on him."

"Just the antivenin derivative!" Mat choked and spluttered until Aych released their grip dropping him to the floor. "He's not in any danger! The dose I gave him only has the extracted proteins in it …"

"I don't fucking care." Aych leaned in and put their mouth next to Mat's ear. "If he gets sick or fucked up because you decided to experiment with his life, I'll be taking a fast boat myself to leave your fucking head on the steps of that fucking bundle of sticks and stones the Awy call home. Do you fucking hear me?"

"I wouldn't hurt him! I wouldn't let anyone hurt him!"

"You're a half-assed useless fuck who does whatever those degenerate swindlers and backwoods frauds tell you to do," Aych shoved Mat away from the door. They raised a long finger under the herbalist's face and let a single obsidian claw emerge out of the white flesh until the dagger tip hung between the human's eyes. "I would love to fucking gut you, remember that. I know there's something fucked with you and the Awy. The way you approached Lu for your Rot. You smell—"

There was a knock on the bedroom door and it slowly opened inward. Aych looked over as Lu stuck her face in.

"Bad time?" She glanced at the exposed claw Aych was pointing at Mat's eyeball.

Mat waited for Aych to step back before slipping by Lu. "Call for me if Ruin needs anything," he mumbled quickly as he stumbled down the staircase.

"I expected you back a few days ago." Raising her eyebrows at Aych, Lu walked over to the side of the bed and stroked back Ruin's hair. She peeled off her coat and laid the thick furs over his sleeping form. "Thankfully, you appear to have returned in time."

"That poor excuse for a healer better hope I did." Aych leaned against the bedroom door. "Did he tell you what the cure was? Using your venom like a Solstice prize given out to all the good children this year. Fucker."

"I gave him *permission* to use the antivenin." Spinning on her heel, Lu swiveled and rested her hand on her hip. "You do tend to overreact when it comes to people hurting your favorite. He will be fine. He has survived worse. And if you're worried about the antivenin causing problems, it won't."

"Once you get him to Grava, I'll stop being so concerned." Ignoring her taunt, Aych jerked their chin in the direction of the windows. "There's a blizzard tonight; you still expecting a full house?"

"Every night. Some nights it just takes them longer to get their behinds in the seats." Hooking a finger through the string of lustrous pearls around her neck, Lu glanced from the windows back to Aych. "What happened with the hunter?"

"Long version or short version?"

"Tell me the version that explains why you're …" Lu waved her other hand. "In whatever kind of mood you're in. You're not usually capable of being calm and pissed off at the same time. Mat's lucky he's still got both eyes in his head."

Aych looked back at the bed and watched Ruin's chest rising and falling under Lu's coat. "The hunter ran away from his shitty little town to chase fame and fortune. He's after the bright lights now."

"You accidentally ate him and *that's* your excuse? Is that what you're telling me?"

Aych shot her a grim smile. "I wish I had eaten him. But no, we're running out of time to find a replacement."

"What's changed?"

"He's not a magician, he's worse."

"Worse?" Lu walked over to Aych. "What did he do, pull a rabbit out of his ear? Disappear Betwixt?"

"He's somebody's idea of clergy," Aych avoided her eyes. "A god is protecting him. And he pulled some kind of psychic trick on me."

"You're sure?" Lu frowned. "And you didn't kill him?"

"Oh, I'm sure," Aych grimaced. "No, I did not."

"But you're certain you didn't eat him?"

"I would remember that." Aych moved around her to the bedside. "I vented my displeasure on a convent. That's why I'm late. Ate too many annas and had to sleep it off." They stared down at Ruin.

Lu rocked her hips again and sighed, toying with the pearls. "Who does he belong to, the hunter?"

"That I don't know." Undoing the button of their suit jacket, Aych settled onto the bed and leaned against the headboard. "It gets worse." They stared at Ruin's face. *He doesn't need this shit, he doesn't deserve to be fucked with.*

Lu glanced up at the seagulls painted on the ceiling. "How much worse?"

"You're not going to like it."

"I didn't like it the minute I walked in and caught you about to maim the only human able to make what we need to get the job done."

"Like I said before, our boy's seeking the bright lights. The hunter's here, in this city."

Lu stared at Aych in disbelief. "You have got to be joking."

"I wish I was." Aych shrugged. "The lure is tracking him now. It was created to return to the candidate if they tried to get rid of it. I didn't expect anyone to leave it and simply run away."

"Is he coming after you on his own? Is he still even in his right mind? You killed his friend and you've been terrorizing him. After your fight, he's got to be unhinged at the very least."

"And I faked taking the kid he employs hostage. Add to that a convent full of very real, dead annas."

"If you pulled that crap with me, I'd want to end you."

"That was the plan."

"How long until your pet finds him?"

"Any time now."

Lu paused. "I don't like it. If he is skillful enough to come looking for you here, he could be more trouble than he's worth. Who else knows about him? Anyone that could've tipped him off?"

"The Caretaker would know our plans." At the mention of the name, Aych felt a sharp pain stab the base of their skull and winced as it increased. "Doesn't matter, he passed the interview. We use him, no matter what else is going on. If he can rattle me for a few minutes, he'll do just fine."

"I don't like anything to do with your so-called Caretaker. I tell you what else I don't like: a hunter smart enough to run away is one thing, but one crazy enough to hunt *you?*" She grimaced. "That's not hubris, that's obsession. Or his protector has a grudge."

"That could be the lure. That's how it is supposed to work, dragging him to me. Whoever he belongs to, they're a babysitter, not a player. Could be any number of assholes out there wanting to fuck this up for us. Hell, they don't even need to know about our plan. It could be Fate, for all I know."

Lu made a rude noise and shook her head. Then she wagged a finger back and forth. "The reason I agreed to this at all was you said it would be quick and clean. That you could get what we want without ever having to go inside. Now you're telling me there's a whole group of unknown Gods trying to get in on this?" Shaking her head, Lu headed into the minuscule bathroom and turned on the sink faucet. "Pure idiocy. And no, I'm not having anything to do with this. You can do whatever you want, but if that's the case, I'm out. You can play games with the hunter on your own. If there's other players getting involved—"

"We can handle outsiders." Getting off the bed to follow her, Aych leaned against the frame of the bathroom door. They watched as Lu washed and dried her hands then checked her make-up. "You think I want to use a human as part of this? Believe me, I'd kill him and leave him for the crows if I could."

Lu glanced in the mirror to meet Aych's gaze. "I know you don't want to talk about it, but it's likely this Caretaker of yours has tipped him off. They are the only other source who could even know the hunter exists. Could they be protecting him?"

"We don't know if it was them. If it was, they have never interfered before." Aych winced as the migraine-level pain pressed on the back of their eyes.

"Leaving that subject aside." From the corner of her eye, Lu watched Aych grimace again. "Let's say the lure finds him." She pointed at Aych's reflection. "Would he last fifteen minutes out there?"

The migraine halos around Lu's face faded from Aych's vision as the pain lessened. "Ten probably. He uses homemade bombs, which should work as a distraction along with his magic tricks. Those and his babysitter might keep him alive for ten. For an added bonus, he doesn't give a shit about living. Classic survivor guilt complex and trauma baggage. All the cracks I could hope for. He's looking for death. I can smell it on him."

A Holy Venom

"We never considered him staying alive. That's not the plan." Lu clicked her tongue. "The hunter was always going to die out there. You should've just eaten him and saved us all the trouble."

"Always the smarter option." Walking along the foot of the four-poster bed back to the windows, Aych pushed the curtains away from the glass and resumed watching the front of the Velvet. "The way he fights now, he's not going to hold his own for too long. He'll be dead before I make it over the garden wall. But he's getting information from somewhere. He showed up to our fight in a blindfold and recited lyrics from one of Ruin's songs at me."

"He fought you *blindfolded?*" Lu's voice, incredulous, rang from the bathroom.

"To prevent the hook being set in, I suspect. Like I said, he was tipped off." Aych rubbed the throbbing at the base of their neck. "He's not going to show up at your door fully unhinged, shouting about monsters like he just rolled fresh out of the Stat, if that's what you're worried about. He's not rattled or spooked. Well, not by me."

"That would still be fine," Lu called from the bathroom. "As long as you can still point him in the right direction on the hook then get in and out safely. Without going into the House."

"No reason to go inside." Aych rubbed the back of their neck stretching against the ache. "Like I told you, the garden is easy. No one ever tries to steal anything out of it. Not even the weird sorcery collectors like the Awy give a shit about what's in there. No one knows about the fountain. Well, not the legit one."

"If this hunter is an ignorant fool out to kill you, then he deserves to die. But if you get caught in the House, I can't help you. It would be betraying you, sending you to take all the risks, and then to leave you in there to die. And you know I won't do that. Not to anyone, not even to humans. If it's a risk, I can't let you go through with it."

"I know." Aych watched a limo pull up and deliver a load of high-class tourists to the Velvet. The exposed flesh of the out-of-towners' fashionable gowns worn without winter coats made Aych's jaw clench. "You don't do betrayal. Rule number one of Lu's School of Charming, Well-Behaved Butchers."

Lu came out of the bathroom and leaned against the doorframe. "You can't go anywhere near that House."

"Believe me, I have no desire to ever go in it ever again."

"You would if you had to." She glanced at Ruin. "Anyway, we will need to find the hunter and then keep him hooked. Keep him from getting too feisty until Mat has the second batch done. I'm not letting you go in without the second dose as insurance." She walked over to the bed and briefly rested her fingers on the sleeping human, then stepped back with her coat in hand.

"Will it work?"

"Don't ask me. You're the one that said it would work," Aych frowned. "You've used it before."

Lu caressed the wooden bedpost, her expression troubled. "It should. Mat's close to finishing the last batch now. Making the antivenin for the *gaesu* took him away from finishing it. We have to wait until he has both doses."

"If you believe he knows what the hell he's doing. Not that I'm complaining that I'm risking my ass on that fool's ability to make a quality product. But this one is almost out of options," Aych glanced at Ruin.

"Do you trust me?" Slipping her hand off the bedpost, Lu stared into Aych's eyes. "Do you think I'd let anything happen to you or to him?"

"I didn't mean you'd screw me over. It's the Caretaker I'm not so sure about." Smiling ruefully, Aych tried to hide the crippling migraine flaring behind their skull. "As for them, if they wanted to step on me, they could've done it ages ago. When I didn't have you to tell me I was being set up for the long play."

"I don't like it. The way they're rolling you right now for even mentioning they exist." Her eyes searched Aych's.

"You've never liked it."

"True, I think it's garbage, the way …" Lu stopped. She looked away from Aych's face. "It's your business, not mine."

Aych nodded and watched her. "The question now is, are you still in?"

Leaning her back into the bedpost, Lu shrugged. "It doesn't change anything on my end, besides having to potentially wait on another human for a few days. Is this hunter at least attractive?"

Snorting, Aych shook their head. "He knows how to use soap, but if his divination leads him to the Velvet, Vetch might not let him in."

"He looks like a salt?"

"The opposite. The way he dresses, he might have a hard time getting into The Cellar."

"Does this unpolished gem have a name?"

"Ky."

Lu slipped on her fur. "I'll have a word with Vetch, tell him to keep an eye out for this Ky, in case he's been pointed in our direction." Out of the corner of her eye, she watched Aych. "This doesn't appear to be bothering you as much as I would've expected. Even without the hook, you must've worked him hard enough by now that he'd stick a dagger in you on sight."

"He doesn't know what I look like except when I'm Big. Not likely to run into me in that form unless I wish it." Turning back to watch Ruin sleep, Aych shrugged. "What else can I say? Eating sixty-plus humans makes me mellow. If he shows up and tries anything, I'll give him a pass. One time, just for you."

"You're terrible. Don't you have any self-control? A whole convent! You fiend." Lu slapped at Aych's arm. "How many humans can you eat? No, don't answer that." With her hands up, Lu started for the door. "I'm sorry I even asked."

"I always save room for dessert."

"You cannot eat the hunter, even when you find him. Don't even think about it."

"If I did, we could look for a better one."

"No. We don't have time for any more interviews. Ruin needs us to finish this job now, not later. You will not eat the hunter. Promise me?"

"What if he does try and stick a knife in me or hit me with another of his toilet cleaner bombs? Can I get a morality clause on that promise?"

"What are you, an entertainment lawyer now?" Laughing, Lu shook her head. "Fine, if he manages to actually injure you, you can eat him ... *after* the job gets done."

"Won't be anything left of him after. Shit," Aych scowled.

"We cannot be waiting on the lure to find a replacement. You and I have things to do before we can even start the real work. And don't you forget about—"

"Like I could."

"Walk me back, since you're making me late. Get yourself to the tables and be useful until you're needed back here. I don't want you hanging around the front door if the hunter does show up." Lu wagged her finger at Aych. "We don't want him starting a brawl with you straight off. I don't want to have to explain any of this to Violet if I don't have to."

"He won't recognize me. Not a quick thinker. I'm amazed he can practice magic at all."

"If he's protected and psychic, he might be getting tipped off. If you find him, let me work on him before renewing your acquaintance."

"Now you're changing the plan ..." Aych glanced at Ruin. "I said I'd be here when he—"

"And you will be. Don't you worry, we'll get this done, one way or the other."

"Yeah, we will. We have to, right?"

Lu gave Aych a dazzling smile. "Exactly. Now, let's go find Vetch and see if the hunter's found our lair."

TWELVE

KY EXITED the Velvet's revolving door, troubled by his new occupation. The head of security had been amiable enough, and the other security guards welcomed him with the same kind of comradery a new recruit could expect in the best barracks: casual assessment of capability, an invitation to join in via friendly banter, genuine acceptance held in reserve until they could see how the new pair of hands shook out. The tin of charcoal pellets in his pocket, the casual questions about his military service and his specialties, the smooth ripple of polite questions; all of it, including the staff's calm professionalism, painted a different kind of picture than what Mudon had pitched on the train. These people were the mop and bucket brigade called in the aftermath of others' poor choices. As Ky had listened and watched the group, none of them, not the newer ones in their cheaper suits or the more seasoned in their tailored expensive clothes, seemed particularly parasitic, psychotic, or sadistic. More importantly, none of the theatre staff gave off the hurricane force of rage and fury he had encountered in the convent garden. None of them carried the tell-tale sign of contamination.

Stepping onto the red carpet, Ky angled sideways out of the path of incoming guests while shrugging his loaned overcoat over his shoulders. The winter night slipped under his scarf and he thought to take his knitted cap out of the duffel slung over his back. He considered if he had made a mistake letting Mudon chivy him along with a salt's tale of unchecked crime and a detailed map of Ky's guilt complex. Thoughts of Haw's widow and children, living in the farmhouse that now must seem too empty to them, all of it slotted right into a long list of terrible things he had been powerless to prevent. Regret and self-loathing, an overabundance of giving a shit, Ky knew these were the tangled bits of himself Mudon had hooked on the line and used to drag him right into the thick of his private war.

Keeping an eye on the trajectories of the taxis, Ky stepped off the curb and into the street. Firecrackers of warning snapped up his spine, the countersignal flaring like struck matches on his nerves. Stiffening, he scanned his surroundings for the incoming threat.

Directly in front of him, outside the Teahouse, a large figure started into traffic with a cloud of blue-tinged smoke trailing off a cigarette. Remarkable for their pallid skin and uncommon height, the stranger stood a full head taller than anyone else in view, their skin shining pearlescent in the neon of the street. A stunning woman in a fur coat clung to the tall stranger's arm. The two took their time as they crossed, as if they knew the traffic would stop for them. Taxis slowed and waited as the pair leisurely talked, plumes of smoke swirling from the tall one's cigarette. As they approached, Ky tried to determine which of the two he was being warned about. Even at a distance, the woman gave off an eerie, phosphorescent glow, while her taller companion's aura appeared dim and strangely contracted. All Ky could glean from the tall stranger was an unnatural stillness, a weird *absence*.

Aware of Ky's scrutiny, Aych took another drag, letting the smoke sink into their lungs. The toxins unwound into their blood, lessening the urge to be confrontational, to get right in Ky's face and open their jaws wide enough to swallow the hunter's entire thick skull. *What a fucking dumbass, standing on the corner with his jaw hanging open.* Anger and frustration set Aych's teeth on edge. *This isn't a sideshow, asshole. You're going to have to learn fast if you don't want to die in under a minute.* Coming abreast of the human, Aych met Ky's eyes briefly and then looked back at Lu and rolled their eyes dismissively.

To Ky, time slowed. He stared for what seemed like an eternity as he locked with the stranger's eyes, one cold blue, the other blazing gold. They burned into him, judging him down to his bones like a Presence weighing his fate, finding him unfit. Ky rushed into the street. A car horn blared. Shaken and panting, he reached the sidewalk outside the Teahouse and fought the desire to look back.

"That was him," Aych murmured to Lu. "The hunter."

A Holy Venom

Lu laughed and threw a quick glance over her shoulder. "He didn't recognize you?"

"He's another half-assed fool."

As Lu and Aych approached the entrance, Vetch nodded in greeting. "Good evening, empress of the night. Any new brews I should know about?" He nodded at the Teahouse.

"Why yes, if you can spare a minute, I'll tell you all about them." Lu transferred her grip to Vetch's arm and playfully pulled him in the direction of the brass spindle.

Aych let the pair head into the first divided section. Casting a look over their shoulder, they waited and stepped into the next junction.

"That one that just left, in the gray coat. He's new to the house?" Lu murmured to Vetch as they stepped into the heated lobby.

Vetch slipped his hands over her shoulders and eased off her coat. "You've got an even quicker eye than I do if you spotted him that fast. Just hired him."

"What can you tell me about our new employee?"

"Rue asked me to give him a chance. Took him in to get the salt off his boots. Bad for leather, just like cars." Vetch gestured to a staff member and handed her Lu's coat and added his own. "He's a soldier wanting to play at being a shepherd. Sets up a good front, and if you weren't casting the right kind of eye over him, you might fall for it."

"Oh?" Lu smiled at the coat check attendant then turned to Vetch. "A ram that thinks himself a shepherd?"

Vetch gave her an elegant half-shrug. "Man's seen some things and hauled his share of iron. Way he carries himself tells me we can use him to right a few tables. Use him as a backdrop, as it were. Like I said, the seats will buy tickets to his show and not check for his strings. Soldier like that is used to taking orders. In this business, you have to be inspired, not just know when to lock a door and when to kick it down." He looked appreciatively at Lu's figure. "That one thinks in straight lines and misses the curves and angles."

"Not exactly what we look for in this house." Lu returned Vetch's appraising look with a sultry one of her own. "You have him coming back tomorrow night, I take it? I might have a use for him."

His eyebrows shot up in surprise.

"I've got an appointment early in the evening before my show. Daisy is driving me up." Lu pressed her hand against Vetch's lapel. "Why don't you have him join me for the ride? I'd like to see how we get on. I could use a good doorstop." She held the human's gaze until Vetch nodded. "Then, if he seems like he might be someone useful, we've got an easy job for him across the street, don't we?" She smiled at Aych then looked back at Vetch. "If you don't mind me taking him off your hands, that is?"

"You had me worried there for a minute, *tau-ve-lm.*" Vetch grinned. "Of course, if he suits your needs …"

"I should head back and get ready for the curtain to rise. So lovely to catch up with you." Lu glided her finger along Vetch's jaw. She smiled back at Aych. "Are you not staying?" She pointedly glanced at their winter coat.

"I need to have a word myself." Aych dropped a hand on Vetch's shoulder. "Then I need to start my shift at the job you were just telling Vetch about."

Lu shrugged her slim shoulders. "You never come watch my act anymore." Pouting, she gave them both a sad look and then sighed dramatically. "I wonder who will walk me in, oh, hello …"

Vetch shook his head as he watched her select a new victim from the admirers standing at a polite distance. Throwing a glance up at Aych, Vetch jerked his head toward the bar. "You got time for a drink, or should we go back outside so you can smoke one of those bug bombs of yours?"

"Time enough to let you defrost," Aych nodded, moving closer. "Besides, it's only right I buy you a drink before asking for a favor."

"A favor? Why that's pure coincidence as here I was thinking I'd have to do the same." Vetch smiled at the security posted by the bar and made a low gesture with his right hand.

The staff opened up a spot for the pair and then lingered behind them discreetly blocking off the area from the overly curious.

The uniformed bartender welcomed the pair with a proprietary smile. "What can I pour you two fine youngsters this evening?"

Vetch returned her smile with one of his own. "Thirty year, please, Bekka. Neat."

The bartender nodded and looked expectantly at Aych.

A Holy Venom

Vetch looked up at them. "Same?"

Snorting, Aych nodded to Bekka. "You should've gone for the hundred year."

"Nah, she'd have to go back to the lock box." Vetch smiled and winked at the bartender.

"He saved me from blowing the dust off the last bottle and kicking up my allergies. Plus saved me a trip to arm wrestle the cask steward at the distillery for a replacement bottle." Bekka cracked a wide smile as she laid two napkins embossed with the theatre's monogram on the marble countertop. She set down two full glasses and went down the bar to chat with her other customers.

Checking over his shoulder, Vetch leaned into Aych. "This about that new pair of boots?"

"No." Tipping the glass back, Aych took a swallow of the whisky and let it burn down their throat. As far as toxins went, alcohol did little to ease the constant restrictive discomfort of their Little form. "We know Boots, though he doesn't know us yet. He's almost on Lu's hook."

"From the way she was working me, I figured it was a setup like that." Vetch watched Aych drink and then took a sip of his own. "What do you need?"

"Set of eyes at the Stat. A set you can recommend that'll look into a paper trail for me." Aych swirled the amber alcohol, catching the reflected lights of the lobby chandeliers in the thick liquid.

"This house business or personal?" Vetch raised an eyebrow and the gold ring in his brow glinted.

Aych dipped their head. "Someone used the Stat's records to find the kid, then stepped on his meds. Looks like they wanted to push him, hoping he'd start up the family tradition."

Hissing, Vetch took a hefty swallow of his whisky and straightened up. "Holy Mother and her Saint. He in trouble again?"

"Only him, no one else got hurt." Anger rolled over Aych and they forced themselves to relax. "We sorted it. He needs a few days to come down off the effects. They stepped on his meds."

"Fucked with his meds? That's vile. Nasty," Vetch caught Aych's eye. "You going to let him know he got stepped on that way? Might put him off ever taking meds again."

"He has the right to decide. His meds, his shit to manage." Aych made a face and tilted their glass. "Won't get stepped on a second time, I can assure you."

"You're not going to make it as a bodyguard with that *a second-time* shit." Vetch looked out over the shoulders of the staff members standing between their private conversation and the rest of the lobby. "Vee and I both remember when the *gae-su* got taken, kidnapped right off the street in front of here. It changed the whole city, what happened to him, how they found him all messed up like that. In Grava, there's a code, but here, vengeance spills out on children. Uncivilized northern fucks," Vetch scowled. "Whatever his family did, he was born innocent. He's been paying interest on his family's debts since he was a baby. Not everyone understands the burdens of that kind of legacy." He swallowed another mouthful and grimaced. "I'll get you those eyes. Should be plenty down at the tables that can find information up on the Hill, given the correct motivation."

"A pair you don't mind me closing afterward." Aych glanced over meaningfully.

"Speaking of, Mudon's taking a run at reserving a spot up the Hill if he's thinking he can drop a whistle in our house." Vetch raised his glass in a salute to the Velvet and then turned back to lean against the bar. "What's the deal with Boots if both Lu and that salt have him hooked?"

"You're sure Mudon sent him over?" Aych frowned. "He didn't come on his own?"

"The salt tried to leverage Rue to get his whistle hired on." Vetch frowned. "Mudon has delusions of being a shepherd so bad, he might as well go sleep in the park under the stars."

Aych frowned. *Someone's stacking the deck, cutting the hunter in.* "Boots has a talent Lu is interested in. Temple tricks, probably the same reason Mudon called him up from the sticks. He's got a knack for calling other people's hands."

Vetch frowned and made a superstitious gesture with his left hand. "If Lu didn't already put an ask in on him, I'd ask you to drop him in the Twins. We don't need a reader hanging around."

"But she did, and you agreed." Aych shot him a sly smile. "Don't worry.

She's going to keep him close and busy until we don't need him anymore."

"Will he be useful keeping an eye on the tables after she's worked her magic?"

"If there's anything left, she said I could have him."

"You've got a nasty streak yourself." Shaking his head, Vetch watched the lobby.

"I take it there's someone else you had in mind for that out-of-season dip in the Twins?" Aych swirled the last of their drink around the bottom of the glass.

"It's a matter of our honor, our reputation as a house," Vetch caught and held Aych's gaze. "Mudon crossed a line dropping a whistle. If he's on the leash …"

"He's too proud, I told you. It's that partner of his. They've got Tosh hooked nice and tight and she's pulling Mudon along as she goes."

Vetch exhaled and set his glass on the marble counter. "Vee extended their hospitality to Mudon. The traditional way of doing business. We let the salts have a taste of honey and petty cash should keep them plenty sweet."

"You changed the business." Aych inclined their head. "Gambling and the rest, the Tank was willing to pass on. But this new—"

"That you two brought in." Vetch threw up his hands. "Not that we're not grateful for the added revenue, but to your point, we changed first. It's true. Out of consideration, we gave the Tank time to catch up. But this trespass, this we can't overlook. New business or old business aside, I don't much care for how the seats can't handle the new trick. We may have to pull back some or find a way to smooth it out. Before the dogs come round asking about it in their particular way."

"How you want to play out, then?" Aych shook their head at Bekka as the bartender indicated the empty glass on the bar.

"If you're right about Tosh, she's going to be a problem. If we punish the Tank, we have to be skillful. Can't give the dogs an excuse to sniff around inside the Velvet. Vee's going to want it done by custom, reinforce house authority. It is a conundrum."

"A shepherd with decent skills knows how to handle dogs," Aych teased the human. They dropped a hand on Vetch's shoulder. "I'll take care of it for you, you get me the info from the Stat."

"Should have it for you by tomorrow. If the kid needs anything, you let us know. In Grava, we've always considered his family off limits, protected by both the Saint and the Shepherd. Even the dogs won't go after that family. Though given their proclivities, you'd think they'd have ended up in their kennel long ago." Vetch finished his drink. "His dad used to bring him over to sing at the Summer Solstice charity show. He ever tell you that? Only time of the year we drop the dress code and let anyone in, including the underage. Vee would let the whole lot of them park their loud machines up on the sidewalk. With his talent, he belongs on a stage like this one." Vetch nodded in the direction of the theatre. "Not living the rest of his life in hiding or locked up on the Hill."

"Agreed." Setting a large bill on the bar next to the empty glasses, Aych nodded at Bekka. "If Lu likes Boots, she'll have him keep the kid company for a few days."

Surprised, Vetch gave Aych a wide-eyed look. "You trust him?"

Aych laughed. "No, but I do know he's protective, probably a decent bodyguard."

"Kid's going to wrap that one around his little finger like he does the rest of us. I hope Boots takes care of the *gae-su* and stays out of the Twins." Vetch patted Aych on the back. "Can't say the same for whoever stepped on the kid's meds."

☾

Ky unzipped his duffel bag and took out his toiletry case. The weight seemed off. He carried it over to the attic room's single window and opened it, turning it to catch the glow of the streetlight. Through the open zipper, the stone head leered. The impish features appeared to gloat at him.

"Fucking thing..." Annoyed, Ky tossed the bag onto the foot of the steel-framed bed and immediately regretted doing so.

He scowled and rubbed the stubble on his chin with the back of his hand then walked over to scoop the toiletry bag up and deal with the stowaway. Using the corner of the borrowed towel, he extracted the head and looked around the room. Spotting the crumbling chimney intersecting the opposite wall, Ky carried the head over and inspected the bricks. Finding one that shimmied and released a trickle of reddish dust under his fingers, Ky pried it out and looked into the hollowed-out hole.

"In you go, you shitty little fuck." He wedged the head in and slammed the brick back covering it.

Shaking out the brick dust from his towel, Ky retrieved his toiletry bag along with a bundle of fresh bandages and headed for the shared bathroom.

☾

The tiles of the arched hallway flickered into sight as the boy flipped on the light switch. The caged bulbs overhead buzzed and dinged, spreading a pool of white light, and then suddenly popped, burning out. Plunged back into the pitch dark, the boy snapped the switch back and forth and then leaned against the wall. The brief outline of the hallway stayed in his mind, another basement hall with the same kinds of doors further down. The cold tiles numbed his left shoulder and he pushed away to stand and blink in the dark. His stomach growled. He was so hungry he almost wished he was back in the suite, just to eat a sandwich. In the dark, only the sound of his own breathing and the slap of his feet on the floor followed him through the basement wards. He started the routine again, fingers of his left hand on the wall above his shoulder feeling for the next light switch. Ears aching for sounds other than his own, nose and tongue testing for the cool, bright smell of water or fresh air. The last draft brought him to a faucet; the next might lead him out of the depths of the tunnels and treatment wards of the forgotten section of the Statler.

His feet were numb and the numbness crept up through his body, inching from his skin inward. The darkness and silence no longer troubled him. The quiet was comforting and he was used to the ghosts passing by on their pre-recorded rounds. Growing up in a haunted mansion, he was used to the visual whisps trailing out of the corners of his eyes. The sudden squeak of a door might chill him, stopping him with stiff-legged terror, the thudding of the pipes sometimes freezing his heart and lungs. Breath held, heart thudding every time he waited and nothing came reaching for him out of the dark. So far, the worst was stubbing his bare toes and bruising his knees against the tub in the first treatment room. Being alone was better than the endless soothing voices of the therapists and nurses upstairs, all the hands poking and prodding. The endless tests and questions. The dark tunnels under the institute were definitely better than the dumpy hotel room that had been his prison; even better than the creepy hospital suite he had escaped from to roam the underreaches of the institution. He could walk and no one yelled at him … or worse.

His throat closed against the fear of being back in there, in his aunt's suite upstairs in his family's wing of the asylum. He remembered the sounds through the vent grate, his deranged uncle's voice rising and falling in the next suite over, sometimes sounding like a sobbing man and other times, like a petulant woman's angry voice. The voices would argue for hours, tinny and echoing through the vent, the man's voice pleading while the woman's demanded. The boy swallowed again. From the strange whispers and anguished shouting that echoed through the vent between the suites, the boy had guessed there had been something in the room with his uncle, something worse than kidnappers. When the thing that haunted his uncle started whispering to the boy through the grate, he knew he had to make a run for it before it got into his room and started in on him. He didn't want to end up trapped with whatever it was. Now, he was lost in the dark far below and didn't know how to get out.

The tunnel went cold, the draft hitting the boy's feet. He opened his mouth to take in the moist, sweet air. Thirst taught him that water possessed a fragrance, similar to how sunlight carried warmth—telltale signs the body understands and will seek out on its own. Soon his ears heard dripping; without a thought, he stumble-ran, keeping his fingers lightly on the walls, slowing only when the remembered agony of his stubbed toes shimmered along his nerves. He slapped his hand on the wall, hoping to find another switch. The air and the darkness felt wider. The wall curved to the left, painting an image in the darkness of a larger space. The dripping and the coolness collected inside his skull, the stillness radiating back emptiness. He knew he was alone, and his only fear was ending up with more bruises or falling into a hole. Metal clattered as a cart rolled away from his touch, the sound jarringly loud. The echoes carried back as he circled, keeping his hand on the tiles and smelling for the water.

A Holy Venom

His thumb brushed over a metal plate, and then, the stub of a light switch. Jubilant, he toggled the lights on. The snapping, rolling clicks dinged and buzzed as he squeezed his eyes shut and covered his face against the onslaught of light. The white porcelain glowed under the ceiling lamps, harshly and without warmth. Frosted globes hung over the central bath. Below, in the center of the chamber, an empty bathing pool held tufts of dirt and dust. Squinting, the boy made out ornate leaf and wave-patterned mosaics set along the circular walls and repeated in the tiered steps leading down into the dry pool.

The boy was relieved that he'd managed not to fall into the pool. Nodding, he felt proud of himself. So often he had been full of doubt and fear; it was nice to not feel stupid.

The antique light bulbs flickered and dinged. He quickly scanned the large central chamber for the source of the delicious scent of fresh water. A bank of sinks stood between the black holes of two other tunnels. His feet were already marching him to the water as the round globe lights overhead sputtered.

A shadow sat on one of the sinks. The boy stopped and stared. Thirst pushed him, but he waited, trying to figure out what he was seeing. The inky shadow turned and a pair of cat eyes looked at the boy. Smiling, the boy extended a hand to the black animal.

"Can I have a drink too?" He managed to touch the tip of its tail. The cat's fur was fluffy and soft.

The cat flicked its tail away and regarded the boy as if weighing his worth. Then, accompanied by the tinkling of a silver bell on its collar, it daintily stepped to the next sink over.

"Thanks!" Wrenching on the ornate, chubby handle of the faucet, the boy opened the tap and stuck his head under it. Icy and sweet, the water froze his throat as he gulped.

When he had enough and shut the faucet back off, the cuts and stitches in his arms pulled with his movements. He wiped his mouth and looked around for the cat. The last few lights that still worked began to sputter and then snapped off, leaving the boy alone in the dark once again.

"Hello? Are you there?" Loneliness and fear brushed over him.

There was water on the floor under his feet and his fingers followed from the edge of one sink basin to the next. In the dark, unreliable shapes floated in front of his eyes.

"Hello? Mr. Cat?" He heard the desperate edge in his voice and winced, remembering how his uncle spoke through the vent between their rooms.

A faint tinkling sound brought his head around. "Kitty?"

He'd moved past the last sink and felt the tiled wall again. A new draft reached him and he remembered seeing a tunnel edged with vine mosaics. The tinkling echoed, growing fainter. "Wait for me!" he called, hoping the cat might be going outside.

His feet slapped against the floor and his breath rasped. He was running in the dark. *There could be another empty pool and you'd fall right into it like a dumbass.* Unable to stop himself, he chased the phantom sound, unsure if it was the cat's bell or his imagination. Exhausted, he slowed, his chest heaving. He leaned against the wall and breathed deeply. The air tasted colder and the tiles stung his feet. Shivering, he wrapped his arms around himself and took another step forward.

His eyes began to see fluffy gray shapes as the sides of the tunnel formed. The dark thinned. Suddenly the air was fresher and tasted of snow. He blinked and took another step.

Something sharp scraped his foot. He pulled it back just as his eyes adjusted enough to see the shape of bare trees. A rusty thumbnail of a moon gave off a weak light, revealing a snowy forest filled with dark, craggy trees.

Thinking he was outside behind the institute, the boy spun around, expecting the Statler looming behind him. Trees and more snow were behind him, the white ground unbroken—no trace of his footsteps, or the cat's. Frowning, he shivered and glanced around, listening for the bell.

The snow scrapped and burned as he plodded through it. Bone-deep and cutting, the pain from each step radiated up his legs. He willed the numbness to come back. *I'm going to die like one of the explorers who tried to find the North Pole. Only I'm just a dumb kid who ran away from a psych ward.* Head down and leaning forward, his arms wrapped around his stomach, he kept going. It could take hours or minutes, but he knew he had to keep walking until he saw the familiar stone outline of the Statler Institute. *In the movies, the ones who stop and rest in the snow die. You can't stop no matter what. Keep going, dumbass.*

A Holy Venom

He thought of his parents who were already worried about him, about his poor crazy uncle who was always so sad on visiting days, asking if the boy knew how to ride a motorcycle yet, if he had had any adventures, if he had any friends. *If you die here, none of that will happen. You will die having done nothing, tried nothing, been nothing. Keep. Going.*

The boy blundered into something warm and soft. From overhead, an enormous pair of eyes glowed in the dark, too big to be the cat's. Startled, the boy shouted and fell backward into the snow.

The eyes came closer and hot breath cascaded over him. The warmth felt better than anything he could remember. Like a steam room, wet and blistering at the same time. It melted the snow under him and pasted the thin pajamas to his damp skin. The shadowy, hulking thing looming over him smelled like sunshine and a flower garden on a midsummer's day. He stared. The delicious warmth was coming from a muzzle full of long, bone-white fangs. Tall, pointed ears rotated to either side of the massive beast's head. It was looking at him, waiting, one eye the bright blue of frost and the other a warm gold, like honey in the jar at the Teahouse.

"I'm lost. Can you help me?" He didn't care if he was dreaming, or if the monster in the forest wasn't real. The boy reached out to it. "Please?"

☽

Ruin slowly woke to find himself lying in his childhood bed. The winter sky hung outside the windows as fat flakes of snow cascaded out of his line of sight. Warmth suffused his back. The rising and falling of Aych's chest was slow and Ruin knew if he laid his hand against it there would be an absence underlying the rhythm of their breath. Over the years, he had gradually noticed the lack of heartbeat. It had been startling at first but now filled him with a strange comfort. Above his head, the painted seabirds in the ceiling mural flew in place as they always had. The world seemed entirely too well-behaved and rigid, the bleak daylight locking the reality of the garret room into place.

"You need anything to eat or drink?" Aych's voice rumbled through Ruin's torso.

"Water would be good." Battered and hollow, Ruin sat up slowly as

Aych assisted him. The inside of his mouth was cottony and tasted like shit.

Aych handed him a glass, the cool light reflecting off the surface of the water. The liquid was room temperature and something about the taste made Ruin wonder when he had brushed his teeth last.

"I probably smell like roadkill." Feeling self-conscious, Ruin started to roll away. Memories of the subway and snippets of jumbled thoughts threatened him.

Aych pulled him into a loose embrace. "You smell fine."

Their breath warmed his ear. Torn between wanting Aych's warmth and not letting himself want more, Ruin leaned his head back. "You're not hungry, I take it?"

"Not really." There was an edge of laughter in Aych's reply.

Ruin slipped his fingers into Aych's. "Not the fierce hunger in your jaws, killer?"

Aych laughed. "No, nor in my throat, nor in my chest, nor all the way down to my stomach."

"What of the hunger behind it all?" Ruin recited the line from the fairytale. "The hunger that drives you …"

"It sleeps yet." Aych rolled sideways, curling Ruin into the crook of their arm. "Now, what is it you actually want to ask me?"

Ruin gazed into their face; he knew it was one of several. Aych's eyes always stayed the same. "Did I kill anyone this time?" He braced for the answer. Waiting, the dread and hope dared him to lean in to steal a kiss, but he could not bring himself to do it. There was an unexpected thrill to being so close, and he knew he would make excuses to stay like this as long as possible.

Aych closed their eyes for a moment. "No, psycho, you didn't kill anyone. There weren't any new trophies in the crypt, either."

Lying against Aych made Ruin's teeth ache. He wondered what would happen if he brought his face close to their neck and tasted the smooth, impossible skin and let his teeth close as he bit down.

Aych shook him. "I hate to break it to you, but it's not your fault this time. You got stepped on."

Pulling back, Ruin scrunched his face in disbelief. "It wasn't—"

"Not the shit-bag and not your wiring. Not this time." Aych rocked their head side to side against their arm. "It wasn't your fault."

"Stepped on? Like someone slipped shit in my drink?" Sitting upright, Ruin crossed his legs and stared down at Aych.

"They fucked with your meds."

Fear raced up Ruin's back and he instinctively tugged the sleeves of his sweatshirt down over the scars lacing his body. "They found me?"

"Yes, but not through your address." Aych studied Ruin's face. "Mat had your prescription checked. It's safe as long as you don't take it with grapefruit juice."

"What the fuck?" Ruin shot off the bed. "You're telling me they fucked with me without ever being in the same room? That they can just fuck with my medication whenever they want?" He began to pace. If they could find him, if anyone could find him …

"No, they can't. I'm taking care of it." Aych sat up. "You're OK, you didn't do anything. They don't know where you are, only that you need your meds."

"I'd be better off if I did kill someone!" Stomping around the bed, Ruin went into the bathroom and slammed the door shut. "Then the diggers could just lock me up at the Stat and no one would try to fuck with me anymore!"

Closing their eyes, Aych pushed away the desire to comfort Ruin. *Leave it alone, he's not going to listen to anything you say. Few more days, it won't matter. He'll be in Grava with Lu and this will all be—*

Ruin yanked the bathroom door open. With a toothbrush hanging out of his mouth, he glared at Aych. "What if I wanted to be a murderer, what then? If I wasn't your sweet, pure—"

Aych chuckled. "Pure? No way no how, my darling. You're like me—"

Ruin made a face and then spat a mouthful of toothpaste in the sink. Pausing, he looked back, the strain showing in his eyes. "When she tells me to kill people, sometimes I want to do it."

"If you were the one who decided to, not the shit-bag, I'd be right there with you. Humans deserve it. If you want me to be there, I will be. If you want to hunt, I'll make sure you don't get caught." Meeting his eyes, Aych smiled cruelly. "But maybe you're just a different kind of monster than me. Maybe instead of ending lives, you do something much worse."

"Yeah? What could be worse?"

"Giving people reasons to live. To keep going through all this interminable shit. Making music, singing them back into this world, whether or not they want to be here."

Ruin kicked the door shut and turned on the faucet. "It would be easier to be a murderer," he replied, his voice muffled.

"You would hate yourself. You'd hate yourself for being a thief." Aych waited until Ruin opened the door again. "Imagine the feeling of wanting to see the one person you love most. Not a photograph, not a recording, not a memory, but to hear their voice, touch them, be touched, laugh, yell, catch their scent on your pillow. I break people with grief, forcing them apart. Bringing death between humans who long for each other. You're not pure, but you're not sadistic either."

"*She* tells me I am." His eyes haunted, Ruin looked across his childhood bedroom and out the windows. He watched the blizzard blanket the city streets with another inch of snow. "That's what I was born to do. Make people hurt."

"I've told you before, despair and hope are both liars," Aych answered methodically and patiently, their eyes closed. "If you want to kill, then do it. By your own will, your own hand, your own greed. Bring absolute separation, absolute loss. I visit that on humans—young, old, good, bad, cruel, or kind. I take lives ruthlessly, devour them for my own pleasure, knowing there's an ever-widening circle of bereft mourners in my wake. That torment, that utter devastation and curse, is who I am. But there is no room for hope or for despair about the future. Only what is in the moment, what I choose." Opening their eyes, they found Ruin looking at them. He was crying. "Your nature is to create much more than that. You bring joy to this world. Fuck that shit-bag and what she wants. I know what you want and it's not waking up like this every day wondering who you fucking killed last night. You decide, not her. Don't believe her lies about your future."

Dragging in a shaky breath, Ruin dropped his head. Aych went over and took his fingers in theirs. Tugging, they pulled the human toward the bed.

"You need more sleep. It's a snow day. I can stay and keep you company. Streets won't be cleared for a few more hours."

"Keep me company?" Pain and desire mingled in Ruin's eyes. "You tell

A Holy Venom

me I'm your darling, but you won't have sex with me. You'll fuck anyone, but not me."

Fuck, I walked right into it. Again. "You know why I can't agree to that."

"Doesn't mean it doesn't suck." Ruin shrugged. "I shouldn't have brought it up, I know—"

"That I think you're the most beautiful and the most aggravating human I have ever met?"

"It's just ... sometimes I get jealous. People talk and," Ruin pressed his knees against the side of the mattress. "Sometimes it feels like shit to know I can't be with the person I love, while they're ..."

"While they feel exactly the same fucking way," Aych kissed Ruin's fingers. "If there was any way it wouldn't make shit worse for you ... but I can't complicate your situation."

Ruin's face contorted. "Complicate my situation?" He pushed away from the bed. "You mean you won't add another layer of crazy to this carnival ride I call my life."

Suddenly feeling exhausted, Aych spoke as soothingly as they could, recognizing Ruin's spiral into a cycle of self-sabotage. "A single attachment like yours is more than enough to drive anyone insane. You don't need my influence adding to your problems."

"You're not like that thing." Anger flashed in Ruin's eyes. "You say you are, but you're not. If you did possess me ..."

Frustration welled up in Aych. "It won't matter in a few days. Lu will be cured, then she can fix you."

"Fix me?" Ruin growled. "Did you just fucking say that to me?"

Fuck. Sitting up, Aych swung their legs over the side of the bed. "I didn't mean it like that. I meant she will be able to get rid of the shit-bag for you. Not your—"

"Not my what? My mental health problems? Not my behavior problems? Not my low self-esteem problems?" Ruin snarled. "If you really don't want me, just fucking come the fuck out and say it. Don't hide behind Lu or this horseshit about me being a great musician, because I'm not. I'm a fuck up. I know who I am, and I know that I ruin everything. You do not get to fix me!"

I would drop anyone else out cold on the floor and kick them down the stairs for this. Retreat, hold, or advance? Aych ground their teeth. *Retreat.* "No, I don't. I know that. Not me, not Lu, not those incompetent diggers up on the hill. Not some fairytale god out on the islands and not your whole cemetery full of useless relatives. Nobody is going to fix you. No one needs to." They moved closer until Ruin was glaring up into their face. "You asked me to help you and that's all I've ever tried to do. You're not broken," they reached out and brushed the hair away from Ruin's face. "You can't ruin me; I'm already far more fucked up than anything you could manage." Slipping their hand behind his head, they bowed theirs until their forehead touched the top of his. "Whatever you want, with the people you want to do it with, however I can help, I am here and I'm not going to abandon you. Even if you keep trying to get me to, I won't." *Until you're ready to leave me behind...*

Ruin pressed Aych's hand against the back of his head, sparkling tears falling from his eyes. "What if she makes me, what if she gets inside again and I can't—"

"Then, I will eat her," Aych whispered softly, drawing him against their chest. "I will become Big, then Bigger, and I will eat the whole fucking world if I have to. Until you can be free."

Laughing, Ruin used the fingers of his free hand and smeared his tears away. "Promise?"

"I promise," Aych replied, looking out the window at a World they hated.

THIRTEEN

DUST WHEEZED OUT of the worn brass ceiling grates and settled on the row of file cabinets in the precinct conference room. The central heating system bellowed its mid-morning blast of heat, and the detectives tugged at their collars and ties, uncomfortable in the sudden rush of dry air. The assembly kept their jackets on and passed each other waxed boxes of sugar-coated pastries.

Heavy footfalls echoed down the hall outside. Detective Tosh kicked her partner's chair leg. "Sergeant Pot's here."

Mudon, napping, took his brimmed hat off his face and sat up. Other officers who had similarly checked out also sat up at attention at Tosh's warning. Tosh cracked the lid off her coffee and peered into the remaining dregs.

A woman in a herringbone jacket leaned over Mudon's shoulder. "Your handler going to call you upstairs for biscuits? Maybe a flea bath?" She flicked a spot off his jacket shoulder.

The man next to her snickered and leaned forward. "Woof."

Tosh whipped around in her seat and snarled.

"Was that an attempt at an insult, Stiles?" Mudon smiled over his shoulder at the woman. "Or were you throwing aspersions to distract from being on the leash yourself?" He glanced at the man next to her. "Though, no one would think the black dogs would bother with Jinks." Turning back around, Mudon shot Tosh a quelling look.

Tosh settled back in her seat. Behind her, Jinks narrowed his eyes and crossed his arms.

"I got no need for your fancy tricks, and nobody's got any reason to think *I'm* on the leash." Stiles pushed two fingers into Mudon's shoulder. "Everybody knows the only way a raft builder like you is sitting in here with us—"

Someone loudly coughed.

"If you've got something to say, Detective Stiles, please, come up and share your brilliant insight," Sergeant Pot called out, her tone mocking. She stood tall and imposing at the front of the room, her expression hard as she braced herself against the podium. "Or were you contemplating an assignment at the City Zoo?"

Chuckles rolled through the conference room. Mudon tilted his head, pretending to review his notes. Tosh smirked over her shoulder at Jinks.

"No, Sarge. I prefer my animals dead, on a plate." Stiles ran a hand through her brassy red curls and sat back.

"We have been called on to give an accounting of what we have so far about distribution and manufacture of the street drug charmingly known as the Rot." Hooking her fingers on the edges of the podium, the sergeant looked around the room. "Based on your reports, it appears none of you have managed to gather more than the names of a handful of sources. Those suspects you *have* brought in don't know what they're selling or who's supplying, beyond the next transom window where they get their assigned drop. You're making this department look incompetent and stupid, people."

Chairs scraped as the collective members of S&P's Department of Crimes Against People and Property shifted under Pot's searing inspection.

"And because of your incompetence, the number of deaths from this new substance has become so great that the higher-ups are terminating our provisional autonomy." She waited while the detectives squirmed and murmured amongst themselves. "Against my protests and those of the captain and chief, it has been decided we have all failed to protect the citizens within and outside the bounds of the city. Authority in this matter has reverted back to the Perlustrate. We have been judged and found painfully wanting."

"Fuck," Jinks shivered. "I don't answer to no black dog, Sarge. I'll turn in my badge and walk out before I work under those sick fucks."

The room erupted in shouts and protests as other voices repeated the younger detective's sentiments.

In the front row, Elowitch crossed his arms, stretching his too-small tweed jacket over his shoulders. He shook his head then looked over at Jinks.

A Holy Venom

"You don't get it, dumbass. If they're telling us they're here, that means they've already pushed the chief and captain out. Even if you wanted to resign, they'd just haul you back. By your balls, if you have any."

"Fuck that." Jinks stood up knocking his chair over. Next to him Stiles grabbed his arm and shushed him. He shook his partner off. "Watch me, I'm walking the fuck out right now. Ain't no dog telling me how to do my job."

"You think it's that easy? Like you can throw a tantrum and quit like this was an ice cream parlor?" Elowitch wiped the sweat from his receding hairline. "Try it. Tonight when you're asleep, they'll come and drag your ass out of bed. Maybe only work you over in the tub, if you have one. Or they might bag you and take you down to the Chapterhouse. Show you their toys and bring you in front of the tribunal. Next thing you know, you'll be sliding down the Dog's Gate and waking up in the Stat wearing a diaper and learning the alphabet all over again, if you even know it now."

Jinks went to rush the other detective. Stiles hauled him back.

"Horseshit, they won't come for me, I didn't do shit!" Jinks lunged again. "You fucker, you'd give me to them to save your own ass!"

Elowitch rose and pushed him back, knocking over the folding chair between them.

"Let him go," Pot snapped. "Pick your things up and go over to HR to file your resignation. Don't bother asking for references. You won't need any where you're headed." She glanced around at the rest of the room, pointedly avoiding Elowitch. "If the rest of you don't want to take early retirement shitting yourselves up the Hill, I suggest you drop a few coins, light a few candles, and pray for sudden inspiration as to where the fuck this new drug is coming from. We have one week before they decide we are actively blocking the investigation and start bringing each and every one of you in for questioning."

The detectives averted their eyes as Jinks stormed out.

Mudon lifted two fingers up and waited.

Pot looked him over. "You better not be taking up our remaining time with one of your useless observations, detective."

"Just a standard question, Sarge," Mudon drawled.

"Go on."

"Does the chemistry lab have anything new for us? Should we be focusing on any kind of regular supplier, or similar product? Could it be coming in on the freight trains from abroad? Or is it being brought in by boat? If it's being cooked up here, what kind of lab setup are we looking for?"

"No change on that front," she made a face and shuffled some papers. "All we know is it's a liquid. The low-level transom pick-ups leave it to the suppliers if they want to dispense it on blotter paper or cut it with another substance. Some of the dealers have been selling it in dropper bottles. Nothing traces back. The only drops we've located are always recycled glass in a brown paper bag. Could be in anything from a milk bottle to a whisky bottle. Once it gets to the houses, the shepherds are pushing it to the annas, or vice versa."

Tosh snorted. "Hell, as far as the chem lab is concerned it might as well be flowing out of a pipe in the Basilica."

The tension in the room dissolved into ripples of laughter.

"You want to spend your nights up there sampling the water, be my guest, Grace." Pot shrugged. "Just do us all the favor and take your genius partner with you and keep him from tipping off his friends at the houses." She eyed Mudon. "No one here is going to be surprised in the least when black dogs carry his sorry ass off."

Tosh clapped a hand on Mudon's shoulder. "Now Sarge, that's not fair. Just because he can beat all of us at a table and can get any anna to preach for free, it's just backwater, musty bias to think he's anything but an honest salt."

Pot snickered along with half the room. "Put another pastry in your piehole before you dig yourself in too deep." She glanced at Mudon. "You got any other questions, *detective?*"

Mudon sank back in his chair. "Not right now, but as soon as I do, I'll let you know."

☾

Walking down the steps of the Tank, Tosh yawned and scratched the back of her head. A snowplow wheeled around the parked cruisers dispensing grit and pushing a wedge of snow down the street. "Hey, since we're going to be on the West Side, do you mind if we stop at my place?"

Glancing at his wristwatch, Mudon nodded. "Sure, but it will have to be quick."

"Speaking of, is your boy in place?" Tosh took out a penknife and began cleaning her fingernails. Slivers of grime fell on her overcoat.

"He's in."

"Didn't you say he was the real deal? Spirit medium or some shit? Can't he just dial up the dead and ask them where they bought the stuff?"

"He's a psychic, not a medium." He looked over at his partner. "Never known him to talk to the dead."

They walked around the corner to a parked black sedan and Tosh eyed the inches of snow packed in around the tires from the last pass of the street plows. She kicked the snow clear of the wheel wells as Mudon did the same on the other side. Once in, Mudon clicked on the radio and they listened to the calls coming in and out of the station.

Tosh slid in and started the engine. "Are we going to tell the Tank about your whistle?"

"No," Mudon replied as he tabbed through his notebook.

"If there's a connection ..."

"We wait until we have evidence."

Tosh glanced at him. "If they find out later we sent someone in without clearing it first ..."

"When we have information, we'll tell the Tank straight off."

"What if your whistle ends up in the Twins? What if there's no connection between the Velvet and—"

Mudon shook his head. "They're behind it, I'm certain. No one else could run an operation like this without fucking up and dropping all the pins for us to find."

"Would you just fucking hear me out for a minute?" Tosh shot him a look.

Flipping his notebook closed, Mudon gestured for her to continue.

"If that's true, we should raid the theatre, bring them all into the Tank."

"On what grounds? We got nothing solid yet."

"You heard the sarge, shit's *reverted*. That means no due process, no lawyers." Tosh smacked her hands on the steering wheel. "We bring the whole lot of them in and shake them down one at a time until we find out what we need. Where the Rot is coming from. We might as well use this opportunity—"

"To what? Kill off Twalum and ship the rest of the Velvet to the mines? Are you out of your fucking mind?"

Tosh shook her head. "They won't kill anybody. Just after we have a go, any of the ones that seem like they know more than what they're telling us will get interviewed by the tribunal. You know how this works. For fuck's sake, you didn't believe that horseshit Elowitch was spouting, did you? The Perlustrate isn't some hit squad. They're part of the Church. The Church doesn't kill people."

Mudon turned his head to look out at the Silver Axe as they drove by the restaurant. "Violet Twalum is over eighty years old. Bringing in an elder of the community under normal circumstances is not advisable. We don't break down doors unless we've got proof they are involved in criminal activity. Now, with everything else blowing up, it's damn well dangerous. Could start something ugly, something with a higher body count than this new kick. So keep it to yourself. Unless you don't give a shit, which clearly, you don't."

"I'm not the one making money off the desperate, now am I?" Tosh shot a heated look at her partner and then stared at the road. "I know the dogs aren't the ideal way to go about this, but we need to find out where the Rot is coming from and stop it. Before more people die. Holy Mother, the morgue is filling up as it is."

"Ky will get us what we need." Mudon went back to his notebook. "If they're making the drug or distributing it out of the Velvet, he'll know soon enough."

"What about the Teahouse across the street?"

Frowning, Mudon studied the side of Tosh's face.

Tosh glanced over. "What?"

"I can't decide if you came up with that because you know how tea is prepared or if you're just a prejudiced Northerner after all."

"You pour hot water over some fucking leaves," the younger detective shot back. "Come on, the Awy own the place. It isn't exactly a major leap to wonder if they're in on it. Their fucking name is on the sign, Saint's sake." She glanced over. "I'm not the only one who thinks we should raid their place too. They're the best equipped to make this new shit. They hate the Church and every god-fearing person on the Continent."

"Tell me, do all the city-raised detectives sit around discussing which of the foreign-owned businesses they should raid for evidence?"

"Yeah, on our days off, after we do the dogs' laundry. Come on, it's not like that. You have to admit after the Velvet, the Teahouse is the most likely place this shit is coming out of. Every other moneymaker in this city leads back to Twalum's pocketbook. If the Awy and Twalum are in on it together..."

Mudon smiled. "It's being managed out of the Velvet, I'll give you that. But it's not stored on-premises. That much I can assure you."

"Are *you* psychic now?" Tosh tapped on the turn signal and passed a plow to get onto the exit ramp.

"Won't be at the theatre or anything close by like the Teahouse. They'll have it off-site. Somewhere unexpected."

The sky was shading to a false twilight as Tosh parked on Grizel St. near the corner of Tanner. Getting out, she grabbed a metal trashcan lodged in a snow bank and carried it up the steps of a disreputable-looking brick building, then went around the side. Coming up the walkway, her partner cast a careful eye at the massive icicles sprouting from the iron balconies on the third floor. Inside, Solstice lights winked on and off in the ground floor parlor.

Tosh held the side door open and then tromped up the stairs to the second-floor landing.

Taking off his overcoat, Mudon slung it over his shoulder and consulted his wristwatch. "We've got twenty minutes."

Dropping her coat on the peg outside the door, Tosh bent and untied her boots. "You think anyone will notice if we're five minutes late?" She moved aside a pair of children's rain boots and unlocked the inner door.

Mudon eyed a pair of men's boots and put his own next to them. "The dogs are watching. You heard Pot."

"Fuck the dogs." Tosh dropped her keys on the side table and loosened her tie. "Anyone home?" Her voice carried through the apartment.

Kiarna Boyd

Hand-painted toys and overgrown houseplants filled the living room. Tosh glanced at her partner and walked over to the kitchen. Checking the bathroom next to it, she moved down the hall to the pair of bedrooms.

Mudon hung his overcoat on the stand. He stared at a plush, orange lizard toy lying in the worn chair by the window. Tosh walked back to the door of the apartment and shot the security bolts. Turning around, she stepped up behind her partner.

Catching her hand, Mudon shoved Tosh up against the wall. Their hands moved in a rush of motion. Tosh groaned as Mudon bent his head and bunched up her dress shirt. Tosh closed her eyes and knotted her fingers in her lover's hair.

Standing back up, Mudon kissed her roughly. He grabbed her by the hips and dug his fingers in. Taking a step backward, he moved closer to the couch. He shoved the other detective onto the cushions and stood over her looking down. As Mudon took out a condom packet, Tosh stared hungrily up into his eyes.

☾

Aych sipped their tea and stretched their long legs alongside the low table piled with bowls and plates of vegetarian food. Across from them, Ruin slowed his devouring assault and set an empty bowl aside. He fell back against the overstuffed embroidered pillows. On the walls above his head, whimsical depictions of wild forest creatures cavorting adorned the cedar panels of the private tearoom. A string of wooden slat lanterns hung over the oval table, casting dappled light on the murals and Aych's shadowed bulk. The rushing splash of a waterfall muffled the conversations taking place in the Teahouse's main dining room.

Ruin leaned forward and wrapped his long, calloused fingertips around the sides of a teacup. Carefully he drew it back from the cluttered plates and into his palm. Eyes half-lidded, he inhaled the aroma of the opaque brown infusion.

Aych grinned at Ruin's elaborate enjoyment of the brew. "If you want a bath of the stuff, I can ask your uncle to prep something."

"Fuck off," Ruin smiled and opened his eyes. "Just because it all smells

A Holy Venom

the same to you …"

"Please. I can still beat your ass at identifying any of the dried shit Mat has stashed in all those jars."

Ruin laughed.

Aych stopped and narrowed their eyes. "What?"

"I just pictured you carrying a basket up that fucking mountain harvesting with him."

"Not likely." Aych frowned over the lip of their teacup. "But if you want a picnic this summer, I do know a lovely spot nearby."

Head back against the wooden wall, Ruin laid his arm over his knee and dangled the cup from his fingertips. "I bet you mean one of your red glades where you eat people?"

"Humans aren't the only ones who like to eat outside." Aych watched him and waited.

Ruined nodded distractedly and rotated the teacup. When he lifted his gaze, the humor was gone from his eyes. "Are you going to kill them? The people who fucked with my script?"

"Up to you. You could go to the salts or take it to the papers."

Scoffing, Ruin shook his head. "That never does shit. No one gives a fuck if some relative of a solved murder case comes after me. No one even fucking believes it half the time. Or when they do, some asshole covers it up." His knuckles showed white as he squeezed the ceramic.

Aych sipped their cooling tea. *Just let him vent.*

"I want them to know what it's like. To feel like that, to fucking wake up and not know …" Ruin stopped and gazed up at the lamps. He dropped his head to look over at Aych. "Fear and madness, that's what I want them to have. That sick feeling of not knowing what's real anymore. Then I want them to die so they can't do it to me or anyone else." His eyes were angry and haunted. "But I want them to suffer first."

And I love you all the more for it. "Easily done." They set their empty teacup amid the leftovers. "Everything we need is at hand. If you want, I'll show you how to make it happen."

Ruin waved his other hand over the table. "Here? You going to use Mat's stash to mix up some sort of curse powder or some shit?"

They smiled and shook their head. Rising to their feet, Aych buttoned their suit jacket and looked pointedly at the musician. "After my shift on the floors tonight, I'll come find you. Then out in the garage, I'll show you how to do magic. *My* kind of magic."

☾

At the Velvet, Aych stood on the balcony above the casino floor, watching the players. Long strands of magenta crystals dangled from the high ceiling, refracting pink light over the plush moss-green carpet below. Upholstered walls and the thick carpet muffled the shouts of jubilation and the cries of loss rising from the lacquered gaming tables. Groups of eight players sat at each of the circular tables, jealously guarding their cards or inlaid blocks of bone. Aych leaned their forearms on the railing casually, but eyed the humans carefully, watching for cheats. They spied a few counting cards, one pretending to be drunk and looking at their neighbor's hands, and a salt trying to winnow the house by palming bone tiles, no doubt holding out for a High Seat run that would automatically beat any other play. Aych made eye contact with the Velvet's security staff stationed along the walls and near the exits and flashed them subtle hand signs. One by one, the guards left their posts and entered the press of bodies around the gambling tables. Servers carrying trays of complimentary drinks and sumptuously dressed sex workers evaded the trajectory of the security staff with practiced agility. Of the guests the guards approached, a few received a few quiet warnings whispered into their ears while others were forcefully lifted from their seats and frog-marched off the gaming room floor.

Aych glanced over their shoulder as the balcony door opened and Vetch stepped out to join them. With a flourish, Aych indicated the table below. "Come to warm yourself on the embarrassment of others?"

Vetch sauntered to the balcony railing next to them. He gestured at the man arguing with the security staff blocking his way back to the gaming tables. "You'd think they'd be grateful for our lenience. In Grava—"

"I'm always happy to remove a few limbs if you're feeling nostalgic." Aych looked back at the man who had palmed tiles hoping for an easy win. He was struggling and arguing vehemently with security. They heard the salt complain and threaten until he was finally escorted through the gaming

A Holy Venom

hall and deposited into the street.

"If the salts wanted an excuse to take the house ..." Vetch frowned.

Shaking their head, Aych put a hand on the man's shoulder. "The order isn't going to come from S&P. When it comes, it's going to be from the other end of the leash."

"You feel this or know it?"

"I know it." Aych pointed to the tables. "Same way I know before a seat decides to try their luck at romancing the cards. Minor indications telegraph the bolder move being prepared. That salt felt bold enough to disrespect your hospitality. Read it as a sign of desperation, the need to prove his worth to his owners. They'll be putting on a show soon enough."

Vetch stared at the gamblers laughing and drinking at the tables below. "How much time you think we have before the dogs come around?"

"Couple of days, maybe less. Enough to clean the place up, maybe run a full rehearsal with all the snaps. Get Vee out ..."

"They won't go, you know that. It would be dishonorable."

"Can't hurt to ask. Even if they say no, at least you flagged it. Due diligence and all that shit."

"What about you and Lu?"

"That's all arranged. Lu's patron will thrash the dogs for stepping on Lu's house, but that's not going to do you any good if they find so much as a thimble full."

"Not to mention your promise to Vee." He eyed Aych uncomfortably. "Way I hear it, you're the one keeping the cleaners in retirement money."

"Only when the house wants a show. You know I'm an adult and can clean up after myself just fine."

"One of these days, I'm going to figure out how you manage your tricks." Vetch caught Aych's elbow. "If you're wrong about Tosh being on the leash and Mudon ..." He dropped his hand.

"Then I cost you a couple days of sales. Bill me. You know I'm good for it. You got that name for me yet, up at the Stat?"

"Branch." Vetch looked at Aych sideways. "Took the liberty of asking him to find out who stepped on the kid's file. Works out of legal. Owes us more than he'll ever make." He pushed open the balcony door and held it.

With a snort, Aych pressed by and started up the stairs. "Funny how someone so good at math as yourself lets that happen so frequently."

Vetch paused on the landing and looked up at Aych. "Don't get yourself or any of the suites too messy. If those visitors you're expecting show up, and you're wearing half a bottle or spilled a whole one on the carpet, it won't look too good."

"You worry too much." Aych smiled back down at the man. "I'm only going to have a drink with one of my admirers."

"Who would admire *you* when they could admire *my* sweet ass?"

Aych nodded at Vetch. "You do have a great ass."

"Don't be a nuisance and scare the talent, you hear me?"

"You sound like Lu."

"Your fault for being such an asshole." Vetch yelled back as Aych continued up the stairs, then clicked his tongue disparagingly.

☾

In the last hours of the night before dawn, Aych roused Ruin from his bed in the garret and brought him to the quiet, frigid expanse of the garage. Squatting between two skeletal motorcycle frames inside the garage, Ruin glanced from the tray of congealed motor oil on his left to where Aych was sitting on the edge of the lawn chair in front of him. A mound of shop floor sweepings with electrical cable snippets sticking out of it sat on the stained concrete. "Now what?" So far all he had accomplished was gathering up trash under the hard thrum of the fluorescents and shivering from the cold.

Aych lit the end of their cigarette and snapped the lid of the lighter shut. The exhaust fans whirling by the open bay doors sent the trails of smoke sailing outside. "Now, take that," they indicated the heap of dirt and refuse, "and use the oil to mold a ball."

"With my hands?"

"With your hands." Aych sat back and mulled over the stronger flavor of the smoke. A languorous mood came over them, melting the tension from the back of their neck and taking with it the ache of confinement imposed once again by being Little.

"You're just fucking with me now." Dipping his hand into the cold, thick goo, Ruin scooped some of the oil out and dripped it over the heap.

A Holy Venom

The slimy mixture fell apart as he attempted to squeeze the dirt into shape between his hands.

"Add more, it will start sticking together." Watching, Aych carefully exhaled the lungful of smoke upwards toward the second story of the carriage house.

"This is fucked up, even for art therapy." Shooting Aych a disgusted look, Ruin put his right hand back into the oil tray.

"It's not therapy. It's magic … Or it will be." Aych tapped cigarette ash off onto the remaining pile still lying on the concrete. "Let me see."

Separating his oil-smeared hands, Ruin held out the gritty clump. Aych turned away to grab a bag off the floor from the other side of the lawn chair. Turning back, they poured clay cat litter into Ruin's cupped hands.

Groaning, Ruin wrinkled his nose. "Now, it's definitely not going to stick together …"

"Yes, it will. But now you have to sing to it. That's *your* magic." Aych started taking off their suit jacket and laid it over the top of the striped fabric chair back. Rolling up their shirt sleeves, they puffed on the cigarette letting the smoke roll in and out of their mouth.

"Any requests?" His tone sarcastic, Ruin watched as Aych finished the smoke and ground out the ember into the wet dirt he was holding. It stank of the garage and motorcycles, of bitter herbs and ash, and burnt electrical tape.

"Not mine to pick. Fear and madness, that's what you said you wanted, isn't it?" Placing their hands above Ruin's, Aych let the restrictive skin unravel off their fingers and palms, the white flesh melting in rivulets and dripping like hot wax into the inky mess Ruin held. "The last one of these I made, I created to find the correct human for a job Lu and I have planned. I wasn't specific about the kind of human to find, only that they could do the job I needed." Aych scowled. "Problem with an intent like that is magic tends to take the long way around if you let it. So be specific, but not too specific."

Ruin inhaled sharply and watched, mesmerized, as Aych's fingers lengthened, the white bones cracking like sticks breaking as they tore through the white skin of the fingertips, scarlet blood and black ichor seeping from the wounds.

"Sing." Prodding him with the toe of their boot, Aych slowed the transformation as the white-hot needles of claws punctured and blossomed from their finger bones. Fibers of muscle began to weave and the tendons wrapped like vines along the bone. "All your pain, all your anger, your desire, everything you hunger for. Sing it into the ball in your hands, tell it what you wish. Sing your revenge into it. The doom of your enemies, the terror of your prey. You don't have to use words unless you want to."

In his heart, Ruin experienced a flutter of doubt, the whispered boundary of transgression policed by his shame that always tried to shut him out. It threatened to close his throat, deflate his lungs, drag him down. The shame would kill his breath, stifle it under his ribs, and compress his diaphragm. Against the drowning anguish of being silenced, he instinctively gasped a lungful of air. As it rushed in, his long hours of practice prompted the expansion of his chest and down into his belly. Coiled there at the base of his spine, seething and vicious, he found his rage waiting ready to spring out.

Listening, Aych wrapped their transmogrified hands around Ruin's human ones and squeezed the mixture of filth, flesh, and fluids. Poetic and savage, the song shaped the form of the rough ball as Ruin's voice boomed and the human screamed the lyrics of his song through the garage.

Aych grinned triumphantly as the ball began to harden. They piggybacked their own malice onto Ruin's, lending a vital strain of strength to the enchantment. Ruin's rage and resentment summoned some *thing* through the bubbling alchemy. Aych kept the spell stable as the human channeled his fury. The clump of filth yawned, squirming as the song compelled it to take form.

An unexpected movement in his hands, and then a new squalling voice that echoed his own, caught Ruin off guard. Aych tightened their grip and locked eyes with the human, prompting him to continue. Instinctually, Ruin accommodated the new voice as he would another singer, improvising and riding the wave of curiosity and frenzy, only afraid to make a misstep and break the shared flow of music. A part of his attention marveled at the strange alliance, partially Aych and a third influence he could not identify. The electric shiver of creative surprise blossomed and was caught up in the spontaneous unfurling. *Find them, tear their minds apart, shame them, torment*

A Holy Venom

them, make them pay...

Aych's toothsome smile split along their cheeks and a wicked joy shone in their eyes as the second voice grew harsher and stronger, mimicking Ruin's to fill the garage as if amplified. The bloodlust magnified, ripping itself free and then falling silent as Ruin let the last howling note die.

Dripping sweat and staring at nothing, Ruin trembled as Aych released his hands and gently pried his fingers apart.

"Did it work?" He tried to focus on the suddenly heavy weight in his palm. Whatever it was, the dark shape caught the light, slick with sweat and muck.

"Of course. You're a natural at this." Aych tapped the new stone head. The grimacing face was contorted into a frozen and fiendish howl. "Now, time for it to go hunting out in the cold, cruel world."

Exhausted and pleased, Ruin matched Aych's grin with his own. "That was more fun than I thought it would be. Better than art—"

"Told you, it's not therapy. Now, stand your ass up and throw it as hard as you can while willing it to find the fucker you're after. It's your hunt now." Aych leaned back in their chair and took out the tobacco pouch. "The real fun starts after it finds them. Trust me."

FOURTEEN

THE WET ASPHALT of the avenue glistened as the usual evening traffic of cabs and limos picked up. Ky hunched his shoulders under his wool overcoat and looked over the pack of tourists in front of him, checking for a clear path forward. As he walked, the soundtrack in his head switched to match his pace. Survival in the large and complicated city required altering the baseline of what he perceived as normal behavior. Intoxicated tourists stumbling along the sidewalks required only avoidance, while the skilled pickpockets mimicking the same inadvertent bumbling required direct and threatening eye contact to fend off. He needed to adapt to his surroundings and assess the inhabitants' intentions to achieve his goals, especially if he prioritized staying alive.

Tires from passing cars threw slush and ice water onto the sidewalk and pelted the pedestrians too close to the curb. Ky edged along the stone buildings, avoiding the ice falls suspended from the gutter spouts, angling to get ahead of the crowd, his body language signaling that he had a destination and would not be stopped. A billow of hot air hit him as the Velvet's marquee appeared around the corner. The fronds of the potted plants moved lazily in the artificial breeze under the outdoor heaters, the green foliage dancing in time to the languid strains of music trickling from the theatre. Ky quickly sidestepped the oblivious patrons and ducked through the revolving entranceway.

Inside the Velvet's bustling, shining grand lobby, the sudden warmth and sensory overload pushed out the frigid unpredictability of the streets and replaced it with a beguiling, threatening glamour. He needed another kind of vigilance to survive amid the perfumed guests sporting sparkling gowns and lacquered hairstyles. Ky spotted Vetch emerging from the main office toward the back of the lobby. Unwrapping his scarf and undoing his overcoat, Ky angled through the press of patrons and waiters carrying trays of sparkling wine and felt the weight of the security guards' gazes on him.

Vetch saw Ky approaching. His eyebrows raised in surprise. The head of security looked Ky over, taking in the well-pressed tailored suit under the heavy coat and Ky's new professional bearing. "Not bad, not bad at all." Waving a hand, Vetch walked further out into the lobby area. "Not too early, not too late. Right on time—I appreciate that." He gestured for Ky to walk with him along the wall of carved sandalwood screens.

As they approached the opposite end of the lobby, an attendant opened the vintage elevator's accordion gate. Ky noticed the woman's face was heavily scarred with what looked like combat wounds. Watchful, she nodded as Vetch waved Ky ahead of him into the small, caged interior.

"Evening, Willow." Vetch nodded back. "Top floor, please."

"Top floor, cleaning department," the guard smiled playfully as Vetch waggled an eyebrow.

Taking off his overcoat, Ky glanced down at the lobby through the rising gate. "Don't tell me you've already decided I'm only good for pushing a broom after all?"

"It's where the talent unloads the remaining contents of our guests' wallets." Vetch shook his head. "In your case, Lu wants to have a word. Seems you caught her eye." He shrugged and adjusted one of the gold rings on his hands. "If it goes well, and she still likes you, you'll be on her security detail tonight. Nothing too difficult for the first night. Keep your answers to her questions to the point and let her ramble her way into charming you. If she likes you, you'll be her shadow while she runs a few errands. Make sure none of her fans gets too close. No one talks to the talent without an appointment. Strictly bodyguard detail." As the elevator came to a stop, Vetch met Ky's eyes as Willow opened the gate, "And remember what I told you before—watch your language. Lu doesn't care for gutter talk and I don't want her chewing my head off if you use a naughty word."

Ky nodded and assessed the hallway with its flocked wallpaper and vases of tropical flowers on high stands between the suite doors. Another guard stood by the fire door to the left at the back of the hall and he winked at Vetch. There was a strong, strange turbulence close by and Ky's skin prickled with static electricity. The thunderstorm quality lingered in the air.

A Holy Venom

Vetch waved two fingers to the guard at the end of the hall. "Nice to see you're early tonight, Spruce."

"Nail's switching with me at ten," Spruce shrugged. "Thought it wouldn't hurt to be on time."

"You make it sound like we have you watch the trashcans in the alley all night." Vetch shook his head and waved Ky to the suite door on the right. As Ky turned, Vetch flashed his hand behind his thigh.

Spruce nodded and leaned against the doorframe, tracking Ky with his eyes. Vetch set a knuckle against Lu's door and rapped twice. His relaxed smile stayed in place as he eyed Ky. Once Lu called out, Vetch turned the doorknob and waved Ky forward.

As the door slowly swung open to the star performer's opulent quarters, Ky's mental background loop of music cut out. A vibrant, electric signal boomed along his nerves, followed by a wave of oppressive heat. The sheer volume of the incoming psychic signal verged on migraine-level pain. He grasped the doorframe to steady himself. The sumptuous drapes and gilded furnishings wavered and the geometric patterns in the wool and silk carpet swam as his vision blurred.

Vetch smirked. "Good evening, Lu. I've brought a new member of the household to join your entourage tonight. Lu, this is Ky. Ky, may I present the one and only Lutauvelm." Vetch eyed Ky suspiciously as the other man, breathing heavily, steadied himself. "The heat's a bit much at first, but I'm sure you'll get used to it."

"Good evening." Standing by the lit fireplace, Lu smiled at the two men, her eyes lingering on Ky. "So kind of you to bring him up for formal introductions. Please, make yourself comfortable, Ky. It's still early, so I thought we could get to know each other over coffee." She gestured at the silver service laid on the low table between the arched marble fireplace and the couch. "Unless you'd prefer something stronger?"

"I'll leave him to you then, gorgeous," Vetch winked and stepped back into the hall, shutting the door to the suite with a quiet click.

"Coffee is fine," Ky managed to whisper. The psychic pressure, like a maelstrom of lightning and raw power, made his knees tremble. The air was thick with incense and the musk of coming rain.

He cleared his throat and looked over at the greenery cluttering the window. Pots of orchids crowded the windowsill, the thriving exotics tangling up support rods held in place by tiny clips. The slender bamboo sticks pushed back the expensive silk drapes, allowing a riot of lobed pinkish, spotted blooms to tumble from slender, emerald vines. Barely able to stand, Ky tried to focus on the darker purple spots inside one of the open-throated hothouse flowers. Next to the window was an array of potion bottles and decanters of various sizes. Alcohol, he figured, eying the bottles as the psychic noise in his head dropped to a buzz.

"I see you're admiring the *tau-ve-gae-elm*. Most people don't know that this particular variety glows at night. Isn't it wonderful? I'm always surprised what people don't know. Did you know they are also used in the distilling process to make Constalia? They give it that distinctive pink color it's famous for. You've had it before, haven't you? We go through *cases* of it downstairs, it's so popular. Good for an angry heart." She watched him stumble. "I find it too sweet, myself."

Lu walked over and sinuously extended a hand to him. An aura of silver surrounded the star's proffered fingers. Her entire persona crackled with the energy of an imminent storm. He stared, dreading her touch. Through the buzzing in his head, he heard the rumble of distant thunder. He turned back to look at the orchids, ignoring her hand.

With an amused lilt in her voice, Lu gestured at the coat still draped over Ky's arm. "May I take your coat for you? Is the heat too much? I keep my rooms even warmer than the rest of the house. Vee indulges me by overlooking the added expense. Come, sit, and relax."

Ky nodded blearily, unable to meet her penetrating gaze, and extended the coat to her.

Lu's eyes flashed with delight as she gently slipped the wool coat from Ky's grip. "Do sit down, before you fall. I'll pour you a cup of coffee."

Ky kept his eyes averted as he came around to the couch. Steady tongues of flame licked over the ceramic logs of the gas fireplace. Ky balled his fists and cleared his throat again. Ozone and enormity emanated from his hostess, threatening to overwhelm him.

"Cream? Sugar?" Alighting on the couch near the serving tray, Lu daintily lifted the silver-spouted coffee pot.

"No." *Damn it! If I keep this up I'm going to blow my cover.* He smiled weakly, as polite as he could, and willed himself to block out the noise. The mental static quiesced, suppressed under the looping cadence of a classic hit song. Its lyrics reminded him to slow down and proceed cautiously. "Thank you, no, I take it black."

"It's not every day I meet someone with your talents." Lu poured out two cups and set the pot aside. "Maybe decades, even. I truly can't recall." She moved one of the porcelain cups and saucer closer to Ky. "Do take your time. I understand if you need to adjust. We'll pretend it's the heat. It can be quite overwhelming at first, I'm told."

Ky reached for the porcelain handle, surprised by her admission. The countersignal flared shooting painfully along Ky's arm a split second before Lu touched her fingertip to the back of his hand. He had no time to respond before the potent rush of her energy hit him. He trembled.

"You'll have to forgive me. I was curious." She picked up her cup and saucer and settled back against the couch. "Try the coffee. You'll feel better after you drink it."

The buzzing permeating the air around his hostess retracted, condensing into shimmering ripples. He glanced at her to find only a beautiful woman in an expensive cocktail dress smiling demurely at him.

Ky considered excusing himself and leaving, but he knew there was little chance of making it out to the street without the guards responding. Keeping his gaze on the cup, he reached out a shaking hand for it.

"I understand you've been hired on here?" Slipping her feet out of her heels, Lu tucked her stockinged toes up under her thighs.

Ky took a sip of the coffee. The song vanished, the loss of background music yawning into unexpected silence as the residual psychic noise disappeared.

"I told you you'd feel better," Lu gave him a puckish wink and set her cup onto the tray.

Ky blinked and opened his mouth then hesitated, remembering Vetch's admonishment not to swear. "What *are* you, lady?"

Lu's laughter rang out, filling the suite with chiming peals. "Oh, you are a rare one!" Her elbow on the couch, she held her head in her palm and looked at him and smiled. "Let's just say I'm special like my orchids and leave it at that. For now. You're accustomed to encountering all kinds of unusual people, aren't you?"

Carefully setting the cup on its saucer, Ky stared at the fire and felt the sweat beading on his face. "Recently I met a nightmare that tore apart a convent. And now its dirty tricks are haunting me, following me around. You tell me if that's unusual."

"What's unusual," Lu frowned, "Is after all that, you are with me, drinking coffee as if nothing occurred. Does this sort of thing happen to you often?"

Still feeling the aftershocks of her touch, Ky checked for the countersignal. The skin under his shirt and jacket was numb and sweaty. "I'm only staying long enough to decide if you're planning to seduce me or eat me."

"Either would be impolite. We've only just met," Lu turned her head to look at the fire. "This nightmare you mentioned—are you running from it?"

"Not running as much as trying to find a safer vantage point."

Lu nodded sagely. "Strange that you'd come here to the Velvet looking for a job." Her eyes wandered to the ceiling. "Unless you think this theatre is safer, that it offers the protection you're after?"

"Lots of dangerous people in these parts. I thought it'd make it easier to avoid being eaten. At least I did."

"Until you met me? I'm flattered," Lu tipped her hand toward herself. "Tell me, if you did run into your adversary again, what would you do?"

"It's a monster. Kill it. Or seal it. Anything, as long as I stopped it."

"Stopped it from what?"

Ky frowned and leaned back against the couch, pondering how to leverage the conversation. "At the risk of being rude, I don't condone monsters eating people."

"I'm not sure if you're insinuating something unkind about my person," Lu gave him a haughty smile. "Instead of pressing you on that point, I will ask the more polite question: why do *you* want to stop it?"

"I told you, it's a monster." He stared, watching the firelight reflect in her eyes. "It killed a friend of mine and ate her. I'm being factual. It's done it before, probably to hundreds if not thousands of people. It's evil."

Lu frowned as she returned his scrutiny. "*You've* killed hundreds if not thousands and tormented countless others, haven't you? Are *you* evil? Or would that only be the opinion of the farm animals that end up on your plate?"

Ky stiffened. "I didn't eat my enemies. I didn't terrorize their children."

"Wasteful perhaps," her lips formed a disapproving moue. "And that second statement sounds more like propaganda than anything honest. You're a killer. Terror comes with the territory."

Ky knotted his fingers. The memories of the war came back in flashes and he inhaled, trying to push back the familiar wave of guilt. So many dead and injured; the faces of the civilians in Bravada, searching, pleading, and praying. The sight of severed limbs lying in the rubble of buildings he had destroyed, condemning him. The jackal prints in the dust along the charred concrete. Scavengers feasting on the dead. "Anything I did, I did to protect people. If there had been other options …"

"And you think this creature doesn't have a similar cause?" Lu replied in a low, mocking tone. "Does it really matter, having a cause?"

"It enjoys the slaughter. Revels in it." Ky pushed his past away and focused on Haw's family, their loss and fear. "It gets off on it."

Lu purred. "Do you think the dead and the devastated give a dog's rump if you feel ashamed or happy when the outcome is the same? They're still dead. Maimed. Bereaved. Damaged."

Anger washed over Ky. "I'm not the same! If you're going to mock me about the war, I should walk out and bail on this job. I know not everyone understands what we did to protect them. There are bad people in this world and someone has to—"

"You're *not* the same, are you? That nightmare of yours is honest about its desires. *You've* constructed an entire city's worth of justification around your participation in atrocity."

He felt her eyes rake over his face.

"Believe me, they're not the only one whose victims call them a monster."

Furious, Ky shot up from the couch. Stalking over to the orchids, he resisted the urge to pour himself a drink. "It killed a wonderful, kind person. She was my friend. She was a *good* person." He looked over and caught Lu's eyes. "It tormented her children, polluted them. Should I accept that?"

Lu slipped her feet back into her heels. "Did they harm your friend's children? Physically?"

"No." He put a fingertip on one of the mottled flowers and stared at the rings of color circling each spot on the petal. The Velvet's star performer was clearly bad news, and highly dangerous. In the back of his mind, Mudon's threat lurked, a counterweight to Ky's intuition to run. He knew he should leave this nest of horrors, but the Tank would pick him up. Maybe he could act the part a little longer and get the information he needed. Lu was clearly protecting someone—or something.

Behind him, Lu murmured. "Did they have the opportunity to do so?"

"Why?" Ky glanced back at her again. "You think going after children is fun? You need a playmate?"

Rolling her eyes, Lu sighed and stood up, rounding the end of the couch. "Tell me, how many children do you think died in the war?" Setting one hand on her hip, Lu ran her other hand over the back of the couch as she walked closer. "In particular, how many do you think died because of the bombs you deployed and triggered? Oh, yes, we checked up on you, Staff Sergeant. Or did you delude yourself into thinking all the hostile forces under the age of eighteen all serendipitously escaped?"

Clenching his jaw, Ky turned his eyes back to the orchids, avoiding his hostess's challenge. "We had orders and a reason. Either our forces took control of the region or the famine—the artificial famine—would have continued until everyone was dead. Thousands dead. Everyone here on the Continent had the same cause; only us, the pathetic draftees who couldn't bribe our way out, had the means to carry out the mission. Civilians always play the blame card when they want to make themselves feel better, that we're the murderers. If the Crisis continued, hundreds of thousands of people would've died. Ours *and* theirs." He shot her a pained look. "Starvation, in-fighting on both sides. So yes, I hauled iron and brought war to those who would rather have lived in peace." He remembered the screaming faces, the hands grasping at the side of the personnel transport as it passed through the devastated desert streets, begging for food, for water, for help. He dropped his gaze back to the delicate, tropical plants. "People I cared about gave their lives, and if you're going to blame us for fighting, you might as well spit in all our faces. But remember, you and yours sent *us* out to die."

A Holy Venom

If she knew his rank and details of his military career, she might know about his connection to Mudon. If she did, he might be trapped between the two of them with nowhere left to go. "If you've got a point, lady, you better make it quick. I've had about enough of your hospitality."

"You've got it all wrong," Lu smiled and pulled the cut crystal stopper out of a decanter. "I'm not blaming you." She poured two fingers of fragrant alcohol into a pair of cut crystal tumblers. "My point is, it's not a matter of who kills who, or how. It's a matter of if you believe they're right to do so." She picked one of the glasses up, dangling it from her fingertips, and leaned enticingly against the arm of the couch, accentuating her figure. She watched Ky over the rim of her glass. "War is never what it's sold as. It's always a distraction from the real show that's happening off-stage. That main performance is far uglier."

He took a deep breath, centering himself, and looked at her. "What exactly do you want from me?"

"To know if I can trust you. If you are a man of morals as well as means." She tapped a lacquered fingernail against her glass. "There's a friend of mine, a human, if that matters, who needs protection. *Your* kind of protection. Just for a few days. He's not safe on his own."

"All this because you want a bodyguard? Who is he and why does he need a babysitter?"

Lu shrugged. "He's a local musician. Not a criminal, if that's what you're wondering. It's true, I could ask Vetch for another member of our household, but I thought you might be a better fit."

"Why don't you ask S&P?"

Lu's mocking laugh shivered the air. "When have those greedy bullies ever managed to save anyone from anything?"

"Then why not someone you already trust?" His hand was around the unclaimed glass before he realized it. As he raised it, the smoky aroma made his mouth water.

"I could say it's because you have things in common. A love of music, for one. Or maybe my friend will feel comfortable with you, that you'll be less conspicuous in their company than any of the others."

The scent of the whisky uncurled from Ky's mouth as he breathed. "And the real reason?"

She watched him through half-closed eyes. "You get angry when people are treated unfairly. My friend has been through the worst you can imagine, and I want him to be around someone kind." She watched Ky. "You're kind, but not pitying. Not coddling or currying favor, but also not prone to harsh judgments. He needs that sort of kindness. Not someone who'll sell his location to the wrong people. And your *talents* would be helpful in keeping an eye on him."

A hunch prodded Ky. He knew his hostess was not the creature he was looking for, but he was sure she knew where it was. "And the monster I mentioned, the one that tore up the convent. Do you know them too?"

Lu pouted. "You're going to make things more difficult if you insist on using that term." She finished her drink and returned the glass to the bar.

"What should I call them then, your other friend?"

A slow smile spread across his hostess's face. "Oh, I'm sure you'll think of something a bit more accurate. But that's a matter for another time. Tonight, I'd like you to take a ride up the Hill with me."

"Why?" Ky considered if he could keep working her for information on Haw's killer as well as what Mudon was after. If anyone at the Velvet knew about that other business, it was Lu.

"There's a piece of religious art I'd like to show you. Not many know the story behind it and I think you might appreciate it."

"What about your friend? The human one?"

Lu glanced in the direction of the window and then back at Ky. "When we get back from my errand, I'll introduce you to each other. He's staying across the way at another friend's place. Also a human." Her tone still mocking, Lu went to the coat rack and lifted Ky's coat.

"And this errand?" Ky watched her, unsure of his next play.

Holding his overcoat out, Lu replied, "All you have to do is keep me warm in the back of a limo and then wait on your own for an hour or two until I'm ready to leave."

Ky glanced at the flames burning around the ceramic logs. "You just going to walk out and leave the gas on?"

Her eyes sparkling, Lu's mouth again curled into a moue of pouty disdain. "We have an agreement, Fire and I. It doesn't burn the house down and I don't flood the fireplace. Now, are you coming or do I need to find

A Holy Venom

another bodyguard?"

☾

The wind picked up in the alley behind the Velvet. Ice struck the dumpsters and pinged off the railing along the loading dock. Ky cast a long look at the shiny limo as the driver held the door for him. Impatiently, Lu leaned forward from the backseat and waved him in. Bundled in furs, she patted the limo seat next to her, her mouth set into an inviting smile that failed to reach her eyes. Ky slid in and settled himself against the leather. Surprised not to feel his countersignal flaring, Ky watched Lu out of the corner of his eye. Her aura shimmered as if echoing her mood.

Suddenly, she laughed and smiled as if they were old friends. "Tell me, Ky, do you know anything about shepherds? Specifically, how they set up their target to gain their confidence?"

Ky looked ahead as the limo eased out of the alley and avoided Lu's gaze. "Is that what you do? You're a shepherd?"

"Before I answer, let me ask you another question. Do you think I'm human?" Her eyes glittered.

Ky considered the question and suppressed a twinge of panic. "I don't know *what* you are, but you're not one of us."

Looking pleased, Lu relaxed and snuggled into her furs. "I'm going to tell you a few stories that might not seem related, but I assure you they are."

"You're going to try and sell me a load of bunk?"

She shrugged. "Time and observation will clear up any misunderstandings."

Ky glanced back out his window watching as the marquee lights fell away behind the car. "If I'm on the clock, I'll listen."

Scintillating laughter filled the back of the limo. "When ticket holders come to the Velvet to see me perform, they want it both ways. The thrill of the impossible trick and a brief moment when they wonder if it's real. They're eager to truly believe, for the split second when they don't think they'll look like a fool. All that delight made possible, with the comfort of knowing it's all sleight of hand, legerdemain. Awe and the ability to dismiss that awe before it's inconvenient. Before they feel gullible or ashamed for *wanting* it to be real. They applaud themselves for figuring it out. They're in love with the mechanics of how they were willingly and happily conned by the illusion because they gave their permission to be misled. Every human wants magic to be real, but not so real that it's threatening. They want to be in control of the mystery."

Ky turned to look at her. Her eyes were full of impossible lights. "When you perform, is it real? Or is it a trick?"

She returned his look with a coy smile. "I'll ask you that after you see my show. Then you can tell me."

He sank into the limo seat and resumed glowering. "If I'm still here. I might shove off any second."

"At least stay long enough to see me perform once," Lu pouted. She flicked her fingers dismissively. "Where was I? I was telling you about the seats. It's not only about the magic shows … the dance troupes and solo acts operate the same way." She watched him for a moment and then continued. "A person like you eases into watching because, again, there's skill, grace, expert artistry. It's how you rationalize paying our extravagant ticket prices. It's the world-class performances you're showing up for. Then, you have a drink or two, maybe three, as the acts start to heat up and the dancers' costumes come off. Beauty glues you to your seat, but your lust peels your eyelids wide open and desire seduces you with every step and shimmy. Once you've peaked, your desire holds you in that sweet spot, between lust and the voyeuristic thrill of watching. Of being seduced willingly, knowingly. All pleasure, no guilt. Those lips, those eyes, all those perfect bodies of every shape and size under stage lights grinding, whirling, shimmying, shaking … just for you."

She gave him a knowing smile and ran her eyes over his half-turned face. "At the pleasure houses, it's a related bit of sleight of hand we run on the seats. Our clients want the fantasy of shared desire and intimacy. In reality, the genuine, vulnerable, real version overwhelms and frightens them. On stage, they want the illusion of the real, but off stage in their arms, they make sure the door to their heart is locked against that most powerful, dangerous authentic emotion. Can you guess the very special difference between experiencing the divine, the numinous, or the magical as real, versus having it presented as charmingly, and safely, false?"

A Holy Venom

Ky shifted his head to hold her gaze without blinking "Control. The seats feel safe because they believe they're in control."

"Perfect. And …"

"That's the con y'all are running. Because they're not. You are. They pay for the seats, but they don't run the show. If you wanted to roll them over the edge, you could, easily."

"You're good at this!" Lu applauded and then gestured out her window. "When I first came to the city, it was because I was told about the healing water of the Saint's sacred spring. Do you know it?"

"Saint Anna's well in the Basilica. We went on field trips in school."

"That's where I'm taking you tonight. Up to the Basilica to try the famous spring water and hear your expert opinion on it." Lu propped her chin atop a gloved hand. "If it seems at all magical to you, *do* let me know." She looked him over. "Tell me, did you grow up in an observant family?"

Ky thought of the plain chapel where his mother ministered. The stout, simple hymns and memories of church picnics in the grassy meadows outside the whitewashed brick church. Butterflies in the sunlight and watermelon slices after the weekly sermons. "My parents are Reformists." As always when thinking of the past, his thoughts turned to the war, and what he'd done. Now, his only access to holiness came after the soul-shivering release carried off in billows of smoke.

"Oooh, you're a heretic!" Lu pressed her fingers to her lips. "Best not to mention that to anyone while we're in the Basilica or they'll start proselytizing." She winked. "One can't get away with saying they're not a believer in the Saint's own house without starting up the annas' engines of persuasion. Nothing like a heretic or an atheist to fan the flames of their devotion. You should listen to them set upon me when they get a chance to tell me all about their missing God." Lu smiled and fanned herself with her hand as if flustered by the image.

"If I'm a heretic, then what are you? An atheist?"

Lu erupted into gales of laughter. Pressing a hand to her chest, she caught her breath and then set her slim purse on her lap. While retrieving a compact from the designer bag, she shook her head. "I haven't laughed that hard in ages." She shot him an amused look and touched up her make-up. "No, I am not. Though, Aych you could call an *antagnostic*—someone who hates the gods."

"Gods, plural?"

Snapping the mirror closed, Lu regarded Ky for a long moment. "Surely you of all people don't think the Holy Mother is the only deity in this World?"

"Not something I've thought about," Ky lied.

"You've never been to Gravagaedoon, then? Beheld the temples of the Ten Thousand? Not even read about them?" Sighing, she gave him a pitying look. "What do they teach in schools these days?"

"In textbooks, sure, we learn about other cultures and all, but we didn't exactly go on an educational tour when we were drafted."

"Do you believe in the Holy Mother? That God and her saint are real? That the passion and the promise of the Saint and the Shepherd literally happened? Do you even understand the importance of that story? That the promise and the passion weren't between the Holy Mother and her Saint like everyone in these modern times assumes?"

"Can't say I ever gave it much thought." Ky was being honest; he'd never considered scripture in any real way.

"If you don't analyze what you're taught, what you're expected to accept, you'll just be another member of the flock, taken in by the show." Lu glanced out the tinted window. "Humans want religion to be like a magic show. Whether it's on stage or up close, it should be safe and thrilling and numinous at the same time. Real mystery isn't safe. It can't be, just like real love, or real passion and intimacy. You can't be in control *and* open yourself to the divine. To willingly do so is a kind of insanity, and anyone who surrenders in that way lives forever as an insane mystic. Neither gods nor humans can fully trust each other because love can always lead to betrayal and disappointment. Religion is a record of the never-ending tragedy written by whichever side successfully betrays the other first." Bitterness filled Lu's voice. "The original con. One in which the loser is condemned to a false reality and the winner recreates themselves as a singular point of existential purpose."

To Ky, the emotion in Lu's voice manifested as jagged edges in the field of her aura. "I knew an ex-priestess, a real anna, in the service. She said shit like that. But she still prayed before we engaged the enemy. Before the dying started. Hated God, but still believed."

"In Grava there is a proverb: *'Lu tau su vun vik. Love is a holy venom none survive.'* It comes from an ancient myth about humans who once tried to imprison a god. Do you know it? Most people don't tell each other the important things, only the things they think will get them what they desire."

Lu looked from Ky's face to the window, her gaze distant and contemplative. After a pause, she continued. "Every year, a rain deity visited Gravagaedoon's summer feasts and brought a gentle, nourishing rain. Every year, the humans worried the god might not return and a drought would follow. Afraid and faithless, the humans designed a temple to ensnare the god. It took many human lifetimes to erect and it was lavishly beautiful. Precious jewels, painstaking carvings, and more gold than you could imagine. Because the god loved the humans and thought well of them, they thought the humans created the temple as an offering, a monument to mutual adoration." She turned back to look at Ky and her eyes were dark. "The god was deceived. The humans had run a long game of flattery and seduction. In the god's defense, they thought only true love, true devotion, could inspire such effort. Once the temple was completed, the priests created a potion from a sacred flower and mixed it with wine, as an offering. While the god lay in a deep, drugged sleep, the humans hobbled the deity so they couldn't escape the temple. They trapped the injured god in a magnificent opulent prison without windows or doors. There was no escape and no chance the other gods would be able to find them."

Frisson lifted the hairs along Ky's arms and neck. "But the god escaped."

Lu shot him a strange look and then glanced back out the window "Oh yes, they escaped. Destroyed the temple soon after they woke and cursed the humans before crawling into Lake Tauvemalum. Now, instead of a moderate, beneficial rain, there are typhoons and floods that ravage the humans' paltry excuse of a modern city." Lu regarded her nails for a moment. "The god occasionally drowns people, after capsizing their dinky, pathetic, little boats."

The mention of boats triggered Ky's recollection. "Wait, isn't that the story of the lake monster Grava is famous for? Mlolm?"

"A monster? Is that what *you'd* call an angry, wounded god?" Looking over her shoulder at him, Lu arched an eyebrow and her lips formed a disapproving bow. "I told you to be careful with that term."

The limo slowed. The other vehicles on the street dropped away as the car turned to enter a colonnade line with granite pillars. Ky looked out the window. A guard, bundled in layers and wearing a pointed cap, raised a barrier arm to allow them through. The night sky was thick with flurries of snow and the white fluff stuck to the stones and the hurrying guards as they returned to their heated nook inside one of the pillars.

Lu glanced out at the snow. "I shan't speak of this more as we're approaching the Basilica. Gods, as a general rule, are quite territorial. It's rude to discuss non-local deities in the region's major pilgrimage site."

"You make it sound like they can hear us," Ky said only half-jokingly.

"I assure you, even absentee landladies are paying close attention." Lu laid her hand on the door control panel and toggled the limo's back windows down. Cold air carrying snowflakes whirled in and landed on her furs. "We're about to enter the mountain entrance. It's worth enduring the cold to see it as the pilgrims on foot did centuries ago."

The freezing temperature caught Ky off guard and sent shivers along his spine. Enormous stone lanterns replaced the pillars that lined the colonnade up the ancient pilgrimage path. Round-bellied granite with flared caps, each multi-ton lantern contained a patinaed bronze cauldron roiling with gas-fed flames. As the limo inched along the processional way, Ky leaned out to look up at the carved archway surmounting the tunnel entrance into the mountain. Jets of gaslight illuminated the ancient script hewn into the living stone. High above, the mountain summit was lost in the storm clouds. His school trip memories only included riding the funicular in the daytime. At night, the whole mountain appeared strangely alive, the otherworldly light from the lanterns making him shiver from more than the cold.

As the limo entered the tunnel, Ky's skin tingled, as if he'd passed through an electric field. The air warmed, the tunnel cutting off the mountain winds. Hammered gold decorated the relief sculptures adorning the stone walls. Gaslight wavered in plumes of copper as drafts of humid air flowed out from further ahead. The limo's headlights birthed strange lunging shadows that slid and stirred on the wet paving stones.

"And so it was that the Saint, chosen by the will of God, did meet the most dread and dire guardian of the holy place," Lu began to narrate the scriptures depicted in the panels:

> 'To gain access to the healing waters of the sacred spring, so all God's children might know full health of mind, body, and spirit, the blessed Saint did supplicate the Shepherd.
>
> 'Would thou not drink of the sacred water and be healed? Would thou not allow others to also be healed?'
>
> 'Nay, I would not allow it. I will not allow it, not on this day nor any other.'
>
> 'Why has thou turned away from the love of thine own kind?'
>
> 'What love hast thine kind ever shown me and mine?'"

Lu glanced over to Ky. "The Shepherd has a bad reputation for being unduly cruel, but I have it on good authority that he had a righteous grudge." She pointed out the window on Ky's side of the limo. "There's a section coming up in a minute that's important." Sliding closer on the backseat, she tapped the limo's intercom button. "Can you stop up ahead, Daisy, if no one is behind us? Marker thirty-seven."

"Will do," the driver replied.

Lu leaned in to watch the monuments and panels pass in the flickering half-light of the passage. "Whatever the game, there's always a moment when the truth is a better hook than a lie," she looked past Ky out into the tunnel, her eyes intent. He followed her gaze. "It's in this section out here in the tunnel, not anywhere else; not in the Basilica proper, and certainly not in the written scriptures. Since the funicular started bringing pilgrims up the mountain, people don't walk under these walls. No one has read this version for a hundred years. It's all here, yet entirely forgotten."

The limo inched up, stopping underneath a towering panel. This section seemed darker, older, but no less impressive to Ky's eyes. The stone was pocked, worn with age and the touch of pilgrim's hands, but the ornate scrollwork and gold inlay on the immense carving stood full and vibrant.

The relief depicted two figures facing each other, surrounded by alternating forms of hounds and sheep seated in a circle.

"Look closely at the Shepherd on the left and Anna on the right. You can see his face. This is the only image—anywhere—of the Shepherd without his hood." Lu pointed past him to the figures.

Ky craned his neck to see.

> *"Thus spoke the holy saint chosen of God: I shall promise to give thee all of my passion and do so for all of time, for thou will be as my beloved. And like the sacred flock, all of the children of this blessed Earth shall be entrusted to thee to love and protect. All shall offer unto thee their love and obedience. Thou will be as a parent, both mother and father in one, to all of our kind. Thy dread countenance hidden, the bloody way of fear replaced with the sacred water of compassion."*

She turned to him. "Let me guess, this is not the version of the passion and the promise you were taught at your parents' knee?"

Staring at the two figures, Ky recited the prayer he'd memorized as a child. "Our Holy Mother who delivers us from villainy, hallowed be thy heaven and thy earth. Thy blessings come as thou accept our follies and forgive us our failures. Give us this day thy sacred milk of compassion so we may show others mercy in thy name. Guide us to understanding and save us from deception. Lead us always to thy divine embrace. For thy love is eternal, the passion and the promise, now and forever, amen."

Lu sat back and eyed Ky. "Ever wondered what exactly that phrase meant? *The passion and promise?* It's not explained anywhere in the scriptures, only here carved into this tunnel. Why did 'sacred water of compassion' become 'milk of compassion?'"

Ky looked down at the seat in front of him, unable to meet Lu's gaze. "Maybe this is wrong? Maybe the sculptor ..."

Giving him a disappointed look, Lu toggled the intercom. "You can keep driving, Daisy, thanks. Can you crank the heat up back here, please?"

"Will do," the woman replied.

"This tunnel was sculpted by hand five thousand years ago. Your reformist scripture has been edited countless times since this was carved. Which version do you think is closer to the truth?" She slid back to her side of the seat and toggled the window up, leaving Ky's down. "Remember, '*save us from deception.*' Ironic, really, to put that part in."

"So your big reveal is Saint Anna convinced the Shepherd to dress up as– "

"Don't be obtuse. People change genders all the time; it's nothing remarkable." Lu flicked her hand at him. "This isn't about something so common. The Shepherd was feared in his own right for punishing people for attempting to access the sacred mountain and drink from its healing spring. Anna offered him *everything* to get safe access for her people. And where was her God, the Holy Mother, while Anna preached to the Shepherd?"

Ky watched as the tunnel opened to reveal the astounding interior of the mountain summit. The underside of the dome was carved from the cavern ceiling, illuminated by thousands of jewel-encrusted lamps. Magnificent gilded statues of life-sized priestesses holding offering bowls aloft surmounted the tiered stairs leading to the Cathedral entrance. The containers overflowed with geothermal spring water, a cascade of steam rolling off of them. As the water spilled out, the cascading stream trickled down chains of golden bells, filling the dome of the Basilica with ethereal music. Late evening tourists took pictures as they waited for the funicular to take them back down to the city. A few noticed the limo and pointed.

"Water everywhere, but no milk." As the limo pulled up to the grand stairs, Lu toggled Ky's window up. "Now I'm going to take you to the very scene of the crime."

The limo deposited them at the bottom of the tiered stairs and Lu led Ky up to the Cathedral's entrance. Bands of white quartz and gold alternated in the variegated marble, creating a stark contrast to the natural granite of the cavern.

Delicate ridged arches buttressed the interior of the sacred structure. The peaked centerline was obscured by clouds of incense, the perfumed air punctuated with the heavy fragrance of resins and beeswax. At the far end of the cathedral, a towering altar gleamed resplendent with treasure. A few people sat in the high-backed pews. Some focused on the altar and others stared up at the grand paintings that illuminated the far peak of the Basilica. Looking at the looming majesty of the place, Ky relaxed, the palatial sanctuary holding for him a sense of deep peace and quietude. Thousands of years of celebrating high mass had imbued the sanctuary with a calm and restful atmosphere.

The echoes of the late-night worshippers and tourists dwindled as Lu headed off the main carpeted path to a gated side passage. A guard in ancient livery opened the gilded gate to allow her and Ky to enter. Ranks of beeswax candles burned under hammered gold memorial plates affixed to the ancient walls. The embroidered carpet glittered, its red and gold threads reflecting the light of countless rows of votive candles as it muffled the sound of their footfalls.

Ky looked over his shoulder at the security guard they passed at the gate. "What do you need me for here?"

"You can't expect me to walk around all by myself, can you? The guards here are purely ceremonial. Their claim to fame is that they can manage a tipsy High Priestess." Lu unhooked the fur at her throat. "Are you going to light a candle?"

"Why?"

"For the dead, of course," She stopped and looked at him. "Either your friend who just died, or all the ones you're so gut-wrenchingly miserable about killing."

Ky shot her a sullen look. "Not getting into that with you again."

"Your choice," Lu shrugged the fur off her shoulders and kept walking. Ky followed. "No matter how much you protest, I can feel it, your extravagant guilt. Not so much that I'd say you hate yourself, but enough that I'm surprised you haven't taken up a few bad habits so you can sleep at night."

"I sleep just fine."

She turned briskly and locked eyes with him, her face only inches from his own. Searching his eyes, she frowned. "And despite your perch on the moral high ground and your precious sense of purpose and ethics, you know how many lives you've destroyed." Adjusting her fur, she looked away and went over to a rack of candles beneath a plaque. Lifting a new candle to a burning one, she transferred the flame and set it in an open holder. "Have you always been able to see and feel things other humans don't notice?"

Ky watched the flame sputter and then become stable. "Not much when I was young."

"Does it run in your family?"

"Not that anyone wants to talk about." The mingled perfumes of incense and beeswax blended with the living flame. Heat swept along his spine and he took a step closer to the rows of lit candles. He stared at the flickering light with hungry, distant eyes. With a quiet hush, every flame in the corridor bent in his direction, then straightened. Ky blinked and shook his head, breaking the trance.

Lu watched the candles from the corner of her eye. "You don't even know what you are, do you? Or who protects you? Typical." She went along the passage to a second gate and spoke in a low voice to the guard there. The man nodded and opened the gate. Her white furs swept over the descending stairs and Ky felt uneasy following her into the narrowing section. As the gate clicked shut above, he ground his teeth against the uncomfortable feeling of being trapped.

Lu's heels clicked on the bare stone floor. She waited for him to follow and then headed off under another archway. Ky heard the water first. The splashing echoed and murmured through the arches as he passed. The passage ended in another archway that opened up into a cavern ablaze with golden reflections. Aligned with the altar on the main floor above, an enormous statue, at least a hundred feet tall, of the Holy Mother dominated the subterranean chamber. The robed figure was veiled and poured a cascade of water from her cupped hands into a wide stone basin below. Tiny by comparison, a second, human-scale statue knelt in supplication, the Saint, with her eyes blindfolded and hands lifted in prayer.

Lu pinched Ky's sleeve and hauled him over to the kneeling statue. Her voice was pitched louder to be heard over the noise of the cascading water. "The Saint, of course. Upholding her end of the bargain." She pointed up at the towering statue. "And who do you suppose that is?"

"The Holy Mother." Ky looked up at the veiled figure. "Pouring out the milk of compassion."

"But it's not, is it? Unless you want to discuss transubstantiation." She tugged on his sleeve again. "And where is the Shepherd in all of this?"

"I thought you said it wasn't about—"

"And I told you not to be obtuse." Lu dropped his arm and pouted. "I'm going to ask you a question, and I want you to think about it before you answer. Can you do that?"

"As long as you're paying me."

"What if the beliefs you've held for your whole life turned out to be lies? What if the Saint convinced the Shepherd he could have everything he ever wanted if he joined her in running the biggest show of them all?" She pointed at the statue of the Holy Mother. "If I could prove that your religion, your Saint, your God, have all been lying to your people for thousands of years, would it change anything? Would you even care?"

"I thought you brought me here for the water?" Ky ignored the uncertainty and discomfort he was feeling.

Lu rolled her eyes and tapped one of her boots. "Answer my question. Then you can try the water."

Ky looked again at the statues. "It wouldn't change anything."

"Why?"

"The story is just a way to explain the unexplainable. It's not meant to be taken literally."

"After our conversation earlier, when you made such a big deal about reasons for killing people, you're telling me that the Gods' reasons don't matter? Do you even feel the presence of any God here?" With both arms, Lu gestured at the statues and fountain.

Ky shook his head. "It's peaceful, but ..."

"Nobody's home." Lu crossed her arms. "And before you start telling me that it doesn't matter, think about all the resources that went into making this place. All the treasure hauled from other countries, taken from other people. The labor, the effort, the hopes and prayers of the people making offerings. How many children do you think this gold could feed? How many of the sick and poor could be housed with the offerings that went into this," she pointed up at the gilded ceiling. "Where do you think all this gold even came from? A community art project? Now you tell me how all those people deceived by a story would feel when their reasons for killing for this gold, and I do mean actual killing, were revealed as a lie? That they were conned into it? Does *that* matter?"

A Holy Venom

Ky felt the air pressure shift as Lu's anger blossomed. There was a sudden smell of ozone and he stared at her as silver shapes darted in a nimbus around her body. He took a step back. "You really are—"

"Don't say it." Lu snapped her fingers in front of his face. Her aura quiesced. "Etiquette, remember. We don't discuss such things inside someone else's house. Even if they're not home." She flipped her fingers at the fountain and walked away from him. "There's a place to dip a cup over here. Do let me know what you think."

Ky followed her around the base of the rippling basin. "People died for this gold?"

"They were murdered and the thieves brought it as tithe to give to the Church—to earn forgiveness. Does that surprise you? Miners died too, and their families, after they starved to death when the mines diverted farmers away from growing food. Murders over the gems, of course, murders over the imported marble. And that's not even counting the millions of lives devoted to propagating the lies, to keep the deception attracting more and more believers." Dipping her fingers into the water, Lu shot him a look over her shoulder. "Remind me, what was your war even about? Oh, yes, a separatist group. They had a different idea about how government should represent the people. They withheld supplies to get what they wanted?"

"It wasn't about their politics. It was about food."

"I phrased that poorly. They had a different belief system, didn't they?" She shook her fingers, sending droplets of water over the marble. "The way they viewed the world was, what's the word—*incompatible?*"

"They were killing their own people."

"I see. That makes all your reasons to kill the same people suddenly so very noble. Try the water."

Ky sighed and glanced at a bronze ladle resting on a bracket attached to the basin. "I don't see how any of this matters."

"That's putting it mildly. You can't see what's right in front of your face. Not that that's always bad, mind you. It makes it easier to mislead your kind." She pointed behind him at the statue of Saint Anna. "She's wearing a blindfold. Do you know it used to be a requirement for a newly elected High Priestess to cut out her own eyes and offer them to the Holy Mother? Oh yes, even with the veil over the God's face, the risk of seeing the divine truth was considered too dangerous. No human could know the truth about the usurper's secret identity."

Thinking about his divination and the warning to cover his eyes before going to the convent, Ky frowned. "There are some things you shouldn't see."

Lu gave him a teasing smile. "Or taste?"

Taking the hint, he took the ladle from the bracket and dipped it into the basin. Lu watched as he brought a mouthful to his lips. The water was cold, sweet, and clean, without a trace of the mineral content he was expecting.

"Feeling any mystical healing kicking in?" Lu watched him splash the rest of the ladle's contents into the grill beneath the bracket.

"Not particularly."

"Over the years, I found six other supposed 'holy springs' on and in this mountain. Including the one under the Statler. The first hospital on that site was originally a plague clinic or a leprosy camp, I can't remember which. Did you know that? Can you guess if any of the springs I located had mystical powers?"

"None of them did, or I suspect you wouldn't still be here."

She raised an eyebrow and smiled at him. "Correct. Now that you've tasted the water, and we've discussed the longest-running magic show in town," she gestured theatrically, "you can go back and wait in the car. Daisy will come around in a few minutes and pick you up out front. Feel free to take a nap."

"You're staying here?"

"I have a client appointment to keep in the Palace. This is my discreet way of being let in." She winked. "We can't have the press snapping photos of my lovely form dancing into the Palace's main entrance. Too scandalous."

"Can I ask you something before you go?"

Lu sighed. "Very well."

Glancing up at the gigantic statue, Ky shook his head. "Do you have proof that it's a con? That the Saint and the Shepherd colluded ..."

"When I said Anna offered the Shepherd everything, I meant she offered him the entirety of herself and her people. The entire world, you might say." She winked at him. "But there's more than that. After all, you know the

A Holy Venom

saying: *'Dogs don't make deals.'"* Turning her back, Lu waved over her shoulder, leaving Ky to stare as her heeled boots clicked over the flagstones. "Have a nice nap."

☾

The sun rose slowly over the frozen city, apricot light glittering over the accumulated fresh snow. The warming light touched the top of the mountain first and slowly spooled under the blue shadows of the pines bordering the garden behind the Statler Institute. The carved dome of the Basilica towered above the tree line.

An unhappy-looking man tucked his hands under his arms and looked around the deserted winter garden. "Couldn't we have met in the parking garage?" He stepped up into the stone pavilion overlooking the city. The wind picked up and piled snow tumbled off the ice-covered plinths onto the burlap-wrapped shrubbery below. Alarmed by the noise, Branch's eyes swept over the burlap and the marble statuary before darting back to Aych, who stood lounging near the pavilion's inner archway. The human's expression soured as he backed away from their imposing form.

"Cameras in the garage. None out here." Ignoring the human's scrutiny, Aych stared out at the sunrise display painting the clouds and gilding the tops of the buildings below. Wet, fat blobs of snowmelt started to fall around the stone structure. "Besides, you can't beat this view."

"I'd rather see it in the summer." Branch nervously edged closer and gazed out over the bleak winter forest descending the slope of the mountain peak. "This gets me out from under? If I give you this, I don't owe the Velvet?"

"Depends on what you found for me."

The man swallowed a few times and then took an envelope out of his pocket. The plain paper shook in his gloved hand as he extended it. "Only one person accessed the record for the earlier date. They didn't do much to cover it besides using a different system. Looks like they tried a few different logins and then got in with their secretary's credentials. Sloppy."

Aych pocketed the name. "Arrogant fuck probably thinks no one will notice." They leaned against the ice-crusted archway and looked out at the snow-mounded flower beds and the lines of the funicular cables. Dark shapes darted over the snow and the distant sounds of birds carried through the trees. "Tell me, do you know what's under this part of the mountain?"

"What?" Caught off guard, Branch stared back. "Nothing. It's all under the main institute and the historic hospital wings."

"Wrong," Aych shook their head. "The original thermal springs and the baths." They pointed at the back of the pavilion to an iron door set in the wall. "If you go through there and follow the tunnel down, it leads to an iron gate set in the granite. Go through it, down the stairs and you can be sitting in the hot springs all by your lonesome on your lunch break. Have to bring your own towel, of course."

"Really?" Branch smiled nervously. "I mean, is it safe? I heard the original baths aren't maintained." He frowned. "Didn't they close off the hot springs because of the lead pipes?"

"That's what they said," Aych shrugged nonchalantly. "But it was a cover-up. People kept sneaking down and getting drunk and falling asleep. Thermal water is hotter than you think if it's not mixed with cooler spring water. Very easy to boil yourself."

Grimacing, Branch shook his head. "That can't be true. I've worked here thirty years, I would've heard about it."

Aych cast a cool look over the man. "They closed it off a hundred years ago. Long before your time. Which is a shame, because it was much easier to feed the dogs that live down there freshly cooked meat. Mind you, I hate the smell of cooked meat. You could say I have a strong aversion. Now I have to bring in bags of overpriced kibble. It's a pain in the ass, but I prefer the way the dried food smells. But I do miss how happy the fresh meat made the dogs. Raw meat's trickier. Too much upsets their digestion. So I stick to kibble mostly."

"What dogs?" Branch stared as Aych took a step closer.

"The strange thing about superstition is that it has unexpected repercussions." They dropped a hand on Branch's shoulder. "Nobody in this city wants to own a black dog, but they don't want to kill them either. So any time a litter has a black pup, some asshole human leaves it in a park or dumps it in the Twins. Either way, they *think* the ones that don't drown get hit by cars or die of hunger. In truth, a few find their way in through the sewer access tunnels following the thermal heat and the scent markings. They end up down there, eating rats and trash and making more black puppies. Think of it: Hundreds of hungry, feral black dogs under the streets you walk every day."

"Really?" The man's voice trembled. "Sh-shouldn't the city do something?"

"Like what?" Aych brought their face close to his. "Kill them? They've tried. Lot of nasty accidents happen in the sewers."

"Maybe people should start a fund … have—have them neutered? Or adopted?"

Patting his shoulder, Aych nodded. "That's a good idea. You're a kind person, and it's good that you want to help the puppies. All those hungry dogs down there with nothing but a few scrawny rats and some drowned, bloated corpse floating in from the Twins. That's what's hard for me. Sure, the vets say kibble is the healthiest, but the dogs, they've got a strong preference for meat. *Human* meat. Must be bred into them. Their ancestors ate anyone who dared trespass on this mountain. I feel compelled to share. I'm paying my share of the rent."

Branch mumbled something about having to go and tried to step away from Aych.

Aych's hand tightened. "What's that? I can't hear you."

"I-I've given you what you asked for. I should be going. My office opens s-soon and I'll be missed if I'm not there."

"Oh, no." Shaking their head, Aych let their grin widen up until their white back teeth were visible.

Branch's expression froze as he stood petrified, too terrified to move.

Aych patted the man's shoulder. "I promised the pack a guest for breakfast. I can't go back on my word."

FIFTEEN

A SENSE OF FISSION ran along Ky's skin, lifting the hair on his arms and neck as he stepped into the Teahouse's rustic foyer. He noticed a lightning bug, oddly out of season and in the wrong locale, dancing in the air. Low, recorded folk music mingled with the soft hiss of sliding wooden doors and distant chatter as he watched the insect bumble along the glossy wooden wall panels and flit under the leaves of a substantial fern next to the vintage cash register. The tiny spark winked and floated away down the corridor into the interior of the Teahouse and then returned, lazily drifting over the shoulder of an older man wearing a linen work smock.

"Would you like a table or a seat at the counter?" The man glanced at the duffel bag Ky was carrying, then to his eyes, sizing him up.

The man's accent gave Ky pause until he placed it as from the Archipelago and not Grava. He hesitated, then shook his head. "Lu sent me. Told me to ask for Mat." Ky realized the green winking light was not flickering as an insect would; this was something different, something strange, a nature spirit. The tingle intensified as Ky stared at the sprite and the man it circled.

"She called just now." Mat came around the end of the counter, slightly scowling. The wee sprite climbed out of the man's collar and rested on his shoulder. "I'll show you where you can leave your things and then introduce you." He flapped an impatient hand and started back down the cedar-lined corridor.

Ky followed in Mat's wake. Snippets of conversation flowed out from the private tea rooms and into the narrow passage. Ky glanced over the waitstaff's shoulders, attempting to dodge the servers carrying trays and cleaning supplies. Decorated with lanterns and low, painted furniture, the windowless cubbies with their panels illustrated with woodland scenes struck him as dangerously confining.

Mat glanced back and caught sight of Ky's expression. He pointed at the closed door of one of the occupied tea rooms. "Each room is named after the mural inside. The wolf or fox den has added soundproofing, and every chamber has an emergency exit. All were brought over from the Islands. Hand-painted there, then disassembled and reassembled here."

Ky glanced down at the corridor, watching for further incoming traffic. "You're from the Archipelago?"

Mat nodded. "Moved here about twenty years back. The Teahouse was built over two hundred years ago. I brought new panels and equipment with me over on the ship, then had the tea ware and the medicinal herbs sent over. We get shipments every month, fresh and dried, seasonally harvested from the main island." The herbalist raised his voice as the sound of rushing water echoed down the hall. "The main chamber is up ahead, next to the apothecary and kitchen. Can I prepare some tea for you?"

"I'm more of a coffee drinker," Ky glanced ahead to an archway leading into the noisier, brighter interior of the eatery.

Surprised by the burbling of water, he came to a halt in the archway and stared at a waterfall flowing out of slate panels, over river stones, and into a pond complete with live plants and fish. Glass tabletops and padded stools floated like islands, each oriented toward the waterfall. A high wall at the back covered in shelves of rough-hewn wood dripped with verdant plant growth. Tucked among the greenery, glass jars filled with dried herbs reflected the golden glow of the oversized lanterns hanging above the tables.

Efficient staff swept through the tidepool of tables and tended to guests. The Teahouse was alive with conversation and laughter, the light warm and the waterfall soothing. Ky noticed the usual emotional stagnation of continually occupied spaces was absent and everyone appeared to be relaxed and happy. He guessed someone frequently purified and blessed the restaurant and glanced at Mat.

Oblivious to his guest's scrutiny, Mat charged across the dining room through another archway and into the apothecary. Ky trailed a few feet back, staring up at the floor-to-ceiling apothecary shelves crammed with ceramic canisters and wooden boxes. A few herbalists working on orders looked up from their tasks as the two men passed the work tables. Mat waved brusquely to his staff, only slowing to pass through a smaller archway into the clattering, steaming frenzy of the kitchen.

He pulled Ky out of the way of a woman carrying a large platter and then pointed at the fire door at the back of the kitchen. "Only a few people use this entrance. Wipe your boots when you come in. We don't want any snow tracked in making a mess." Mat pushed open a door, letting a gust of cold air churn the steam billowing in the kitchen. With another glance at Ky, Mat stepped out into the freezing night. Clasping his arms around his thin smock, he jerked his chin at the carriage house across the turnaround. He clambered over the knee-high lip of snow out into the plowed driveway. "We keep the backyard lights off unless there's a delivery. The backdoor's usually not locked." He led Ky over the gravel and to the side of the two-story garage.

Ky glanced through the porthole windows in the bay doors and caught sight of the motorcycles. "You ride?"

"Was a courier a long time ago." Leading him to the side entrance Mat shrugged. "Work on a few for a hobby these days. Take a couple out when the roads are clear. Short riding season over here. You?"

"Not in a long time."

"If you're around when it warms up, come by and borrow one." Stopping briefly to shove his shoulder into the side door, Mat smiled sadly at Ky. "They get lonely." The herbalist lingered in the entranceway to stamp the snow off his boots before heading up a set of creaking stairs. "You'll have the upstairs to yourself. Hot water in the shower takes a minute after you switch it on, sheets are clean. If you're hungry, come through to the counter."

Frozen in place at the foot of the stairs, Ky stared at the miasma seeping through the exposed wallboards. Contamination emanated from the garage, spilling through the cracks in the ancient wood. The shadowy tendrils, feral and skittish shifted just as they had at Haw's house.

Mat followed his gaze and frowned. "Everything alright?"

Ky forced himself to put his hand on the railing and start up the stairs. "Thought I heard something."

"You might, but hopefully you won't if ..." Mat cleared his throat and resumed stomping up the stairs. "There's good insulation up here. Used to have friends stay so we made sure there'd be a way to keep it quiet if we kicked up a ruckus and to keep it comfortable no matter what the weather was doing." Pushing open the door at the top of the stairs, Mat snapped the lights on and waved Ky in ahead of him.

Ky stopped and looked around the room. He wasn't sure what he had been expecting, but it wasn't this. Band posters and moth-eaten wool rugs lined the walls and ceiling while the wide floorboards gleamed under the glow of countless strings of lights. The lingering feeling of stored-up joy and shared comradery permeated everything from the broken-down leather chairs to the over-stuffed couches. Whatever evil was in the garage below, the upstairs was sanctified with the same kind of protection active in the Teahouse. The division was startling.

Hauling open the tapestry drapes at the back, Mat shuffled through into the concealed sleeping area. "Bathroom is through the first door on your right, the other one is storage." After checking over the bed, he pointed across the open space to the corner opposite. "Coffee pot works, but you'll have to pick up milk and keep it on the stairs. If you need to, you can use the phone in my office. From what Lu was saying, I expect you'll mostly be out with Ruin."

"Ruin?" Ky set his duffel bag on one of the cracked leather chairs. "Lu didn't tell me the client's name."

"They're funny about saying words like that across the street." Mat made a face. "Don't want to spoil the luck. Anyway, this side of the street, we call people by whatever they want to be called." He looked Ky over. "That all you've got, those suits?"

Ky pointed at his duffel. "No, jeans and T-shirts ..."

"Those would be better. He'll want to check in with his bandmates and if you're dressed like a salt, you'll stand out, might not even get into wherever they're at. I'll give you a few minutes to change and then send him over. The two of you can figure things out on your own."

"Is there anything I should know?"

"He's not troublesome," Mat snapped defensively. "Ruin is a good person."

"Sorry, I didn't mean it like that. I meant, is there anything you can tell me about why he needs protection?"

Mat sighed and shot Ky an apologetic look. "People are assholes and they want to hurt him. That's all you need to know."

☾

Ky heard the downstairs door open and then the thud of boots on the stairs. He looked up from contemplating the sad state of the coffee pot and set the mineral-stained container back on the burner just as he heard a perfunctory knock on the door. A shaggy head poked through the doorway.

Wavering, darting threads of etheric currents chased around Ruin's body. The nightmarish taint from the garage was languidly coiled around his neck and twined through his hair, like an oil slick. The contamination was a thousand times worse than what Ky had encountered on Haw's children and there appeared to be competing factions within the hazy mix surrounding Ruin. Ky tried to focus on the younger man's face and got the impression of a handsome and extremely suspicious person staring back at him. The warping effect slowly diminished until Ky could see shaggy hair pulled back in numerous loops and ties, the silver rings in Ruin's ears and nose, and the scars of former piercings around his lips and eyebrows. Ky blinked as his charge warily looked him over.

"You're Ky?" Ruin glanced around the room. "OK if I come in?"

"Yeah, sure. It's more your place than mine." Dropping his gaze back to the coffeepot, Ky wondered what the hell kind of human he agreed to protect.

"Don't bother with that fucking thing. It got trashed when we used this for a practice space. If you want coffee, there's a good place around the corner."

Ky glanced forlornly at the pot. "Don't know what your plans are, but if you could point me in the right direction, I'd appreciate it." He gave Ruin a relaxed and somewhat desperate smile. "I'm not going to be much use without a cup or two."

Ruin smiled. "Easier to walk you over, there's a short cut."

"If it's no trouble. Mat was telling me you were likely headed out." Ky debated standing up and offering a handshake and then decided against touching the man. "I've been asked to tag along and make sure no one fucks with you."

"Nothing personal, but I don't want a babysitter." Ruin exhaled and looked around the room. "I don't know what anyone told you, but …"

"That there's a bunch of assholes causing trouble for you and you need an extra set of eyes and hands," Ky shrugged. "All you need to know is I'm on your side. Don't think of me as a babysitter. I'm here to back you up. Maybe in return, you can tell me if there are any good bands I should check out while I'm in town. Maybe point me in the direction of a few good record stores?"

Ruin ducked his head and scuffed the toe of his boot on the worn floorboards. He looked over. "There's a show at The Cellar, a couple of local bands."

"Friends of yours? Are you in a band now?"

Dropping his gaze again, Ruin nodded and then turned his back, walking away with his hands laced behind his head. "Maybe." He stopped and stiffened. "Couple of people I might want to see."

"And maybe a few you don't?" Standing up, Ky watched as silver serpents snapped at the red threads floating in his charge's aura. By his count, there were at least two, maybe three different contaminants adhered to Ruin. However many there were, they were clearly from different sources. Ky wondered if Ruin's enemies were numerous and skilled enough to be layering so many curses. "You want to see your friends but you're not sure if they want to see you?"

"Yeah." Vulnerable and angry, Ruin met Ky's eyes. Ruin's expression changed quickly into a roguish smile. "But I fucked up, so it's on me to apologize to the ones I give a shit about."

☾

The Velvet's house lights were up at the soft mid-level, denoting a pause between acts. Ticket holders took advantage of the intermission to visit each other's tables and flirt with the staff. Aych reached Violet's alcove and nodded to the pair of security guards on watch.

Aych caught sight of Lu in the alcove and smiled. "Hey gorgeous, I came to watch your show."

A Holy Venom

Violet opened their arms wide in greeting. "Ah! *Tau-vik-lm!*"

"You look well, *tau-lm*." Aych nodded to Violet and waited for the man next to Lu to vacate his seat. While the human apologetically moved over, Aych winked at Lu. "You look ravishing, as always."

"*She's* a genuine goddess of beauty. In my case, it's all make-up and professional lighting." Violet fluffed the silk scarf at their neck. "I appreciate you joining us, in case we have a sudden… infestation." They waved at the man who had relocated. "Why don't you take a turn around the floor, Rod? See if any of our *gaedoon* require assistance?"

"Of course, *tau-lm*." Rod inclined his head and smiled at Lu. "Thank you for allowing me to speak with you, *tau-ve-lm*." He nodded at Aych but kept his eyes fixed elsewhere.

Violet waited until the man was far enough and then rolled their eyes. "*Pik-een*, that one. Cousin of mine sent him to be trained up." They inhaled quickly and watched as Aych settled next to Lu. "Thank you for your help the other night, by the way. Legae said you left it enough of a mystery to keep the *doon* on their toes. A mess in another room, but nothing in the expected suite?"

Aych smiled as Lu offered them a fluted glass of pink liquor and took a sip. "Mixed some business with pleasure. Glad I could be of some assistance, Vee." They set the sweet alcohol aside and glanced at Lu. "Constalia? You expecting me to be in a bad mood?"

"Not that you need it." Lu purred and put her hand on Aych's. "Or am I wrong? You've fed."

"Right as always." They brought her hand to their mouth for a formal kiss across the knuckles. "Just ate, as a matter of fact."

Violet laughed. "How listening to your divine and demonic banter chases away my boredom, my dears. What secrets you must share!"

One of the guards dipped her head under the curtain. "Vetch and a pair of salts are on their way, *tau-lm*."

Sighing, Violet plucked the lacy frills escaping the cuffs of their brocade jacket. "Places everyone."

While Lu arranged her silk shawl to fall off her shoulders, Aych stood up and leaned against the back wall away from the screened theatre lights. Violet and Lu began laughing and conversing in their native language.

Vetch emerged through the beaded curtain and slightly bowed. "*Tau-lm*, Detectives Mudon and Tosh wish to pay their respects to you this evening." He held the curtain back and allowed the two detectives to pass into the alcove.

"Detectives, so lovely for you to think of an old person such as myself. I am touched. Truly touched."

"*Tau-een, tau-lm tu gaedoon*," Mudon took Violet's hand and kissed their knuckles. "You're looking radiant, Lutauvelm." His eyes strayed to Lu's cleavage and then up to her face.

"Won't you join us, please?" Violet indicated the seats next to their right. "Drink with us and allow our house to bring you delight." They glanced at Vetch as the two guests drew back the chairs to sit.

Vetch nodded and stepped out. Once on the other side of the curtain, he spoke in low voice to the staff members and then stepped back in. He shared a look over the table with Aych and raised an eyebrow.

Tosh pulled a handkerchief from her wrinkled suit jacket. Blotting her forehead, she reached for a glass of ice water. "I never get used to how hot you people keep this place."

Lu smiled. "You should visit us more often. A hot stone massage would improve your circulation."

The detective's eyes widened and she quickly shoved the cloth back into a pocket.

"I wish we could visit you more often." Mudon leaned on the table to look at Lu. "As it is, social calls are harder and harder to justify, what with the trouble coming out of here on the regular."

Pressing a hand to their breast, Violet pantomimed surprise and shock. "My dear *pen-lm*, whatever could you mean?"

Mudon looked from Aych to Vetch and back to Lu. "Could be you don't know, *tau-lm*. That would be a pity. A member of your house is abusing your hospitality, possibly taking advantage of your kindness."

Smiling, Lu shook her head. "*Tau-lm* is our *ku-olm*. Nothing goes on in this house without their knowledge. From the slates on the roof to the anchor blocks in the cellar, every person and every thing in this house is loyal."

The detective leaned back with one arm over his chair. "Then we might have a problem. It would be one thing if you were unaware, but if these things are happening with your blessing, then..."

"I appreciate your delicacy, *pen-lm*, but I'm quite at a loss about what you're referring to?" Violet flamboyantly waved a hand.

"Drugs." Tosh glanced from Violet to Mudon. "We got a tip that the Rot is coming from here."

Lu gasped as Violet reeled backward. She caught the elder by the shoulders and began fanning them. "How dare you come in here and make this accusation?"

Violet waved a hand and sniffed. "No, no, my dear, let them speak. If something that awful is taking place in my house, it's my duty to be punished." They wiped tears from their eyes. "I assume you have a warrant to search and find the culprits to apprehend at once, detectives?"

Mudon shot an annoyed look at his partner. "We're not quite at that point, *tau-lm*. I wanted to extend you the courtesy, to ask if you might cooperate and hand over the responsible party." He glared at Aych. "Possibly a foreigner not from here or from Gravagaedoon. Someone ignorant, possibly dangerous—a known troublemaker." He looked back at Violet. "If you handed them to us now, we could avoid further complications. You've always been reasonable, and we've appreciated that. It's not your fault if someone took advantage of your kindness."

Aych snorted as they sprinkled herbs into a rolling paper. "If you don't have a warrant and you don't have a name, then all you've got are fantasies of promotion. You think you can come in and disrespect the house, maybe try your luck at more than the tables. Maybe you're playing fetch to appease your owners ..."

Mudon frowned. "I don't like what you're implying."

"I'm not implying anything." Aych shrugged and licked the rolling paper then sealed the cigarette. "Everyone in the city knows the facts."

"Now, now," Violet crooned. "We're all friends here. The detectives came to ask us politely to cooperate. This is a public safety issue and they're only doing their jobs, isn't that right, *pen-lm*?"

Tosh narrowed her eyes. "Public safety, yeah. The Rot's through the whole city now and it's killing people."

Mudon glared at Aych. "It was a nuisance, but now that there's deaths…"

Violet and Lu both shuddered and reflexively flicked their fingers against their drinks, making the glassware ring.

"My apologies, *tau-lm*." Mudon inclined his head. "But there have been many. Between the beds filling up at the hospitals and the morgue, we have to catch whoever is making it."

Aych sneered. "I'm curious, detective. Did you go up the Hill and have this same conversation at the Palace, or did you think of us straight away?"

Tosh looked mortified. While Vetch remained silent and rotated one of the heavy gold rings on his right hand, Lu raised her glass to her lips and barely concealed a smile.

"Watch the things you say," Violet swatted at Aych. "You'll forget you heard that for my sake, won't you, *pen-lm*? This demon of ours is a troublemaker."

"The Church isn't suspected, no." Mudon held Aych's gaze. "No sane person would even consider that a possibility."

"Then I'm not surprised you haven't caught the culprit, detective. You're too busy airing your prejudices and playing dress up with your paper dolls to get the job done."

Violet groaned. "Enough. Why don't you escort Lu backstage? It's getting close to her next performance and your company will keep her admirers away." They smiled at Mudon. "They have their uses, you see."

Lu kissed Violet on the cheek and started to stand. "I'll see you later, Vee."

Patting her hand, Violet nodded. "*Tau-een tu*."

Mudon stood and Tosh slowly followed suit as Lu adjusted her glittering shawl.

"*Tau-een tu*, Lutauvelm." Mudon inclined his head to Lu and then narrowed his eyes as Aych fell into step behind her.

"Have a good evening, detectives. I do hope you'll stay for the show." Lu inclined her head.

"Stick around, maybe visit the tables since you're here." Aych patted Mudon on the chest. "Maybe I'll come over and we can play a few hands."

Tosh took a step forward.

Mudon met his partner's eyes. "Sure, no one will care if I win some

A Holy Venom

pocket money off scum like you." He leaned into Aych. "We've got enough to bring you down to the Tank right now."

Aych leaned closer and stared into the human's eyes. "If that were true, we wouldn't be standing here, would we?"

"*Le-lm*, are you coming, or shall I ask Vetch to accompany me?" Lu drawled in a bored voice.

"Sorry, beautiful. I was just wishing the detectives good night." Aych pushed Mudon out of the way with a fingertip. "See you at the tables, *detective*."

☾

Inside the crowded basement club, patrons jostled shoulder to shoulder as jarring beats boomed from the cramped stage. Tub leaned forward to yell into Ruin's ear. "You doing OK? What's with your date?" Tub looked over at Ky, who was sipping a beer and watching the dance floor.

"Friend of my uncle's. Offered to show him around," Ruin yelled back.

"You going to go talk to Shine?"

"Yeah." Ruin stared into his glass, trying not to look over at the bar where his boyfriend was flirting with another man.

Tub patted Ruin's arm and glanced at the crowd dancing under the oscillating lights. "Busy tonight!"

Over the thumping of the bassline, Ruin heard a scream. A woman laughed and swatted at her friend before the pair resumed dancing together. He looked at Tub and then at the other people standing close by. Upending his glass, he tapped Tub's elbow. "I'm getting another," he pointed at Tub's glass.

"Yeah, the same." Tub finished his beer and passed it over. "Thanks!"

Pushing gently through the press of people near the bar, Ruin shivered as bare limbs and hands brushed along his body as he passed. Setting down the glasses roughly on the bar, he called out, "Sun, can I get two more?"

From her post mid-counter, the bartender flashed her fingers in acknowledgment. A spot opened as two people headed for the dance floor. Ruin snagged the opening and set his back against the brick wall. Sun set a shot and a beer on the bar and waved Ruin closer.

"Squash is looking for you." The woman tilted her head toward the other end of the bar.

Ruin handed her cash for the drinks. "Thanks." He watched Shine laughing as the other man leaned in closer. A classic love song thumped through the speakers as Ruin caught Squash's eye.

She pushed away from the group and ran through the dense crowd to hug him. "Where have you been? We were fucking worried!"

"Sorry, I …"

Squash made a fist and playfully mashed it into his jaw. "Your uncle told me you got sick again. Feeling better now?" His bandmate's eyes were full of concern.

Ruin looked over her shoulder at Shine. "Did you know?"

"Know what?"

Ruin jerked his head in Shine's direction. "He's fucking that guy, isn't he?"

Squash looked away and gulped her drink.

"Tell me."

She scrunched up her face. "You haven't been around. He gets lonely too."

"I fucking knew it." He grabbed his drink off the bar and threw it back. "I'm right and you don't fucking want to tell me."

"You've got to ask him about it, OK? Besides, it's not like you want to stay with him. So what? You've been friends for ages and ages. We're still a band. You're fucking around too." She nodded in Ky's direction.

"No, I'm not." He glanced at his boyfriend—could he even still call him that? "Maybe he's seeing someone else because I'm a stat."

Squash put her hand on his back. "It happens to people who aren't, you know."

"Being cheated on, or being lied to?"

She sighed and looked over at Shine. "He probably thinks you won't notice. You're not around anymore."

"I'm mentally ill, not stupid," Ruin growled. He watched the other man touch Shine. A rush of adrenaline kicked in, pouring electricity up Ruin's spine. His free hand tightened into a fist.

Stepping into his line of vision, Squash poked him in the chest.

A Holy Venom

"Everything's an extreme with you. Either it's fucking amazing or you've got to fucking trash it. Instead of starting a fight, maybe go dance or, I dunno, fuck the guy you brought tonight?"

"I told you, we're not together. But you're right. I'm selfish. It hurts to matter so little that he can't be bothered to break up with me."

She hugged him. "Maybe he's putting on a show for an audience of one, ever think of that? So *you* can break up with *him*?"

The last fragments of Ruin's anger dissolved into sadness. Tears burned his eyes. "Band's not going to last. Either I'm going to trash it or …"

"Everything has its season, hon." She kissed his cheek. "Go home and get some rest. You still look tired."

He squeezed her tightly. "It's too early. I wanted to dance tonight." He forced himself to not look at Shine. He could feel the two men laughing at him. He was a joke they shared after fucking, someone to laugh at and mock; *poor stat, unable to get it up, probably cutting himself for attention*. Self-loathing blossomed, tendrils of jealousy burning and running under his skin.

"Hey," Squash reached out and shook his arm. "Don't think about them." She jerked her head at the bar. "Even if the band doesn't work out, you'll just start another one. Or go solo."

The kind words burned into him. The walk through the crowd was a blur. Suddenly, he heard water dripping. He looked around. He was in the bathroom, the sink under the vandalized mirror leaking steadily. He had no memory of how he got there. He yanked open one of the two stall doors. Inside, he stared at the graffiti above the toilet and then fumbled the lock on the door. At the click, a remembered pressure barreled into him. The hot press of skin and wet lips, kissing, hands on skin, and a musky odor. Shine fucking him in the stall. The noise of the club faded out. Ruin heard a pair of voices arguing distantly, as if from a long way off. A man shouted at a woman, and she shrieked in response.

Someone banged a fist on the stall door.

"You OK in there?" Ky called.

"No," Ruin answered as everything pushed in on him at once. The dead and the living making their demands, the imp chorus resuming its song.

Aware of the currents swarming around Ruin, Ky tried to think of a way to help. "Talk to me. Tell me how you're feeling." He wedged the overflowing waste can between the sink and the doorknob and sealed the bathroom off from the rest of the club.

"I don't want to talk." Grasping for an anchor, Ruin closed his eyes and leaned back against the stall door.

"I don't care what it's about. Just keep talking or I will take this door off and check on you."

Ruin blinked back tears and smiled ruefully. "What should I talk about, then?"

"Whatever you want."

"Ask me something."

Ky had an idea. "If you know Lu, you must know Aych. What can you tell me about them?" The question triggered a flood of emotions in Ruin. Ky could feel conflicting waves of sadness and happiness peak and ebb as Ruin stayed silent.

"You could say we share an affinity…or maybe, an affliction."

Surprised by the change in emotions, Ky thought of his next question. "When did you meet Aych?"

"When I was a kid." Ruin closed his eyes and was silent. Memories of the kidnappers shook him. It was difficult to think of meeting Aych without thinking of them, but he managed to shut them out of his mind. "I was staying at the Stat, for treatment. One night, there was an emergency, and all the nurses and attendants got called away. I wanted to get the fuck out. Leave, go home."

"You walked out?"

Ruin laughed, "No, they do lock the doors on the ward. I mean, they were in a rush, but never careless with their VIP guests. I had this stupid idea that I could get out through the ventilation. Probably got it from a movie."

"How old were you?"

"It was right after," Ruin's voice cracked. "Ten."

"Did you get out?" Ky glanced at the bathroom door; someone pounded on it. He braced the trash can with his boot.

"Almost. I ended up in this fucked up area in the basement. Body bags on a couple of hospital gurneys. Empty ones, thank fuck. With restraints, like they used for violent patients, all of them positioned under these metal chutes. Reminded me of trash or coal chutes, like bodies were going to come tumbling down and land on the stretchers."

"Was it the morgue?" Ky considered changing the subject but the miasma surrounding Ruin seemed to be quiescing, drawing in as he calmed down.

"No, there weren't any freezers or autopsy tables or shit like that. Just the gurneys under the chutes. There were these creepy cast iron bells shaped like dog heads, triggered to ring if the chutes opened. Scared the fuck out of me, imagining those bells ringing and the body bags sliding out."

"That's where you met Aych?"

Ruin laughed. "No, I got the fuck out of there and ended up getting even more lost. The main building is crazy old and there's a shit ton of subcellars. Every time I tried to find my way out, I ended up further down in the abandoned treatment rooms. I slept in the stairwells and hoped someone would find me."

"How long were you lost for?"

"Couple of days," Ruin grunted. "Maybe three, just wandering around scared shitless."

"Did you have anything to eat or drink?"

"There were therapy tubs in the main halls. Massive submersion tubs and individual ones, I think those were for ice therapy. The faucets still worked. I guess the natural mountain spring water was a big deal when the Statler was built. Before they had drugs, they used the water. My last digger told me it's high in lithium and some other mineral shit. The subcellars are bathing therapy chambers. Creepy as fuck down there. Kept expecting to see ghosts."

Ky considered if he should get Ruin out of the stall or keep him talking. Eventually, security was going to check on the bathroom and roust them out. "Sounds pretty traumatic."

"Oh, it was. I was exhausted and starving. Hallucinating my ass off. I can't even remember how I got outside, but I ended up in the woods at night in my pajamas, barefoot in the snow. The cold was worse than anything. Just tried to find my way to the gardens, figured I was out back behind the main building, halfway up the mountain. Trying not to die, trying to keep going up. There was a movie I'd seen with my mom about Arctic explorers. Frostbite and the dangers of falling asleep outside, death by hypothermia. I figured I was a goner if I stopped moving and they'd have to amputate my toes and I'd end up with those freaky boots, the ones with built-in wooden toes."

Ky imagined the child version of Ruin scared and wandering half-frozen through the backside of the mountain. "That sounds rough. I'm glad you survived."

"I almost didn't. The hallucinations can be overwhelming. I mean, sometimes I know when it's my head fucking with me, but other times it's real. Hyper-real. Ultra-vivid, and if it's really bad, there are these compulsions to do things. I can't explain it properly, but they're like imps controlling me. My digger said I shouldn't feel like a failure because I can't resist the compulsions, but I do. It's like watching yourself turn into a puppet…" Ruin's voice trailed off uncertainly.

"I know how that feels." Ky thought of his own struggles with self-control. "Like you're enthralled, or under a spell."

"Yeah, similar, I guess." Ruin sounded reassured. "Anyway, I was outside freezing to death and I thought I saw someone standing in the garden looking up at the moon." He turned his head to where he thought Ky was outside the stall. "It sounds like you've met Aych now?"

"Yeah, in passing."

"Well, I walked up to them, not sure if I was seeing shit or if they were real, and then I said the most fucked up thing." Ruin smiled, remembering looking up to see Aych's fangs and claws and their dark fur. All that impossible warmth. Aych's eyes burning in the night.

Ruin's laughter echoed off the bathroom tiles. "I said, *'Can you help me, please?'* Can you imagine? Scrawny little shit in pajamas walking up and saying that *to them?*"

Ky imagined a boy at the brink of total collapse approaching the tall, pale shepherd alone at night. "But they did help you?"

Thinking of Aych, Ruin felt all of his anxiety fall away. He unlocked the stall door and pulled it open an inch. Looking at Ky, he nodded. "Yeah. Took me back to their place and treated my toes for frostbite and the rest of me for hypothermia. Then they brought me home—not back to the Statler, but my own bed in my house and tucked me in. Told me not to wander around at night anymore. But being me, I did the opposite so I could meet them again."

Ky backed up to give him room. "You don't have to keep talking about it if you don't want to."

"That's OK. I'd rather tell you about it so that if you're freaked out, you can blow me off now rather than later."

"I won't blow you off."

"I don't mind anymore. Really. When it's bad, I don't want to be around me either." The sadness in Ruin's voice increased. "I'll probably end up like my real uncle, my mom's brother. He died in there, in the Stat. My family mostly dies in there. Or in accidents."

The despair in Ruin's voice colored Ky's vision. The darting threads pulsed and spun around the younger man, snapping.

Ruin looked up, embarrassed. "Sorry, I should've probably gone off on the local music scene or started listing record stores you could check out."

"I want to know more about you." Opening the stall door wider, Ky looked down at Ruin. "I'm not exactly standard issue either." He lifted his T-shirt up under his jacket.

Ruin's eyes followed the lines of scars and mottled skin over Ky's torso. "Can I ask what happened?"

"You can ask whatever you want," Ky shrugged. "Some are skin grafts and others are burn scars. It was an explosion during the war. I was caught at the edge of it."

"Does it hurt?"

Ky pointed at the thicker keloid over his ribs. "Doesn't stretch and this part's numb from nerve damage. Occasional nerve pain. There's a sanded-down patch on my back."

"Like road rash?"

Ky smiled. "Yeah, industrial strength road rash."

"I have these," Ruin showed Ky small burn scars and thin cut scars on his arms. He dropped his gaze to the floor and paused. "I'm not good with fire. Both my parents died when our house was burned down. My digger told me I was lucky to escape, or I would've died too."

"I'm sorry. That must've been difficult, losing them that way." Ky moved the trash can away, unblocking the bathroom door. "Feeling like you want to go back out?"

"Yeah, this isn't the best place to hang out. People will get the wrong idea." Looking embarrassed again, Ruin moved past Ky and headed for the door. "We should go back to the Teahouse. Unless you need more coffee?"

"It can wait. You go on out first." Stopping to wash his hands at the sink, Ky grinned and looked at Ruin in the mirror. "So no one gets the wrong idea. I'll meet up with you in a minute."

Ruin nodded and headed out toward the dance floor, looking for Tub. The sound of the club burst back into normal volume. Suddenly, the dancers' bodies slowed, leaving colored trails. The notes of the song pounding through the club warped and droned. Dazed, Ruin stood still. Bodies jostled him as the lights above the crowd began singing a faint, lilting melody.

"Ruin, hey!" Tub called as he squeezed through the crowd. "Thought you might have left! Sorry, I only got myself a drink." Tub dropped his hand on his friend's shoulder. "You OK?"

Shaking his head, Ruin shouted back. "Got a piece of music stuck in my head."

Tub nodded and took a hefty swallow of his cocktail. "I think I saw Gerdy." He clapped Ruin on the back. "You're sure you're OK?"

"Going to get out of here. Want to get home before I forget."

Tub hooked a thumb in the direction of the crowd. "They want to hear it too."

"See what I can do." Ruin threw a cautious glance at the people standing by the stairs to the exit. Taking a deep breath, he pushed through and nodded to the group. A few smiled in recognition as Ruin made his way up the stairs.

Pretty, pretty, pretty. A woman's voice repeated in time with the music. Instead of ignoring it, Ruin imagined layering it into a song. He stopped on the landing to listen, the cool air from the street above calming him. In his head, the repeating choir of the lights and the voice began assembling over the borrowed bassline.

"There you are." A man's voice cut through Ruin's reverie.

A hand gripped his arm. Ruin shook it off. "Fuck off, Flox. I'm with someone tonight."

"Not with Shine anymore. I saw him with Cane. And you're staying

A Holy Venom

until I talk to you." Flox grabbed Ruin again and forced him to the side of the landing. "You haven't returned my calls. You're avoiding me."

"I told you, fuck off." Ruin growled and shook Flox's hand off a second time. "Touch me again and I'll—"

"You'll what?" Flox leaned his face into Ruin's. "Go crying to that shepherd friend of yours? You owe me."

Ruin pushed the man backward with both hands. "I don't owe you shit." He clambered up the stairs and vaulted the last few steps to the street.

Catching himself on the railing, Flox sneered and came up the stairs after Ruin. "You fucking little shit, I almost fell!"

Ruin wedged sideways, dodging around the line of people coming into the club. *Why are you running? Running, running, always running. He doesn't scare me.* The female voice cooed. The winter air slapped against Ruin's chest as he came up onto the sidewalk. *You never have to run again if you would only say yes, say yes, say yes to me.*

Glancing at the Velvet's marquee up ahead, Ruin shoved his hands into his pockets. He knew Aych was working tonight and that was why Lu had Ky babysitting him instead. He concentrated on the crunch of his boots on the mix of grit on the plowed sidewalk. Shooting a quick look over his shoulder, Ruin saw Flox coming up from the Cellar's stairs. "Fuck."

"You owe me, you piece of shit!" Flox yelled. "Don't think I don't know where you're going! I'll tell everyone who you are, what you are, and where you are. You'll never play anywhere again!"

Fear and adrenaline hit Ruin. He stopped as the panicked rush crested and slammed through his body. A surge of anger and rage hit Ruin as Flox's hand clutched onto his arm. As the bigger man dragged at Ruin, the music in Ruin's head crashed into a crescendo. He spun and gut-punched Flox. The phantom imps' chorus responded to the violence with an onslaught of music more beautiful than anything Ruin had heard under the stage lights, off vinyl, out of speakers, or out of a human throat. Gasping for breath, Flox fell to his knees with a shocked look. Ruin grabbed him by the collar and kneed him in the face.

Droplets of blood spun from Flox's mouth and nose as Ruin's incandescent rage turned the world red. Ruin hit the man again, fists and knees rising and falling in time to the internal music of his violence. With every strike, the music intensified. The rhythm of it, the pain in the knuckles of his hands, the hammering of his muscles in his back, stomach and thighs, felt exhilarating.

"Enough. That's enough." From behind, Ky grabbed Ruin's wrist. "Whatever he did, you're done." His hand burning from the psychic backlash, Ky tugged the younger man along the sidewalk.

Flox lay on the ground, coughing and spitting blood. The blood-thirsty miasma surrounding Ruin shimmered and flared. Ky dropped the younger man's wrist.

Careful not to touch him, Ky stepped around Ruin to open the Teahouse door. "C'mon, let's go inside."

With his head down, Ruin raced through the hall, away from Ky.

"Hey!" Ky shut the door and chased him.

Waitstaff and customers jumped back as the pair slammed through the hallway of tea rooms and into the dining room. Ruin sprinted into the back section and Ky followed through the apothecary.

Mat shouted, "Slow the fuck down!"

Ky followed Ruin out the back door and watched him run to the garage. After a moment's hesitation, he jogged across the packed snow, pushed through the side door and went up the wooden stairs. Lights flicked on and Ky paused as he heard Ruin arguing with another person. A woman shrieked and yelled in response. Pushing open the door, Ky stepped into the guest room and discovered Ruin alone.

Ruin was oblivious to Ky's presence, his head down.

"Are you OK?" Ky watched him. The younger man's knuckles were raw and bloody, and his hands were shaking. "Why did you run from me?"

"Sorry. I have to get this …" Ruin began humming. "I have to …" His voice erupted.

Waves of grief and psychic imprints poured in a torrent that threatened to drown Ky. He slumped to his knees as the song overwhelmed his senses, far worse than any physical contact. Paralyzed, he watched as, next to Ruin, a gray silhouette formed. The streaming, misty outline coalesced into a skeletal figure trailing gauzy filaments. The monstrous thing hovered, caressing the singer like a beloved prize. Repulsion and nausea hit Ky as the filthy, hate-filled emanation entangled Ruin. The spirit turned and leered at

A Holy Venom

Ky, the withered mummified face materialized wearing a megalomaniac's expression of triumph.

As darkness overtook him, Ky heard himself screaming.

SIXTEEN

DR. WINNOW ASH SMILED at the janitorial staff polishing the grand staircase. The scent of the lemon oil hung in the air and the Statler's director inhaled deeply as he plodded toward his office. Through an ornate beveled panel mounted into the eastern windows, golden light pooled on the office carpet. Taking his seat behind the cleared surface of his desk, he straightened his eyeglasses and glanced up as someone knocked on the open doorframe.

Dr. Ash smiled at his new secretary. "Ah, Mixter Tuvlm. What can I do for you? Are you finding everything you need?"

The young person smiled apologetically and carried a small brown paper-wrapped parcel to the desk. "This arrived for you last night, sir. Security has cleared it." Looking up, they stared at the sculptural mask hung on the wall behind the director's desk. They stepped back from the lupine mask's grotesque, contorted features.

"Thank you, please leave it on my desk." Dr. Ash followed their gaze and smiled. "Stunning, isn't it? A former patient of mine spent years making it." He gestured at the mask's snarling fangs. "She was not allowed anything sharp, so it is fashioned from linen soaked in boiled wheat paste, including the teeth. The fur," he gestured at the mane of black hair circling the rippling muzzle, "is the patient's own hair. Each bundle is a little plug, tied like a fishing lure, and inserted through the fabric. It took her a decade to harvest enough without going bald. Tore it out in patches by the roots. She made it to ward off her nightmares."

He chuckled and glanced over his spectacles at his secretary. "By your features, I'd say you appear to have some Ornish ancestry in you. Are you familiar with stories of the Ourma, the sea witches, or the Awy, the forest witches?"

Tuvlm tore their gaze away from the mask. "No, sir."

"With your family name, I imagine you're more familiar with the Doonese tales. Mlom and other tauviklm." He nodded and waved his hand at the mask. "The patient in question was convinced she was a member of the Awy, a legendary and feared Ornish clan. Quite delusional." His gaze lingered on the mask's gaping eye sockets. "It is an amazing work, especially considering she was blind at the time. Clawed her own eyes out before she was committed. One of our more tragic cases sent over from the Archipelago. Historically, quite a surprising number of visual artists from the Archipelago become our patients. Curious statistic, actually."

Tuvlm started to back away from the looming sculpture. "I'm sorry if I've interrupted your work, sir." They pointed over their shoulder. "If you don't have anything for me, I should get back ..."

"Of course, of course. Thank you for bringing me the parcel." Dr. Ash smiled. "Do close the door on your way out."

"Absolutely, sir. Have a good morning." Tuvlm hurried out, quietly shutting the heavy oak door behind them.

Sighing, Ash glanced back up at the mask. "Another dim bulb, I'm afraid. Ah well, we're used to it by now, aren't we?" Humming, he reached across the desk and drew the package closer. His name was written on the plain brown paper in an elaborate, calligraphic style he was unfamiliar with. Frowning, he noticed the absence of a return address or postage mark and set the package down. He took out a letter opener. Once sliced open, the paper revealed an unimpressive cardboard box tied with string. He cut through the twine and opened the flaps. He reached in, his hand searching the paper packing material. "What have we here?" He held up what appeared to be a rough stone head. The director carried it over to a beam of morning sunlight streaming through the window for a closer examination. He considered who might have sent the charming, if unsettling, gift.

"Aren't you an odd fellow!" The impish features of the deformed human head stared back at him as a long, sinuous shadow wavered on the carpet, unnoticed. "You will be a prized addition to my private collection!"

☾

Inside the neighborhood diner, patched vinyl booths surrounded a long,

A Holy Venom

curved chrome bar. Ky looked up from his plate of pancakes and hash as Mudon dropped his hat on the seat opposite.

"You look like shit, *pen*." Mudon glanced away as the waitress appeared. "Good morning, Hyacinth."

"Good morning, Lwen. Your usual, or just coffee?" The woman refilled Ky's mug then placed a clean one in front of the detective and filled it. "Your friend here's been drinking the pots dry all night. Finally convinced him to put something solid in his stomach before it paid the check and left without him."

"Cast iron military issue," Mudon winked. "Just coffee today. If I ordered anything without bringing something back…"

"That one's got no excuse." She poked a varnished fingernail into his arm. "Could've gotten her lazy ass out of bed if she wanted a hot breakfast."

"It's for the best." Mudon glanced back at Ky. "It's too early for me to manage them both."

"Let me know if you change your mind," Hyacinth waved as she sailed back to the kitchen.

"You bring it?" Ky mopped up the last of the berry compote and took another sip of coffee.

"I was surprised you asked for something like that. Clever. You think it will work?"

Feeling exhausted and not at all social, Ky pushed his plate aside. "Won't know until I try it."

"What happened?" Mudon leaned over the booth table. "They mark you?"

Ky snorted. "I feel like I got marked by a truck, tell you the truth." He shook his head. "They had me playing bodyguard last night. The way I figure it, it was a test of some kind."

"You pass?"

Thinking of Ruin's solo performance and the demented spirit possessing the younger man, Ky shook his head again. "No. My first mistake was letting an admirer get too close to my charge. It could've been worse, but it was bad enough. My second mistake laid me out cold for most of the night. I woke up, peeled myself off the floor, and went to the first phone booth I could find and called you. I can't be around those … people anymore." He glanced

287

at his cup. "This place has the best coffee I've had in town, so I figured I might as well wait here for you."

"Good thing. No one will talk if they see us having breakfast." Mudon leaned back and stretched his arm over the vinyl bench back. "Neutral ground, plenty of parolees having informal chats here rather than down at the Tank." He made a shaking gesture with his fingers. "Nothing to see, no one to whistle about it. Pies here are better than most, especially the raspberry peach. You should try a slice."

"I'd rather get this over with and go home."

Mudon looked him over. "You think even if I let you walk, that fake werewolf of yours will? If they killed Haw over her nibling, they'll come for you."

Ky stared out the window at the early morning foot traffic starting to fill the sidewalks. "It's all too fucked up. Here, in Thursby, wherever I go, it—*they* will follow." He looked back. "If I have to fight, I'd rather choose the location. And this city isn't it."

"But Thella is?" Mudon reached over and took a packet of sugar from the porcelain bowl under the window. "That's where you'd go. Back to the desert and the long nights under all those stars. Not as chilly as it is here, but cold enough that you won't fall asleep easily." Shaking the packet, he sighed. "You still think it's real, what you fought at the convent?"

"I *know* it is." Ky cradled his coffee. "You wouldn't believe me if I told you half the shit I've seen in this city."

"Yeah, you got marked alright. Took the fire right out of you. Well, not all of it, I imagine." Mudon stirred his cup and then set the spoon aside on a napkin. With his other hand, he took an envelope out of his inner suit pocket and passed it across the table. "You can manage without opening it?"

"Holding it is all I need." Ky set the envelope on his lap. "How old is this sample?"

"Took it off a donor about twenty minutes ago. She was a little unhappy to lose her morning dose, but I couldn't exactly walk into Evidence and ask them for a donation to our cause."

Ky felt for the envelope's contents. A bright trickle prickled his fingertips and he closed his eyes, focusing.

"If this works, maybe I should keep you around." Mudon offered. "Put you up on stage so I can retire off the seats."

"If this works, you can keep your word and leave me the fuck alone," Ky exhaled, letting the energy signature blossom and unspool. The mingled scent of cut grass and an unknown floral scent reminiscent of honeysuckle erased the syrup and berry from his palate. Sharp, crackling, and stinging, the sample seemed to recoil in his hand as an image of Lu lying in bed flickered behind his eyes. Her eyes opened and she stared back at him. Ky sat bolt upright and slapped the envelope on the table.

"It's Lu. You want Lu. She's the source."

Picking the sample up and then putting it in his pocket, Mudon studied Ky's face. "If I thought you could act, I'd be worried you were setting me up."

Ky opened his mouth to speak but Mudon shook his head.

"It tracks. Even without your expert opinion." The detective sipped his coffee. "Everything is already in motion, so all your confirmation does is set my mind at ease about calling their hand."

Ky grabbed the straps of his duffel bag, suddenly uncomfortable. "If we're done, I'm heading out. There's an eight o'clock I'd like to catch." He started to slide out of the booth.

Dropping a large bill on the table, Mudon leaned forward. "So long as you're clear of the Velvet tonight, where you go is your business, *pen*." He caught Ky's free arm and held it. "You could stick around, just so you know. Leave the one-twos where they belong. If someone is after you, I—"

"If Haw couldn't kill it, you sure as fuck can't." Ky shook him off. "In the desert, I've got options."

Mudon bit off a reply and sighed. "If you say so. Enjoy waking up with sand between your teeth." The detective sat back against the vinyl booth seat and flashed a salute. *"Tau-een, pen-lm."*

☾

Wild birds flew through the iron support struts and under the train station glass cupolas. Ky sat on one of the wooden benches, watching the multitude diving and squabbling over the crumbs dropped by the deluge of travelers. Crows chattered, rattling their beaks at each other while the mottled iridescent wings of pigeons opened amidst their coos. Bright, electric plumage of the castaways flickered above the market as the tropical birds sought resting places in the fronds of the imported palm trees.

In the waiting area below, vendors waved their wares over the railings, crying out their specialties over the drone of the station announcements and the drawn-out train whistles. With his duffel against the back of his calves, Ky glanced over at the station clock and closed his eyes. Nearby women's voices made him glance over. He watched as a group of elderly priestesses in vermillion habits and veils shuffled through the waiting area. Flashes of the fight in the convent garden returned and Ky scrubbed at the stubble on his face, suddenly exhausted. The sensation of a burning brand was set against his back. The countersignal flared an urgent alarm, prompting him to swivel around.

Beside him, a priestess sat on the bench, a crimson veil obscuring her face. "I'm sorry, is this seat taken?" The tenor of her youthful voice was lower than expected, while her inflection was rounded and soft.

Ky shook his head, unsure of what to say. "No."

"I'm sorry, I can't see very well through this." She inclined her head and then leaned in his direction. "If I'm honest, I hate it, but we're supposed to keep it on whenever we travel outside the cloister. Outmoded ideas of holiness, or maybe it's keeping up appearances. Jeans and a warm coat would be my preference. At least our shoes are sensible." She angled a chunky snow boot out from under her robes. "Hot, though."

Ky suppressed the urge to leap up out of his seat. Whatever his new neighbor was, she was throwing off a low thrum like bees trapped inside a porch on a summer afternoon. Her Presence, honey-gold and rich, made the countersignal pulsate.

"Don't try and pass yourself off as one of the sisters." Ky jerked his chin in the direction of the elderly women in similar scarlet vestments. "You're not human."

"Listen to you! Suddenly an expert." Her demeanor changed as she laughed at him. "How do you know what I am and what I'm not?" She raised a gloved hand as if to pull away her veil and then paused. "Don't forget, humans used to go about as all sorts of animals and all sorts of things went about as humans. Your new friends pretend as well, do they not?" She folded both gloved hands together over her knees. "When judging another's agenda, ill or benign, one should look to the other's heart. A human heart will reveal itself no matter the outer form. A human in an animal's skin still maintains a human heart. But something pretending to be human may not have a heart at all."

"And you?" Ky glanced around trying to assess his chances of escape. Her proximity made him sweat and the pain in his back made it difficult to breathe. "Is yours human?"

"I have a very tender heart. These birds for example," she pointed up at the slim bodies flying overhead. "I'm glad they're warm and fed in here and not pent up in a smaller cage. A few born in here might even believe this is the whole of the world. Though you and I know, this shelter they've found for themselves is not quite as expansive as the open sky. They long for it, you know. Perhaps even knew it once. Perhaps some remember the spring rain and the winter Gales and choose this human-wrought compromise. Perhaps a few were captured in the jungles and then brought in on the trains. Maybe they managed to escape, or maybe they were released." She turned her head toward him. "My heart tells me a few remember and hate the hands that caught them, while others only remember, and love, the hands that opened their cages. Using the name they call the sky, they sing praises for the one who released them. Freedom."

A train whistle sounded, the long, mournful song of the locomotive filling the station. When Ky glanced back, the priestess had vanished. In her seat, a feisty young crow wrestled with a stolen piece of muffin. Flustered by the human's attention, the young bird flew off with its prize.

Ky watched the crow bob over the head of a seated child. The girl shrieked happily and pointed up while tugging on the hand of her caregiver. Something about the child's expression kicked at Ky's chest with tremendous force. For the first time in a while, he thought of Haw's children and widow. A turbulent mix of regret and shame tormented him. Having failed to find Haw's killer or accomplish anything significant to protect her children from further harm, he needed to get out of this city, away from all its strange and awful inhabitants.

The schedule board slates flickered and clicked as incoming and departure times and tracks changed. He eased out of his seat and collected his duffel. Heaving the bag over his shoulder, Ky made his way through the waiting area and back out to the busy mash of commuters and produce sellers.

He moved his head away as an exuberant man shoved a citrus fruit up for inspection. An electric buggy tooted and forced the pedestrian traffic to the sides of the walkway. Pressing closer, Ky shook his head at the fruitmonger and then held his hand up, making the gesture for a phone.

The man smiled and shouted over the ruckus, "By the food court, next to the bakeries!"

Ky held up a hand in thanks and stepped out into the throng. Navigating the market, he continued in the direction the man had indicated. He could've followed his nose. The smell of baked goods laden with butter and spices gave rise to the hope of decent coffee.

Ky forced himself past the coffee and tea stalls with their tantalizing aromas. The lines of people queued at the bank of closet-style payphones turned over quickly. When his chance arrived, Ky wedged himself and his bag into the wooden booth. He managed to wrench the folding door closed, minimizing a fraction of the station noise. He dug out a fistful of coins from the pocket of his winter overcoat.

The droning dial tone in the earpiece was replaced by ghostly dings as he punched in the phone number. The coins dropped, clattering into the collection box as the other party picked up. "Hello?" Ky moved the coiled phone cable and glanced out of the booth.

"Who's this?" Berry's girlish voice demanded.

"It's Ky, do you remember me? I'm a friend of your parents." Ky leaned against the door and watched the birds through the smudged glass. "Can I talk to your mom?"

"I remember you," Berry replied, her voice less wary. "Everyone is outside having a snowball fight. I came in to get a drink. Well, that's what I told them but really I came in to get a cookie, but I didn't want to have to share."

"I see," Ky smiled sadly. "Well, I can call back some other time."

"Did you find the monster that killed my Madda?"

For the second time, Ky felt like he had been punched in the gut. He took a breath. "No, honey. I found some others, but not that one. I'm sorry."

A Holy Venom

"It's OK. You're probably not strong enough to kill it anyway. It killed my Madda, so it must be invincible." The girl managed to sound proud and sad at the same time. "Plus you can't even find it. It probably went back to the Silent Woods."

"That's the forest from the story it told you, right?" Ky wondered what he should say.

"Yeah." Berry paused. "But even if you could get there, you're not strong enough to kill it."

Ky realized the girl was really talking to herself, not him. "I appreciate you saying so. I was feeling bad about it, not being able to find them or stop them."

"If you wanted to stop them, you'd have to trick them, like in the fairytales."

"Sounds like you're an expert?"

"I've thought about it a lot, yeah." Berry's confidence rang down the line. "I read all the books in the library on monsters."

"All of them? Wow."

"Well, the ones in the sections I'm allowed into. The librarians told me I had to wait to go in the older kids' section. To read the werewolf stuff. But I found the intel."

His heart squeezed at the child's use of military vocabulary, picked up, no doubt, from her parents. "Care to share it, Home Office Agent B?"

Warming to the game, Berry answered seriously. "Well, you have to trick them into owing you a favor. Or you have to save them from something like an iron trap. Or break the curse they're under. Then, you can make them do what you want. Like not ever eating anyone's parents again. But," she said, "that might make them starve and go extra crazy."

Ky wondered if the girl had gotten access to a horror novel for older readers after all. "That sounds bad."

"The worst, Agent K, *the worst*. Because then they eat everyone and then the sun itself! What you have to do is," the girl lowered her voice and whispered into the mouthpiece. "Trick them into owing you a favor and then make them promise not to eat everyone all the time. They have to promise to leave some people. You know, like not eating all the cookies in the jar."

"What if they promise but aren't telling the truth?"

"Oh, even if they lie about other stuff, they can't break their promises when they owe you a favor. But you have to be very, very careful. Because they might still eat you."

Ky managed to not laugh. "But how do I find them if I can't get into the Silent Woods?"

"That's not a big deal. They will find you." Berry fumbled with the phone, her hand muffling the mouthpiece. "The twins are coming back in. I have to go. Good luck!"

Ky lowered the receiver and stared at it. *First, a supernatural being dolled up as a priestess gives me the once over, and then a little girl gives me an old hand's advice on fieldwork.* The dial tone droned as the connection was lost, shaking him out of his reverie. He settled the receiver back in the cradle. Thoughtful and not a little disturbed, he slid open the folding door and walked out into the noise of the station.

The station boards started shuffling again, the clicks and rumbles coinciding with station announcements. Ky sighed as the slot with his train departure details started flickering. The boards stilled to present a new later time.

Glancing down at his borrowed winter coat, Ky sighed again. The delay removed any excuse he had not to go back to the Velvet one last time. He headed toward the cab stands, sure he'd regret this choice later.

☾

Lu's heels clicked on the stage flooring as she inspected the new cabinet centered under the lights. She tapped the lacquered wood of the new stage prop with a dagger-sharp fingernail. "Show it to me with the sapphire filter, Cee," she called out.

The lighting designer switched the white spots to a deep azure. In response, the enameled vines decorating the tall, lustrous conjuror's cabinet gave off an eerie, silver glow.

"Try the next." Lu took a step forward and swung open the lacquer doors.

As the lights bathing the stage shifted to a golden yellow, Ky walked into the theatre. The seated security staff members who recognized him nodded before resuming their card game at the circular table closest to the cantilevered bandstand.

"Too bright, need it about half that. Bring it down?" Lu waved her hand as she opened and closed the box's satin-lined interior compartment.

Coming up to the stage, Ky called out as he set his duffel on the parquet dance floor. "Sorry to interrupt, Lu, but I need to talk to you."

Lu waved her hands and flipped her long, loose hair over her shoulder before resuming her inspection of the equipment. "I'd love to chat, but as you can see, I'm in the middle of—"

"It's important."

She came over to the side of the elevated stage and then raised her voice. "I need five minutes, Cee." She looked down at Ky pointedly. "Five."

He watched as she maneuvered to jump down to the parquet dance floor. Dropping his coat on the lip of the stage, he offered her his hands and braced for her touch.

Gracefully, she accepted his assistance and lowered herself down sliding against his chest as she stared into his eyes. "Everything alright with the *gaesu*?"

Ignoring the sizzling tingle of her touch, Ky shook his head. "Everything is definitely *not* alright with him, but it's not that. Last I saw him, he was asleep in the apartment above the garage and seemed fine, physically. Spiritually, the kid's fucked."

Lu frowned.

Pressing her close, Ky whispered in her ear. "There's a raid planned for tonight. For the Rot. They're coming for you." Shamefaced, he stepped back, setting her on her feet.

Tugging him back, Lu made as if she was adjusting his shirt collar. "You're sure?" She studied his expression. "Of course you are." Sliding her hands behind his neck, she resettled the silk of his necktie. "What time?"

Shaking his head, he caught her hands and held them. "I only know it's tonight, nothing else."

She let go and moved back to lean her elbows against the stage. "I've got nothing to do with—"

"Oh, come on," he snapped. "Don't play innocent! It has everything to do with you!"

She held up her hand and the security team settled back into their chairs around the nearby table. Tilting her head, Lu returned Ky's intense gaze. "You've got me all figured out, have you? If you did, then why bother coming here and telling me? Was it your over-developed and misplaced sense of justice?"

"It's wrong." He moved closer to take his coat off the stage. He glanced into her face. "All of it is wrong. But I can't let them cage you—or even try it." He hesitated, hefting his bag up off the floor. "I'm sorry. I'm sorry they did that to you then, and I'm sorry that you're still so hurt by it that you'd do this to them here and now." He glanced away. "If you can help your friend, the one I shouldn't name in here, you should do it. He really is in trouble."

Lu watched as Ky walked away. "You think you can leave and no one will drag your self-righteous, pitiful behind back here? That you can play both sides and leave when it gets too complicated? That we… that *I* will let you?"

"Not my concern. Never was." Ky replied. He stopped and half-turned to look back at her. "Not my house."

"Then why?"

"I thought I should return the suit and coat." Remembering the train station, the conversations with the inhuman priestess and Berry, Ky stared up at the gilded ceiling of the theatre. The plaster and molding framed a starry night sky replete with shooting stars and southern constellations. "Maybe the problem is you shouldn't be here at all. Maybe the problem is you're under the wrong sky. Maybe I'm doing you a favor to save someone else's ass."

Lu watched as Ky pushed through the curtained passageway to the backstage then turned her head to the security team surreptitiously keeping watch. "If one of you would go find Vetch in whatever plush bed he's still snoring in and tell him I need him here, *right now*, it would be appreciated." Turning back to the theatre, she raised her voice. "Cee, if you would, let's try it with the next combo."

☾

A Holy Venom

Patches of clear sky appeared and disappeared between the ancient rooftops. Ky, back in his street clothes, exited through the Velvet's back door. He failed to find Haw's killer, he had left Ruin in the grip of multiple curses, and now he was walking away from Lu and the Velvet. Hell, the only things he was even remotely OK with this morning were talking to Berry and telling Mudon to fuck off. If Mudon kept his word, at least the Tank would leave off trying to find him for a few weeks. He could use that time to swing by Haw and Olive's place and spend some time with the kids, maybe for the last time.

As Ky reached the sidewalk, a woman's voice called out from behind him. "Funny, I heard you were leaving on the eight o'clock."

"Got delayed to eleven." Ky stopped and turned toward the voice. An imperious salt stared back. She was bundled up against the cold, but Ky could feel the icy heat of a bully's conviction seeping off her. "Enough time to pick up my last paycheck."

"Convenient, your train being delayed then." The woman eyed him suspiciously. "I take it you're not in any hurry? Now that you have your paycheck?"

He moved away from her, angling toward the street. "Trying to catch the eleven."

She shook her head. "Hope you can exchange your ticket. You need to come down to the Tank. We've got a few questions for you."

"Who are you?" Ky considered if he could outrun the salt. She was wearing a bulky winter coat and boots, but looked at least twenty years younger than he felt.

"I'm Detective Tosh. I take it Mudon didn't mention me." She cocked her head and looked away, clicking her tongue. "The train can wait." She put her hand on her waist, drawing back the folds of the overcoat to show her S&P badge. "Car's around the corner."

"What's this about, detective?"

"Your questions can wait until we get to the Tank." Tosh came up behind him and smiled reassuringly. "Don't worry, we'll get this over with as soon as possible."

"Just doing your job?" Ky grimaced as they approached a parked sedan.

"Exactly," Tosh sneered and opened the back door. "Watch your head, please." She slammed the door closed and went to the driver's side.

A redheaded woman in the front passenger seat looked Ky over. "That's him? From the way you were talking, I expected him to be seven feet tall."

"That's him, alright." Tosh flashed a smile in the rearview mirror as she got behind the steering wheel. "Detective Stiles, I'd like you to meet Mr. Kyanth Drew. Mudon's whistle in the Velvet."

Stiles snorted. "Mudon really thought …"

"Oh, but he wasn't wrong." Tosh waited for a commuter bus to roll past before pulling out into traffic. "Not about your skills at any rate. Just about your vulnerability to picking up bad habits from bad people."

"I have no idea what the fuck you're on about," Ky snapped.

"Quite a change from the country life you've made. One minute you're a stat out in nowhere doing nothing. The next minute you're rubbing elbows with celebrity crazy in the big city." She gave a low whistle.

Stiles snickered. "You could've played it differently, you know? Plenty of people would've offered you real high numbers for access to the stat." She threw a look back at Ky. "Too bad you decided to start pushing the Rot. You could've taken it easy. Traded one protected loser for a lifetime of comfort."

"I don't know who you're talking about and I'm not pushing anything." Sitting up, Ky glared at the two of them. "If you're suggesting I'm selling drugs, you're out of your damn minds."

Tosh nodded and thumped her hands on the steering wheel. "This should be fun." She shot a look over at Stiles. "Couple of hours from now, he'll be using his new performance skills and listing all the names we need."

☾

Tosh and Stiles herded Ky up the stairs of the granite armory that housed the central S&P station. Uniformed officers leaving the building greeted the two detectives, some averting their eyes and some staring openly at Ky as they passed. Inside, the fluorescent lighting glared off the striped tiles as more officers filed by. Stiles took Ky's bag and dropped it into the waiting arms of a uniformed officer while Tosh put her hand on Ky's back, hurrying him along the painted path on the floor.

A Holy Venom

An officer behind a glass screen buzzed them through a metal security door.

"You've had a long morning, huh?" Tosh patted him on the back and then held his arm as Stiles swung one of the interrogation room doors open.

She tilted her head. "We'll need his file."

"And coffee." Tosh playfully pushed Ky into the room. "I'll go."

"Thanks." Stiles stepped into the room and watched as Ky took off his leather and slipped it over the back of the metal folding chair. "Too hot in here? I'd expect that you'd like it, after—"

"Can we get started?" Ky looked away and studied the three blank walls.

"You're in a world of shit," Stiles smiled cruelly and pulled back the opposite chair. "Can't wait to get the fuck out of here. How much they pay you to keep an eye on the stat?" She pointed at Ky's jacket. "Not that it's worth it." She leaned back and put an arm over the back of her chair. "You ever been in a closet like this? Ten by ten. That's two feet more than what you'll end up in." She interlocked her fingers and smirked.

"You mean a jail cell?"

"No, I mean the Statler." Stiles pointed both her index fingers at him. "If you don't tell us everything we want to know, we're going to turn you over to the Perlustrate. When they get done with you, they'll dump you through the Dog's Gate. Even a stick farmer like you has heard about the gore hounds."

Ky considered what he should say to get out of the station as quickly as possible. "Whatever you think I've done, I haven't…"

Stiles watched him. "The Church considers the Rot overdoses to be murder. Did your new friends tell you that running drugs is a crime against God herself?" She smiled maliciously. "Double points—you can be tried for heresy *and* murder."

"I don't know anything about drugs."

"Right about now, Officer Myrtle is finding quite the haul in the bag you kindly brought in with you." Stiles jerked her head at the door. "Tosh will be back in a minute and then anything you say will be on the record. Right now, you've got a chance to tell me whatever you want. Unless you repeat it in front of both of us, it stays off the record. There are no cameras or recording devices in here. If you tell me the truth now, I can coach you about what to say in front of Tosh. Then we can get you out of here before the dogs get involved. You can trust me; I have no interest in little fish like you. Or the stat."

"I told you the truth. I don't know anything."

"If that's how you want to play it," Stiles shrugged and sat upright. "You just *happen* to be staying at the Awy Teahouse as a guest and spending time at The Velvet Door? They just *happened* to think you ought to chaperone—"

"Yes." Ky scowled, wondering how Ruin fit into everything.

"And you just happened to be skipping out of there this morning after telling Tosh's partner you were on the next train out of town?" Stiles set her forearms on the table and slid her hands closer to Ky. "I gotta ask: do you actually think anyone buys your carnival sideshow act? That you're psychic? I mean if you were, why didn't you leave town before we picked you up? Why the fuck would you be hanging around the Velvet this morning if you knew?"

"I don't—"

She cut him off. "The Awy! You're a guest of the *Awy* and you want us to believe there's no connection between you and the drugs coming out of the Velvet? That it's all a big coincidence?"

"Detective Mudon asked me to come here," Ky stated firmly and held the woman's gaze. If nothing else, he'd been through the grinder when more skilled hands and minds were churning the blades.

"Because you're pals, served together back in the day and he knows all about your ability to do… what exactly?"

When the detective sat back in her chair, Ky clenched his hands under the table.

"Mudon doesn't give a shit about you, you know that, right? You're a corpse waiting to happen. Disposable. He's trash. He'll use anyone or anything in order to look good. To keep the dogs off his own throat. He'll give them you, that's for sure."

Ky sighed and wondered if maybe at least the coffee here was decent. "I wanted to help. That's all."

"Help? The way I hear it, Mudon dragged you by the neck." The detective eyed him and then tapped on the table. "The only thing on your mind should be whether you're going to talk to me or let the Perlustrate handle this." She pointed at the door. "If you tell me, you can spend the night in a jail cell while we check your story. If you won't," Stiles dropped her hand and tapped the table again. "You can spend the rest of your life as a vegetable at the Stat. Unless they get a little too rambunctious and torture you to death. That does happen."

She leaned over the table and brought her face up to Ky's. "They're here, you know. All I have to do is walk out of this room and leave you alone and you're fucked. No second chance, no trial. Just the sick freaks fucking around inside your head until they get what they want. They'll make it look medical. Clean. But it will hurt much more than you can imagine. They'll take you apart inside and out until you're a limbless, sightless, tongueless chunk of meat hooked up to tubes and living out your days as a fuck toy at the Stat. Remember, asshole: *dogs don't make deals*."

A shiver went down Ky's spine. "I told you, I don't know anything about drugs." The staccato warning of the countersignal rippled over his right shoulder.

The door opened and Tosh came in carrying a file folder and a cardboard takeaway tray of coffee. She smiled at Ky. "Didn't know how you take it, so I brought packets of creamer and sugar. Non-dairy OK?" She glanced at Stiles and then set the tray on the table and handed the folder to the other woman.

Flipping the folder open, Stiles extracted three glossy black and white photos. "Just so you know, we're starting the formal interview. Anything you say can and will be used against you." She laid each of the photos out in front of Ky. "Since you don't seem to know anything about the Rot, let's talk torch party." She squared the photos of charred buildings and picked up one of the coffee cups out of the tray. "As of today, you've been named as a suspect in each of these ongoing investigations. You've got a background and a psych profile that aligns, and with the most recent fire, we can put you within twenty miles of the location on the day of."

Willing himself to remain calm, Ky reached for one of the two remaining cups of coffee. "I'm sorry detectives, I don't know what any of this is about either."

Tosh offered Ky a packet of sweetener. "Arson is a lesser charge than murder, but with what we just found in your bag... If you help us with locating the source of the Rot, your assistance will go a long way in reducing your prison sentence." She glanced at Stiles. "What'd that last firebug get? Fifteen years of hard labor in the mines? That was for one charge of property destruction. This is…" She craned her neck to look at the photos.

Tapping the photo of a burnt-out church, Stiles caught Ky's gaze. "This one was holy ground. That's thirty years, easy."

Ky swallowed a mouthful of tepid, black coffee. It hit his stomach with a sour churn and he instantly regretted drinking it. So much for the salts having decent coffee. "You've got the wrong person."

Stirring her cup, Tosh leaned against the wall behind Ky. "There's a lot of sympathy for veterans, especially when their crimes only involve property damage. Everybody feels poorly about the draft, you know. So long as there's no causalities. You've damaged only a few abandoned derelict properties, acting out because of difficulty reintegrating, that sort of thing." She looked over at Stiles. "The Rot though, that's the opposite. Too many have-nots dying. And the haves, too. Rich young fuckers."

"Ever sampled it?" Stiles watched Ky and sipped her coffee, then dangled the cup from her fingers. "Maybe you're withdrawing. Maybe if we ran a blood test right now, we'd find it in your system." She gestured with the cup. "If we had the local Tank in Thursby go to your place, we'd find all kinds of things."

Ky shrugged. "Can't find what's not there."

"Doesn't need to be anything *there*. We can find all sorts of stuff. Gas residue in the trunk of the car, tire tracks at the crime scene, witnesses who remember unusual visitors." The detective smiled. "In fact, it may surprise you that we've already collected enough to keep your ass in this chair for as long as we want. Security camera at a gas station in Delmont has footage of you filling up a container ten minutes before a torch party started down the road."

Stiles set her coffee down and the bottom of the waxed paper cup clipped the edge of the table and spilled onto her lap. "Damn!" She wavered in her seat and shot Tosh a startled look before her eyes rolled back in her head and her body went slack.

Tosh caught her limp torso and gently folded the other detective's head onto the table over the open file and smiled at Ky. "Any minute now you'll

A Holy Venom

be napping too."

Panicked, Ky tried to get up as he felt his limbs go numb. The antidote charcoal pellets were in a tin sitting in the suit jacket he'd left at the Velvet. His coffee cup dropped out of his hand. He watched the brown liquid puddle under the table as the white walls of the interrogation room crumpled.

SEVENTEEN

THE TOUCH ON HIS NECK was soft at first and then grew firmer. Ky's sense of self slowly resurfaced from its muddled pool of formless dreams. His skin felt freezing and boiling in alternating patches over his entire body and he realized he was naked. He blinked rapidly, trying to clear his mind, and opened his eyes. A blurred silhouette loomed over him, framed by the smooth wall behind. A stranger's face snapped into clarity and Ky reflexively pulled away.

Ky tugged his wrists and ankles. He was restrained, tied to a gurney. He craned his neck to see where he was, but a bright overhead light shrouded everything outside it in shadowy darkness.

"Is the petitioner awake?" An elderly woman's voice drawled from the end of the chamber.

He moaned and shuddered.

"He is, madam." The figure standing over Ky turned away and retreated into the shadows behind the surgical lamps ringing the gurney.

The older woman's voice echoed off the hard surfaces of the chamber. "Very well. This session is now commencing. Let the record show we are conducting an interview with Mr. Kyanth Drew, formerly of the Western Division, in the ongoing investigation related to the creation and distribution of the illegal substance known by its street name as the 'Rot.' Mr. Drew has been documented consorting with known distributors of the substance in question. Evidence has been submitted that incriminates the petitioner in several other crimes. However, as those alleged crimes are property-based, they are outside the jurisdiction of these proceedings. Mr. Drew, I am going to ask you a series of questions. For your own sake, I encourage you to answer immediately and truthfully."

"Who are you? Where am I?" Ky struggled against his bonds. "I'm not answering anything without a lawyer."

The figure stepped back into the light and rotated the gurney with a quick jerk. Nausea slammed into Ky's stomach as he was abruptly pulled vertically. His guts roiled as he squinted against the bright white light.

"No lawyer or other representative is allowed to speak on your behalf in these proceedings. You will answer for yourself directly." The woman sounded both bored and annoyed. "If you are unwilling to cooperate, appropriate measures will be taken."

"That's not entirely fair, is it?" a third person murmured somewhere to Ky's right. "He's asking reasonable questions given the circumstances he's in."

Ky turned his head, trying to see and feel where the speaker was in the room. "I haven't done anything."

There was a rustling of paper and the older woman spoke again. "You, Mr. Drew, have done a considerable amount, including, but not limited to consorting with the Shepherd's—"

"He doesn't understand, Lustrate," the other interrupted. "Perhaps Mr. Drew believes this is merely another kind of Safety and Protection interrogation. Or possibly," amusement filled the silky voice, "he thinks he is still asleep and this is all a dream?"

The last word was spoken directly into Ky's right ear and his heart leapt. The voice's proximity made him panic. "I haven't done anything."

A hand slid over his left arm and gripped it tightly, the fingers digging into his skin. "Do you hear that, brethren? The admitted murderer and accused arsonist pleads his innocence." The speaker's breath grazed Ky's left ear.

Chilled, Ky tried to shake off the contact. "I'm not a murderer."

"All the things you are and are not are of no interest to me. God herself knows you've killed her children."

The fingers dug deeper, practiced placements pinching nerves against bone. Ky grunted from the pain as it shot up and down his arm. "What do you want from me?"

Silence. The movement of papers and the quiet noises of human motion ceased. Ky felt the leather straps cut into his wrists and thighs, the heat from the brilliant lamps and the basement chill coming off the floor underneath his bare feet.

"There is only one thing we wish for," the speaker's voice suddenly rolled forth. "The redemption of your soul and your return to the flock."

"Amen," Several voices intoned together.

"Conciliator. Proceed."

The interrogator grasping his arm shifted their grip, the fingers pinching up along Ky's shoulder, capturing the nerves up into his neck.

Ky gasped as the icy numbness in his arm shifted to blazing, stabbing agony. "I didn't sell the Rot. I don't know anything about it."

"Mr. Drew," the older woman replied, disapproval coloring her voice. "We have a clear record of your activities before your arrival in the sacred precinct. We also have documentation on items collected at the long-term residence used in your previous criminal activities. It is of no use, and frankly, a waste of this tribunal's time, to deny your participation in organized criminal efforts and heresy. What we want now is an accounting of the activities you have engaged in since your arrival here, the names of your associates and any affiliated persons, and the details of your co-conspirators' plans and criminal activities against the Holy Church and her authorized subordinate organizations. If you do not comply, we will use extreme, and unpleasant, techniques to acquire this information. Do you understand?"

"I came here to kill a monster. A werewolf. That's all." Ky dropped his head back against the gurney and blinked back tears. Even with his left arm numb and tingling, the nerve pain had quelled his nausea.

Papers rustled again and the older woman spoke. "Were secondary inducements administered?"

"No, Lustrate, they were not," a younger voice murmured.

"Is there a history of mental illness ..."

"There's a werewolf in the city! It killed Major Hawthorn and who knows how many people over the years. Thousands." Ky shook his head. "Lu is some kind of monster too. I don't know if she's a rain god or a lake monster or just a shepherd. They eat people. Kill and eat people. Mudon brought me here to find the Rot, where it was made, who was selling it. I told Lu I knew; I told her I didn't, I couldn't do it." His eyes snapped open. "It was there. Right in front of me, if I hadn't listened to the songs, if I hadn't kept the blindfold on, my eyes closed, it's like nothing you can imagine." The memory replayed bringing back the stink and the terror. Madness seeped into Ky's voice. "It tore Haw apart. That's what it, what *they*, do. If you get either of them, then you'll have what you want. The drugs, that's all theirs. I don't know why or how, but Lu is who you want."

A deep, listening stillness hung in the chamber.

"I know it sounds crazy. I know you don't believe me, but it's the truth." Ky spit the last word out. "They hunt and eat people."

The pinching in his neck vanished, leaving only hot pulses of nerve pain behind. Ky hung his head limply, grateful to be left alone.

"There are no monsters here, we can assure you," The Conciliator's silky voice started in Ky's ear as a gloved hand grasped his chin and forced his head back up. "Do you think yourself some kind of vigilante? A hunter, perhaps?"

Ky had to force his jaw open to speak. "No."

The hand dropped to his chest and lay over his heart. "There are three kinds of hunters, Mr. Drew. Those who hunt animals for food or sport are the most common. Those who hunt other humans for reasons of insanity, or possibly a malignant sense of justice, are second. Perhaps they have a misplaced community loyalty, such as your heretical military career illustrates. Those are all thin veneers over the desire to kill, stretched over a framework to justify actions that nonetheless wear the varnish of cruelty. What you are describing is the third category: the hunters of the nonhuman violators of God's only true law–simply, no one but the Holy Mother herself may end human life. Whatever reason any killer hangs on the outside, on the inside, the true reality is that murder is an abomination."

The hand tapped Ky's chest. "Permission to administer the secondary round of inducement."

"We haven't the time to indulge Mr. Drew in his fantasies," the Lustrate replied. "Names, affiliations, activities, and locations are all we are interested in. We require a full confession of all criminal activities. Conciliator, this tribunal grants you permission to use all methods at your disposal. As Mr. Drew appears to be uncooperative and operating under the assumption he can mislead this investigation, I utilize my authority as Lustrate to authorize full abnegation."

A Holy Venom

Ky stiffened as the emotions in the chamber rippled with shock and horror at the pronouncement. A kind of pleased inspiration infused the Conciliator. Once the muttering and waves of emotional disturbance died down, he flinched at the intense eager anticipation from the people standing closest to him.

In the dark, beyond the ring of surgical lamps, the Conciliator's silky voice murmured happily, "I shall restore this ram to the flock."

A cold, wet sensation in the crook of his elbow caught Ky off guard. He glanced at his naked arm just as the tip of a syringe slid into a vein.

"There, now, Mr. Drew. That will move things along nicely." The Conciliator stroked Ky's arm with their gloved hand. "While we wait, I assure you that after you provide the Lustrate with the information the tribunal requires, I have all the time in the world to listen to your bedtime stories about monsters, whether they are under your bed or hiding in your head."

The lights blurred and became haloes around moving shadows. A disturbing, hypnagogic paralysis gripped him. He felt disembodied, yet horrifyingly present as he listened to himself reply to an endless stream of questions. The questions themselves were too far away from him, each a wet bubble striking somewhere on his bare skin. There was a pattern, a repetition of pinching until he wanted to scream, and then a popping that brought strangled sobs up out of his chest. The pain and discomfort rose and fell moving across and inside his body. The torment goaded him to speak and then hurled him into gibbering silence. Child-like confusion and terror shook him as a reassuring touch transformed into precise torture. Someone wiped sweat and blood off his face and the corner of the cloth scraped his open eye. The sensation wrung a howl of supplication from him.

"Please stop, please!" The voice was both his and far away as if he was hearing it carried on the wind. Time felt lost to him. Only the anticipation of the next cruelty linked the moments together.

The room cooled as several of the lights snapped off. Ky hung limply in his restraints, eyes wide open and unseeing as fragments of fire and dust storms filled the edges of his vision. There was a maddening jolt as the gurney rotated. Feeling as if he'd been flung into a concrete wall, every joint in his body screamed, filling his mind with the suffocating memory of being crushed and waiting to die. Hands and fingers stroked his legs possessively, the Conciliator's desire swathing Ky in a different kind of foulness.

☾

There was a rattling clatter and his body jostled violently. Every nerve flared with pain. Everything was gritty and sharp and stabbing. Ky was exhausted, but sleep evaded him as his thoughts raced in endless circuits. He struggled to move a finger or toe, anything. The pressure inside his head and his chest made him hallucinate he had transformed into one of his homemade bombs, a vulnerable ball of flesh, like a rubber balloon, inside a glass bottle, his body and mind primed to puncture. He was both accelerant and catalyst. Under the agony, a sense of movement: he was on a gurney. It jerked to a stop and someone threw a thin sheet over his body. He screamed.

"I will only be a moment, and then we will continue our conversation regarding your new friends," the Conciliator whispered. Their breath scalded Ky's ear.

A heavy door slammed shut, the noise making him whimper and cringe. The cell was dark and he wondered if they had removed his eyes. He tried to click his tongue against the back of his teeth. Helplessness swallowed his efforts. He knew the darkness was all there was left. His brain was removed, his skull scoured clean, only a faint shred of his mental capacities remained. Sadness for his lost life welled up and he sobbed knowing there was no escape left to him.

His grief was interrupted by a loud thud and then clawing, scrambling sounds. Terror raced through Ky as the scratching and scampering got closer. The sheet slowly slid off his skin, burning as it slipped to the floor. The cold air was a relief, for a moment. Then a deep chill crept into his bones. The gurney shook and his heart pounded. He screamed again as tiny needles poked at his ribs and something boiling hot and hard rolled along his side, coming up into his armpit.

A sudden spark of color appeared in the darkness. The singular dot danced and expanded and Ky found he could breathe without pain. The spot grew, as if he was rushing toward a hole, falling through an opening. The illusion of movement overwhelmed him and his body thrashed as the

A Holy Venom

sensation of falling overtook him.

He sat up in his childhood bed, clutching the sheets. Ky stared at the familiar astronomy mobile hanging overhead. The glow-in-the dark orbs bobbed and whirled as he squeezed the flannel sheets in his child-sized hands. Feeling small and afraid, he backed up until he was cowering against the headboard.

A noise from the toy chest in the corner made him shrink back. His favorite toy, a stuffed animal, clambered out, pushing aside the other toys. The nubby, olive-green dragon waddled out of the stack and flung itself onto the floor. Ky watched in amazement as the familiar toy approached his bed. Something pulled the sheets taut and Ky sensed movement on the bedside. After a moment, two stubby, felt-tipped arms appeared. The toy hauled itself onto the bed and made a strange growling noise.

The toy made the strange noise again and tugged at Ky's kitten pajamas. Holding the cuff of his sleeve by one of the blue cats, the dragon tugged him and started walking backward. With its other paw, it gestured at its mouth, miming a shushing motion.

Ky let the toy guide him off the bed. His bare feet touched the cool wood and the dragon tugged him toward the bedroom door. Gazing around at the details of his old room, Ky focused on each step, avoiding the squeaky floorboards and the toys strewn between him and the door.

Reaching the closed door, the toy pointed at the knob. Ky reached up and turned the brass knob and held his breath as he eased the door open. The dragon scampered through the gap and Ky pushed himself through after it.

The dragon waddled a few steps and then stopped. There was a tearing noise and a long spindly black leg appeared from the right leg and then the left. Two clawed hands tore through, leaving stuffing dangling out of the dragon's stumpy arms. No longer entirely confined to the stuffed toy, the thing inside it adjusted the stuffed head like a mask and gestured emphatically at Ky to follow it. Zigzagging down the hallway, the strange toy checked each of the doorways the pair passed before waving Ky on to the next. When they both reached the bathroom, it madly flailed an arm and pointed under the claw-foot tub.

Ky stopped in the doorway, looking at the coppery sickle moon shining through the window over the toilet. The toy hissed and violently waved at him to join it under the tub. A distant fear of closed, cramped spaces haunted Ky, a dream he could not remember. He wondered how the toy thought a boy could even fit in the narrow space only a few inches high. There wasn't enough room to get his head under the tub. Being squeezed in was bad, the worst.

He heard someone coming down the hall, the footsteps growing louder. With a backward glance at the doorway, Ky dove for the impossibly narrow space between the belly of the tub and the black and white checkered tiles.

Strong beams of light bobbed along the hallway outside the bathroom. Adult voices called to each other as the flashlights glared through the doorway.

"Is he already gone?"

One of the adults swung their light along the bottom of the tub, temporarily blinding Ky. The dragon toy clamped a filthy clawed hand over his mouth. Ky tried to hold his breath as the pungent odor of wet dog and potato crisps clogged his nose. The other hand quickly shoved Ky further under the tub until he was crushed up against the wall.

"He's still in there. The dose wasn't great enough for abnegation to take effect so soon."

Ky recoiled from the sound of the second voice. Using both hands, the toy dragon gestured for him to keep retreating further back. Confused, Ky made himself as small as possible along the length of the bathroom wall.

"What's this?" the unknown adult voice asked, surprised.

The beams of the flashlights snapped together, illuminating the stuffed dragon's back. The black spindly arms and legs contracted back into the toy disappearing entirely as adult hands reached under the porcelain and dragged out the dragon.

"Where did it come from?"

"Throw it away, then bring me the stimulant. We will get his attention and resume the interrogation. So many more things to discuss with this one. We can't let him slip away from us quite yet."

Ky stuffed his hands in his mouth and tried not to whimper. Something moved in the corner of his eye. He saw a grubby child waving frantically to him from behind the pipes at the end of the tub. The child gestured again

A Holy Venom

and pulled back into the recess panel for the plumbing. Ky squirmed along the tiled floor pushing with his legs.

The child was filthy and dressed in rags. They grabbed Ky's arm and tugged him around the copper water pipes then the child put two claw-like fingers to their mouth and Ky nodded. They needed to stay quiet.

With a rough shove, his rescuer pushed Ky into the dusty wall and carefully replaced the access panel. Once the recess was dark, Ky felt hot fingers wrap around his wrist. An impatient tug started him moving as the child snuck through the bathroom wall.

Ky tried not to cry out as his feet caught on rough wood and hard pieces of fallen plaster. The tight space scared him and the warning sizzled along his nerves: *this is bad*. Through the dark, narrow confines of the walls, the strange child dragged him further into the dark. A sharp fingernail scratched Ky's cheek as his guide put up a hand to stop him from hitting his head on a beam. Roughly pulling Ky's head down, the other child pushed Ky ahead through another panel.

Candlelight flared and Ky looked around the hidden cubby under a set of stairs. Barely wide enough for both of their small bodies, the den was lined with stolen blankets and food containers. The child pressed a snack pack into Ky's hand and handed him a dented bean can filled with water. Everything caught up with Ky; a sob shook his small frame and he almost dropped the food. The walls were too close, he couldn't breathe, and soon the house would start squeezing in on him.

Alarmed, the child hissed at him and snatched back the food and water. They shoved Ky into the far corner, close to a dense pile of moth-eaten blankets. Something about the other child's proximity allowed Ky to take a deep breath. Someone was trying to help him and, most importantly, he wasn't alone in the dark.

The child scowled and plopped down next to him. "You OK?"

Ky nodded, ashamed to explain his fear of tight spaces.

The other child brought their dirt-covered face close to Ky's head and whispered their name. "Hyrinth," they pointed at their chest.

He tried to smile at his new friend. "Kyanth. Ky," he whispered back.

Footsteps on the stairs above made him gasp. Hyrinth smacked a hand over Ky's mouth. Their hot fingers and grimy palm sealed Ky's mouth and partially blocked his nose. Tugging frantically, Ky gasped for air.

"You're a crybaby." Hyrinth cracked a mean smile. "You afraid of the dark too?" Their white teeth shone in the candlelight and they leaned over to snuff out the flame. "We have to put the light out to save it for later."

"I'm scared of the dark," Ky admitted. He was ashamed, but he could feel the dark pushing in, taking away his breath.

"Could be worse," they leaned closer to Ky. "If you stay quiet, I will tell you a story. Then you won't be so scared. Hiding here is easy. There are worse things to be afraid of."

"Won't they hear us?" Ky glanced up.

"I'll whisper so only you can hear." Hyrinth pulled a musty blanket over Ky's shoulder. "You're a crybaby, so no one probably told you this, but there are terrible things that happen to kids all the time. They just do. Like getting eaten by monsters and buried in ditches. Or if you're very, very unlucky, getting shoved in an oven while it's hot. Crying doesn't help. The only thing that helps is getting stronger and meaner and bigger. Getting bigger and stronger than what you're afraid of is the best thing in the whole world. But it's hard to do. If you listen and stop being afraid, you can learn the secret too."

✻

A long, long time ago, there was a kid who got treated like shit for no reason. All the adults ever did was yell and hit them until the kid learned to hit back. One night, they crawled into the back of a closet to sleep in what they thought was a safe place. It wasn't. Because a lot of places are traps that monsters use to hunt children. It was through the back of the closet the kid fell—or was dragged—into another place. A terrible place, one all kids fear more than being kicked and told they're stupid or having to go days and days without nothing to eat or drink, even stale bread or water from the toilet bowl. This dumbass got caught and fell into the House in the Silent Woods, a stinky, horrible, and bad place In Between.

They wound up under a huge wooden bed with a lot of other children, all hiding from the giant hands and paws that tried to drag them out. Each day, one of the kids would be tricked, and they'd be grabbed. The monsters would laugh and laugh and then there would be screaming. Those that stayed under the bed

A Holy Venom

watched as the Heavy Blade came down on the Bloody Stump and the kid who'd been grabbed was chopped up for the Pot. The House filled with the stink of roasting flesh, which is the most gross stink you can imagine, like old shoes and dog farts but way worse. Then the House filled with evil laughter like cartoon witches cackling.

One by one, the kids were tricked with promises of food, or by traps with scraps inside. If you were dumb and tried for a piece of cheese or bread—BAM!—the trap would catch you right on your leg or arm and cut it off. If you were thirsty and tried to go for the sink, you might get wrapped up in webs and then bit on the ass by a hairy, ugly spider. Then you'd die all bloated, your fizzing guts leaking out onto the floor. Starving, those hiding under the bed shoved rags into their mouths. Thirsting, they sucked on buttons torn from their clothes. This went on until at last there was only one kid left, too wild and too angry to go to the Pot. When a hand or paw came for that kid, they hissed and spat and stabbed at it with an iron nail stolen from the floorboards. They stayed under the bed in the dark, starving and thirsty and feeling like they were dying. If you think it smells bad in here, it was a thousand times worse under that bed, full of thousands of years of children's tears and pee and blood.

When the House was quiet, the kid watched the monsters nap in front of the Stove or go out the back to the Garden to hunt under the rusty moon or drink from the magic fountain. The House's nasty Owner might nap in her chair by the Stove or pretend to make things at the Workbench or sit above on the crap heap of the bed, which crushed down almost to the floor when sat on. Sometimes during the long nights, the Owner taunted the last kid alive under the bed. "I wasn't the one who left you in the Woods, my dear," she said. Or, "Nothing in this house can kill me!" Or she tried to trick the child by saying things like, "If you come out now, I will kill you quickly, and then it will all be over," or even worse, "Don't you want to leave this place?"

There were other things in the House. Monsters. Wolf might sniff along the end of the bed and growl in his big scary voice that there was still a child underneath. And Cat might answer that the child would die soon, leave it alone. From high above, Owl might say something cryptic, or Spider might say something shitty, like that the other monsters' laziness was why the child was still alive. But all were silent when the Owner was there.

One night, all the monsters were outside, except Spider, and the Owner was out—or at least invisible. That was the worst, not knowing if she was actually in her chair by the Stove and had pretended to have gone out. That night, the risk was worth it; the kid raced from under the bed to the door leading to the garden. There were always traps and tricks in the House, but this time it was a trap laid by Spider, who was jealous that Wolf and Cat and Owl always got more praise for killing thieving adults. Down, down Spider came from her web high up in the rafters. Down and down, rushing to catch the child. So stupid! She even shouted, screaming that she, not the others, would get it. She plopped her hairy and squishy body to the floor, blocking the garden door. Spider turned her eyes to the scrawny, boney kid and advanced, hopping like a fat turd. Too far from the safety of the bed, the kid tried to fight off Spider with the nail but was driven back against the Stove. Spider spit venom and it burned the child's eyes. Blind, and with Spider so close, the child squeezed themselves between the burning hot iron Stove and the stone wall of the House. The child's flesh cooked and their hair burned. Spider laughed and went back to her web where she gloated, swallowing the ghosts of dead kids, their souls caught long ago in the sticky strands.

Spider thought the last kid was dead, but they weren't. Cooked and crippled, the child ignored the pain. Blind, they dragged their bloody and burned body out the garden door. Crawling through the deadly flowers and bitter herbs, they found a sweet spring of fresh water and drank until they might burst, not knowing it was magic. While they were guzzling, Cat came and sat on the garden wall above them.

"Do not worry, I shall not harm you," said the huge and sleek Cat. "I shall tell you a secret thing, though it is up to you what to do about it."

"Why would you help me?" the child managed to mutter from blistered lips. "You eat kids like me."

Cat huffed and fluffed up. "Have you ever seen me eat a child? I only eat the adults foolish enough to try and steal things from this House. Once, a very long time ago, it was my purpose to aid the children who came here. But it has been a very, very long time since then. If you will do as I say, you will live, though not as you have or could have. Do you want to live?"

"Yeah," said the child. "So I can beat the shit out of Spider."

"Be that as it may," Cat flicked his tail. "Go back into the House and use the Heavy Blade to cut out your heart and feed it to the Fire that burns in the Stove. Do that and you will no longer be human."

"If I cut out my heart I will die."

A Holy Venom

Cat winked at the child. "You have just now tasted the water of this spring and so you shall not die. Had you been wounded by anything other than the Fire or a Guardian, the Water would have healed you completely, but it cannot undo injuries given by those that dwell here. But if you do as I say and cut out your heart and feed it to the Fire, none of the Guardians of the House can kill you. Only the Owner of the House will be able to kill you."

"Why should I trust you?"

"Do as you like. I have said what was mine to say. In time, you shall remember my kindness." With another flick of his tail, the Cat leapt off the garden wall.

The blind child dragged themselves back into the House and found the Heavy Blade on the Bloody Stump, still wet with blood. With the last of their strength, the child cut out their own heart, and it hurt like the worst thing you can imagine! With their heart all gross in their hands, they opened the iron gate to the roaring Fire and threw the scrawny bit of meat in. It burned bright red like a coal and did not stink like the other children's meat boiled in the Pot. It smelled like flowers. Just believe me.

As Cat had said, the child did not die but only grew stranger. Under the Workbench, they scavenged parts forgotten in the dust. They found glass eyes—perhaps spares that once belonged to Cat, or Owl, or Wolf—and pressed them into their empty sockets. They scraped up spare fur shed by Wolf and Cat to replace their scarred flesh. They scavenged and scraped until at last, they were no longer human but instead a stumpy patchwork thing of leftover parts. They practiced growling and fighting, waiting to catch hold of Spider and put out all eight of her beady eyes.

From the garden, they ate the sour leaves and starchy roots and drank the magical water from the Fountain. Finding all the ways through the House, they watched as Wolf and Cat and Owl fought and killed many humans who came to steal things. The child-thing got angrier and angrier every time an adult knocked at the door or tried to sneak in. The humans never came for the children trapped in the House. And even though they had changed into something no longer human, the child tried to protect the kids who came to the House. But the new ones were always too afraid of them or too hungry and stupid to resist the traps. For years and years, the patchwork child tried to save even one kid, but they finally gave up. Their only happiness was either winning fights with Spider or watching Wolf, Cat, and Owl tear apart the shit-bag human thieves.

Kiarna Boyd

One time, the child watched from behind the woodpile as Wolf tore a whole calvary of armed humans apart and splattered the snowy ground with their blood. Wolf shook out the humans' blood like a red rain, until even the patchwork child was covered in it, like in a horror movie. The child tasted blood and felt a new hunger. They no longer ate the garden plants. The magic of the House had messed them up, so they craved human flesh and blood. Nothing else could satisfy them.

The child grew and grew and feared only the Owner of the House. The giant came in many shapes. The Owner cackled her horrible fake laugh when she caught children, and then made fun of them before butchering them for the Pot. Sometimes she looked like the ugliest grandmother, with warts and a chin like a butt. Other times she looked like a beautiful and wise old priestess. She used magic to look like some of the children's parents, or teachers and siblings. But most of the time, when no one was around, she became invisible and looked like nothing at all, falling still like a clockwork toy run down. The wild little patchwork child watched her, gnawing on their hatred for the Owner's cruelty. The House changed inside and outside to confuse the kids; then the Owner would vanish and reappear, scaring her current victim before killing them.

It was awful in there. And if it wasn't awful, you had to watch out, because that's when it got really, really, bad.

A wooden step creaked over Ky's head and his new friend fell silent. Ky waited in the dark under the stairs. Next to him, Hyrinth seemed to dissolve into the dark.

There was a strange sound like a small bell jingling, then another completely different voice spoke in the darkness, the melodic male voice startling Ky. "And so it was that the child was changed and thought themselves no longer human but a thing of stolen parts and hatred. They found the paths of magic between the worlds and learned to hunt humans to feed the cravings that had been with them since the Wolf showered them in blood. They think themselves heartless and cruel, raised in the Silent Woods and the House of Sorrow. Listen now, for this is the thing you must hear, that I must tell you. This is the important secret no one knows. Their heart was not consumed by the Fire, but concealed from the Owner, hidden in the flames, burning as bright as the Sun and as big as your fist. The heart dreams of the child still and seeks to fetch them back to the House, no matter

A Holy Venom

the risk. The child grew and met others and planned to fetch water from the spring to heal the ones they loved. For though they have been separated from their heart, it is theirs still.

"If you would be brave and strong and grow bigger than what you're afraid of, you will help them steal back their heart. For long before the First Owner taught the House what it was and confined the Fire inside the Stove, the Fire was there. Before Water was corralled into a pool, the Water was there. And before the House stood, Stone was there. From before there was a beginning, there was Fire and Water in the place of Stone. Since the beginning of all things and before time itself changed, there was the House of Sorrow. All children went and all childhoods died there, just as all adults were bathed in Fire and in Water and born again from Stone, having given the death of their childhood to the House of Sorrow in exchange for their true life in the Hunting Grounds. Why the Second Owner never returned, I do not know. You must discover how to help the children trapped in the House and that can be discovered only from the heart that lives in the Fire."

EIGHTEEN

KY WOKE WITH A START and found himself lying in a four-poster bed in a strange hotel room. He clutched at his chest and ran his hands along his arms, neck, and face; he felt the familiar scars, the worn lines of his brow. The weight of the childhood dream slowly dissipated. The clock high on the wall struck the hour, calling his attention back.

He considered the satin duvet on the bed and the painting above the fireplace. Tiny rainbows from the chandelier reflected over detailed murals depicting sloping forest hills and a cone-shaped mountain painted in hues of blue. A formal landscape painting of a forest stream hung above the mantel. A pair of matching wingback chairs stood in front of a fake fireplace. A glass of water was carefully placed on a small table next to the bed.

Ky tried to get up but found his limbs unresponsive. He slumped back against the headboard and attempted to piece together what happened.

"Hello?" He managed to croak and roll his head, looking across the room for a sign of another's presence. He could feel someone was there with him, but that feeling was confused, tangled.

"Awake at last, I see," Ruin said, exiting the bathroom located on the other end of the fireplace. He smiled possessively at Ky and walked closer. Running a hand along Ky's face, Ruin smiled and stared into his eyes. "Feeling any better?"

"Where?" The word stuck in his throat and Ky swallowed; there was something terribly wrong with Ruin. Ky wasn't sure if it was the effects of whatever the dogs gave him, but the younger man's eyes were sickly bright, and vague lines traced his movements as if he were slightly blurred.

"We're in my rooms, silly. Safe as can be, where no one will find us." Ruin gently picked up Ky's hand and then dropped it.

Ky's limp hand smacked against the bed. He tried to summon the strength to lift it again. He needed to get the fuck away from Ruin, of that he was certain. The musician's aura was swamped with sickly, web-like filaments.

"Don't worry. I understand that you can't embrace me." With a sly smile, Ruin began undoing the buttons on Ky's shirt. "Your helplessness is quite alluring, you know." He glanced at the doorway in the far corner of the hotel room and back at Ky. "We have some time to ourselves and I plan on using it to the fullest before anyone can interrupt." His glittering eyes narrowed. "No one is going to take you from me, not this time." He slipped a hand under Ky's shirt and touched the burn scars. "And I won't let you get away like you did the other night."

Chilled, Ky managed to pull his head back as Ruin's features clouded, flickered, and disappeared under the ghostly vision of a woman's face. Ky inhaled sharply and tried to shout.

Ruin clamped a hand over his mouth and frowned. "I've told you before, there will be none of that. We're in my rooms. They brought you here for me and you're not going anywhere. You're *mine!*" The woman's face hissed. She snagged her hand in Ky's shirt, tearing the buttons as she wrenched the fabric apart.

The door to the room flung back with a crack against the wainscoting on the inner wall. Aych entered, growling low in their throat. "Leave now, before I fuck you up permanently, shit-bag."

The spirit screeched and Ruin's possessed hand pulled a scalpel out of his pocket. Shoving Ky's head against the headboard, she pressed the blade against his throat. "You put him in my bed! Mine! Everything in here is mine! This body, his body, this soul, his soul! Mine!"

"The dead don't own shit, lady," Ky managed to grunt.

She snarled at him and squeezed his throat. With a squeak, she dropped the scalpel and stared at the blood dripping from her hand. "*Something bit me!*"

Aych laughed as the woman threw herself off the bed and scrambled backward on the wool rug. "It does more than bite." Aych strode the rest of the way across the room and lifted her up by her shoulders. The wraith struggled in Ruin's captured body, kicking her feet and thrashing wildly. "Easy, easy, this isn't your body, now is it?"

A Holy Venom

"Mine!" The wraith howled, her voice shrill and unreal, echoing through the room.

Aych shook her and the skeletal shape of a woman unfurled from Ruin's body.

The spirit shrieked and tried to reenter her host as Aych snapped their Little jaws together and bit into the misty form.

Ky recoiled. "Fucking hell!" An overpowering scent hit him. Memories of the fight in the convent garden flooded back and triggered a rush of adrenaline. It was the same musk from his apartment stairwell and apartment. The uncanny animal aroma mixed with floral perfume. He stared at Aych.

"You dare!" The wraith stabbed her bony fingers at Aych's eyes. "My rightful prey! Mine, mine!"

"Shut the fuck up. Like he said, the dead don't own shit." Aych's mouth opened wider and tore again at the wraith, ripping away at the ghostly filaments binding themselves to Ruin.

The painting and the clock face rattled, banging against the walls. The ceiling fan shuddered and the lamps dimmed as Aych tore sections of the wraith apart like cobwebbing. Ky felt the bed shaking and the mattress juddering sideways.

"You cannot keep me from my prey!" The woman screamed and disembodied hands tried to claw Aych's face. "Before he was born, he was mine. He belongs to me!"

Ky heard an animal chattering and looked down to see the stone head lying against his side, smeared with blood.

Aych lifted the wraith higher. "You've been saying that all this time, and every time I throw your bony ass right the fuck out. You don't own anyone and no one owes you shit. If you want a body so badly, go stitch one together out of bed sheets and newspaper." With a last snap of their jaws, Aych bit through the wraith's head.

Ruin's vacated body fell still and his limbs went limp. Aych lowered Ruin gently and hugged his body close, cradling his head against their own. "Last time you have to go through that, I promise." They carried the unconscious human over to one of the wing-backed chairs and carefully settled him into a sitting position.

"What the fuck is going on?" Ky croaked as his heart rate slowed. He tried to sit up again. "You're the werewolf? You killed Haw?"

Still kneeling in front of Ruin's chair, Aych shot Ky a look of scorn. "A round of applause for the winner of the *It Took You Long Enough, Dumbass* contest."

"Fuck you," Ky coughed and reached for the glass of water on the bedside table.

Lu suddenly strode through the open doorway to the suite. From behind her, Mat entered and shut the door before walking over to the bed.

"Here, I'll help you. Sit back." Mat eased Ky back against the pillows. "I told you he would need help sitting up, and needs plenty of fluids." The herbalist shot Aych an angry look and then stopped. "Why did you bring Ruin with you?"

Lu glanced from where she was standing by Ky's side over to the chair and raised an eyebrow. "I thought we agreed—"

"I didn't bring him. They were both in here when I got back," Aych scowled at Mat. "I thought you brought him."

"Me?" Mat yelled. "I wouldn't bring him in here! Of all places!"

"Ruin said this was his room." Ky pressed his empty glass into Mat's hand. "Though he wasn't exactly himself at the time."

Lu walked over to the chair and pressed her hand against Ruin's forehead. "How bad was it?"

Aych leaned against the fireplace mantel and looked at the floor. "Bad enough. I only sensed the shit-bag. Ruin wasn't in there at all."

"Looked like a full possession. That thing was in total control." Ky stared hard as Aych glared at him. "She tried to kill me, remember?"

"Damn." Mat absently set the glass on the nightstand. "How could you let it get that bad? You told me you were going to protect him. You promised."

"I did, didn't I?" Aych glowered. "She didn't take Ruin, and if you could shut the fuck up, maybe he could get some sleep."

"Language!" Lu walked over and put a soothing hand on Aych's elbow. "He's only worried, just like you. No reason to get angry at him about it."

"His face is enough reason to get angry," Aych scowled. "Don't you have some chemistry shit to be finishing? We need that second batch. We're out

A Holy Venom

of time. Ruin is out of time. It was on the verge of a full possession."

"I came up to check on Ky. The antivenin should clear everything out, but Lu said you needed him functional." Mat threw a hurt look over his shoulder. "I'm trying to help."

"Antivenin?" Ky pulled away as Mat checked his pulse.

Lu walked to the side of the bed. "The Perlustrate's cocktails can cause long-term damage. After Aych rescued you, I asked Mat to purge you of their filth." She smiled reassuringly. "Mat is an expert on poisons and their antidotes."

Aych scoffed. "Like hell he is. Shit for brains over here is just a bag of fucking useless opinions. He should fucking experiment on himself."

"Don't make me put out a swear jar! You curse so much that not even you could afford it." Lu shot a quelling look over her shoulder. "And shouldn't you be a bit more appreciative right now? Be grateful the hunter's in one piece and talking sensibly. You could have lost him to the Chapterhouse."

"We don't need him sensible, just wriggling on the hook." Aych dropped their gaze and then looked back at Ruin. "When you're done with bright boy over there, take a look at your nephew. He should've woken up by now."

Mat nodded and took a glass vial out of his smock. He caught Ky's eye. "Only side effect I can think of will be vivid dreams."

Ky laughed.

Lu eyed Ky over Mat's shoulder. "I never knew it was an antidote for the dogs' bite. You never mentioned that before."

"Neither you nor them," Mat shot a look at Aych, "are vulnerable to the Perlustrate's compounds, so there was no reason to mention it."

"But the Aya knew about it." Lu's eyes glittered. "What else aren't you telling us about the Rot?"

"The Rot?" Ky looked up, alarmed. "You're giving me that shit?"

Mat sighed. "I told you, I gave you the antivenin form, not the venom-based compound."

Setting a fingertip on the herbalist's shoulder, Lu leaned closer. "What else are you not telling us? Anything about the other complications you'd care to share details about?"

Mat shifted uncomfortably. He yelped suddenly and pulled his hand away, surprised.

"What?" Ky glanced down at the bed as Mat recoiled from it.

"Something bit me." Mat showed them both the angry welt on the side of his hand.

"Didn't even break the skin." Aych snickered. "You're lucky you taste like shit, herbalist."

Mat glanced at the sheets next to Ky's shoulders and saw the grim features of a stone imp head leering back. Across the room, Aych frowned.

Ky stared at the sleepy expression on the stone face. He felt a slight vibration where the head made contact with his body. "Is it me or is this thing alive?"

Lu peered closer at the head and then laughed. She covered her mouth and looked over at Aych. They narrowed their eyes and turned back to Ruin.

"What the hell is that thing and why did it bite me?" Mat got off the bed, massaging his hand.

"Well, it was a lure to find a hunter, but now..." Lu laughed again. "I think it likes him. Protecting him."

The vibration increased as if the stone was cooing, tingling through Ky's side and settling pleasantly in his stomach. "It's purring?"

Aych shrugged off Lu's amusement. "It's telling me about you. It's a type of enchantment." They turned back as Ruin stirred in the chair. Aych carefully placed their hand on the human's arm. "How are you feeling?"

Ruin smiled weakly. "Like shit." He glanced around the bedroom, his expression troubled. "Why are we in *here*?" Ruin casually wiped the fresh blood off his hand and gestured at the room.

Stroking back his hair, Aych frowned. "Short version is we needed to hole up where the salts won't look."

"Here?" Ruin pushed himself upright and looked at the others in the room. "But she'll find Ky if he's in her room. She wants to hurt him, maybe even kill him."

"It's OK." Aych knelt next to the chair and rested their hand on Ruin's knee. "I got rid of her. You don't—"

"She'll come back! She wants to get back at you for hurting her!" Ruin tried to stand. "I need to go. You need to get him out of here. Away from me."

"It's really OK now." Lu held her hands up and gestured at Ky. "Mat's taking care of Ky and Aych has sent her back to wherever it is she hides. You don't have to worry. You can rest."

"You don't understand." Ruin pushed himself up onto their feet ignoring Aych's concerned expression. "If I'm here, she'll come back. This is her domain, the place where she died."

Lu glanced from Ruin to Aych then back again. "No, it isn't." Taking a few steps, Lu closed the distance and picked up Ruin's injured hand. Running her fingertips over the small bite, she looked deeply into his eyes. The puncture wounds faded, replaced by unbroken skin. "I didn't want to upset you, but the entity isn't your aunt. It's only pretending to be. It has her memories. I know this is confusing, but it's been attached to your family for a long, long time." Lu held onto Ruin's hand. "It was attached to her, but when she died, it moved to your uncle."

"Then me," Ruin's eyes went wide and he slumped back against the chair.

Aych stood up and shot Lu a stern look. "What's important is that shit-bag is gone now. And soon we'll be able to get rid of her permanently." They glanced back at Ruin. "You don't have to concern yourself with any of this right now."

"If you both knew this, why didn't you tell me? Why can you get rid of her permanently now, but not before?"

Lu smiled. "Aych is going to go get something to bring back my true power. We were waiting for Mat to finish making us a potion and then for Ky to be able to help us—to help Aych—get my cure. Once we bring it back, I'll be able to give you a unique medicine to protect you from the *pikma*." She reached out and touched Ruin's cheek. "Then I'll always be able to protect you. She won't be able to attach to you anymore and no one will ever be able to hurt you like that again."

Ruin's eyes darkened as he looked from Lu to Aych and back. "But she'll just find someone else to torment and possess, won't she?"

Aych growled, "Who gives a shi—" They caught themselves. "A crap about other humans? Not your problem, not mine, not Lu's. So long as she's not able to mess with you, that's all I care about."

Lu rolled her eyes. "What Aych means is that once you're free of the attachment, the entity will be forced to find another host."

Ruin pulled his hands free. "How is that OK? You're telling me this thing fucked with my aunt and uncle and who knows who else in my family. Won't it just find another relative and drive them insane?"

"You are the last. Once Lu's able to give you her protection, there won't be any lawful prey left. It will starve to death or shrivel up … I don't care."

"I'm the last? What if you're wrong and there is someone? Or what if I have kids?" Tears welled in his eyes. "I don't want anyone else to have to have that thing crawling inside of them."

"Fine." Sighing, Aych closed their eyes. "Once you're free of it, I'll find a way to kill it permanently." They opened their eyes. "I promise."

Lu looked at Aych. "If you go down that path …"

"I fucking know." Aych snapped. "Sorry." They gave her an apologetic look. "But what else can I say?" They brushed back Ruin's hair with their fingertips. "You see how stubborn this one is. If I don't promise, he's going to worry himself sick over some asshole he doesn't know or isn't even born yet. Won't you, psycho?" Smiling, Aych let their fingertip linger on Ruin's ear.

"Probably." Ruin blinked back tears and nodded. "I just don't want anyone else to have to—"

"I know." Aych bent and kissed the top of his head. "Just rest now. Come tomorrow, this will all be sorted. You'll see."

Watching the exchange, Ky remembered the dirty, claw-fingered child from his dream. He looked at Aych and recalled the brusque kindness the child under the stairs had shown him. The stone head, the dream of the House with the stranger wearing his face, all of it came crashing together in Ky's mind. "Aych … H! H is for Hyrinth. That's your name, isn't it? Your heart, you have to get it back, Hyrinth."

Everyone in the room stared at Ky.

"Are you fucking talking to me?" Aych turned and glared at Ky. "Between the dogs using you as a chew-toy and Mat's so-called cures, your head's finally turned to mush, pal."

"You admitted you killed Haw. You're the monster that was at the convent. Just now, when you were fighting with the *pikma*, I saw it… I saw *you*. You smell the same!" Ky set the stone head on the nightstand next to the water glass. The countersignal beat a staccato rhythm along his back and he considered if the window adjacent to the bed was shatterproof. He could throw the stone and find out.

"Your timing is a little off, hunter, but if you want to do this now..." Aych glanced at Mat. "The second dose, is it ready?"

"It is, but..." Mat looked from Aych to Lu.

"Might as well fully set the hook. We are conveniently in a locked insane asylum." Aych smiled viciously at Ky. "You can bounce around in here until I need to drag you out into the Woods." Aych began to release their Little form. "Just need to crack your head open a bit wider, won't take much ..."

Alarmed, Ky shouted at Mat and Ruin. "Close your eyes! Don't look at them!"

Wide-eyed, Mat ducked his head and covered his face while Ruin started up out of the chair.

"*No.*" Lu grabbed Aych's arm.

"I'm finishing what the Perlustrate started. Giving our boy here a push over the precipice to set the hook. Then, once I tug, he'll follow me straight to his grave, just like we planned."

"What's happening!" Mat yelled, crouching with his eyes closed.

Ky tried to think of options. His body was still unresponsive, sluggish. The aftermath of the earlier adrenaline had made him even more tired. Aych was between him and the exit. The other humans were vulnerable. If they saw Aych transform, they'd go insane. He couldn't justify leaving them to die in his place.

Lu stepped between Aych and Ky. She poked Aych in the chest. "Stop. Right. Now."

Aych looked down at her. "Why? Everything is set. He can spend a few hours working himself into a lather and then in the morning, I'll drag him over to chum the water. You can't be seriously worried about the herbalist? Ruin—"

"I won't let you." She put both her hands on her hips and tilted her head at Ky. "He tipped us off about the dogs."

"So what? Just because he and Mudon hate each other's guts is no reason for us to change the plan," Aych growled.

Lu stood on her toes and got in Aych's face. "Because I said so."

Ky felt the air crackle with energy like storm clouds gathering.

Snarling, Aych threw up their hands. "Fine. Now what? You going to have the herbalist play decoy instead? Or should I pull Mudon out of the dogs' dinner bowl and see if he'll last five minutes?"

"Can I open my eyes yet?" Mat opened one eye. "I'm likely immune..."

"No, you're fucking not!" Aych snapped at the human. "No human can see me Big and not fall into madness."

Ruin gave a choked laugh. "That's why you get so fucking weird on me. You think because I saw you that night in the garden, that you're the reason—"

"He saw you Big?" Lu looked at Aych in alarm.

"When he was still a kid." Aych looked at Ruin. "That's not why—"

"You don't have to drag anyone else," Ky looked over at where everyone was standing. "Not Mat, not Mudon. I'll do it. Whatever you brought me here to do. If it will help Ruin and Lu, if it will get rid of that shit-bag possessing him... and get rid of *you*."

Aych growled at Ky.

"You have to get your heart out of the Stove," Ky said, meeting their gaze. "You know you do."

"What the fuck are you even babbling about?" Aych brushed by Lu. "You came out of the Tank with only half a brain left. Are you looking for me to spill the rest for you?"

"You cut your heart out and fed it to the fire. It's in the Stove in the House. You need to get in and take it out."

"Oh no, we are not talking about that." Lu crossed her arms. "No one, and I mean *no one*, is going into that evil place for anything." She reached over and pushed Aych back a step. "You cannot go in there."

"Believe me, there's no fucking reason I would." Aych spit the words out then pointed at Ky. "You want to play, hunter?" They waved their arm at the suite door. "There's a whole janitor's closet in the hall full of supplies so you can make your toilet bombs. As soon as you're ready, I'm more than fucking happy to throw your—"

"You have to bring him back." Lu looked up into Aych's face. "If he goes, he comes back."

A Holy Venom

Aych grimaced. "That wasn't the plan, how the fuck am I supposed to—"

"You said he could beat the clock. Well, he's just going to have to now, isn't he? And you're going to have to move quickly and get him back out before they tear him apart."

Watching Lu and Aych argue, Ruin shook his head. "No one has to go anywhere if this is for me. I appreciate you all deciding how I should live my fucking life, but don't do me any extra favors."

"It's not like that." Mat held his hands out to Ruin. "The Awy wanted Lu's venom, and they offered to make her a potion in exchange. They had me make it so Aych can get what Lu needs from the Silent Woods."

"Wait, what?" Ruin stared at him and then the others. "First you make it sound like you're doing me a favor—"

"The Awy wanted Lu's venom." Ky interjected. He shakily sat up as Mat's antidote began to work. "To make the Rot. Why?" He looked at the herbalist.

"How would Mat know?" Ruin asked.

"Because he makes the shit," Ky slowly reached for the glass of water, wincing as his muscles screamed. "He's the Awy's expert in poisons."

"At the Teahouse? You make the Rot at the fucking Teahouse?" Ruin got in Mat's face.

"No," Mat put his hand up and moved away. "I make it here, in the abandoned levels. There's nothing incriminating at the Teahouse."

"Why the fuck would you do that? Why would you..." Ruin looked from Mat to Lu and then Aych. "Do you just hate all humans enough to want to kill all of us?"

"It's not like that," Mat pleaded as he moved closer to Ruin. "The Awy use herbal and magical remedies to heal people." He motioned at Lu. "Her venom, in its debased form, is still holy. It amplifies the plant magic that causes the change. The Aya layered it with sacred herbs that have strong protective spirits. It's not meant to kill people. Given enough time, it frees them. It releases the change in them. It calls descendants of the clans home."

"That's an elaborate way of describing death," Aych rolled their eyes.

"You're not helping," Lu snapped and glared at Aych. She put a gentle hand on Mat's arm. "Neither are you."

She looked at Ruin. "I'll tell you what you want to know. The Awy made the Rot so it would magically affect the humans who take it. How it does that, or why they wanted it to, I don't know and didn't ask. They knew about me and my…condition. And they knew about Aych. Apparently, word gets around when you eat hundreds of people indiscriminately. Anyway." She looked back at Ruin. "We made a deal, the forest witches and me and Aych. My venom in exchange for a special poison. And yes, I agreed to set up the Rot distribution because, yes, I hate humans."

She smiled at Aych. "Imagine my luck finding the only person in this frigid, boring city who knows where the sacred healing spring is hidden. My venom only works on humans, but the Awy know other methods." She pointed at Mat. "Your uncle found the method to remake the other potion we need so Aych can get over the garden wall and back in one piece. We thought roping in a hunter would provide some extra insurance." She looked sideways at Ky. "It's a tried-and-true ploy. Nothing like a little floorshow out on the sidewalk to distract the front of the house while the talent cracks the safe in back."

"Once Lu's restored, her venom becomes a sacrament again. The Rot wouldn't work with it." Mat tried to catch Ruin's eyes. "No evil can withstand it."

Ky shot Mat a look. "You might want to consider what it means if the purified venom steps on your magical drug."

Ruin looked up into Aych's face. "You were planning on breaking up the band after all."

Aych looked away. "If he's up for it, I say we do it in the morning. Get this over with. Before the shit-bag reassembles itself."

"No one's going inside that House," Lu stated firmly.

"*They* have to," Ky shook his head and then looked at Aych. "You know you do. You have to get it out of the Stove, out of the Fire—"

"You need to shut your mouth." Lu made a silencing gesture at Ky. "Not another single word about the House."

"Why? If he knows something…" Mat glanced at her.

"There are things we don't talk about." Lu shot Ky a look and glanced meaningfully at Aych. "Things we don't say out loud where others can hear us."

A Holy Venom

"What others?" Ky glanced from Lu to Aych. "Who else is involved?"

"It doesn't matter." Aych snapped. "The plan stays the same. As soon as you're not a bag of jelly and unsolicited opinions, we'll run the job."

"It's easy," Lu kept her eyes on Ky. "Aych will give you a sack of goat meat laced with the sleeping draught Mat distilled. They will then bring you through to the front of the House, where you'll distract the Guardians by offering them the laced meat. That will keep them busy for the time it takes for Aych to get into the garden, get the water from the spring, and then come get you back out. No one needs to go anywhere near that House. The draught will work within three minutes."

Lu stepped over to the side of the bed and stared into Ky's eyes. "The Awy seek justice for the thousands of Ornish clan members who died when the islands were taken from their people. For the countless human lives stolen and taken back to this hell of a frozen mountain range to work in the mines. For all that gold I showed you."

"You don't care how many lives are destroyed by this deal of yours?" Ky balled the bedding up in his fists. "People are dying from the Rot. The addiction is destroying their lives, their families – "

"I know I said I won't do this, but you're asking for it." Lu sat on the bed and draped herself along Ky's body. An electric storm cloud zapped through him until his eyes watered and haloes of light blinded him.

She murmured into his ear so only he could hear her. "Once I loved humans and they betrayed me. Like any relationship that ends in betrayal, the only way to overcome it is by embracing the truth. And the truth always hurts."

Ky's head lolled back as visions of a winged, scaled serpent undulating through lightning clouds filled his mind.

"You're cooking what's left of his brain," Aych grumbled. "I need him to walk and talk, remember?"

Lu got off the bed and flicked her hand as Ky gasped for breath. "He made me mad."

"Why does he think you need to go in the House?" Mat recoiled from the look both Lu and Aych shot him. "If he's just a decoy, why does he know things like that?"

"Whatever he thinks he knows, doesn't matter," Placing both hands on her hips, Lu looked down her nose at both Ky and Mat. "No one is going in the House and that's the end of it."

Aych snorted. "Bright boy needs to rest, and you and I need to prep for tonight. I should check on Violet."

Ruin put his hand on Aych's arm. "I can help."

"You can help by promising you won't follow us. Before you tell me off, remember: the Owner can look like anyone. If I see anyone that looks like you in the Woods, and there's the fucking slightest chance it *is* you, I could get tricked into going into the House. Promise me you will stay here, in the Hunting Grounds."

"What if you don't come back? Then I'm the only one who could…"

Aych shook their head. "Promise me."

Ruin relaxed against Aych and they drew him into an embrace.

Ky watched as the emotions rippling off Ruin steadied into a strong undercurrent of rebellion.

Aych turned to look at Lu. "I should check on the Velvet and do divination. Little bit of forewarning never hurts."

Mat cleared his throat and looked over at Ky. "Physically, Ky should be fine by morning, but you'll have to ask him if he feels up to it, after what he's been through."

"Oh, his little sojourn with the dogs wasn't much of a bother, was it?" Lu smiled at Ky. "Good night's rest, a decent dinner and breakfast, and you'll feel right as rain. That rejuvenating bolt from the blue I gave you will sort out anything the antivenom can't handle."

"I should go pack up the equipment." Mat looked over at Ruin. "Since you're here, maybe you could come downstairs and help me? I need to get it all packed tonight."

"Sure, why not." Ruin shrugged and slid out from Aych's arms. "Since we can't go back to the Teahouse, I might as well embrace a life of crime. Though, I'm not OK with killing people for no reason. Or poisoning them. That's fucked and needs to stop."

"Not to worry," Lu brushed her hand along his arm. "The dogs won't be rummaging around in your home. Once they ascertain that Ky's flown, they'll focus on the Velvet and try to pick up the scent there. Nothing will lead them to our business here. It's why we decided to utilize this facility."

A Holy Venom

Lu scrunched her features. "I'm sorry if our intrusion into your family's wing has brought up painful memories. It wasn't our intent to be disrespectful."

"It's OK, it was shuttered," Ruin shrugged. "Not like anyone was using it." He patted Mat on the back. "Come on, show me this mad science laboratory of yours."

"It's not like that," Mat replied gruffly and started for the door.

"I should go," Aych glanced at Lu. "If everything looks good, we will need to…"

"Of course. I've been quite looking forward to it." She smiled lasciviously.

Mat cleared his throat.

Aych and Lu looked over as Mat pointedly nodded at the locked door. In response, Aych snapped their fingers and the lock clicked open.

"Really should be knocking over banks or at least raiding Church vaults with that talent of yours," Lu winked at Aych. "Think of all the expensive things you could walk away with."

"As long as I can keep walking, you can use me for whatever you like."

Ruin stopped on the threshold and looked back at Ky. "If you need anything, we'll be downstairs. We could … "

"I'll stay and watch over our hunter," Lu offered. "Don't worry. If he needs anything, I'll fetch it."

"Can't really imagine you in a kitchen is all." Ruin looked at Aych. "See you later?"

"I'll tuck you in." They winked. "Wherever you end up, I'll swing by before dawn."

Nodding, Ruin closed the door.

Aych glanced over at Ky and then back to Lu. "About two hours then? Before we go fetch the goat?"

"Enough time for me to have a chat with Ky here and be bored out of my mind while he sleeps." She flounced dramatically into one of the chairs.

"If you try to run, the lure will let me know." Aych held Ky's gaze. "It will stay with you no matter where you go."

Ky considered throwing the stone head at Aych. "I don't want to hear you bellyaching. You can take the damn thing back anytime, regardless if I blow."

"And separate it from its best friend? I'm not that much of an asshole." Aych turned and winked at Lu before stepping In Between and disappearing from the room.

Vertigo hit Ky and he found himself grasping the bed. "What the hell was that?"

"First time seeing Aych's party trick?" Lu pillowed her chin on her hand and watched Ky from half-lidded eyes. "When it comes to me, you always react like I'm a bomb about to go off, no matter how well-behaved I am."

"You broadcast, they don't. Not when they're human-ish."

"Ish?" Her eyes opened wide. "That makes sense. I suppose that's the best way to say it. Human-ish." Her eyelids drooped. "Now then, why don't you tell me why you're suddenly volunteering to help us? And by us, I mean Aych, who … how did you say it? Killed your friend? A strange change of heart. You're not going to betray them once you're over there, are you?"

"It took me too long to figure Aych is your other friend. The one you don't like people calling a monster, even though that's what they are." Ky inhaled slowly and then exhaled. "The thing is, Haw would be pissed if I left Ruin to get possessed by that thing. Or if I left you without helping." He glanced over and nodded at Lu. "She would want me to stop Aych from killing people, that's for damn sure. But as you've pointed out, and I've seen firsthand, that's above my pay grade. I can scratch that phony skin they're wearing, sure, but not enough to slow them down if they decide it's snack time at a retirement convent. Maybe if you're fixed up, you'll do something on your own about them." Ky tried to figure out if it was safe to tell Lu any part of his dream. Chances were, she would agree with Aych that it was all a result of the Perlustrate's torture.

Lu shook her head. "Me? Control that beast? Oh, darling, you continue to flatter me. Besides," she winked at him. "It's so much more fun when they don't behave."

"If you say so. It looks to me like carnage and misery are their meat and potatoes." He shrugged. "When there's a human you care about trampled underfoot, you might sing a different tune."

"I'm not enough of a fool to love any human again." She watched him from under her lashes. "Now, why don't you tell me exactly what you meant about Aych needing to go into the House to get their heart?"

"I thought you didn't want me—"

"Not when they're around."

Ky looked at her in confusion. "I'm not following."

"Since you're risking your life to help our disreputable cause, I'll share a little secret." She drummed her fingertips along the edge of her jaw. Sitting back in the chair, she watched him steadily. "There's another party involved. Well, potentially involved. I'm a little short on evidence."

Ky thought about Mudon's warning not to trust anyone. Could be Lu was about to pour out another mess of lies and expect him to drink it down like the good agreeable target they'd pegged him as. "Could be any number of unsavory factions."

"Unsavory? Oh, I know it's not the Awy. They don't have any hold on Aych."

"That leaves me all out of guesses, lady. I don't know who you're in cahoots with or if this is all more bunk."

"We all feel that way, to be honest," frowning, Lu looked around the room. "We don't know exactly who it is, or even *what* they are. Aych calls them The Caretaker. Whoever it is, they've always tidied things up around Aych. Procured supplies, apartments, cars; disposed of bodies, arranged cash, travel, even filled refrigerators with human organs or goat meat on occasion." She glanced back. "Doesn't mean either of us trust them. In fact, I actively *distrust* them."

"Wait, someone's been taking care of Aych for years, and you don't know who they are?" Ky stared in disbelief.

"Centuries. I have my theories and I'm sure Aych does too. But they're under a compulsion not to speak or even think about the Caretaker for more than a few seconds. The longer they keep their attention on that topic, the more they're punished for it."

"Punished?"

Lu flicked her fingers. "A headache that becomes a migraine, and, on the one occasion I tried to force them to keep thinking about the Caretaker, that migraine becomes something like a seizure. They lost control over their form." She glanced back. "If there's anything I have learned from my time with Aych, the one thing you do not want is for them to shift from Little to

Big without someone on hand to eat. Especially if they size up to their Biggest. If they start going all cloudy-wispy on you, run."

"I don't follow."

"The important point is we can't discuss certain things around Aych because then the Caretaker will know it too."

"Are they eavesdropping now?" He tried to feel if another influence was still present in the room.

"No. Whatever they are, they seem to abide only with Aych." Lu uncoiled herself from the chair and stood up. Pointing at the stone head, Lu gestured for it and waited until Ky tossed it over to her. "This connects you to Aych. But it doesn't seem to be broadcasting in general." She looked at the head for a moment then tossed it on the bed. "Since we've established we're alone, tell me what you meant about Aych's heart and getting it out of that House."

Ky considered if he should hold anything back. "It was a dream." He picked up the stone head. The vibration tingled along his forearm and traveled into his armpit. "When the dogs were working on me. I think this thing came to protect me and in the process, it fed me intel about Aych."

"Or your own dream, the result of the dogs rummaging around in your head." Lu waggled her fingers at him.

"Maybe. But it felt like a true vision, a true knowing." Ky ran his thumb over the rough surface of the canine face and felt the uncanny heat coming off it. "Doesn't matter. What does is that I know without a doubt Aych needs to get their heart back out of the Fire in the Stove in the House where they left it. I'm sure of that as I am of anything."

"And you think, if Aych has their heart back, they might find a new approach to life that doesn't involve murder buffets?"

"Like I said, above my pay grade." Ky kept scrapping his thumb over the head, turning it in his hand. "But they need to get it." The child's admonishment to that effect stayed with him, as clear as if Hyrinth were sitting next to him.

"Even if that was a thing, and let's be honest, it sounds like utter dream nonsense, but if it was true, that House is not something even Aych can go in or out of easily. The garden is one thing, but all the way to the Stove? No way no how."

"You seem to know a lot about the House." Ky slumped back against the pillows. "I don't know how long you two been planning this job. Or when you decided to try it. But Aych could go into the garden any time, if what you say is true. They don't need your sideshow ploy for that. From what I've seen, they could pop into the garden, get the water from the spring, and then pop the hell back. So why this?" He held up the lure. "Why do they need a hunter to distract the guards? Do they know on some level they need to get into the House?"

Lu was silent for a moment. "Aych found you inside the Chapterhouse because the lure was with you. Let's say for a moment, just for a moment, your dream was the product of that same magic. It doesn't change the fact that we don't have a plan to get them in and out of there safely, nor does it change that they might already be going into a trap."

"The Caretaker. You think they're setting up Aych."

"I don't know. Having been betrayed once, I can tell you I wouldn't risk it."

"But you're letting them go on in anyway. For your medicine."

Lu exhaled. "You have eyes. You saw how those two are, Aych and the *gae-su*. Any time I try and talk Aych out of it, they insist they can get the water for me. Because they want to save him."

"Because Aych wants to free Ruin." Ky corrected her. "Isn't there any other way?"

"Oh, there might be, but Aych doesn't want to do it." Lu sighed and threw up her hands. "Because they think it would be unfair. Even the worst people have their limits, it turns out."

It was Ky's turn to be silent. "Or it could be that Aych knows they have to go into the House. They're either lying to themselves or to the rest of us. Or both."

NINETEEN

BRIGHT HALOGEN LIGHTS snapped on as Mat opened a thick metal door into the vaulted chamber. Ruin stepped around him and gave a low whistle. Set up throughout the vast cellar, stands of metal work lights illuminated tables covered in glassware. Mat crossed the room to a second door set in the inner wall and unlocked it. Ruin trailed after the herbalist gawking at the vast basement.

The second cellar room was bathed in a soft, tangerine glow and full of rolling shelving units draped with heavy tarps. Mat walked to a metal worktable in the back lined with hundreds of brown medicine bottles and waited for Ruin.

"What is all this?" Ruin lifted the corner of a tarp and peered at several trays of moldering soil.

"Leftovers. Nothing to concern yourself with. This is what we need to move." Setting a wooden crate on the table, Mat began to carefully wrap the amber glass bottles and tuck them into the dried moss lining the box. "Lu's venom won't be usable as the base after she takes the cure. This is the last of it."

"You made it? The Rot?" Coming around to stand next to his uncle, Ruin carefully lifted one of the bottles. "Has anyone changed from taking it? Like in the legends?"

"Not yet." Mat furrowed his brows and kept packing. "The Aya developed it from a mixture the Awy use. They take the herbal tincture when one of their own has difficulty changing. They use the exact same herbs to change and don't die from it. I followed their decoction. The only difference is Lu's venom. Here, wrap it like this," he demonstrated, padding a bottle. "I don't know why people are dying from it. They should be changing ..."

Ruin obediently began adding bottles to the crate. "Do you believe it?

What you said upstairs? Does it help people at all, or is it just a way to ..."

"Kill people?" Mat shot Ruin a mournful look.

Ruin focused on the bottles for a moment. "I don't think of you as someone who murders people. I was hoping not all of my family did that. Aych—"

"I don't think of myself that way either." Mat's hands kept moving at a steady pace. "But I can't deny there are people dying because I made this. Ky was right, people are suffering because it's addictive. It shouldn't be—it should only cause the change to start—"

"That's why you made it?" Ruin stopped and looked into Mat's face. "You made it as a remedy? Like your teas?"

The room's tangerine light made Mat look far younger. "I made it as a medicine that can cure. It can kill, depending on the dose and the person. Their choice, their path. If they take too much ..." Dropping his gaze back to the crate, the herbalist continued speaking, clearly distraught. "Plants make medicine. Even when it's a defensive toxin or a hunting strategy, it's still a medicine. Animals make poisons, often from ingesting plants or sometimes all on their own. Humans who are in pain need help or their own poisoned souls will kill them. The difference between a poison and a medicine isn't just the dose or the source. It's understanding the nature of the healing it offers. You can either resist or accept. But getting people addicted wasn't part of the plan and I don't understand why there are so many overdoses." Mat fell silent.

Ruin stopped and held a bottle. "You should get rid of it. It's hurting people."

Mat sighed. "But what if it does work? What if it can bring them home?"

"You're fucking people up gambling on a chance some of them might survive." Ruin shook his head. "If you wouldn't use it, or let me take it, you shouldn't make it."

The two men worked in silence until the crate was full. Mat tapped the lid shut with a rubber mallet and hefted the crate onto the floor. He replaced it with an empty one and they continued working. The sounds of rustling moss and the clink of the bottles filled the air between them. The repetition of the work and the sounds of packing formed a song-like rhythm. For a moment, Ruin forgot everything else.

A Holy Venom

Mat broke his reverie, catching Ruin off guard. "I was younger than you are now when it happened. A woman I loved very much died unexpectedly. Tragically. I couldn't handle it. Then a few years later, another woman I admired died." The older man's hands kept the rhythm of movement as he spoke, his voice dropping into the soft cadence of recalled pain. "When she died, everyone was sad, depressed. Your father was the only one who gave a fuck about me, how I felt. He was kind to me when no one else remembered I existed." Mat flashed a sad smile. "Even then I was too fucked up to understand my grief. I was broken and had been for so long. I'd been sober for a while, but after she died... I went right back to drinking. To the poison I knew. I was an alcoholic and I wanted to die." He hefted a glass bottle, turning it in his hand, watching the liquid slosh inside. "Everyone was getting back to their lives, to the courier routes, to earning bonuses and their petty, shitty lives. But there was this hole, bigger than it had ever been, and I just fell right through it. Next thing I knew I was riding inland, stopping at gas stations to fill my tank and buy beer. Middle of winter on the islands." He paused and caught Ruin's eye, his tone shifting back to conversational. "Not like it is here. Usually it only rains on the coast, with some snow. But inland, where I grew up, it's the mountains."

"Awyton?" Ruin imagined the great peak in the center of the main island.

Mat nodded and pulled up another hunk of moss absently as his eyes unfocused. "Blue Mountain. Awyton's at the foot. Only town, real town, up there at the source of the Mam." Shaking his head, he looked back at the bottle and resumed packing. "I was maybe fifteen miles out when the snow started. Too drunk to stop, too miserable to care, too fucking cold to think. Ended up coming off the pavement doing about seventy and ended up ass over tea kettle in a ditch. Snow coming down through the trees, headlight fading out over the snow as it was starting to stick..."

Ruin imagined a younger version of his uncle, dazed and lying next to the still-running motorcycle, alone on a deserted road at night in a snowstorm. "Did you pick the bike up or did you flag someone down?"

"Neither," Mat chuckled. "Passed the fuck out from exhaustion and pain. Coming off, I'd cracked three ribs and had a fourth puncture my lung. Would've died drowning on my own fluids or gasping for air like a fucking fish pulled from a pond."

Ruin stopped and stared at him. "You cracked up that badly? You never—"

"I'm telling you now." Mat tapped Ruin with his elbow, prompting the younger man to keep packing. "Obviously, I didn't die. Instead..." He sighed. "I grew up in Awyton and we heard all kinds of shit about the Awy. Some kids think it's cool to claim to be part of the clan and scare the others. That flies until you're around twelve or so and then you learn to shut the fuck up. Not that they care who says what, but well, you pick up that it's not a good thing to lie about. Scary as fuck walking by that lone mansion out in the forest. Bigger than your family's and built right into the mountain. All kinds of rumors of tunnels and whatnot. Anyway, the kids that are from that family stand out no matter what names they use. Everyone knows them, everyone is afraid of them." Mat shook his head. "You stop lying about belonging the minute they look into your eyes and know you're lying, that you could never be one of them or know what they know."

"Was it one of the Awy that saved you?"

Mat looked startled and laughed sharply. "Oh, hell no." He stopped. "I don't know what they would've done if they'd found me. Maybe finished me off and buried me, if I was lucky. No, when I woke up, I was sixteen or so feet off the ground, swinging back and forth like a ragdoll in a dog's mouth." He laughed and the echo bounced off the basement ceiling. Wonder filled his voice. "There were these huge legs moving through the snow. One was like the feathered leg of a giant bird, banded and scaly like a raptor's, and the other was furry like a bear's. I didn't see the back, but whatever it was walked with a gait like a quadruped, and I remember thinking it should smell terrible, but it didn't. *He* didn't. He smelled like sap, like when I was young and snapped the heads off dandelions. That bitter, milky green fragrance, but golden like the dandelion sunshine fluff of the flower head." Mat's expression changed as his eyes sparkled. "Summer and spring smells, rich, loamy soil, and rotting leaves, but always green. People say cut grass, but it's like this." Mat lifted the packing moss up under Ruin's nose. He laughed again and grinned. "Sounds crazy, doesn't it? Like I clocked my head against a tree and hallucinated the whole thing."

Ruin smiled back. "Yeah."

A Holy Venom

Mat laughed. "I tell you the single most important memory of my life and that's what you say. 'Yeah'." He shook his head again. "Look." The older man dragged his smock up and showed Ruin the side of his ribs.

Leaning closer, Ruin stared at the indented scars running along Mat's ribs and back. "What the hell made those?"

"Teeth. Well, fangs, really. He carried me as carefully as he could, but his teeth are sharp. Carried me those last few miles to the Awy and left me in their care. The Aya said they found me bloody and delirious on the stone altar outside the sacred entrance to the caves, like a dead mouse left on a porch." Mat's expression dimmed and he looked back at the amber bottles in silence. "One of the Eldest saved me—Amrwyn. The Awy say his original skin was stolen because it was the most beautiful of all and he had to make a replacement from his dead children's cast-offs. That's why he looks like that. He wears a skin stitched together from leftover parts of the dead."

Ruin stared at him incredulously. "The Earth Father saved you and the forest witches trained you. Now you're here doing this? Making the Rot?"

"Aya got the sickness out of me. Not just the alcohol, but the original sickness. I've been ill since, well, since before I was born. I'd spent my life being an asshole, seeking something I couldn't put into words. I thought it was love." He gave Ruin a rueful look. "I thought I loved those women, but all I was doing was trying to find someone stronger, someone worth living for because I hated myself. When I looked at them, I saw beauty and strength. Everything I wanted to be and knew I wasn't. But the Awy made me fix myself, *be* myself. Taught me the way of the outcast clan—power for power, medicine for medicine, and change for change." He smiled at Ruin. "You must've been a few years old when they sent me here to the Teahouse. Your parents brought you over the water a year later and your dad came to see me. We'd talk shit about the old days and go for a ride together."

"You mean hide from my mom in your garage," Ruin laughed. "Dad always came to the Teahouse to get away from her when she tried to get him into one of the family businesses."

"That too," Mat frowned. "Your mother was never overly fond of me, but she was better than some others I could mention …"

Ruin grimaced. "Uncle Bee and Uncle Dee couldn't leave—"

"They're pompous assholes full of their own self-importance." Scowling,

Mat furiously packed the last few bottled into the crate. "Thankfully, we won't run into them in Grava, fucking assholes. Neither of them ever called to check on you, never wrote, never sent you—"

"Grava?" Ruin glanced at the crates. "Is that where you're going?"

"Where *we're* going." The herbalist paused. Tamping the lid into place, Mat grumbled under his breath and placed the next crate on the table. "Nobody said anything about your new relationship to Lu either, did they?" He studied Ruin's face and then shook his head.

"What are you talking about?"

"Never mind. If they didn't tell you yet, then I'm not going to say the wrong thing and have Aych jump down my throat. Or worse."

Ruin leaned over the worktable and stared into Mat's face. "What the fuck is going on?"

Mat avoided his gaze. "Not for me to say. As it is, I told you too much about the Rot and about other things. Better for you not to know."

"That's not fair. If you know something, you should tell me!"

Mat paused, uncertain. "All I know is Lu is going to put you under her protection once she's able, once Aych is back with the sacred water. Then Lu will be restored."

Ruin watched him. The herbalist began packing with rushed, nervous movements. "There's something you're not telling me. I'm not a kid."

"I told you everything. Honest."

"No, there's something else. Out with it." Ruin turned Mat to face him. "What else besides we're all going to Grava?"

"We're not all going," Mat added guiltily. "Just Lu, you, and me. I don't know what they're planning to do with Ky. Once Lu's restored and you're under her protection, you'll need to stay with her."

"What about Aych?"

"I don't know. They didn't tell me anything. Lu said to pack what I could and that the three of us were going alone. When I asked the Aya, she said Aych couldn't be around you, that you could only be around Lu…"

Ruin dropped his hands and numbly stared at the glass bottles in the half-packed crate. Silently, he took another bottle, wrapped it mechanically and tucked it inside.

"It's an important thing that Lu's going to help you with," Mat said softly. "You won't have to worry about the—"

"I understand," Ruin replied, his voice flat. "Everyone is doing what they think is the best for me ... like they always have."

☾

Aych dropped Tosh's limp body into the chair next to Mudon and tied the hands of the two unconscious detectives. The hum of multiple industrial vacuums began to die as the theatre staff stopped their work and watched. Vetch stared at the detectives then raised his head and whistled. At the sound, the security and stage crew converged a few feet from the only table standing in the middle of the wreckage. Seated across from the two detectives, Violet set a silk bag embroidered with flowers on the tattered tablecloth.

Aych looked around the theatre at the gathered humans' solemn expressions. "If you're ready, Vee, I can wake up the salts."

"You may," Violet nodded and folded their hands onto the table. "Let us begin."

Aych made a show of slapping the two detectives awake and withdrew their enchantment. "Nap time is over." The detectives groaned groggily.

Vetch reached over and slapped Mudon. "Wake the fuck up."

"Easy, *pen-lm*," Violet admonished. "See, they are coming around."

Tosh's eyes opened. She shot up from the chair. Aych dropped a heavy hand on her shoulder and pushed the detective back into her seat. Next to her, Mudon stirred and looked up, licking blood off the corner of his mouth.

Mudon nodded. "*Tau-lm*." He looked across to Violet. "I apologize for the damage done to your house."

Violet shifted in their seat and looked across the jumble of overturned tables and broken chairs and the shattered mirrors behind the bars. Only after they had swept the entire theatre with their gaze did the elder look back at Mudon. "This is nothing! When Honey and Ruby fight over a client, it takes days to fix. This will be a few more hours. By tomorrow night, there will be only beauty, only music, only pleasure."

They looked at Tosh and then back at Mudon. "But tonight, I'm afraid…"

Tosh turned her head and laughed. "You can't be planning anything that rough. Too many witnesses." She tried to get up. Aych thumped her back down into the chair.

Nodding, Vetch leaned into the detective's face. "It's tradition. They are as much the house as the doors you assholes kicked open, the costumes you ripped and threw on the—"

"Don't waste your time," Mudon cut him off. "She doesn't care if the Tank disrespected your house."

"So we messed your pretty things?" Tosh bared her teeth at Vetch and then at Aych. "We hurt your feelings? Pulled your VIP party down into the dirt where it belongs?"

"Oh, young woman, I should say you rather did more than that!" Violet leveled a piercing stare at Tosh. "My family creates an oasis of joy out of their hard work, their endless effort. From the scullery to the attic, everyone here produces exceptional art." They looked at Tosh in disgust. "While you and yours," they waved at the damaged furniture, "only remind people of the despair waiting outside."

"You think you can intimidate us?" Tosh glared back.

"It is tradition," Mudon shot her a quelling look. "On the Night of Two Doors, to have justice delivered in public."

She stared at him. "You're just going to sit there while these fucks—"

Vetch slapped Tosh across the mouth. "You will too, unless you want me to tape your mouth shut, *pikeen*." He pointed at a roll of duct tape on the table.

Mudon closed his eyes and then looked at Violet. "If I offer to accept responsibility…"

"That will come later. First, we let fate tell us what they wish." Violet undid the strings on the silk pouch and withdrew a deck of cards. With practiced dexterity, the proprietor shuffled the deck with a smooth flourish.

Aych leaned next to Tosh's ear. "I love this part. How they get the cards to dance around like that. Don't you?"

"Fuck you," Tosh growled.

Aych squeezed Tosh's windpipe.

"*Tau-vik-lm*, your patience, please," Violet gave Aych a pleading look. "Once the cards decide, you may have one of them."

A Holy Venom

Aych shrugged and released Tosh.

"Now, your senior already knows this, but you do not." Violet cut the deck into thirds and then restacked it before looking at Tosh. "High card goes out the front door, low card goes out the other way." Violet glanced over their shoulder to the pile of broken wood lying on the stage. "I should have very much liked to have had Aych use Lu's new magic cabinet for its intended purpose. But as you children seem to have broken it," they glanced from Mudon over to Aych, "I shall have to impose on you, *Tau-vik-lm*, to find the correct exit."

Aych patted the top of Tosh's head while looking at Mudon. "I'm hoping this one goes out the front."

Stricken, Mudon opened his mouth to protest.

Vetch laughed and looked at Violet. "He gets it...but this one," he jerked his head at Tosh.

"Ah, yes, always a disappointment to have to explain the trick." Violet rolled their eyes and smiled apologetically to the theatre staff. Looking back at Tosh, they dealt two cards face down in front of both detectives. "What Detective Tosh fails to understand is that the dogs have been watching the Velvet. All of our entrances into the venue tonight were observed and recorded, except two." They tapped the backs of the cards. "When one of the salts manages to walk out the front door unharmed, there will be questions. Whatever story they give will not be believed and they will be at once on the receiving end of the dogs' displeasure."

"A short stay under their tribunal getting chewed on, and then the rest of your life at the Stat," Vetch stated as he crossed his arms.

Violet laid the rest of the deck aside. "However, the other one of you will go out the secret way you both came in. Given as payment to our Demon to do with as they wish."

"To drop in the Twins, you mean," Tosh glared up at Aych. "Fucking murderer, we know all about you, you sick fuck."

"You must think so poorly of me, that I'm so unoriginal." Aych pressed a hand against their chest. "Not tonight, gorgeous. Tonight, the lucky winner gets to help me ask fate my own questions. Human entrails reveal the future—even under streetlamps." They smiled at Mudon.

"You heard that!" Tosh yelled. "Now you're all accessories! They threatened a—"

Vetch slapped a piece of duct tape over Tosh's mouth. "Been wanting to do that for a while now. Sorry, Vee."

Violet gave a demure shrug then reached for the card in front of Tosh. "One can never be too sure of the outcome when using inexperienced actors." With a manicured fingernail, they flipped over Tosh's card.

Aych grinned. "Oh, the irony." They shared a look with Vetch.

"Not over yet." Vetch glanced at the card in front of Mudon. *"Five hundred says his card's higher,"* he yelled to the crowd.

Violet leaned back while the other staff shouted their own bets.

"That's a tough call," Aych said, looking into Mudon's eyes. "If he goes out the front, and his junior with me, it will cut him to the bone."

"Really?" Vetch put both his hands on Mudon. "Way I see it, he can go to his grave with a clear conscious. Tipped off his real *pen-lm*, that whistle he sent in." He smiled malevolently at Tosh. "Mudon saved Ky, his favorite, and you found out, so you got revenge by handing Ky over to your owners."

"I did it so Ky would warn Lu," Mudon glanced at Violet. "I knew he would warn the house in advance, *tau-lm*." He looked back at Tosh. "I've always known you were on the leash."

"After that, how can Fate not walk him out the front door like the shepherd she is?" Aych shook their head at Vetch.

"You're not taking my bet, then?" Vetch leaned forward and set his finger on the card in front of Mudon.

"Not that one. Try this instead. Five hundred says the senior tries to go swimming in the Twins before the dogs pick him up."

"The dogs are going to get him the minute his foot hits the red carpet," Vetch shook his head. "I'll wager a grand he doesn't make it off the avenue."

"Done," Aych smirked at Vetch and then nodded to Violet.

The theatre staff crowded close as Violet turned over the second card in front of Mudon. Shouts and groans echoed through the theatre.

☾

Stepping out of In Between, Aych paused and adjusted the cuffs of their formal dress shirt. Behind them, snow tapped against the glass doors leading out onto the ceremonial balcony of the Basilica Palace. In front, heavy drapes, embroidered with images of the Shepherd's tale, hid them from sight. Recorded music swept through the curtains while a fire snapped in the ancient hearth at the far end of the chamber. Over the recorded drums and woodwinds, live cymbals and bells rang as a woman's silhouette danced across the flagstones. Smiling, Aych waited patiently as Lu performed before the roaring flames, their inhuman sight caching the echoes of serpents writhing in the shadows.

As the music ended, a single set of human hands applauded wildly. Lu's whirling silhouette became still. A young woman's voice murmured compliments as Aych inhaled the scents of opulent incense, fine wines, and mingled sweat over the aroma of burning oak.

"Then if you're certain, I shall call for them," Lu's voice rang out. "Come then, oh dread spirit of the mountain, for you are at last summoned."

On cue, Aych stepped out and inclined their head to their audience. The young woman at Lu's feet gasped and brought a startled hand to her mouth.

Lu dropped a soothing hand to the woman's head and smiled. "Be not afraid of the Shepherd's emissary. Have I not promised you that no harm shall come from their hands to your person?"

The High Priestess stood up, the firelight shining through the silk slip covering her body. Aych moved their gaze to meet Lu's and smiled. "You called, and I've come, sorceress."

Growing bold, the young woman let go of Lu's hand and stepped closer to Aych, her face lit up with excitement. "You are not human, then?" She glanced back at Lu and, seeing her smile, the High Priestess looked at Aych. "Are you the Shepherd himself? There is a prophecy that he will return, reborn. His bloodline is sacrosanct—"

"I am myself. What that is—it is not for me to say." Aych winked.

Lu stepped over to a table set close by the fire and poured a glass of wine. She held it out to the High Priestess. "Offer the spirit a cup of hospitality and speak your desire."

Excited and caught up in the moment, the woman quickly took the wine glass from Lu's hand. With quick steps, she carried it to Aych.

Violets and woodsmoke, sex, and snakeskin. Aych gently caressed her hand as they took the glass. "What would you have of me, servant of the Saint?"

The trace scents of other humans, hidden in concealed locations around the chamber and watching, amused Aych. *They think this is all staged for a fantasy setup. Some group sex, which they're more than happy to observe. Perverts and fools, every last one.*

"Our mutual friend," the High Priestess gestured at Lu. "Tells me that you are a dread spirit, birthed from this mountain, much like the Shepherd. Are you truly such a thing?"

"I am." Aych smelled the wine. The odor was without a secondary scent, only fermented grape and the ghost of the grape must. "What of it?"

"Will you show me?" A girlish joy shone in her eyes. "I long to see a true miracle. It's not that I don't believe," her gaze dropped to the crystal glass and the pale wine. Shyly, she looked back up. "But I want to see with my own eyes what the Saint saw when she came to this sacred mountain. When she met the Shepherd and gave him her promise."

"And passion," Lu murmured.

"And passion." Blood rose to warm the woman's face and with the heat, her scent was infused with desire.

"There is a price to pay for such things. Are you willing to pay it?" Aych closed the gap between their bodies and gazed into her eyes. "It is not a small thing, not a trinket. Not a thing you can bargain out of later."

"My very life itself." The woman, barely out of girlhood, breathed the words, carried away in the drama of the moment.

Lu stepped up behind the human and placed a hand on her shoulder. "It is not a game, not now. What stands before you is indeed death. Not an actor, not a safe charade that will leave you with a memory in the morning." Lu looked up into Aych's eyes. "I name you Eater of Bones, Eater of Blood, Eater of Flesh. You are Death itself. Are you not so?"

"I am," Aych replied. They leaned closer to the human's face. "Your advisor speaks the truth. Let there be no lies or betrayals between us. Should you ask this miracle of me, then by your own hand you shall give me your life and I shall take it to do with it as I will." *The perverted sacks of lust hiding under the bed must be squirming by now.*

Girlish foolishness shaped the woman's answer. "My life for the miracle of seeing you as you are in truth. Spirit of the mountain, I give you my life as the Saint gave hers."

A Holy Venom

Lu leaned and whispered in her ear. "Be warned, dear one. Never again shall you lie in my, or anyone's embrace. Never again shall you wear the vestments of the Saint, nor shall you grow old or wield power in the Palace. I warn you one last time," Lu looked up at Aych. "Death stands before you in truth. Do not think yourself safe from them."

"So be it. I shall see God's miracle as the Saint did before me," the High Priestess whispered. She leaned against Aych. "I pledge my life, my flesh, my blood, my very bones, to you. Do with me as you wish. Only show me the Shepherd's true face."

"I can only show you my own, and then only one of them, for the other would be unbearable, even for a moment. Agreed?"

"Agreed!"

"Pledge it to me then, with this cup of hospitality offered with your own hands."

Lu stepped back as Aych brought the glass of wine to the High Priestess's lips. The woman drank it down eagerly. Moving away from the fire, Lu began to sway, the bangles and bells in her costume chiming as she danced.

Releasing the restraint of being Little, Aych watched as the High Priestess's eyes widened. The white skin of Aych's face tore as their muzzle ripped through, the flesh dropping bloody gobbets of meat on the carpet. The pain swirled as their fangs erupted and the swelling agony began. *Five, four, three, two ...* They delighted as screaming erupted from the hidden panels in the chamber walls. *Let madness take the fools.* As the human in front of them began to swoon, Aych caught her, their monstrous body tearing free of the last vestiges of their human form, spraying the High Priestess with blood and ichor.

Laughing, Lu leapt behind the priestess and wrapped her arms over the woman's gore-coated torso. Embracing them both, Aych indulged in a long undulating howl, louder than the screams of the Palace staff. As the guards tumbled through the chamber doors, Aych carried Lu and their shared prize In Between, the wine glass slipping from the Priestess's hand and shattering on the flagstones.

☽

Kiarna Boyd

A boy startled awake. Bitter smoke stung his eyes. The ceiling around the drapes of his four-poster bed was hazy. Coughing, he threw back the blankets and bedding, covering his mouth and nose with the sleeve of his pajamas. Smoke slithered across the ceiling and crept in through the edges of his bedroom door. He fell to his knees and crawled under the bed, away from the churning smoke. The wide wooden boards of the mansion felt hot under his belly. Trying to keep one sleeve over his nose and mouth, he crawled to the far side of the venerable bed. Stars twinkled through the leaded glass windows in the reading nook, the light wavering as his eyes teared up. Panic propelled him out and up onto the window seat. Smoke burned his lungs as he slapped the window lock open and threw back the swinging panel. Crisp autumn air rushed in, and then the smoke began streaming by him as the draft pulled it. Flames licked through the cracks of his door.

Unsure if he was awake or asleep, the boy sat on the windowsill and stared out at his family estate. The lawn below was awash with shadows and leaping golden light. Pillars of roaring flames jutted out of the windows to either side of the boy's bedroom; more spilled from the high, peaked roof. He pulled back his head as slates fell from the roof.

Over the roar of the fire and the sound of glass breaking, there was a weird absence of noise. No fire alarms squealed with tyrannical insistence, nor were there any incoming S&P sirens like the shows on television. No adult voices called out for him. Only the creaking and thudding of the ancient timbers and heavy stone that comprised his home, now falling apart.

He opened his mouth to yell for his parents and inhaled a lungful of smoke. Coughing, he watched as the inner wall of his room peeled open and ragged tongues of flame ran along from floor to ceiling, seeking fuel.

The lawn swept down the hill to the dark edge of the garden hedges. No emergency lights or S&P vehicles raced up the gravel drive, and the distant lights of the city were only a faint glow through the billowing haze. A window one floor down shattered, and flames reached upwards clawing for the boy. Fire at his back, fire below, the smoke stinging his eyes; the boy felt trapped. There was no water in the room to wet his shirt with—like in the drills they taught at school. Suddenly, he remembered his mom showing him what was stored in the window seat. In a rush, he threw the cushion

A Holy Venom

pad off and tried not to stare as the flames leapt to grab the fabric. Hypnotic, the white and golden serpents were eating the drapes on his bed, clambering over the mantel of his unused fireplace and marching in a line across the braided rug relentlessly toward him.

The boy heaved the heavy, rolled bundle of the rope ladder out of the seat and threw the bulk of it out the window. The anchored ends went taut inside the exposed chest. The rungs slapped against the stone wall, the length of the ladder disappearing into the flames rising from the floor below. The sight of the burning ladder cracked the boy's heart. He knew the lack of his parents' voices signaled something bad. Everything had gone wrong; no help from outside, no S&P, no fire department, no alarms. He knew firsthand people hated his family and wished them all dead.

If he tried to jump, he would break all of his bones. If he tried to climb down, the fire would burn him; but if he stayed, he would die from the smoke—if the roof didn't collapse on him first. He wanted to curl up under the bed and wait to die, but some angry, awful part of himself was waking up. It was screaming and fighting, like a furious toddler, hysterical and implacable in its demands. *Someone, anyone, help me!* The scalding heat of frustration and resentment shook the boy. *No one is coming this time. No one.* Grabbing the edges of the window frame, he stared at the night sky and the long drop to the ground and threw himself out of the burning house. Falling, he closed his eyes and braced for the coming waves of agony.

Instead, he heard rough laughter and something hard pushed him backward. There was a lurching, disorienting sense of falling and then being still, being held. Wool scratched under his cheek, and recognizable perfume replaced the stink of smoke. When he opened his eyes, a stranger smiled at him, their face not clearly a man's nor a woman's, the skin ghostly white. The reflected flames of the burning mansion shimmered in the stranger's mismatched eyes. The boy recognized those eyes. They weren't human eyes.

Setting the boy gently down on the ground far from the house on the edge of the lawn, the stranger took their wool coat off and draped it over the boy's shoulders. "If you'd waited a minute, I would've gotten you down here the easy way."

"I hate being burned." Sitting on the grass and leaves, the boy stared at his home. It had become an inferno. "You're not going to save my parents?"

"There's no one alive in there."

"Are you sure?"

"Yes, I'm sure."

"I remember you," the boy glanced over. "You smell the same and your eyes are the same, but you looked different last time." He tried not to think of his parents asleep in their bed. He tried not to think of anything.

"I was Big then. Now I'm Little." The stranger's tone was matter-of-fact.

Inside his head, the boy knew he was broken. A normal child would be crying and trying to save his parents. *A normal boy would...* He stopped and stood up. "Why are you here? Did you set the fire?" His voice sounded strange, like a recording. *Like the therapists' voices when they ask hard questions...*

"No. I don't like getting burned either." The stranger shrugged. "You asked me to help you, so I came when you called out."

I called out? When? Stunned, the boy stared up. "Will you always come? When I need help?"

The stranger paused, their expression troubled. They shrugged again. "When I can, sure. When I can't, you'll have to manage on your own."

The sirens were finally coming up the hill, the long whines bouncing off the gravel, the red and blue lights dappling through the leaves of the trees further down the drive. The boy watched, wondering if someone had been bribed to slow the response time. There was a terrible realization creeping up about what life was going to be like, and he wanted to scream. He knew if he did, the people in the cars would put him in a backseat and drive him to the Statler and he'd be locked in his aunt's suite again, next to his sad, screaming uncle.

Resolute, the boy pulled the coat tight and looked into the stranger's eyes. "Will you take me some place again? Like last time when you brought me here. Can you take me to a Teahouse in the city? It's across from a theatre called The Velvet Door. My uncle," the boy paused. "He's not my real uncle, but he's my dad's friend, he runs the Teahouse. He can pay you if you bring me there tonight. I have a room there and everything."

"You don't want to go with the salts, is that it?" The stranger was watching the firetrucks and the emergency crews slowly start their duties. "Not that I blame you. Fuckers," they said, closing their blue eye and watching the boy with the other eye. "I'm not a cab service and I've got money enough. You can walk or take your chances with the salts. One favor per night is more than I'm comfortable with."

"I'll trade you something you don't have." The boy squared off, facing them. "I can sing pretty good. I even won a competition. I bet no one has ever written you a song. If you take me to the Teahouse, I'll sing you a song. Just for you."

The stranger stared and then laughed. "You've been sucking smoke like a chimney tonight, kid. Save your pipes." They held out a hand. "If you want to get out of here that badly, I'll oblige. But don't make it a habit. We'll be going In Between and then I will become Big to get us to the city faster. Don't scream or piss yourself. You can keep my coat on."

The boy put his chin up. "I didn't freak out last time when you were Big, did I?"

"No, you did not." The stranger held out their hand expectantly. "You coming or not?"

"I can sing when…"

"It's called The Silent Woods for a reason, kid."

"My name is Ruin." The boy took the offered hand. "Not kid."

"Is it?" They looked at him for a moment. "You can call me Aych. Do us both a favor and zip it until we get to this Teahouse of yours. Got it?" Before the boy could reply, Aych carried them In Between.

☾

Ruin stepped out of the bath in the Unity Suite, toweling his long hair dry, and found Aych in front of the open balcony door, smoking. "You found me. I was taking a nap earlier and dreamt about you."

"You don't sound particularly happy about it," Aych glanced over and flicked their cigarette out into the frigid night. They shut the glass doors. "Would you prefer to be alone?"

Quietly padding across the harlequin floor tiles, Ruin went over toward the massive bed piled high with pillows and bolsters. "I wasn't sure you'd think to look here."

Aych watched him for a moment and walked over to the opposite side of the bed. "Process of elimination. The salts are likely watching the Teahouse, so Mat would have warned you off going there. You wouldn't want me going round to your apartment, in case your boyfriend is there. And you wouldn't want to spend the night in the Stat in your uncle's suite. Then I remembered you telling me you could always get a room for free at the most expensive hotel in the city." They paused and looked over the expansive luxury of the room with a thoughtful expression. "I did check and see if you were at my place first."

"You don't have any plumbing. And after what happened earlier with Ky and my ... the shit-bag, I needed a shower." He held Aych's gaze for a moment. "And Shine's my *ex*-boyfriend now." Ruin sat on the edge of the bed and lowered the towel. "Were you going to tell me? Or were you going to disappear tomorrow and leave it to Lu to break the news?"

Aych wrinkled their nose. "I may yet kill that herbalist."

"Mat didn't do anything wrong," Ruin shot Aych an annoyed look. "He assumed I already knew, that's all." He turned his back and studied Aych's reflection in the mirrored closet doors. Ruin searched for something neutral to say. "How did things go with Lu tonight? Is everything all set?"

"Lu's happy. She got to do the performance she's always wanted and roped me into a starring role." Aych sat down on the bed. "Finally got me to say her tawdry lines."

Ruin shrugged on a thick bathrobe, dropped his towels on the floor, and looked over his shoulder. "You make it sound like you don't like it, but I know you enjoy playing those fucked-up games with her. You'll miss all the drama when she—when *we*—leave."

"It's true." Aych leaned back on the mammoth assortment of bedding and opened their arms, gesturing for Ruin to come and lie down with them. "She's got a flare for the dramatic, that one. Terrible playwright, though. The over-the-top shit she had me say."

"You're used to acting," Ruin closed the fluffy hotel robe, laid back into the crook of Aych's arm, and nestled his head on their shoulder. "You're always pretending to be something you're not. Both of you."

"Can't stampede the herd." Aych pressed their lips against the top of Ruin's damp head and inhaled the scent of their favorite human. "Lu gets mad if I make a scene she didn't write."

A Holy Venom

"Why does Ky know about your heart and I don't?" Ruin shifted to look at Aych. "Is it true?" He spread his hand over Aych's chest, feeling through their dress shirt. "Does he know your real name?"

"I didn't tell him," Aych let Ruin feel the breath rising and falling and laid their hand gently over his. "The hunter's got magic of his own, the prying fuck. It's not like I want him to know. Or you. Such things only cause trouble."

"You never talk about it. About the House and what happened to you there." Ruin slipped a finger through the buttoned edge of Aych's shirt.

"What would you have me say? Once upon a time, there was a ..." Aych caught his hand and sat up roughly. "It doesn't matter. None of that shit matters." They gave Ruin a teasing smile. "You should understand, considering how much you hate your given name."

"At least I told it to you." Glancing away, Ruin paused. "You never told me yours ... or about your heart."

"It's gone. All burned up." Kissing his fingers, Aych winked at Ruin. "The only thing the hunter would find in that Stove is his own stupid ass being slow-roasted."

"I don't even know how to pronounce it."

Exasperated, Aych sighed. "Who fucking cares? It's not important. Getting Lu what she needs so she can give you what you need. *That's* all that matters."

Tugging his fingers loose, Ruin shook his head. "You only let me get so close and never even an inch closer." Rolling away, he moved to the edge of the bed, his back to Aych. All the pent-up emotion, the ache and the fear whispered harsher words than the imp chorus ever could. *Aych doesn't want you. You're not good enough—not smart or glamorous like Lu, not strong or fast like Ky. What are you? A constant shit show. Just a kid they've been supervising; now they're tired of you. Yet here you are, pushing, always pushing.* The grasping, shameful desire flared again. "Do you even know how the fuck I feel? What it's like to want someone to want you. I feel fucking desperate all the time. Like I'm going to say the wrong thing and you'll leave. Or I'll miss my chance to say the right thing and you'll leave. You have no idea what it's like to have the one person you give a shit about so close and yet further away than the ends of the fucking world."

His breath caught in his throat at the thought of going to Grava. *Where would Aych go? Back to the Silent Woods? Stay here in the city? Did it matter? They wouldn't be with him; they wouldn't be looking for him. Not anymore.* The pain of it, the shadow of separation loomed large. "I'm not talking about fucking. It's the wanting, the desire to be important, to have that returned. It hurts more than not being *allowed* to have sex with you. Everyone else in this city can fuck you except me. You want everyone in this city except me. The one fucking person I love the most doesn't want me."

"I'm not having this fight." Aych swung their legs over the edge of the bed. "I don't want to fight about this again. Not tonight."

"Last chance, then. After tomorrow there won't be any more fights, any more anything. Will there?" Ruin's voice went low and ragged with anger. "You're going to run the job like you do anything else with Lu and then expect me to be a good kid and do what I'm told and never fucking see you again. When you say you want me to be free, you mean free of *you*. Free of me." Ruin rolled the pain over his tongue, scalding himself with more unspoken accusations. *Anything I say will make it worse. There's no magic words to bring them closer, to make them want me.*

Aych paused. "You'll be free. Free of that shit-bag, free of this place. I get why you might resent having to go with Lu, I do. But that's not forever. Eventually, the bond will be strong enough and you can go wherever the fuck you want, and her influence will protect you. Like Mat. He doesn't have to stay on his shitty, backwater island, he can travel the damn world and you'll be able to do the same. So yeah," they placed their hands on Ruin's shoulders and turned him. "It is unfair right now, but in the long run, you'll be free of all the shit. I'm sorry if it hurts to hear, but I'm not going lie. Not tonight. Tomorrow you'll go with Lu. Without me."

"So you do mean I'll be free of you." Ruin's body shook with anger and grief. "And you'll be free of me."

Aych's gaze remained steady. "I'll never be free of you. Would never want to be and can never be." Their expression softened. "The hunter might know a thing or two, but he's dead wrong about the important shit. You can't trust a human with mystery. They fuck it all up, trying to tell it so it makes them sound important and they end up spitting out garbled nonsense. You have my heart—or whatever the fuck is left of it."

A Holy Venom

The tears came hot and fast, blurring Ruin's vision. "Then why won't you stay with me? Why send me with Lu? Are you lying when you tell me that you love me?"

Instantly Aych's arms were around him. Ruin felt their lulling, inhuman aroma envelope his senses.

"I've told you before, if we get too close, I'm afraid the same fucked up shit will happen between us. I don't want to pull your strings, get in your head, make you kill people. My influence can be as evil as—"

"I don't care if you possess me. I don't want you to not be with me." Ruin shoved Aych roughly onto the bed. "I want to fuck you. I want you. Always." He half yelled and half growled as he climbed over, his tears and anger spilling out uncontrollably. "I want you with me. You belong to me."

"I want you too," Aych stroked Ruin's face. "But I need you to be free. I can't have you with me because of that shit."

"I don't want—"

"Too bad." Aych leaned up and kissed him. "It's not fair and I'm a monster and it snows too much and Mat's an irritating idiot and Lu gets cold too easily. And Ky's a dumbass and he's going to slow me down and fuck everything up tomorrow. It's all stupid and a pain." They cradled Ruin's face between their massive hands. "But I love you and that means I'm not going to do to you what that piece of shit attached to your family has been doing for generations. I can't change what I am, but I'm not going to start haunting the human I love like a third-rate ghost because I can't control myself. We tried. This doesn't work and it sucks, but that's the truth." They glanced at the pile of pillows. "You can sleep next to me or I can leave now."

Leaning over Aych, Ruin braced both arms against the bed. He sat back straddling Aych's waist. "If your plan tomorrow works and Lu's restored, she's going to claim me so no evil spirit can possess me. If that's all true, give me one good reason we shouldn't do whatever the fuck we want tonight." He brought his face to Aych's and stared into their eyes. "If she can permanently sever the connection between me and the shit-bag tomorrow, she can sever it with you, can't she?"

Aych blinked slowly and then stared back in stunned silence. *Retreat, hold, or advance?*

Ruin bared his teeth. "Right. Then if you've got nothing to say, you can nod your consent, and I'm going to do to you all the things I've been waiting all these fucking years to do." He grabbed the edges of Aych's shirt and ripped it open. "And don't tell me I'm not old enough or some shit. You're either in or you're out."

Throwing back their head, Aych laughed and then growled, stretching their long arms up under the pillows. "This is a very bad idea ... so how can I not be all in?"

Advance!

TWENTY

THE CITY SLID BY as Lu's limo rolled through the snowy early morning streets, skirting the slower snowplows. Dawn-painted clouds glowed silver amid the spires of the academic district, the sunrise muted by the limo's tinted windows. In the back of the car, Lu, Mat, and Ky huddled, anticipation heavy in the air. Ky yawned and nodded, holding out his mug as Lu offered him more coffee from her thermos.

Mat eyed the duffel bag by Ky's feet with suspicion. "You're sure they won't break accidentally? That's a hell of a chemical reaction waiting to happen."

Lu rolled her eyes.

Ky shook his head at the herbalist. "I used disposable gloves from the nurses' station." He gulped down a mouthful of coffee. "The impact will need to be strong enough for the shrapnel to slice through."

"But if the knots you tied…"

"Mat, it will be fine." Recapping the thermos, Lu leaned over and looked out the window. "Nothing is going to blow up, explode, catch fire, or leak."

"If you say so." The older man glanced uncomfortably at the bag on the floor.

Ky took another pastry out of the cardboard box on the seat next to Mat. The powdered sugar left a thin trail on Ky's leather and dusted his faded black jeans. "Won't we be walking in during the middle of morning mass?"

"We'll have an hour to ourselves." Lu sipped her coffee. "Aych will meet us inside and review the plan." She glanced at Mat and Ky. "We'll keep an eye on things on this side while you two slip over to the Woods. You'll have fifteen minutes—more than enough time to get in and get out before the poor deluded flock shows up on this end."

Mat focused on Lu and folded his hands. "You used the *tau-ve-vik* potion to kill the High Priestess last night? Aych didn't eat them?"

Lu laughed. "I can assure you and your employers, the exalted and dearly departed High Priestess died from your distillation of *tau-ve-vik,* not from any other injury."

"Wait! You *murdered* the High Priestess?" Ky looked back and forth between his companions. "Putting aside how fucked that is, won't S&P be looking for you?"

"Don't concern yourself." Lu glanced out the window as the car slowed and a guard opened the barrier to the mountain passage to the Basilica. "There weren't any witnesses. No coherent ones, at least. We put on a show that left the seats trying to separate the illusion from reality. I staged it such as to imply she's merely been kidnapped. Searching for her should occupy their efforts for at least a day or two." She lifted a shoulder and dropped it in an elegant half-shrug. "If her death bothers you, think of it as an overdue assassination in a long, drawn-out war."

"And you two are just hired mercenaries lending a hand?" Ky glowered at her. "To get paid by the Awy, *per your agreement.*"

Ignoring Ky's comment, Lu turned back to Mat. "Quite ingenious how you managed to resurrect that particular potion, by the way. How did you ever figure that out?"

"That it could be made from Constalia?" Mat looked pleased to be asked. "The vine orchid came to me in a dream." He glanced at Ky. "It's a liquor they make in Grava; they use the vine orchid as coloring for authenticity. The real recipe was lost thousands of years ago. But the compound, it's preserved in the alcohol, if you know how to extract it. Takes a vast quantity—"

"Forty cases of the stuff, to be precise," Lu interrupted. "Virtually untraceable through the Velvet and the other clubs at our disposal." She smiled. "My orchid chose to tell you her secrets. Impressive. No wonder I like you!"

Looking embarrassed, Mat huddled in his winter coat. "It should grant a painless death to a human, but prolonged sleep to any inhuman…god or other." He glanced up at Lu. "Did the High Priestess suffer?"

"Quite painless, I assure you. Gave her the entire vial, per our agreement.

A Holy Venom

Honestly, one or two drops would've sufficed."

"One vial for you to kill the head of the Church, one vial for Aych to lace the goat," Mat half recited. "That was the deal. The Awy do not want any more out in the world."

"You brought the second vial?" Lu asked Mat in a light, offhanded tone.

Mat nodded. "I wouldn't forget, not something that important, not this morning. Aych would kill me."

Ky cradled his coffee mug and looked at Mat. "Why are the Awy helping Aych and Lu? I get the *'your enemy is my enemy'* aspect, but was it all for the High Priestess's assassination?"

Mat glanced uncomfortably at Lu. "I don't know why the Awy do what they do. I go where I'm told and do what I'm told. They want Lu's venom, and they're interested in Aych and Ruin. That's all I know. If I could go home, I'd be happy to ask, but…"

"Now, now, Grava won't be that bad," Lu patted Mat's hand reassuringly. "You'll both see. I've had the townhouse cleaned and prepared for the four of us. It's got an outdoor pool with views of the original city and the lake. I'm sure you'll feel better once the chill of this frigid hell is out of your bones."

"Four?" Ky glanced over. "Us and …?"

"Ruin," Mat added.

"He'll need to stay with me for a year or so, not too long." Lu shot Ky a speculative look. "Not that you'll mind having him around, I'm sure."

"Not Aych?" Ky glanced between Lu and Mat. "Why aren't they coming with us?"

"You'd have to ask them," Mat muttered.

The limo slowed to a stop. "We've arrived, Lu," the driver announced over the intercom.

"The anticipation of opening night. It never gets old." Lu slipped her sunglasses out of her fur jacket and settled them across the bridge of her nose. "Come along, gentlemen. We are expected in the main chapel."

The trio alighted from the limo and onto the steps of the Basilica. The chimes spilling from the water chains on the statues echoed under the carved dome. Mat nervously looked over his shoulder, watching as the car pulled away. Next to him, Ky crammed the remainder of his pastry in his mouth and brushed powdered sugar off his leather. Ahead of them both, Lu marched up the white stone steps.

Sentries outside the cathedral doors kept their gaze at ceremonial height as the group approached. Mat skirted away from the guards and looked up at the vault of the cathedral as he crossed the threshold. "I don't – "

Lu slipped her arm through the herbalist's and guided him into the massive stone building. "Nobody's home; don't worry if you didn't get an invite." She eased her sunglasses down and glanced around. "And don't worry about the guards. They couldn't stop an infant from stealing candles."

The Basilica hummed with the soft murmur of the Church's early morning routine. The upper recess of the buttressed ceiling was obscured by incense from the new day's sunrise offering. As the sun rose higher through the rose window, a rainbow-colored glow streaked through the churning smoke.

Ky hefted his duffel bag over his shoulder and considered if he had time to light a candle and then catch back up. Relinquishing the whimsy, he followed the others across the marble expanse toward the golden lattice that marked the sanctum.

Mat was whispering to Lu as Ky caught sight of Aych and Ruin seated together in one of the back rows of pews. The pair appeared to be oblivious to anyone else in the main chapel. Ky noticed Ruin's aura was polluted with the same nightmarish black taint he saw seeping out of the Teahouse's garage bays.

"Well, don't you two look blissful. Good night?" Lu slipped into the pew in front of them. Lu glanced back and forth between the two and swatted Aych's arm. "Not such a powerful fount of corrupting influence after all, are you? You still need to run my errand."

"A deal is a deal." Ignoring Lu's teasing, Aych pointedly looked at Ky.

Ruin sat forward, planting a kiss on Lu's cheek. "Oh, they're a bad influence alright." He looked at Ky and motioned to his mouth.

Ky self-consciously scraped a knuckle over his lips, brushing off the crumbs of his breakfast. He reexamined Ruin's aura. The sickly webbing was still present but submerged under the thicker murkiness.

Aych looked at Ky. "You sufficiently recovered enough to play squeaky toy this morning?"

A Holy Venom

"Less squeak, more bang," Ky patted his duffel bag. "As long as you don't keep me waiting, I'm fine." He glanced at Aych's casual outfit and leather coat. "Dressing down today?"

"Not a day to be wearing a suit is all," Aych dropped a kiss on Ruin's head and started to get out of the pew. "Let's get this over with."

"You'll need this. For the goat." Mat slipped his arm over the back of the pew. He glanced at Aych. "Our deal is complete."

"I must be in a good mood. I don't even feel like telling you to go fuck yourself." Aych palmed the vial then glanced back at Ky. "Come on, bright boy. Clock's ticking."

Ky got up and joined Aych. "You going to tell me your plan, or am I improvising?"

"For you, it's simple," Aych pointed ahead at the main altar. "Once we're in front of the House, I'll give you a bag full of meat. Dump it out, ring the dinner bell like I told you, and get your ass behind the woodpile. It's always night in the Woods, so you'll be at a disadvantage when they come at you." Aych pointed at the duffel. "Use your toilet bombs to buy some time. This should only take a few minutes." Aych stopped and put a hand on Ky's chest. "Only thing you have to remember, no matter what—"

"Don't go in the House. I got it." Ky glanced at the altar. "What's the plan if you don't come back and I run out of things to throw?"

Aych shrugged. "If that happens, you'll get torn apart like a goat tossed into a pit of hungry beasts."

"Nice." Ky glowered. "No backup extraction? Can Ruin come get me?"

"No, he cannot." Aych glared. "I'm your one and only ride home. Any other questions, or can we get this fucking over with already?"

Ky looked at the statue of the Holy Mother towering in the back nave of the chapel. It was a half-scale version of the enormous statue Lu had shown him in the chamber below. "I should've lit a candle." Bracing himself, Ky squared off facing Aych. "There's one more thing. I know we're on a tight schedule so I'll make this quick. I don't claim to understand your war against humans and gods, or why you've decided to fight them, but despite the harm and misery you've visited upon people I care about, I'm willing to undertake this mission even if it kills me. But it's going to cost you."

Aych sneered. "Give me one good reason why I shouldn't just throw your ass in as bait right now."

Grabbing Aych by their jacket, Ky yanked them close. "Might be I know the one thing that can hurt you. Maybe you throw me in there and I get you some unwanted attention from the one person you're avoiding."

Aych narrowed their eyes and smiled coldly, glancing down at the human's hand on their chest. "You're bluffing. You wouldn't survive either."

"Then we both die and there are two fewer monsters in this world." Ky stared back into Aych's eyes and let go of their jacket. "Toss my ass in there as bait and you'll find out. Fast." He nodded in the direction of the others. "Then you'll have nothing to bring back. Not even your own ass."

Aych glanced over and met Lu's concerned gaze. "What do you want? Make it quick."

"You hate us so you kill us. I'm not going to ask you to change, but I am going to ask you to honor the risk I'm taking." Ky inhaled and thought of the jackals running off in the evening dust of the desert. "Promise me you'll remember what I do for you today. Honor the risk I'm taking on your behalf by letting some of your victims go. Do that for me and we'll be even. Whether I live or die over there. Don't visit despair and madness on all of those that cross your path. Let a few humans escape. Leave a few cookies in the jar. Let them die another way."

"Bright boy here wants me to go on a diet," Aych snorted and laughed. "Fine, I'll let some run off my plate. Now, you try and not get eaten yourself." Gripping Ky by his shoulders, Aych hauled the hunter In Between.

✳

Calf-deep in snow and buffeted by blustery nocturnal wind, Ky screened his eyes from a flurry of ice crystals and quickly assessed his surroundings. In front of him stood a rustic A-frame cabin built of charred cedar, surrounded on three sides by a weathered porch rising above the snow. The first-floor windows were dark holes in the flat front wall overlooking the porch. The peaked window caps looked to Ky like eyebrows, lending the structure the semblance of a face. At his back, a double row of stacked wood concealed

A Holy Venom

Ky from the tree line. He noted the snow covering the top of the logs and the lack of a trail between the building and the reserve of fuel. No smoke exited the stone chimney that protruded from the steep slate roof. An ominous and oppressive glamour suffused the structure of wood and stone. Malevolence pulsed in waves of feverish hunger. All the residual foulness he had encountered at Haw's home and in Mat's garage, even the taint on Haw's kids and on Ruin, all of it was a dim echo of the swirling vortex of oppression and misery before him. The building felt as if it was expanding and contracting, alternately repulsing Ky and compelling him towards it. The menace beat out in a silent rhythm: *Run. Come. Run. Come.* Ky realized it was matching his heartbeat. The undulating enchantment churned his stomach and pushed the background music out of his mind. He was vaguely aware of a high stone wall to the right of the House that obscured any trace of a garden.

Reaching In Between, Aych pulled out a large burlap sack, handed it to Ky, and then tapped their own wrist with two fingers. Taking the added weight of the bag, Ky felt himself sink further into the snow. He nodded and hefted the heavy bag over his shoulder, keeping watch on the front of the House. Out of the corner of his eye, he saw Aych sprint a short distance and then spring over the high stone wall.

He dumped the contents of the bag out. The meat thumped out onto the snow and Ky glanced down. "Fuck!"

A young woman's severed head stared back at him. Her torso and limbs leaked fresh blood, turning the pristine snow black as he unconsciously took a step away from the High Priestess' remains. Around him, the trees creaked and shuddered as the coppery scent of fresh blood unfurled into the night air.

The staccato of the countersignal flared along the muscles of his back, snapping him to attention. Then the thunder of wings filled the air as an enormous shadow sent ice and snow gusting in a whirlwind across the yard, stinging Ky's face and momentarily blinding him. A gargantuan bird landed on the roof of the cabin. The monstrous Owl's head swiveled to look at Ky as her clawed talons gripped the crest of the roofline. Her eyes glowed and refracted the minimal light. To the left of the yard, the crack and thud of falling trees echoed through the woods. Suddenly, the barren trunks at the tree line splintered as a huge, shaggy Wolf pushed his way out into the clearing, his eyes of eldritch blue fire locked on Ky.

Ky stared back at the colossal beast and cried out, "I offer this to you!" He gestured at the human remains lying in the snow.

"So thoughtful ... a guest to bring us meat," a purring voice murmured over Ky's shoulder.

Ky spun to find a ten-foot-tall ebony Cat balanced on the woodpile behind him. Silver claw tips gripped the exposed wood. Each of the monster's paws was larger than Ky's face.

The feline's massive head snaked down at him while one paw gestured at the decapitated head lying in the snow. "Indeed, now that I see it more closely, you *have* brought us a rare treat!"

"It is not for you, Cat!" Wolf growled. "He offered it to me!"

Cat lashed his tail and narrowed his amber eyes at Wolf. Turning back to Ky, Cat smiled, showing his fangs. "Who did you bring this for, human?"

"I brought the meat for all of you," Ky pushed his legs back through the snow, trying to keep the three beasts in his line of sight. With Cat behind him, Ky had nowhere to run.

"We can see that," Owl blinked her glowing golden eyes. "But such a small morsel is not enough for all of us."

Wolf huffed. Cat laughed a throaty trill, jumped over Ky's head, and started over to the remains. The snow was melting from the still-warm blood.

"I'm warning you, Hairball, don't touch my food!" Wolf raised his hackles and took a stiff-legged step.

Pausing, Cat tilted his head. "We can be civil about this, Brother, can't we? Say, the torso for you, the legs for Sister Owl, and the head and the arms for me?"

"The torso has all the best organs, 'tis not fair!" Owl called. She ruffled her feathers, sweeping her wings over the slate roof in protest.

"The legs have the most muscle," Wolf narrowed his icy, blue eyes at Cat. "You are giving us the prizes. The head and the arms are so paltry. What trickery do you have planned?"

Cat's eyes swept over Ky. "Consider it a race. The first one to finish the main course has an early start on dessert."

A Holy Venom

Owl hooted and bobbed her head, her golden eyes locked on Ky. "True, true! Wolf eats the fastest, so the torso will take him the longest, while you gulp down the head and the arms like wriggly fishes!"

"Your sharp beak will make easy work of the legs, my dear. Perhaps you might even beat me," Cat beamed up at her. He glanced back at Wolf. "What say you then? Is my suggestion to your liking, with the true prize going to the one who finishes their share first?"

"Is it safe to eat?" Owl cocked her head at the bloody snow. "Is it a trick?"

Wolf sniffed the frigid air. "It is holy meat. Stinks of a god's blessing and sacraments: perfume, wine, and sweetness. A life of leisure fed well with fine foods and little work. The meat will be tender and quick to tear. Safe enough for our kind. What say you to Cat's division of it, Owl? Is it fair?"

Owl bobbed her head excitedly. "As I am above and must come down, let us take our shares and begin at the same time."

"Well said, well said," Wolf nodded and looked back at Cat. "We shall each take our meat, then start. The first to finish is the first to start the next course. Agree, us three?"

"Agreed," purred Cat.

"Agreed," cooed Owl.

Ky swung his arms up to protect his face as the three monsters dove for the butchered remains. He gasped as Cat clawed the High Priestess's left arm out and tossed it over the stacked wood. Owl grasped one thigh in her talons, then the second, and lifted off into the air, while Wolf shoved his head in and retrieved the bloody torso. Owl was still in mid-flight carrying her portion away as Wolf snapped his jaws and gulped down half of his. Ky stumbled back as Cat smugly batted the woman's severed head in his direction, her long hair tangling as it rolled through the snow.

Wolf snapped his jaws, devouring the second half of the torso. "How fare thee, my siblings? I have finished mine and now am set to have the prize. I call it." His huge head swung in Ky's direction. "None can complain, for I have finished mine first and earned my dessert!" He launched himself into the air.

✶

AT THE SIDE OF THE SPRING, Aych capped the first bottle and heard the commotion over the high stone wall beyond the garden. The enchanted garden dwelled in summer's twilight dusk within the shadow of the House. While winter reigned beyond the stone walls, bleak and bare and frigid, within the Garden, glossy, deep green foliage and heavy-headed blossoms slumbered in the warmth of the poisonous nocturnal air. Golden-eyed toads watched Aych from their lookout posts along the low stone curb of the spring as glowing, fuzzy-bellied wasps and luminescent speckled bees droned from one deadly flower to the next. Noxious pollen and fatal tufts of seed fluff floated languidly on the calm air, coming to rest on the rippling surface of the pool below the spring's outflow. All was sleepy in the nighttime warmth, the untended beds of flowers and herbs exhaling a perfume of death and dreams.

Suppressing the inclination to stop and check on Ky, Aych pushed the glass bottle In Between, took out another, and unscrewed the cap. The water gushing out of the cleft in the bare rock was colder than the glass and droplets of condensation collected as it splashed into the mouth of the bottle.

Shrieks and yowls of surprise filled the air and Aych looked up. Owl was high over the House, her vast wings sending gusts of cold air into the garden, shaking leaves and raining down ice and snow from the roof. The second bottle filled, Aych pushed it In Between after the first and sprinted for the wall nearest the front of the House.

*

From behind a tree, Ky threw another one-two. As he released it, Owl plummeted out of the sky behind him, her razor-sharp talons spread wide. The countersignal flared up his back in warning. Ky sprinted back into the clearing as Owl swooped down on the tree, her talons grasping empty space. Owl screeched and flung herself back up into the sky. Her wing strokes suddenly became labored and she wobbled. From Ky's left, Cat and Wolf leapt at him. Wolf stumbled as Cat eagerly sprang forward, cutting the larger beast off, and swiped at Ky's head. Holding his duffel bag against his chest, Ky dodged the attack and threw himself sideways behind the woodpile, landing on his side.

Hunkered against the woodpile, Ky readied another one-two. Yowls and growls shook the air. He took a breath, steadying himself. Suddenly, the stack of wood against Ky's back started shaking. The ground under him tipped away as he and half the woodpile fell through a hole. He landed in the bottom of a pit with a thud. Snow and falling wood pelted him as he checked the bag for breakage. Logs and splintered wood tumbled down after him and surrounded him in darkness and the scent of wet soil. Burning colder than flame, a foul-smelling liquid squirted around his head. Ky tried to tear it off as it hardened and he found his hands encased in sticky fibers.

✱

Aych emerged from the wall at a dead run and the ground trembled. They saw Ky's leap and Owl's drugged movements. A second later, Wolf and Cat crashed into one another. Wolf staggered and shook his head, slumping against part of the porch and roof, his enormous head resting over the peak of the front of the House. Cat danced back and then spun about before collapsing flat into the snow. His proud tail drifted lazily then curled against his body and stilled.

As Aych watched the Guardians succumb to Mat's potion, out of the corner of their eye they saw the woodpile shudder and collapse into the ground. Aych rushed over and examined the logs and the abandoned duffel bag below, all strung with a familiar gossamer webbing. The acrid stink of Spider filled their nose. They looked over their shoulder at the House and snarled. *Fucker!*

Aych stood up and flexed their hands, releasing their Little form. Stripping off their clothes, they glanced at Owl, still asleep on the roof. Wolf snored from the side of the porch. A deep depression in the snow stood where Cat had laid, now empty, a deep furrow indicating the direction the beast had wandered off to. Snow swirled around the clearing as the restless wind stirred the sleeping Guardians' fur and feathers.

The steps leading up to the porch were free of snow and warm under the pads of Aych's Big paws. The boards creaked and the House sighed as Aych tapped the doorknob.

"Open to me. No way is ever closed, neither in nor out. I am free to come and go as I please." Aych growled the words and narrowed their eyes as the lock clicked and the bolts inside slid back.

Aych eyed the décor of the quaintly decorated hunting cabin with distrust. "Put it the fuck away, would you?"

The glamour wavered and shimmered, like moonlight on water. The walls sprouted upwards, pushing the ceiling far out of sight. Walls receded darkening from pale wood through a range of grays until hardening into obsidian blocks each taller than Aych. The wooden floorboards slid under packed, hardened dirt and the furniture disassembled itself, stretching and tumbling up the walls to transform into a gigantic worktable, a grubby cot, and a battered chair near the squatting hulk of an iron-bellied Stove. Aych kept watch on the shadows high up in the cobwebbed rafters, moving warily in the direction of the single, small window in the far back above the sink.

The mingled scents of dried herbs, fresh blood, rendered fat, and wood smoke replaced the homey smells of furniture polish and baked goods. Heat drifted in waves from the iron Stove and Aych flexed their claws as they walked past the gigantic cot piled with ancient, greasy sheepskins. The only scent of a living human was that of Ky. Aych stared up at the rafters, sniffing. Near the counter full of crusted bowls and smeared plates, dried blood coated the wooden stump at the foot of the cot. The cleaver embedded in the chopping block was wet with blood. Water dripped quietly from the hand pump mounted to the side of the slate sink, a ring of water pooled around the mounting block. Aych watched as the tattered ghost of a child beat their feeble hands against the dusty glass windowpanes above the sink, trying in vain to escape into the garden. Straggling cobwebs stretched back and forth across the sill and wispy remains of other ghosts struggled within ratty cocoons.

"I'm here, you half-rotten excuse for a bug. Now what do you want?" Aych flexed their claws, longing to stab them deep into Spider's body.

A petulant feminine voice replied from the shadowed rafters above. "I want you to die, slowly and horribly. Preferably in my web, but I'd be delighted if the Owner dissected you and reclaimed all the parts you stole, you foul abomination! You miscreant!"

Aych tried to pinpoint the freshest stink of webbing. "Never going to

A Holy Venom

happen and you know it. So cut whatever line of shit you're trying to get over on me and tell me what you want in exchange for the hunter."

"You think yourself clever, but I'll have you know that I've been tricking you for a long time, my dear. Who do you think has kept you on the line?"

"Blah, blah, and did my laundry, blah blah," Aych sniffed for the stone head, hoping it was with Ky. "Never managed to get me a pair of fucking shoes that fit correctly. Should have guessed only you would be that incompetent."

Something hurtled down from the rafters. "Hoping to locate him with this?" Spider crowed as the stone head clattered next to Aych's clawed feet. "Petty little magicks made by a petty little thing!"

Picking up the stone head, Aych moved closer to the cot. "If you're trying to keep me here, don't push your luck. I can leave any time, with or without the hunter. We both know humans don't leave this place alive."

"And everyone thinks *I'm* the vicious one."

"We're done. I have what I came for." Aych eyed the end of the cot and the distance to the rafters.

"Almost done, yes. You think I'm only going to kill your hunter? Only going to eat his liquified innards? If you don't do what I say, I'll do something worse, something that will haunt you forever."

"Finally!" Aych rolled their eyes. "Just tell me your stupid fucking game so we can get on with it."

"Go to the Stove and take your filthy, human heart out of it. Then give it to me. Once I have it, I'll simply kill him but let his soul go free. Then he can be reborn once more. If I eat his soul, that's the end of him for all of eternity."

Aych groaned and looked at the bulbous iron Stove. "You dragged me here to do that? For fuck's sake, you live here. You could get that fucking thing out any time you want. You never even fucking leave this House, you dried-up agoraphobic child-eater."

"I went outside and dug the trapdoor behind the woodpile!" Spider screeched. "And the Stove is too hot! It burns! You do it!"

Gotcha, you stupid fuck. Aych groaned again and walked to the Stove. "Fine, just bring the hunter down with you."

"You won't be able to steal him back from me ..."

"No, shit for brains, I only want to make sure you kill him and release his soul." Aych gestured at the children's souls struggling in webbing by the window above the sink. "You think I trust you not to eat it?" Putting their hand on the lever of the Stove, Aych wrapped their claws over their thumb and hauled the heavy door open. Their hand began to burn. The heat from the roaring Fire inside washed over them, singeing fur and blasting hot air through the House. Taking a deep breath, Aych stared into the flames and shoved their right hand into the belly of the Stove. Pain seared throughout Aych's body as it tried to reform the burning hand in the flames.

Spider's giant, bulbous form abseiled from the rafters, Ky's bound form dangling from her front legs. The Guardian's scintillating, multifaceted jeweled eyes reflected the firelight as she hung over the cot, her mandibles clashing in joy at the stench of burning meat. "Show it to me! Show it!"

Aych retracted their charred arm and shut the iron door. They turned their half-burned muzzle to Spider. With their charred hand, Aych held up a beating child-sized human heart. "This what you want, bug?" They nodded at Ky. "You can't have both. Either the heart or the hunter."

"I can too!" She hissed and a long leg flicked out to press a claw against Ky's bare throat.

"No, you really can't." Aych shook their head and then spun around throwing the heart toward the kitchen window.

Spider screeched as Aych's heart crashed through the glass window and went out into the garden. She launched herself, chattering and hissing, in pursuit of the heart. Ky was dangling over the cot. Aych leapt onto the sheepskins and pulled the man down.

"I have to go finish with her or else she'll come right back for you." Aych tore the webbing off Ky with their good hand. The Hunter was paralyzed and delirious from Spider's venom. "You with me? We're not out of the Woods yet." Aych smacked Ky, leaving bits of charred fur and flesh on his cheek.

"Your family sucks," Ky mumbled.

"Not all of them," Aych pulled the two water bottles out of In Between and put them in the inner pocket of Ky's leather. "Give these to Lu and tell her you've been bitten. She'll fix you right up. Congratulations, you're the first human in a very long time to make it out of here alive." Aych slapped

A Holy Venom

Ky again and pushed him In Between.

In the garden, Spider hissed and chattered. She ran back and forth, pushing aside the tall stalks and feathered fronds. When Aych jumped through the broken window and landed on the moss behind her, Spider reared up, venom dripping from her fangs.

Keeping their eyes on her, Aych walked to the fountain and made a show of slipping their seared arm into the cooling water of the pool. The flesh and fur rippled out, healing as Aych rested against the wet curb stones.

"Where is it?" Prancing forward, Spider menaced Aych with her claws. "You threw it out the window, I watched your hands…"

"That was a fake. I left the real one in the Stove." Aych smiled, showing all their fangs. "Bit of rock with illusion wrapped around it. Go on, look again in the bushes. I'm sure you'll find it. Use your damn eyes. You have enough."

Hissing in frustration, Spider danced back and forth.

"Why do you want it anyway?"

"Because I want to eat it!" Spider thrashed through the ferns.

"I told you that's a fake." Aych watched as Spider chittered in frustration. "The real one's still in the Stove."

"It's another trick! You think I'm stupid!"

Aych groaned and went to the garden bed and picked up a broken piece of the lure. "I'm leaving; either take the heart out yourself or fuck off. Makes no difference to me if you eat it." They showed the irate Guardian the chunk of the broken lure. "A lump of flesh wouldn't have broken the window, shit for brains. I threw this lure."

Spider wobbled back and forth, dancing on the tips of her legs, and then pounced at Aych, pinning them against the fountain. Glossy black hairs stood straight up as she swiveled her abdomen and shot webbing at Aych.

Aych grimaced in disgust. "You shouldn't have picked another fight with me. I always win now."

Spider answered by biting off Aych's hand, swallowing it whole.

"Fucker!" Aych kicked Spider in the abdomen and sent her flying across the garden. Hissing, Aych shook their amputated stump as their clawed hand reassembled out of the gushing ichor and blood.

"I hate you!" Spider wheezed and pulled herself up against the stone wall. The arachnid wobbled, her glittering eyes spinning. "You think you're better than the rest of us!"

"Smarter than you, maybe. That rock I was holding, the one you just swallowed? Another illusion. You just ate a full vial of *tau-ve-vik*. Saved it just for you, dumbass. Enjoy sleeping it off outside, where anything under the sky can find you and kick the shit out of you."

Spider clashed her mandibles and wavered on her rear legs. "Why? Why do you hate me? You admire the others, but you hate me!"

"They don't eat children and their fucking ghosts, you sick shit. They don't torment the kids like you do." Aych shook their new hand out and flexed the claws. "I should fucking gut you, but you're not worth my time."

Spider staggered into the thorny brambles along the wall and crashed to the ground. Her eyes dimmed as her legs contracted and folded up.

"Not to interrupt your childish moment of revenge," Cat murmured from the stone wall above the spring, "but you're out of time." They pointed a paw at the front of the House. "The Owner has returned. You best leave now while you can."

"Shit." Aych glanced in the direction of the House. *Retreat*.

TWENTY-ONE

KY CAME TO IN THE REMAINS of a splintered wooden pew. Ruin was shaking his shoulder and Mat was peeling back his eyelids. The opulent cathedral chamber reeled and his body screamed, like it was burning from the inside.

Ky batted Mat's hand away. "Where's ... Aych?" His breathing was labored.

"Not back yet," Ruin answered as he stripped spider webbing off Ky's face. "We have to get out of here."

Ky strained to catch a glimpse of Lu, his vision blurring in and out. He made out her sinuous form flanked by ceremonial guards and Perlustrate agents, their shouted commands only echoes in his buzzing skull. "I ... Lu. Spider ... bit me." Nauseous and sweating, he started to convulse violently, a trickle of foam breaching his lips.

"I did not kill the High Priestess and I am not going with you for questioning!" Lu stamped her boots and bared her teeth at the Basilica guards surrounding her.

The nearest Perlustrate moved in and grabbed Lu's arm and held her fast, restraining her. "Enough! You're coming with us, heretic." They brandished a syringe and moved it toward Lu's neck. "Hold her!"

"Shit! I don't have any anti-venin here!" Mat cried, forcing his wallet into Ky's clenched jaw. "Lu! Ky says he's been bitten by Spider!"

Lu glared at the Perlustrate agent holding her and the guards standing between her and Ky. She sighed and her normally coquettish expression turned grim. "Fuck it."

Searing silver light erupted from Lu's form. The Perlustrate agent holding her screamed and reeled back, dropping the syringe as they covered their blinded eyes. The guards fell back with confused yells.

Delirious, Ky watched as enormous silver coils formed around Lu's diminutive body. The looping curve of her tail swung out, effortlessly knocking pews and enemies away. Ky dropped his head back against Mat's hands as the convulsion stopped. Lu's face came into focus—and then her second, much larger, serpentine head appeared in the air above, the vertical pupils of her reptilian eyes staring down into Ky's. He weakly tried to move his hand and retrieve the bottles from his jacket. "The water..."

Mat fumbled at the leather and found them. "Quickly, drink!" He uncapped one and held it to Ky's mouth.

"Give it here." Lu plucked the bottle from Mat's hand before any could spill. Swinging it back, she downed the contents.

Mat sat back on his haunches, stricken. "You're just going to let him die?"

Ky felt the storm he always felt around Lu, but now it was amplified. The air in the Basilica crackled and then went still and heavy with ozone, like the moment before a cloudburst. He gasped as the countersignal scorched through his torso, arching his back with crippling fiery pain.

"He's going into cardiac arrest!" Mat shouted.

The numinous head of a giant sky serpent floated in front of the cathedral ceiling, framed against the majestic mural of a clouded dawn sky. Lu's human body was gone, her true form brought forth. Raising her head, the serpent slammed down, striking at Ky. He screamed, arching his body into the dazzling, ecstatic pain as her phantom fangs sank into his shoulder. Visions filled his reeling mind. *Should be a painting of a night sky up there, at dusk, not dawn. The stars are wrong.*

"Holy Mother!" one of the guards cried out.

Ky seized and thrashed on the marble floor of the Basilica.

Mat tried to keep Ky's head from hitting the splintered wood. "Call an ambulance! He's having a heart attack!"

"He'll be fine, relax." Dusting off her hands, Lu, appearing human once again, stood up and glared at the remaining guards. They stood frozen in place, watching in disbelief. Frowning, she poked Mat with the toe of her boot. "Where's the *gae-su*?"

Naked and wrapped in what appeared to be the altar cloth, Aych pushed through the guards. They glanced from Lu to Ky. "Is he going to live?"

"Who? That one?" Lu looked at the convulsing human at her feet. "He'll be fine once the effects of my venom subside. Not my first choice for the clergy of my restoration, but he did risk his life to deliver my cure. That's worth a reward, even if it means I co-own him with a desert god of war. I am not looking forward to *that* conversation. I'm feeling parched just thinking about it." She looked around on either side of Aych. "The *gae-su* is not with you? Don't tell me he went—"

"For fuck's sake!" Aych snarled. Turning around, they went In Between.

✹

The biting cold hit Ruin first. An unexpected silvery afternoon sky overhead threatened foul weather. He stared at the undifferentiated cloud layer in surprise, expecting to see a night sky over the Silent Woods. For a moment he worried he was in the wrong place.

His boots settled into the wet, slushy snow and he shivered. He cautiously walked over to the shattered woodpile and examined the hole behind it. Dropping into it, he grabbed Ky's duffel and heaved it over the edge before pulling himself out.

In front of him stood a brick house painted matte black, with a porch with plain white railings. It took him a moment to realize the building lacked windows. The gingerbread-style white trim adorning the roof blurred in places, hanging in unfinished wedges.

It looks like teeth. Gripping the handles of the bag, he pushed his way through the snow, watching for any signs of movement. He circled to the right, where he thought the garden should be, and found only a few bare branches sticking up through the smooth expanse of the yard. He circled to the left. The windowless House bothered him in a way a barn or a garage without windows never could. Sinister and refusing to give up its secrets; the structure shut him out.

The wind cut him to the bone and rustled the dry leaves on the trees. He stared back at the line of trees, unsure what to do if anything rushed out at him. Unzipping the duffel, he took out one of the bombs and clutched the glass in his freezing hand.

"Fuck it," he muttered. Returning to the front of the House, Ruin stomped up the steps and rang the modern-looking doorbell. Knocking the snow off his boots, he set his finger on the button and pushed it a second time. He listened for the bell inside the House. A reckless compulsion struck him and he shifted the duffel bag so he could knock with his free hand. The sound of his hand striking the door echoed out into the Woods.

Ruin stepped back and looked around. *Should just go the fuck back to the Basilica, everyone is probably looking for me.* Feeling foolish, he walked backward to the porch stairs and retraced his steps to the yard. Picturing the Basilica, he tried to step In Between but only stumbled forward, barely stopping himself from pitching headlong into the snow. The one-two slipped out of his fingers and fell uselessly into the slush. From behind him, he heard the unmistakable noise of a door creaking open. He closed his eyes, trying to block out the sound. *Don't go in—you promised.*

Curiosity and a strange urge pulled at him. He turned and let the duffel slip from his arm, forgotten. The sensation of a dream—or a nightmare—crept over Ruin. He was compelled to take a step toward the House. Then another, then another. He was on the porch and then the brink of the threshold. Unable to resist, he stepped inside.

He was inside a stranger's home, uninvited, and he moved cautiously. Uncertain if he should call out, Ruin looked around at the pale cream-colored walls and the polished, dust-free furniture. The apricot fringed lamps were on in the living room, and he walked across the wool braided rug to look out the windows at the yard. When he had been outside, the windows had been missing. The spicy tang of cinnamon hung in the air and he spotted a bowl of dried flowers and reddish sticks of the spice in a bowl by a bay window.

"Lovely doll's house you've made for yourself," a woman called out from the doorway. "Not at all like the shitholes and palaces you've actually lived in."

Ruin spun on his heel. It was his aunt, her long hair unbound over a satin cocktail dress. Young and arrogant, she looked as if she'd stepped out of a photograph in the family albums. She turned her back and walked out of the sitting room.

"Wait!" Ruin wondered why he would want to try to catch her. What would he say?

There were pieces of unopened mail on the table in the hallway and umbrellas resting in a stand near the front door. *Were those there before?* Ruin stumbled further into the House. Low conversation punctuated with angry tones floated from behind the staircase to the second floor. His parents were fighting again, most likely about him. The wounded pitch of his mother's voice rose and fell over his father's subdued tones. It all seemed bizarrely familiar, as if Ruin was remembering something that he knew was happening for the first time.

"There you are!" His aunt grabbed Ruin's arm and hauled him into the kitchen. Her fingers dug into his skin, pinching the nerves against the bone of his forearm. She gave him a co-conspirator's full smile of malice and mischief. "I've been hoping to catch up with you."

Wooden cabinets hung above the butcher block counter and an exhaust fan hummed over the white enamel stove. Recoiling from his aunt's touch, Ruin shook himself, falling back against the side of the refrigerator. Magnet clips holding recipe cards scuttled along the surface of the appliance like insects as he pulled himself upright.

"No reason to be like that. We're old friends, you and I," his aunt winked. "Now why don't you tell me what you've come all this way for and we shall see if we can't make a deal. I'm sure you've come for a reason. The House let you in after all."

"To find…" Ruin stopped himself and looked at the electric burners on the Stove. Everything in the pristine kitchen was spotless, but he could smell the coppery tang of blood under the overpowering perfume of cinnamon. Dread sealed his tongue to the roof of his mouth. Suddenly, he remembered his real aunt was dead, her bones sealed away for eternity in the family mausoleum.

Leaning her back against the counter, the thing that looked like his aunt tilted her face and smiled at him alluringly. "Find what, child? Did you misplace a favorite toy? Or your parents? Tell me what you've come looking for all this way. I can help you."

Ruin tore his gaze away from her and looked at the oven. "Aych's heart."

"That banged-up thing? It is yours to take …" Her voice deepened and grew louder, somehow becoming bigger than her body. "Should you pay the price."

Ruin's pulse raced and he stared at the enameled oven. Out of the corner of his eye, he saw his aunt growing taller, her cocktail dress and jewelry enlarging with her, resizing as she grew beyond human proportions. "What do you propose to give me in exchange?"

He realized too late he was shrinking, becoming smaller as the scale of the kitchen shifted and his perspective heaved unevenly. "I didn't bring anything." He tried to think of something to offer.

"That's a shame. You came into my House without my express permission." The looming figure expanded nightmarishly as the kitchen stretched and shifted to accommodate her. "If you have nothing to give me, nothing to trade, I shall be forced to—"

"I can sing! I can sing you a song," Ruin stared as the floor lengthened, leaving him stranded, exposed and terribly small.

The Owner laughed, an eerie haunting sound. The windows in the kitchen darkened. Ruin glanced out as the afternoon sky became the void he remembered. The colors drained out of the House, everything becoming pale and gray. The Owner's cocktail dress faded to match the shadows under the Stove.

Her voice boomed. "No lullaby or sonnet to beauty shall win my approval. Neither shall songs about the seasons nor love's fickle flights. No pining for a lost home or for unknown shores where love dwells. There is no song you can sing of human warmth or human joy that could please me." The giantess lowered her face next to Ruin's, still holding onto the appearance of his aunt. Her glossy lipstick was the fresh scarlet of newly-spilled blood, and her breath carried the putrescent stench of corpses. Her eyes turned quicksilver and reflective as her face shimmered into a liquid mirror.

"You'll say you hate anything I sing!" Ruin shouted. "You'd never accept anything I offer because you hate me!"

The giant's expression stilled, her features becoming flatter, more mask-like and inhuman. Her glassy eyes blinked, the lids clicking like an enormous doll's. "You have a point," she said. Her eyes, a distorted mirror, reflected Ruin's stricken face back to him. "The House shall judge, not I. If you fail to sing a song worthy of this House, I will devour you, voice and all."

"And if my song is worthy?"

A Holy Venom

"Then you shall have your prize," she said, her lips curled into a cruel smile. "There are rules and there are rewards. Sing your song and live or die by your power to sway the House. Be warned: it has no heart and no mercy. No tale of human tragedy has ever changed a human's fate here."

Swallowing, Ruin thought of all the songs he knew. Songs he had written, songs by other musicians, songs he had heard in clubs, in stores, on elevators. Songs hummed or shouted, belted out in celebration and whispered in despair. Crappy songs on the radio, jingles, poems in high school textbooks, and scrawled on bathroom stalls. Songs he had admired and ones he had loathed. But none of them contained what he needed now.

Despairing, Ruin recalled Aych's rant about murder and what it was to kill. He closed his eyes and slowed his breathing. He waited until the one breath came that pushed itself out of his body and with it the music and the words he needed. He sang about death and his desire to kill, his desire to die. Every taunt the imps in his head had lashed him with, every obscene fantasy, every glorious moment of rapture, imagining the taking of a life. He'd finally found the words. The poetry of slaughter spun itself into a murder ballad, using him as an instrument and gateway. He counted himself among his victims and sang the World into its grave.

The pale walls of the kitchen shuddered. The paint ran and dripped, cascading off the obsidian stone underneath. The cabinets spun and fell as the House remade itself, shaking off the disguise of a human dwelling. The House of Sorrow showed itself and listened, bending to hear Ruin's song.

Through half-lidded eyes, Ruin watched the transformation of the white enamel oven as it swelled and peeled, stretching into a blackened iron thing. The leaping outline of flames flickered through the Stove's door. The stench of roasting meat and woodsmoke grew pungent, stinging his eyes and throat. Through the pain and stench and terror, he sang.

Ruin tasted sea salt as the song unfurled. Sweat and tears dripped off his face as he gave himself to the music and the dreadful emotions rising out of him. He sang of grief so horrific it tore his heart to shape the words, to give voice to his inner madness. Aych had been right; the guilt and shame of murder would break his heart. Yet the desire was there, and he gave it to the House. The inspiration flowed, maddening and patient, his ease with it startled him. His body and voice knew the atrocity of the song, the loss and the reckoning, the grave and the dust awaiting all humans. The song was full of despair and agony, not for the loss of love alone, but for the constant loss of all things as the World flowed to its solitary grave, murdered by the ones it created, silenced at last. Holding the final note until his empty lungs brought the song to an end, Ruin waited in the silence. The thing before him was unmoved, standing as it had before he sang. Had he chosen poorly after all?

"The House," she stared at him. "Has accepted your payment." The Owner, still wearing the shape of his aunt, gestured at the Stove. "Take your prize, human." The reflective silver of her eyes followed him.

A compulsion overcame Ruin as he placed his left hand on the iron handle. Terror of the fire, of his parents dying in the burning shell of his childhood home, all of the burning pain, the cigarettes the kidnappers had put out on his skin, the scars from the lighter and the knife, all the pain he had suffered welled up.

He opened the door. Waves of heat rushed out. Ruin reached into the Fire. Pain chewed through his flesh while around him the air shivered with a sudden roiling. There was a shrieking scream in his ears and head drowning out everything except the pain and the all-consuming fear of the Fire. The wraith, still bound in the deepest reaches of his body, restrained by Lu's influence and injured by Aych, seeped from his pores, coalescing grey and sickly in the air next to him. It steamed and writhed around him, screaming until at last, its withered face burned away in tatters.

Realizing he too was screaming, Ruin's fingers caught hold of a cool glassy object deep in the flames. Colder than wading into a river in the middle of winter, the freezing object numbed the pain of the Fire. Panting, he pulled it from the coals. The iron door slammed shut, cutting off the heat and leaving him in a shock of sweat, shaking, and panting. A heart-shaped ruby, flashing with its own internal flame, lay in his unscathed palm.

"Too bad you failed to ask for safe passage home." The giantess's voice whispered in Ruin's ear as her eyes reflected a distorted image of his own. "Now you will go in the Pot and that shiny treasure will—"

Silent as a grave, Ruin plunged the pointed tip of the ruby into the Owner's neck.

A Holy Venom

✳

Outside the House, Aych screamed in frustration, clawing at the formless pile of obsidian stones, searching for a way in. The stones jostled and shook, rising higher from the broken ground. *Fuck it. ADVANCE.* Shaking their entire body, Aych let go of being Big and willed themselves Bigger. The fur and bone slipped off, bursting apart and splattering on the trampled snow. Coiling blackness enveloped the stones as Aych bellowed.

Trees cracked and blew over as the writhing mass of deepest shadow rose higher and dashed against the stones, ripping entire blocks free, dismantling the House in search of their beloved.

A single, long undulating scream echoed from below the ground. In the night sky, the crescent moon dimmed and then vanished. Aych, in their spirit form, uncoiled from the House.

"You'd best get your disembodied self over here, young one," Cat called from the edge of the Woods. His tail tip flicked once and settled on the snow.

Aych's awareness snapped to the Guardian. Their enormous, incorporeal eyes focused on Cat, sitting by the sleeping bodies of the other three beasts.

"Suit yourself. If you get trapped in it, I imagine someone will let you out. Eventually." Flicking his tail again, Cat groomed a nonexistent speck off his glossy fur.

Aych began to shrink, coalescing as they moved back. The smokey outline became dense and solid and they dropped to their claws in the snow, once again Big. "What the fuck …"

"Watch," Cat said. "The House. You'll never have the chance to see this again."

The stones Aych had thrown floated silently over the clearing. The blocks and bricks altered, remaking themselves to join with the slabs of obsidian in the center. With a subtle ripple, the House shook and transformed, drawing carved pillars and glowing stained glass windows out of the stony ground until the structure reformed into the shape of a mausoleum. Gravestones and monuments broke through the snow, a necropolis sprouting in the yard. Through the bare branches, a whisky-colored full moon glimmered, rising up as the snow melted and released the scent of fresh turned graveyard soil, moldering leaves, and autumnal decay. As an icy breeze flung leaves into the air, rusted iron cemetery gates creaked and whined on newly sprouted granite posts.

Cat and Aych looked up as the dead trees behind them unfurled new scarlet and amber leaves. The Silent Woods rustled and sighed, a chorus of new voices whispering in the night air.

"Hello?" Ruin called out from the mausoleum entrance. "Aych? Is that you, killer?"

Still Big, Aych laughed and loped to the ornate brass doors. Candlelight from the mausoleum spilled onto the dry grass. "That you, psycho? What the fuck have you done?"

"He has become the Fourth Owner. Now, we can sort everything out and get back to running things as intended." Cat lashed his tail impatiently. "You didn't think I went to all this trouble so your pet snake could get her wings back, did you? We needed a restoration and that required a new Owner."

"You're the *Owner* now?" Aych stared at Ruin, dressed impeccably in a tailored three-piece black suit, and then at the silver stain on Ruin's right hand. "Oh, for fuck's sake." Aych glared at Cat. "What do you mean, *'you went to all this trouble?'*"

Sighing, Cat rolled his eyes and looked at Ruin. "It wasn't always like this, you see. The killing and the excessive eating. Of course, it happens, especially when certain people get ideas into their heads …" He glanced at the sleeping bodies of the three other Guardians by the edge of the Woods, then back at Aych. "The House was always where children came to, willingly or not, give up their childhoods. To face Death and trade what they could for a new life as mature people who understood certain … priorities. People who understood the need to face their fears and strive to be more for the sake of others. Surviving the House was intended as a sacred ordeal of initiation. The First Owner—"

Aych made a disgusted noise. "You're lying. No one survives."

Cat sighed and looked at Ruin. "This is what I've had to work with; you see how difficult it is?"

Ruin pointed at Cat. "Just so we're clear, I'm not going to cook and eat children. Absolutely no baby eating."

"That was a tale to scare the children before they even arrived." Cat waved his paw dismissively. "It's the root of all terror: all horrible and evil creatures eat children, especially babies. If one wishes to be the absolute worst of the worst, well then, one must have it said one is a child eater. It was intended to be theatrical, not factual." Cat sniffed and spared a sideways glance at Spider before addressing Ruin again. "As I was saying, as there are seeds that require scarifying to germinate, so it is with humans. The young need ordeals to mature. The House's original purpose was to provide children with the ceremonial demise of their childhoods, a child-sized version of death. An obstacle course set up by the First Owner, if you will, to prepare humans for the real event," Cat's mouth lifted into a smile. "Eventually. It was never intended to be the formal death of children, you see, only ... how did your snake friend put it? A show for the seats. Your role now is to oversee initiations with an insight into the necessary mechanics of the young individual's ordeal. A little divine terror goes a long way toward improving human behavior, especially in cases where divine love is not enough. You, my dear, are highly qualified by way of ample experience in the artistry of misery and madness," Cat glanced at Aych. "And mayhem."

Ruin looked at Aych. "Do you believe him?"

Shrugging their Big shoulders, Aych sat back on their haunches. "What do I know? I didn't think it was possible to kill the last Owner. Or that it was option to even get a new one."

Sighing loudly, Cat flicked an ear and looked up wistfully at the full moon hanging over the new cemetery. "I knew once I arranged your meeting that fate would lead you here. You are so very clearly made for each other." Closing one eye, he looked at the House. "But we shall have to address why the children stopped coming. Why the adults started showing up to loot instead ... that's when all the trouble began. The children stopped coming and the Second Owner, the one in charge before the imposter you so recently dispatched, went to find out why and never came back. In their absence, the House decided ... well, perhaps it's best not to go into that particular bit of history. It was clearly a poor choice. The current situation calls for amnesty, I should think." Cat wended his way between the graves. "Though I'm curious to see where the garden and the spring have relocated.

The Water's as essential as the Fire, you know."

"It's in the crypt, down there. The garden too. The Water told me I can use it like my meds. Well, my normal ones ..." Ruin tilted his head. Looking over the cemetery, he smiled up at the golden full moon as the wind blew through the haunted trees and rustled their newly unfurled autumn leaves. "I'm sorry, Aych. I used up your heart, it's gone."

"Wasn't using it anyway." Aych scratched along their jaw and looked Ruin over. "I like your outfit. Vetch will let you into the Velvet if you're dressed like that."

Ruin plucked at his expensive garments. "I think the House ..."

"Oh yes, that," Cat called over his shoulder. "Aych, do ignore what Spider was babbling. She tries to take credit for everything. It's the House that's been looking after you. Though I will admit occasionally dropping breadcrumbs myself. I may have even called in a favor with an old friend to get you a suitable hunter. Owl has looked out for you as well; she's checked up on you in the Hunting Grounds. Wolf is too proud to admit he's been curious about your adventures. You are the youngest of us, after all. Though, I'm not entirely clear if you will—"

"Yeah?" Aych glared at the brass doors of the mausoleum. "Then what the fuck is the deal with the headaches?"

Cat's eyes widened as he looked up at the stone lintel above the new form of the House. "It can be a bit of a privacy freak at times. Rule of silence, and all that. You are made of its magic, so it feels it can impose imperatives on you. Something of a leash, perhaps."

Aych glared at the stone columns. "We'll see about that."

"Can I go back to the Basilica now?" Ruin asked Cat. "I couldn't go In Between before."

"The House didn't want you to leave until you completed your ordeal." Cat slowly closed his eyes and opened them again. "When I first led you here to contract with Aych, the House recognized you as an heir of the Second Owner and allowed you to come and go as you wish. And now, it's yours. You can come and go as you like, as you always have. And Aych, you shall have to assist with Spider's rehabilitation. She must be guided back to the sacred path of terror and awe. Before the imposter's dreadful influence, Spider was possibly the greatest of us all."

A Holy Venom

"The bug can wait." Aych began forcing themselves back into their Little form. "Right now—"

Ruin grinned. "We need to tell Lu and the others."

✽

Pushing himself up out of the remains of the pew, Ky looked at Lu. "I am well and truly marked. What the fuck did you do to me, lady?"

Lu laughed a resonating, otherworldly laugh. The mountain rumbled. Statues and lattice work clattered, skittering across the marble floor. Mat lurched sideways as the chained incense burners hanging over the altar spun madly. The ceremonial guards fled, screaming. The Perlustrate agents recovered and advanced on Lu, their eyes shining with righteous fury. Ky's eyes snapped open, wide and aware. He sprang up into a crouch and maneuvered around Lu. He shoulder-checked one of the Perlustrate out of his way. The remaining two squared off against him and dropped into an attack stance. Ky shot forward in a blur, throwing the shocked agents off. He punched one, who fell to the ground in a crumpled heap. The remaining Perlustrate recovered and attacked. Ky deftly blocked and kicked the agent hard in the stomach, sending them staggering back to fall against the pews, unmoving. Taking Lu by the hand, he ignored the electric shock and ran with her behind one of the columns. Spooked, he instinctively took a step away from her. Someone grabbed his arm and Ky spun around to find Mat covered in plaster dust. The rumbling grew louder and parts of the cathedral's buttresses began to crack. In the eastern side of the Basilica, the rose window shattered. Mat and Ky ducked as splinters of stained glass rained down. From under his raised arm, Ky watched as Lu calmly walked in the direction of the high altar.

"Where's she going?" Mat cringed as a block of masonry shattered on the marble next to Ky. "We have to get out of here!"

"Watch out!" Ky pulled Lu back as a section of the high altar tumbled free.

Lu turned strange amethyst eyes to Ky and smiled serenely. "Thank you, dear one."

"We need to get out of here. Now!" He hesitated before letting go of her wrist.

"And miss the show? Never." Lu laughed again, her voice ringing like water droplets. She stood smiling as the nave shook itself free of the plaster and the bare bones of the mountain appeared through the cracks.

"What is wrong with you?" Ky screamed and pulled her away from the collapsing marble.

Lu's mouth formed the small familiar moue and her eyebrows shot up in surprise. *"Wrong?"* She pointed at the remains of the altar as it crumbled before them. "Can't you see what's happening? I haven't felt so right in such a very, very long time."

EPILOGUE

KY SAT AT THE SIDE BAR in the lobby of the Velvet, hunched over an empty glass. "To tell you the truth, I don't know what the fuck I saw, honestly."

Vetch watched him from behind the bar and nodded. "The whole top of the mountain shook and I still smell smoke. Whatever you saw, you need another drink." He pulled the stopper from the cut glass decanter resting on the bar and added another finger of amber whisky into Ky's glass.

"That I do, that I do." Ky picked up the glass and threw back the drink.

Ruin came out of the restroom and sat with his back against the bar, looking out over the round couches of the lobby. "I wish they'd hurry up."

Vetch cast an approving eye over Ruin's three-piece suit. "My money is on Lu taking over an entire steam room at that luxury spa she favors if even half of what this one's been telling me isn't complete horseshit."

"Where's your uncle at?" Ky glanced around at the vacant lobby. "I know he doesn't drink, but it can't be a good idea for him to be wandering around on his own. The dogs are sure to have him on their shit list, and they'll be watching the streets ... and the Velvet. On the hunt as it were."

"Ha! The dogs wouldn't have the courage to come around here after the disaster that happened up the Hill. As for the herbalist, he's on the phone in Vee's office. Asked to place a long-distance call." Vetch shrugged. "Considering what he just gifted us, Vee won't be asking him to pay the call charges."

"You folks still going to sell that stuff?" Ky locked eyes with the head of security. "It's bad news. It changes people into—"

Vetch cut him off with a flip of his fingers. "Why? You want in? Finally got a taste of the high life?"

"I've had my fill of it, believe me." Ky snorted and shook his head. "If I can, I'm going to Grava and spend at least a year doing nothing but taking it easy. Until I can give Lu the brush off."

"From what I heard, that should be entirely impossible," Ruin winked. He glanced back at the revolving doors and sighed. "They both should've been here by now. Aych needed to eat, but they promised me we would—"

"You can always go look for them if you want. The dogs shouldn't be after *you*. Nothing links you to this mess. Though they might have pulled your name out of me when they were scraping my skull clean. Safer if you stayed here with us." Ky lifted his empty glass. "*I am going to sit here until I drink enough to pretend it was all a dream.*"

"You and most of the city, I should think," Vetch shook his head. "Let me order you some dinner to soak up all that alcohol before you make a mess."

"Offering to buy me dinner?" Ky looked over at Vetch. "I thought you were too good for the likes of me."

Vetch rolled his eyes and laughed. "That I am, son. That I am. But you can ask me again when you're properly dressed and not swimming in a glass."

Mat walked up, smiling. "What I miss? Are they here yet?" He glanced around at the couches.

"Look at you! Did you win a prize?" Ruin pointed at the herbalist.

"Something like that. I've been invited home, back to the islands."

"Good for you, getting a promotion." Ky threw a crumpled bill on the bar. "I myself am getting drunk. Cures most everything."

"Not in my experience." Mat looked askance at Ky's glass and put his hand on Ruin's shoulder. "You can come back with me if you'd like. The Aya said it was time that historic feuds ended. You will be welcome among us there."

"You been fighting with his witches?" Ky shot Ruin a puzzled look.

Ruin looked over at Ky and rolled his eyes. "Nothing like that. Just old family trouble. My kin did bad things to the clans."

Mat shook his head. "You could come back and we could ride all the way to Awyton. The roads will be clear enough this time of year."

"I'd like that, but …" Ruin shook his head. "I have unfinished business here. And Aych …"

A Holy Venom

Vetch rapped his knuckles on the bar. "I'll leave you folks to your goodbyes. Keep an eye on this one for me, you hear?" He shot Ky a quelling look. "I'll have food sent over. No puking inside my house."

Ky swatted his hand at Vetch's back and then looked over at Ruin. "You're still coming to Grava with me, right?"

"I can't," Ruin fidgeted. "I have other obligations now. We have to stay here."

"You don't have to stay with them." Ky pushed himself upright and tugged on Ruin's suit jacket. "You can go anywhere. With your uncle, or with me, for example."

"I know, but I have to stay ..." Ruin's face lit up as Lu came through the Velvet's revolving brass doors. "Lu!" He rushed over and hugged her.

"Hello, darling." Lu turned her amethyst eyes from Ruin to Ky and Mat. "Everyone is here." She gave Ky a dazzling smile.

"Where's Aych? Aren't they with you?" Ruin looked through the theatre doors to the street.

"No, they aren't." Lu smiled. "About that, you might want to have a seat before I—"

"Aren't they coming to meet us?" Mat demanded.

Lu smoothed her hand along the side of Ruin's face. "Oh, they will be along. But first they had a few ... loose ends to tie up. For Violet," she turned to Ky, "and for you. I suspect they'll need to sleep it off."

"Oh, shit! Aych's really gone to the Chapterhouse?" Ruin grimaced. "They are going to be asleep for days!"

"That's what I was trying to tell you," Lu made a flourish with her left hand and gestured at the bar. "Gentlemen, it's going to be a long night and we have much to celebrate."

☾

Trained as he was in the analysis of dreams, Dr. Ash was amused to find himself standing on stage with bright lights dazzling his eyes and a microphone stand placed before him. *Not quite lucid; I should bring myself up a level.* He glanced at his liver-spotted hands and decided he would much rather be his younger, more vibrant self if he was going to indulge in an afternoon session of self-analysis instead of simply napping. Frustrated, he stared at his dream body as it refused to change to suit his preference.

"If you would please continue, Director," a younger male voice spoke through the stage monitors.

"I beg your pardon." Ash folded his arms behind his back, feeling the scratch of his tweed jacket against his aged hands. The spotlight intensified and he resisted the urge to cover his face. "What was the question?"

"What was the purpose of altering the subject's prescription?"

"The prescription? Oh! Of course!" Excited to have an audience to whom he could present his latest project, Ash smiled broadly and stared into the shadowed lecture hall, trying to see the faces of his peers and acolytes. "The family history is fascinating. You see, I simply couldn't resist. Once the lab results were brought to my attention, there was a ready application, a perfect test subject. All that was required was – "

The voice interrupted. "You did it for research?"

He cleared his throat and caught the sound of low conversation and suddenly realized he was on stage in a cheap dive bar, not a lecture hall at all. Flustered by the change in venue, he took out his handkerchief and mopped his brow. It was saturated with thick slime, something akin to motor oil. He threw it aside. "Yes and no, I had my professional curiosity, of course, but it was the perfect opportunity to gracefully and humanely reset the account balances in the institute's favor." *Could these intellectually inferior minds even comprehend the necessity? The imperative scientific mandate set before me?*

"You did it for the money!" a heckler shouted out from the tables near the footlights.

The crowd booed and Ash cringed. Taking a few steps back, he cupped his hand over the rim of his glasses, searching for the heckler. "Is that you, Sal? Surely, you of all people must understand my curiosity regarding your family's dysfunctional narrative and your inherited neurology. I needed to know whether, after all of the trauma you've endured, your early childhood conditioning would win out and manifest as an inward-turning drive for self-abuse rather than become a propensity for outwardly expressing violence? Specifically, would the love and constructive ideals you received from your parents negate the generations of dysfunctional narrative?"

A Holy Venom

Ash attempted to sway his detractors by convincing the patient himself. After all, his successful career was built on the gentle art of persuasion. Surely this was only his mind, his subconscious, testing his resolve. "Could your intelligence override your destructive impulses, or would your family's inherited genetic disposition actuate your self-fulfilling prophecy? If the psychoactive compound removed any lingering barriers your guilt might have created, would you enact the same brutal themes of self-aggrandizing mythology as the previous generation?" He paused and a wave of frustration hit his frail body with a volcanic force. "You of all people should understand! Be grateful!"

Warm breath stirred the director's hair. Startled, he jerked around and found himself standing back in his office behind his desk and under the familiar mask. The long, human hair of the sculpture's creator floated in an oily nimbus along the wall above the wainscoting. Twin flames of blue-gold fire spluttered in the bestial visage's empty eye sockets.

"What should I be grateful for, Director?" Speaking plainly from the other side of the desk, the young man's voice was full of disappointment. "That you made me relive my parents' death and my own kidnapping? Over and over again, for years?"

Spinning about, Ash caught sight of his patient seated in the leather chair on the opposite side of his desk. Formally attired as if attending a funeral, the younger man rested his head against the chairback. He had the same weary, aged gaze that his deceased uncle had worn during his last session with Ash. No longer a child and clearly not believing anything his therapist had said, his patient held him with the same mistrustful and sorrowful gaze.

"You cannot be allowed to hurt yourself or others, Sal." Assuming a conciliatory posture, Ash inclined his head. "You would be well taken care of here. Our facilities are state of the art and comfortable, just as they were when we took care of your relatives…"

"You wanted me to kill someone. Not fantasize about it, not talk endlessly about it, but actually do it. Why?" The man's gaze flickered up the wall to the mask and then back to the director's head. "Admit it: you wanted to make a monster. To see if you could push me to be what they were. Except you wanted the credit. To know you had the power. You did it with my aunt—let her go back into the world to kill instead of keeping her here."

Ash ignored the mention of his former patient. He hated to admit it, but his assessment had been flawed. However, the accusation that he would allow a potentially violent patient to return to an unrestricted life was simply slander. "No, you're projecting, Sal. It is true that I sought to have you committed, that I will admit. But I did not want you to take a life. Not your own and certainly not another person's. It is true your altered prescription medication will cause your behavior to become erratic, then the courts and the trustees will be forced to—"

"If you wanted the estate, you could've asked. I don't want it. I've been thinking of giving it all away for some time now. Reparations." Standing up, his patient dropped an object on the mahogany desk. "Speaking of, my friend here is happy to collect what you owe. For all the years you've spent tormenting me and my family. For the games you played with our lives. If you hadn't signed off on releasing my aunt all those years ago, who knows how many people would still be alive." The young man's features contorted in pain.

Ash looked away and caught sight of the stone on his desk. "You sent this?" Wiping his face with the slimy handkerchief that was strangely again in his hand, Ash stared at the stone head on his desk. "This is your friend?"

"Don't be silly. That's a lure I made so I could ask you about the meds myself." The patient pointed up. "My friend's behind you."

The director glanced up. An open animal's mouth full of wicked fangs hung over his head. Panic assailed his senses and he screamed. The creature smiled and licked the director's face while giant, clawed hands seized his arms.

"It's only a dream, Director. No reason to be alarmed." With his hands on the back of the leather chair, Ruin smiled at the hulking monster drooling saliva over the elderly man. "Though to be perfectly honest, you should be very worried about what happens when you wake up in a minute or two. Aych is coming for you now and they're even angrier than I am."

An agonized scream startled Ash awake. Blinking, he realized it was his own voice that had pulled him out of the nightmare. Still catching his breath, the stout, antique furniture of his home office loomed and twisted for a moment before settling down into recognizable shapes. A second tall-backed chair, the sea captain's desk between the potted ferns, the painstakingly arranged sumptuous curtains all appeared ominous, tainted by the ebbing tide of the tempest of a dream.

In the modern fireplace, flames whispered and sang on the ceramic log. Warmed air flowed over the elderly man, and yet he shivered uncontrollably, aghast by the manifestation of unexpected guilt. *It wasn't my fault that the patient had been released only to cause such devastating loss of life. Surely no one would blame me. Surely no one knew about my current experiment.* He took his eyeglasses off and wiped the lenses with the corner of his clean handkerchief.

At his feet, the steady flames cast an oval of firelight over the hardwood floor. Slipping out like a thief of time, the afternoon was lost, replaced by a frigid winter night, all while he had been in the grip of his subconscious drama. *The experiment has thrown all of this remembered material up for me to reexamine. Internal inventory – that's all.* He settled the spectacles back across the bridge of his nose.

Disoriented and hazy from too much sleep, Ash pulled himself up. The front panels of the cabinets lining his study rippled, their ancient glass pooling imperceptibly at gravity's behest. Emotionally exhausted, he shuffled over the carpet and passed the curio cabinets filled with his treasured collection of patient artwork, the artifacts of ingenuity created from whatever objects the institutionalized could get their hands on. Without pausing to admire the implausible masterpieces crafted from scrounged metal spoons or hard-won mother-of-pearl buttons, he headed to the oak panel hidden behind the desk.

As he swung the liquor cabinet open, the hinges squealed in complaint. Swallowing nervously at the unexpected noise, he reached inside. The tendons in his dominant hand strained as he lifted a decanter off a pewter tray. Appalled by yet another example of his encroaching decrepitude, Ash noted his hand was at least steady as he poured fortified wine into the waiting glass.

The aromatic fumes and a single sip of the restorative were all he managed to consume before a thunderous noise shook the entire house. Startled, Ash lost his grip and the diminutive wineglass fell, fragmenting on the floorboards. From under his feet, the tremors repeated. His heart raced and his mind tried to account for the source of the terrible commotion. His study was on the ground floor directly over the basement, the space given over to the furnace and hot water pipes. *Could the pipes have frozen? Was this tumult the result of the furnace banging in protest?* Ash exhaled in relief. Then his mental blueprint corrected itself. The confines of the basement stopped below the hallway outside the study's entranceway. The far wall of the lowest area of the basement was a granite ledge bulging in layers of mica and quartz, the study an extension the previous resident had constructed over a poured foundation. There was nothing below the concrete except a solid granite ledge.

The shaking came again, accompanied by a bellowing roar. Ash fell back against the open liquor shelf as one of the curio cabinets toppled, the glass door exploding. From the stand next to him, one of the potted ferns crashed to the floor. The cherished contents of the room chimed and rang with the quake. Another roar deafened the director as a massive force slammed into the underside of the room, toppling the remaining cabinets. Shards and splinters flew glittering and raining down among the scattered artwork.

Certain it was an earthquake or a forgotten mine tunnel collapsing, Ash tried to escape. The roaring sounds could not possibly be from an animal. It was something like bursting pipes, surely a catastrophic event, geological in nature or at least scientifically explainable, was to blame. *My mind is grasping to comprehend the upheaval and quaking and drawing false conclusions, false parallels.* As his house slippers crunched through debris, he trampled on delicate matchsticks and felted figurines. He tried to run and a slippery tendril of dread sprouted up his spine and blossomed into crippling fear. A single obsessive thought barreled through his mind. The sound of a heavy body slammed once, then twice, into the underside of the floor.

The slithering fear howled in his brain—he was certain: whatever had caused the rampage was now standing behind him. *It was behind him!* Ash felt the heat of the thing as the air became fragrant with musk. Inhaling the fragrance, a flash of his nightmare returned. *Nothing could be under the floor and behind me at the same time!*

Ash whirled around. There was nothing except the wreckage of his home. The fire wavered on the ceramic log, the blue streams tipped with bright gold. Silence and stillness pervaded the entire house. Nothing stirred

A Holy Venom

or rang. Whimpering, Ash turned in a circle, scanning the shadowed corners of the study, throwing panicked glances at the plaster ceiling. With a clang, the light flickered and dropped several inches from the ceiling. The spiraling wires rotated as the fixture hung loose, the frosted globe tumbling askew to give more evidence of the inexplicable turbulence.

Stumbling, Ash backed out of the room and seized the doorframe. Sagging against it, he tried to comprehend what was happening. *Earthquake, a gas leak, a collapsed miner's tunnel.*

"A conundrum, isn't it?" Aych murmured into Ash's ear.

With a yelp, the human lost his grip on the doorframe and fell.

Jolted, he awoke in his chair by the fire. The contents of the study were undamaged. As he pressed a hand to his chest, he felt the galloping of his racing heart.

"As I said, it's a conundrum." Wearing their Little skin, Aych stared down from over the chair back. "Actually that's what you would say if this was all being retold to you by one of your patients." They slipped a hand onto Ash's shoulder and held the squirming, surprised human in place. "*We will have to work through it together, trust me.* You'd say that to the poor fuck trying to figure out what was real and what is..." Aych let their fingers extend into claws and felt the man's clothing and flesh give way. "Not."

Ash screamed as pain flared in his shoulder. Flailing, he tried to wrench himself away from the intruder.

Lowering their head, Aych gazed into Ash's face. "Is this pain real? If I withdraw my hand, will blood soak your clothing? More importantly, would the pain stop?" They tore their claws free and stepped away.

Sobbing, Ash slumped out of the chair. The elderly man found himself kneeling in shards of broken glass and clutching an uninjured shoulder. Glass sliced into his legs and sizzling pain licked up his nerve endings. He stared in disbelief at his undamaged shoulder and then at the blood wicking through the fabric of his trousers.

"Tricky, isn't it?" Aych stopped near the mantel and gazed down into the flames. "This whole business of sanity. Can't even trust your own body to signpost the truth." The firelight glittered in their eyes as Aych glanced over at the human. "But you're the expert at calling that distinction, aren't you?

A trusted guide for your patients."

"Please, whatever I've done, whatever you want, I can—" the director pleaded.

"I've had time to consider your case history." A mocking smile belied the fury in Aych's eyes. "Once upon a time, I would've driven you insane, inch by inch, dragging your mind back and forth like this until you ended up raving in one of your own VIP suites. Your colleagues all falsely sympathetic about your broken mind." They dropped their hand off the mantel and held it to the heat of the fire, letting it warm their skin and claws. "Or maybe I would've given into the urge to rip you apart for what you've done." Rage frayed the edges of their voice as they turned to Ash.

"I'm sorry. Whatever I've done, whatever my trespass, I'm sincerely sorry." Ash cowered against the legs of the chair, desperately trying to think of a strategy. *Who are they? Who could they be?*

"Ruin told you to expect me, don't you remember?" Glass crunched under the soles of Aych's shoes as they walked over to crouch in front of the human. Firelight glinted off the extended claws tipping each of their elongated fingers.

"Ruin? You mean…"

"That's right, the patient you were just dreaming about." Aych watched as the man tried to concoct a way to manipulate the situation. "One of many you've betrayed."

"I haven't done anything!" Shrill and caught off guard, Ash flinched as Aych leaned closer. "I'm an ethical practitioner…"

"The ghost in your office told me otherwise. Normally I don't bother with gossip, but she told me something even you don't carry around in here." Grasping the man's head, Aych gingerly removed his spectacles and stared into his eyes. "You don't even know how much of a sick fuck you really are. Making your patients tell you their horrors over and over again so you can collect their tales of woe." Keeping one clawed hand on the top of Ash's head, Aych crushed his eyeglasses. Ash whimpered. "You get off on their pain."

Ash screamed. Blood welled up and dripped as Aych's claws punctured his scalp.

"Don't get me wrong, I don't care if you torment other humans. I don't

A Holy Venom

care if you were getting off on listening to them recount every trauma and every heartbreak. I wouldn't give a fuck—but then you started doing it to the one human I care about." Aych snarled. "How many times did you make him relive that fire? Or did you hone in on the death of his parents? What sick questions did you come up with to squeeze his heart that much more? It wasn't enough to see his heart break; you wanted to break the rest of him. His mind, his spirit, even his will to live."

Eyes sealed against the blood running over his face, Ash cried. "No! I never hurt my patients like that! Lies! I would never—"

Aych pushed the man's head away and stood up. "Dig around in your own head for a while and you'll find it. Look under your self-satisfaction, your egotistical sense of accomplishment over your implacable attention to detail." Aych coldly stared at Ash. "She was right. You don't even know it yourself." They watched as the human started to crawl through the wreckage toward the exit.

"Sal's not my patient anymore, I assigned him to Dr. Tansy. I never meant to hurt anyone …"

Rolling their eyes, Aych stepped on the back of Ash's calf and pinned the man in place. There was an audible crack as the bone inside broke and the human screamed. "As I was saying, once upon a time, I would've ripped you apart for fucking with the only person I love." They bent down and grabbed Ash by the back of the suit jacket and plopped him into the seat of the chair. "Or driven you mad until they signed you up for a room of your own. That last option is a bit obvious of a play, I will give you that." Aych returned to lean against the mantel. They watched the sobbing, mewling mess of a man and waited. *But now Ruin is beyond you, beyond all harm from your kind.*

"You're fragile and can't take very much of my attentive care. Therefore, my conundrum is this: putting you out of your misery too quickly isn't satisfying, but now that I've thought it through, neither is rendering you down to one of your own charges." *And I made that stupid promise to that other pain in my ass.* "You hurt Ruin, badly. You made him want to die." Fury and helplessness mingled in Aych, the potent, crippling combination seething through their skin until their Little form smoked and twisted at the edges. They ground their teeth, holding back the release. "Neither a gruesome slow death nor public humiliation is a suitable enough torture for what you've done." *This one doesn't get to escape. Not completely.*

"Please, I don't want to die, not yet," Ash whispered. "I still have things I need to do, people I want to help ..."

Aych's fury curdled and cooled into disgust. "*Help?* Is that what you call it? Well then, I guess we will see how you do with a triple dose of my help." They stepped over to the chair. Bending, Aych stared at the crumpled human. "You've got a few years left in your bones. A little under a decade, maybe a bit more. But not nearly enough. Except when you're asleep and dreaming, we can stretch those into all the lifetimes of suffering you've so eagerly collected. All the tales of other people's trauma you've gathered and curated, ephemera of a life spent *helping* others inventory their pain." Cradling the man's head, Aych glided their fingers through Ash's hair. "In your dreams, I will grant you your dearest wish. Eternal youth—at the cost of a living hell of endless madness. You will sleep and relive all the stories, all the cases you've read and recorded, all the amassed horrors of your long career. A hundred thousand lifetimes of anguish in a hundred thousand bodies. Then you'll die, still in a coma. Maybe you'll notice you're dead or maybe you'll stay in the nightmares I've crafted for you. Forever." *Each nightmare a love letter or a fucked up prayer.*

"Why? Why?" Rising up, Ash screamed, his eyes bulging. "I don't deserve to be punished!"

"Sure, you do." Aych laughed and stroked Ash's cheeks. "Maybe you would've gotten away with fucking over all your other patients if you'd been smart enough to know when to stop. But you didn't ... and now, you're fucked." Aych's toothsome smile extended unnaturally. "Now sleep and tell yourself all the stories you've stolen, in all the rich and nuanced detail you so love, and with all the scrupulous attention you pride yourself on." They watched as Dr. Ash fell into an unfathomable slumber and the first of an infinite number of abysmal lives yawned open to catch him.

A Holy Venom

Author's Endnote:

This story was written and revised while listening to the music of many amazing bands and solo musicians. Thank you!

Acryl Madness, Aesop Rock, Allicørn, Astodan, AXIUS LINK, Beastmilk, Boris, Burial, Calabrese, Cocteau Twins, Dance With The Dead, Faith No More, Frayle, Ghostemane, HEALTH, Hyper, Kate Bush, King Dude, King Woman, Kreeps, La Chica, Leonard Cohen, Lhasa de Sela, Mogwai, Morphine, Nina Simone, Nox Novacula, Orville Peck, Peter Murphy, Prince, REZN, She Wants Revenge, Sisters of Mercy, Star Guided Vessel, and Vision Video.

Special thanks to TEAM BOOK for stunt reading, SERIOUS BUSINESS werewolf logistics, and making friends with my imaginary criminal besties.

Kiarna Boyd

Printed in the USA
CPSIA information can be obtained
at www.ICGtesting.com
CBHW031909060724
11199CB00003B/5

9 781958 669266